Advance Reviews

We are all familiar with the Borgias and such ghastly family sagas, but those atrocities, we've been conditioned to think, happened centuries ago. It is with relief, then, as well as with morbid curiosity, that I've read Getting Away with Murder *because it is fiction. Read it closely, but be warned: this is not for the faint-hearted!*

Guido Mina di Sospiro,
Author, *The Forbidden Book,* et al

A roller-coaster of a read for political intrigue buffs. Emilio Bernal Labrada's tale of material and moral corruption, unbridled lust, and political assassinations plotted in the utmost secrecy by the strangest of bedfellows reveals a side of the "democratic process" rejected with fear and loathing by some insiders and unknown to the public at large; but its revelations, in the garb of vivid narrative fiction, become fast-paced prose of the highest order.

Manuel Santayana, PhD
Author, translator, critic

A dizzying story that lays bare the puzzling assassinations, suspicious deaths and lusty sex lives of famous political, show-business and underworld personalities—with the complicity of a well-known Caribbean tyrant—that have made headlines over the last fifty years. In an astonishing, witty roman à clef *that pulls no punches, the author details unsuspected three-way interconnections among these players, as well as their interface with politics, the world of intelligence and war-making—both open and secret.*

Edward Keen
Writer, translator

aug 23/14
To Roy
with best wishes,
Emilio

GETTING AWAY WITH MURDER

—AND COSTRA'S CRIMES—

IN U.S. PUBLIC LIFE

Emilio Bernal Labrada

SECOND EDITION
September, 2012

Published in 2013 by Emilio Bernal Labrada

GETTING AWAY WITH MURDER
—AND COSTRA'S CRIMES—
IN U.S. PUBLIC LIFE

Publisher: Create Space

ISBN 978-1-47503-110-2

My thanks to Guido, Emmanuele and Carlos
for their invaluable help and support.

CONTENTS

PREFACE

At best, there is but slim likelihood that this book will ever be taken up by a regular publishing house. It is unsurprising that they have all distanced themselves from such a possibility. Although a work of fiction, it's quite clearly based on real people and events, mostly historical but never before so honestly and comprehensively examined. It is, therefore, far too incendiary to be acceptable in "polite society," particularly if one is partial to certain political beliefs or fond of groups or families whose public renown has resulted in the creation of unassailable myths. As a writer friend told me, "the myth far outweighs the truth."

I have, however, made a determined effort to objectively depict wrongdoing by members of all political parties and affiliations, including public figures who evidenced little if any political preferences, regardless of any temptations to tread lightly, or heavily, upon them.

I have also indicted in the court of public opinion—in view of his proximity to and well-known hatred of America—an international outlaw who, not content with leading his own country into social, economic, political and moral ruin, has reached out to kill the President of the United States and other Americans, commit bloody and felonious crimes in partnership with the underworld and overseas enemies, and tear apart our society with drug trafficking and subversion—all of this to undermine his arch-enemy: democracy.

Whenever possible when dealing with theories I have attempted to give those involved the benefit of the doubt. Although surely *doubt* is precisely the reason that many of the countless crimes described in this work have, for decades upon decades, gone unexplored and unpunished. Most never will be, since the culprits are beyond the reach of earthly laws.

To believe or disbelieve any of this is the reader's prerogative. I have simply set forth the results of my research, gleaned directly or indirectly from individuals whose identity I am not at liberty to disclose, as well as from hundreds of books, documents and audiovisual materials. By comparing different versions of the same event from a variety of sources, I have been able to confirm some accounts, discard others, and come up with cogent, common-sense conclusions representing the most likely scenarios, no matter how far-fetched they may sound.

Given enough time and patience, anyone can replicate this exercise. But be forewarned: it has taken the author well over forty years to accumulate all this material, research it, conduct interviews with a wide variety of individuals privy to confidential information, watch films and documentaries, and read or consult hundreds of thousands of pages.

The next step was to digest and absorb this corpus of information, condense it all down to reasonable dimensions, put the basic disarray into some semblance of order, write the manuscript— at first on a typewriter and later on a computer—assemble it into a more or less coherent whole and carefully edit the text before bringing it to the public.

I hope it brings enlightenment to those who have ignored such events and confirmation to those who have wondered about them or all along suspected that the truth was buried under a barrage of deception.

EBL

Chapter I
AN UNEXPECTED VISITOR

August, 1962. Hollywood was enjoying a late afternoon respite from the relentless heat. In her modest home not far from Hollywood, Marie Moore moped about her latest squabble with MGM over her habitual lateness and repeated absences from the set. The movie—her last, the moguls at MGM were thinking—was aptly named *Something's Got to Give*.

Enjoying his prerogatives as co-President, Roland flew in on Air Force One and landed in Los Angeles, nearly unannounced, on a trip that was billed as "taking care of routine Justice Department business." When the phone rang, Marie was half hoping it was the studio.

"Guess who," Roland said playfully.

"Oh...," she said in that breathy voice of hers, pausing only a split second to make sure she did not mistake him for another of her many off-and-on lovers. But his voice was quite unlike his brother's ... or anyone else's.

"Roland! Are you here in L.A.?"

"How did you guess?" He was still uncharacteristically playful. Sometimes he forced himself to turn on what he lacked: charm.

"Oh, I don't know. I just sort of figured..., but I had no idea you were headed this way." She felt like asking him why, lately, he had been avoiding her, rejecting her calls and even changing the number on his private line at the Justice Department, but thought better of it.

"What are you doing?" His question really meant, as well she knew, that he expected an invitation to come over.

"Well..., not much at the moment, really." She fleetingly contemplated putting up some resistance, but did not have the strength of character. Anyway, she reasoned, when dealing with him it was always best to be welcoming. Instant availability—to the Kilmorys, at least—was something she wanted to believe in, against logic, thinking it made her more desirable, although she always toyed with the notion of playing harder to get. It was hard for her to avoid the feeling that she was just too much of a pushover, especially with the powerful "Brothers Karamazov," as she nicknamed them. Literary allusions were a favorite way of hers to bolster her pretense of familiarity with the work of great writers. She liked to think of herself as a serious actress and not, according to rampant stories in the press, just another empty-headed blonde with a beautiful body.

"Well, I'm here just briefly, but...," he trailed off, pretty sure of what she would say next. "You know, the pressures of government, the wheels of justice...." He surprised her by putting on a momentary air of mock importance. Flippancy did not come easy for him, but under the circumstances a little levity was in order. Besides, it calmed his nerves.

"Well," she hesitated with a giggle, "but have you got a little time to...?"

"Stop by?" He cut her off in mid-pause. "Maybe," he said coyly. "Who knows when I'll get another chance, right?" It was good that he had her line tapped, he reflected, even though this particular conversation might—just might—be forever on record and somehow find its way into the wrong hands. That was a long shot considering all the safeguards in place, but then, others might be tapping her line as well. For instance Hooper, the perennial FBI Chief, with his devious ways of finding out everything and keeping files on anyone that might conceivably cause him the slightest inconvenience.

"Well, good. It would be really nice, hon," she cooed, now anticipating one of their delicious sexual sessions after having put her incessantly ringing phone conveniently off the hook. It had been a couple of months since they had seen each other and she was fond of the power trip—more than of his performance, at times mechanical, less imaginative and energetic than she felt her sex-goddess status entitled her to. Still, she felt he had improved a notch or two thanks to her.

"All right. I'll be there around one or two o'clock," he said, knowing he'd be at least a couple of hours late. "Wear nothing but your usual 'Number 5'!" He added, alluding to her famous Chanel perfume and chuckling at one of his own rare attempts at humor.

"Okaaay," she replied cheerily.

Just after sundown they were enjoying their sex session, whispering to each other whatever came to mind in the heat of the moment. Her sensuality was one of the greatest turn-ons he had ever experienced. No comparison to wives—his own or Justin's—and better than most women he had been with, thanks to the insistence of none other than "the Prez"—the family had now given him a new nickname. Justin was much more liberal about sex than he, despite— as Roland liked to put it—the "Big Brother influence" that he exerted on him. The Church might frown on it, but how else, he thought, is a man going to improve his technique than by practicing with a variety of women? And anyway, didn't confession periodically absolve you from all prior sins? He had not yet ventured to think of it from a woman's point of view, *that* being a little beyond his mindset—not nearly as open as he liked to think of it.

They had been at it for no more than ten minutes—though it seemed longer, as sex usually does—when he turned her around and took a suppository from his pants' pocket hanging near at hand. Skillfully, he played an erotic game around her anus with his fingers, inserting first one, then two, then a thumb; finally, he slipped the suppository deep into her through her rectum.

"Hey, what kinky stuff are you up to this time, you Irish devil?" She wagged her behind in step with him to emphasize her playfulness, assuming it was some kind of new anal toy.

"Oh, just a foretaste of what's coming," he replied mischievously. "Which you're going to thoroughly enjoy," he added with a devilish giggle that he surprised himself with and very nearly suppressed.

His sessions with Marie were always great. She was extremely fond of sex, particularly of that type—and especially with him, he fancied. Marie had the gift of being wildly uninhibited, inclined to scream, talk dirty and do anything else that came up as she got into the spirit of the action.

He felt the delightful contractions of her well-trained sphincter muscle around his penis and chose to let himself reach an intense, delicious climax.

"Baby, what happened?" He had not waited for her to reach orgasm first as he usually did.

"Oh, baby, I'm sorry, I just couldn't hold back," he lied, not bothering to sound too convincing. "Do you want me to...?"

"Sure, but let's take a little break." Vaguely, the realization dawned on her that she wasn't getting as much enjoyment as was customary—and, quite suddenly, began to feel dizzy. Did she need a fresh start?

"Fine, I could use it too." He figured that the "break" would soon stretch out.

No more than two minutes had gone by before she was fast asleep. Wasting no time, he was nearly dressed in another minute.

He located her diary—sure enough, in its regular place in her night stand drawer—and dropped it into the bottom of his briefcase, which he had practically emptied out for the occasion. He saw the photo album she kept atop her dresser, glanced through it just to make sure it was the right one and, with no time for selecting pictures that might incriminate him or Justin, dropped the whole thing into his briefcase as well. No time to do any more than that, he reflected fleetingly. He would, as usual, trust his clean-up crew to take care of the rest as soon as he notified them to come over and do a proper job throughout the premises. Before sending them in, he would have to wait until the news became public.

Now, he had to clear out fast. But first he needed to cover his tracks with Mrs. Manderly, her housekeeper. She was familiar with Marie's heavy reliance on amphetamines to get herself up for work and then, at night, sleeping pills. So it would not be too surprising if she had taken the dose accidentally, or even on purpose.

He had told her that they would need privacy until late that evening. So she had been unobtrusive and shown no awareness— acting, pretending?—that anything out of the ordinary was going on.

Once sufficient time had gone by—two to three hours would probably be enough—nothing could be done to bring her back. She would be gone, beyond any medical rescue efforts.

At least, that's what he, with his nearly nonexistent knowledge of medicine, had been able to glean from a quick read on the subject. He had not risked consulting his personal physician, or even friendly CIA agents, about so delicate a subject.

It was, he reflected, an act in flagrant contradiction of what would normally be—and actually had been—a fantastic sex session, as sacrosanct as could be if not for its inherent sinfulness, for which he intended to get absolution without going into detail. *That* he tried to put out of his sometimes overly religious mind. But what else could he have done?

"She's sleeping soundly," he whispered to Mrs. Manderly through the half-open bedroom door. "Better let her get some rest. She needs it for that movie she's doing." At the moment, it bothered him that, under pressure, he couldn't think of its title.

"Yes, sir," the housekeeper said respectfully without looking him in the eye, afraid that he might see a hint of her suspicion that something unusual was afoot. He had never said anything like that before. She quietly determined to follow his advice to the letter, not about to get in trouble with the country's top law-enforcement official.

With that, he walked out and got into the car he had borrowed from one of his assistants. He never used official cars on such occasions, since they drew unwanted attention. Then, he drove a few miles to where his helicopter was waiting.

Too bad, he thought. If only she had kept quiet and stopped trying to contact him at the Justice Department.... But no, she was too intense, overwrought, in turmoil. The Hollywood icon—hot but basically naïve, had not realized she was playing with fire.

Worse, she did not understand the danger she courted when she threw those tantrums and told close friends that she was about to hold a press conference and go public with her very personal, explosive story about her relationship with the two Kilmory brothers. One of those friends, he knew, had even told her that such a move would be an excellent idea: "hit 'em hard." And she was going to show them that she couldn't be trifled with. Roland had once told her how powerful he was: "so powerful," he said, "that I can have people 'taken care of' if they get in my way." It never crossed her ingénue mind that it would ever apply to her, a world-famous movie star.

None of the other Kilmorys had ever personally done anything like this, Roland mused. But anything done for the first time is difficult. Was it easier to throw someone out of a sixth-story window, as he had done in a fit of anger with a black child molester? He had to admit that it was. This was different because it was premeditated and required cold blood. How did those Mafia guys do it on a regular basis?, he wondered. Well, he reluctantly concluded, they probably got used to it and actually began to enjoy it, if that was possible. Or so they said.

No matter, he told himself, trying to brush those intruding considerations aside. What else could he do? There was no other safe way out with an unstable personality like Marie's. Besides, there was no time to lose and no one else who could be trusted to do it without risking letting the cat out of the bag.

Who in hell would suspect the top law-enforcement officer in the country? Besides, the Prez had given him instructions and it was his job—more than that, his duty—to carry them out. It was in the Kilmory tradition to not question authority. Was that analogous to the Mafia's own code? In a way, perhaps.

In any event, Roland figured, he had done it with finesse. No blood, nothing messy. The massive dose of Nembutal and chloral hydrate, quickly absorbed into the bloodstream through the thin intestinal membrane, would have done its job without a trace of his own role in having introduced it. He then put the whole matter firmly out of mind.

Hours later, after midnight, Mrs. Manderly had a feeling that she ought to do *something*, whatever the consequences. Marie had not gone through her regular pre-sleeptime routine and put the telephones "to bed" where she could not hear them. She tried to open her bedroom door but, strangely, found it locked, so she went outside and looked in through the window. Marie had left a night-table light on and she could see her body. It was eerily still, lying on the bed, not covered by sheets, on her back with her legs splayed. She didn't usually sleep like that. It looked, oddly, like a setup.

Her instincts as a confidant of Marie's, aside from other indications, were prevailing over her fears. She was still thinking about a course of action to take without getting herself in trouble when she had heard a car pull up outside.

A couple of men got out stealthily. They came into the house, silently opened Marie's door and made muffled noises, as if making a search. Flashes of light showed through the crack under Marie's door and occasionally out the windows. Fear overcame curiosity and she stayed out of sight in her room, recalling an anonymous telephone warning earlier that day. "Better mind your own business, lady," said a man's steady voice. "Don't go doing anything that might get you in trouble." Maybe it was some sort of burglary, she thought.

Some fifteen minutes later, hearing them clear out, she peered through the shades and saw the two, carrying bags, leave in a dark sedan. After waiting a few minutes to make sure the intruders were out of range, she pulled herself together and picked up the phone. Again, she felt that she had to *something*.

Maybe notify Dr. Grayson, Marie's psychiatrist. He was a close friend and, she knew, one of her many lovers as well. After all, it was on his recommendation that Marie had hired her. Grayson had been Marie's shoulder to cry on every time she was troubled about something, however minor.

"Dr. Grayson, Marie's in trouble. Please come quickly." She consciously decided to heed the anonymous warning and say nothing of the mysterious two-man visit.

"Have you been in her room to check on her?" He tried not to sound too alarmed.

"No, I can't. Her room is locked. I peered through the window and saw her lying there, looking very still. I don't think she has even put her telephones away. I, I don't know what's going on."

"Well, sit tight and do nothing until I get there." He lived only a couple of miles away.

The psychiatrist arrived in minutes, saw her through the window and then broke it to get into her room. In a few moments he opened the door and announced: "She's possibly dead."

"What? Oh, no!" Beside herself, she still couldn't help noticing that he was not that surprised or emotional. And what did "possibly" mean? Shouldn't a doctor, of all people, know a dead body from a live one?

"Isn't there something we can do?," she implored, as confusing thoughts clouded her head. She had had her inklings but had chosen not to think the unthinkable.

"Let's not do anything rash." Dr. Grayson looked at her intently, ominously. "Let me see what I can do." He spoke calmly. It all seemed unreal.

"Do you want me to call an ambulance?" She wondered whether he was trying to calm her down or... playing for time?

"No, let's wait until I finish checking her out." He went into her room and shut the door behind him.

Forty-some minutes later he came out, but seemed indecisive, went back in her room, then out once again. More minutes went by while the doctor fiddled with a syringe, then went back in again as if determined to give her an injection before doing anything else. (The delay in reporting an "accident" was to be repeated some seven years later when a younger Kilmory brother waited about ten hours to report one in which a young girl might have been saved from drowning in a car that he said he was driving.)

"It doesn't look good," Dr. Grayson said evenly when he eventually came back out, picked up the phone and dialed a number. "Miss Moore," he said, "is in need of emergency rescue." He then gave the address, slowly and clearly. "Please come quickly," he added, "she's not breathing but there may still be time to bring her back." His tone was not at all hopeful. By now it was nearly two a.m.

* * * * * * *

The next morning, the news went around the world.... From a safe phone, Roland called his clean-up crew chief.

"I guess you've heard the news about Marie," he mumbled unemotionally. Then, after the expected response, he went on: "I'm awfully shocked." After a brief pause, he continued. "But you'll have to take care of it quickly, before all hell breaks loose. There must not be the *slightest* hint of anything, I'm sure you understand, er, in view of the circumstances."

His inflection reinforced the message. The team, a private, elite Kilmory group sworn to secrecy, was poised to act, having been told twenty-four hours earlier via a call from President Kilmory's executive assistant that there would be a job to do on a moment's notice.

Later, Roland called the L.A. Chief of Police and gave him his instructions, specifying that if "some major event occurred in the next day or so," the file on the case should be put away in a vault and conveniently made to disappear in due course. "By the way, he said, "there is no need whatsoever to involve any other law enforcement branch, not even the Secret Service. Quite the contrary. Just handle it yourself."

Knowing Hooper was devious and slippery, Roland wanted to make sure the FBI Chief and his Bureau were out of the loop. They would pick up the scent anyway, but it was much better to, officially, keep them at arm's length. The man was a dangerous and clever bureaucratic infighter. They had wisely given up on forcing him into retirement—Hooper had the goods on the Prez and, for that matter, on everyone else in the family. For his part, Hooper hadn't forgotten their attempt to ease him out, which he had stopped in its tracks by making his threat of blackmail perfectly clear.

Jeff Kilmory, the youngest brother, was still wondering how closely involved Roland had been in the Marie case. Well aware that his brothers didn't let him in on everything, he still understood what had happened—after all, in private his brothers had, at first, done quite a bit of boasting. But the truth was clearly a secret shared only by Roland and the Prez. No one else in the clan—much less outside of it—knew precisely what had happened, although its members easily figured it out. Lately, the brothers had been complaining about "that pesky bitch of a movie star." Who else could it be?

"It probably served her right!" was uppermost in their mind.

* * * * * * *

A sergeant named Higgins from the nearest police station was the first law-enforcement officer to arrive at Marie's. He immediately observed that the scene looked like it had been arranged. Her nude body, so stunning when alive, particularly in that famous Playboy magazine spread, was stiff and pale, showing that *rigor mortis* had set in hours ago; besides, her legs were perfectly stretched out. An overdose of barbiturates ingested by mouth usually causes contortions as well as vomiting before consciousness is lost. Here there was nothing of the kind, indicating a lethal dose by injection or... insertion of a capsule through the anus? Higgins insisted it was murder, but was overruled by the Los Angeles Chief of Police Patten, who later suspended and fired him.

Chief Patten was not about to upset his own applecart, not after Roland had personally told him that he was in line to be the next head of the FBI as soon as they could get rid of Director Hooper. Patten got insurance for the appointment by immediately seizing the telephone company records of Marie's local and long-distance calls for July and August. No one has since seen them again.

No inquest was ever held nor a grand jury called to look into the event. The medical examination, by a Dr. Naguri, was rigged to reach the pre-ordained conclusion: "possible suicide."

The witnesses were never asked to testify under oath, so they changed their stories and contradicted themselves and each other until finally they cobbled together a cleaned-up, collectively agreed-upon version, consistent with the official version of events. It was put into a report as though it were a verbatim transcript of unedited, unrehearsed testimonies. In short, the word was out from the highest level that all evidence was to be oriented toward a finding of suicide and nothing else.

So the case was open-and-shut as far as the L.A. police were concerned. Once closed, the files on it somehow disappeared.

Marie was dead and buried, never again to trouble anyone, except in the mind of those who saw her sexiness on film or read up on her life and times. She would forever remain the 36-year-old blonde bombshell.

* * * * * *

Justin and Roland, always on the edge of trouble with uncountable sexual adventures, hoped they had set a good example. Word would go out about what Marie had done to bring her to "suicide." Not unlike a Mafia hit, it would act as a deterrent to others who might stray, saving them the trouble of taking care of yet other complications, such as blackmail or stories that might cast suspicion on them in the press. There were consequences in store for those who might dare cross the line. And the press itself didn't worry them too much. Unknown to the public at large, the Kilmory clan had near- ironclad control over the media. Their father, Jonathan, had taught them the ropes of that delicate and vital process.

* * * * * *

"How did it go, Rolly?" the Prez asked Roland when they were in the White House "safe room." In private, he liked to use his nickname.

"Well, I think. The press coverage has been clean." At times a man of few words, he was as brief as if, momentarily, he were concerned the recording system might be on, even though they spoke outside of the Oval Office, where everything was regularly taped.

"As it should be, although some are questioning whether it might have been an accident as opposed to something she did to herself." Matter-of-factly, Justin avoided mentioning "suicide."

"There's bound to be speculation. But, heck, I just slipped that stuff into her," he emphasized the location with a gesture, "right in the middle of it," he said with a mischievous smile that he allowed himself occasionally. "She never knew what hit her," he added wryly, with only a slight hint of what he thought appropriate regret. He brushed his unruly hair back with his right hand, a gesture that seemed to act as a form of punctuation—generally a period—to anything he said.

"A nice touch, Rolly. No traces left behind.... By the way, make sure about the autopsy. We don't want to bring up anything at odds with that...." The Prez let the phrase hang in the air and then slapped him on the shoulder to end the conversation. "Too bad," he added as Roland walked off and shrugged, "but well done. We," he said, generously emphasizing the plural, "had no alternative." Once in a while he felt Roland deserved that physical pat on the back, like a stamp of approval from his older brother. He was well aware of how its judicious use could make him feel good about himself.

Chapter II
CLOSETED SKELETONS

It was bright and sunny that late-summer day in the mid-1980's. The clan was gathering to celebrate Jonathan Kilmory's birthday. But they all knew it was perfunctory, since "the Patriarch," as they all nicknamed him, was increasingly losing his senses after a stroke the previous year.

Roseanne, the matriarch, after giving her usual precise instructions to all the hired help, greeted daughters, grandchildren, in-laws and assorted other relatives as they trickled, in small groups, into the family compound on the New England seashore. At the side of the elder Kilmory was his last surviving son, the only one who, pretending to seriously seek the presidency of the United States, had gingerly sidestepped it.

"Son, uh, uh... you know what to do. I don't have to, uh, tell you to guard our secrets well. The one about the, uh... 1960 election... Justin's. The one about... Marie. The one about your sister Rebecca. And, uh... most important of all, the one about Rantachidick."

"I know, Dad, I know!" Jeff Kilmory was annoyed, even though the old man, he realized, was no longer coherent. He was bringing up subjects that for decades he, and the Kilmory clan in general, had carefully, scrupulously avoided. No one could recall the last time anyone had made even the slightest reference to them.

In his right mind he would not, by any stretch of the imagination, have made the remotest allusion to any of those topics. It was as though the Kilmorys had never had anything at all to do with such things.

"Well, don't you think it's important?"

"Yes, but relax, Dad, no need to, uh, go over that now." Jeff attempted to calm him down. "Remember, we're here to celebrate your birthday!" For his part, Jeff had always wanted to forget those events, to pretend they had never happened. Especially the one in which he had been personally involved. The old man had mentioned it last: Rantachidick.

He had, for years, avoided that subject like the plague; in fact, he hated anything that might remind him of it. The feelings it stirred up were distinctly uncomfortable; he tried to avoid even the thought of the word *guilt*. He still felt the satisfaction—with, at this late date, barely a hint of worry—of a near-perfect cover-up. The net result had been, as far as he knew, that the truth had never even been hinted at—at least in print. Of course, rumors had been whispered around for years, but that was to be expected. Despite the Kilmory machine's power over the media—studiously ignored by none other than the media itself—as well as over the publishing industry, no one could stop the speculation and what the Kilmorys liked to call "irresponsible gossip."

Yet they realized that it would be quite a different situation if such speculation appeared in black and white. If that happened, Jeff was well aware that the story might be out of control. It would surely be printed and reprinted, aired and conveyed in every possible way, throughout the media and in personal communications such es e-mail, texting, etc.

That would affect him directly and perhaps with damning results. It might conceivably cost him his prized seat in the United States Senate, his recurring nominations being—as they used to say about Democratic Party nominees in the South—"tantamount to election."

Back in Jonathan Kilmory's more youthful days, he had been happy to think of Jeff's seat as "a lead-pipe cinch." He was more familiar than he liked to admit with vernacular terms from underworld jargon.

Jeff felt he had shielded himself well from any further investigation into the Rantachidick episode. Only three people, at most, knew the truth about the event. He was satisfied—almost proud—of his television address to the nation: he had come across convincingly, smoothly appearing to assume contrite responsibility for what appeared to be the accidental death of Molly Jeanne. The overwhelming majority of viewers, he was assured by his staff, accepted his explanation at face value. Somehow, he said, he had barely survived the accident himself and then, dazed and suffering from a neck injury, had made near-heroic attempts to save her from drowning in his upside-down car under murky channel waters just off a small island close to the New England mainland.

Of his intermittent but ongoing relationship with her, no hard evidence had surfaced. He had been careful to instruct every member of his staff to never reveal anything whatsoever about his personal life—not one iota—on pain of being fired. Worse, he had threatened to make all possible efforts to make sure that no other employer hired them. So, he was fairly satisfied that no one would likely put two and two together about the truth of their relationship and exactly how the girl had died. All of that, he hoped, would forever remain undisclosed.

As for his father's own shady episodes, of which he had got wind while he was growing up, he noted with some sense of wonder that the old man tended to bring them up more freely as time went on, while remaining more guarded about those of his sons. This was, Jeff thought reassuringly, probably on the ground that he was fairly certain little harm could possibly come to *him* at this stage of his life, whereas his sons—or at least Jeff, the sole survivor among them— could still be held responsible if sensitive information became public knowledge.

His mind went back to what, over the years, he had learned about some of his father's secrets....

Chapter III
DECISION-MAKING

The root of the Marie affair was philosophical. That is, based on principles that had netted Jonathan the MKO and Parquet Motion Pictures corporations and caused the death of people who stood in the way, among them Edna Klinger. Later on this had its sequel with Jeff Kilmory and the girl who died in that peculiar accident at Rantachidick. An observer might have taken all this as just a run-of-the-mill vicious circle.

In retrospect it became clear that in neither case did the Kilmory brothers do anything but what had to be done, according to the rules established by patriarch Jonathan. The Kilmory men were all, individually and collectively, convinced that certain measures were necessary when there was no other sure way to deal with problems. What they did, however, had to be justified by requirements and validated by actual results.

The brothers, however, presented a solid front, making up excuses and alibis for each other, defending their kin tooth and nail. It was the Kilmory way. Jeff, the youngest brother, preferred to assume, when he thought back to the Marie affair—in order to assuage any familial guilt, however minimal—that Roland might have only taken part in an accessory manner, doing none of the really dirty work. What else were his brothers going to do?

Marie had threatened to go public with the whole story of her sexual-romantic involvement with Roland and Justin, which had evolved either sequentially or, perhaps, to some extent, simultaneously. Not that they had necessarily "played" with her at the same time, although that was standard procedure in the Kilmorys' frequent White House swimming-pool skinny-dipping, sex-party romps. But part of the fun was two (or more)-on-one, and the Kilmorys frequently went for this formula, any time they couldwork it in. So a threesome among them could quite possibly have occurred with Marie.

She had also done threesomes and moresomes with Spanitra and his pals—the Brat Pack—including, at some point, the powerful capo Sal Campana. The locales were The Sands or Wilbur Clark's Desert Inn in Las Vegas or, more often, the secluded Cal-Neva Lodge on the California-Nevada border, which was co-owned by Campana, through one of his front men, and none other than Jonathan Kilmory himself. Spanitra's photographs of the occasion have no doubt by now been destroyed by his widows and heirs, thereby depriving the world of important, if salacious, evidence.

It shouldn't have been too hard to arrange those frolicsome goings-on considering Marie's proclivities, her liberal view on sex and the attraction inherent in the power trip of two alpha males at once. That probably turned Marie on more than anything else, once her basic promiscuity overcame her squeamish concern about how it would "look" if it ever came out. And the brothers, of course, no doubt thoroughly enjoyed the romp as much as she freely and mischievously admitted that she did.

In the case of Marie, the brothers Kilmory had also carefully considered the national security angle. She had been privy to top-secret information regarding Cuba and other foreign policy issues, and she had been foolish enough to imply that, above and beyond her love affairs with them, some of those secrets might come out as well. She had no idea of the dangerous ground she was treading.

In any case, her affair with Justin began to get serious when he started seeing her more frequently, whenever he could work her in on his trips or else get her to come anonymously to Washington. After all, he was regularly able to see some of his girl-friends in the White House itself. Among those who did were Judy Campbell Exeter and Marlee Penshaw Meter, the ex-wife of a CIA agent with whom Justin had an ongoing relationship that blossomed, as opposed to his other affairs, into something more than pure sex. The intellectual side of their relationship was unusual and appealing to Justin.

Most of the presidential girl-friends were not celebrities or well-known personalities, so they posed no serious secrecy problem. Some were simply young and naïve White House interns, such as Gigi Harlan, whom the President seduced after a swim in the White House pool by giving her a personal tour of the presidential living quarters. When they reached his wife's bedroom, he pushed Gigi onto the bed and, using an equal measure of the powers of office, personal persuasion, coercion and sheer will, took her virginity. As she later told the story, she was in no mood to resist the advances of such a public persona. In the case of Gigi they remained romantically involved for some eighteen months, although there was nothing more than sex to it. So much, that he even prevailed upon her to service, via oral sex, at least one personal assistant who happened to be around the pool at the moment.

"Gary doesn't look too happy," the President observed. "See if you can do something to make him feel better." In a short time, he grinned through his whiskers like a Cheshire cat.

Not long afterward, the President suggested that she do a repeat performance for his brother Jeff, but at that point Gigi drew the line.

Marie, older and wiser, was not basically in the pure-sex-and-not-much-else category. She did have something extra: lots of Hollywood gossip to relay, and Justin was fond of hearing it.

She usually came to Washington in disguise to keep the press at bay. (Among her fond memories was one of the time when she and Roland, in one of their secret forays, went to a nude beach in California disguising only their faces, thereby sharing in the fun and preserving anonymity.) Publicly unannounced, Marie would slip into Blair House, the special presidential guest quarters across Pennsylvania Avenue and come to the White House via the secret tunnel that connects the two buildings. This handy passageway makes it possible for the president (and on occasion someone very close to him, in this case "co-president" Roland) to get together with VIP's, girl-friends or confidential contacts of whatever kind without any public exposure. The underground passage, concealing everything from prying eyes, was for a long time kept more secret than the White House bomb shelter as a perfect way of smuggling people in and out with no one being the wiser. To a certain extent it remains unpublicized to this day.

Among other playmates of Justin's, and possibly of his brothers too, are a number of Hollywood and TV stars—still alive as of the availability of this book—such as the beautiful and charming Genna Dickson, who has refused to discuss the matter ever since. That makes it a sure thing. Another girl, who was very forthcoming, ran around with the Rat Pack a lot and might have been part of Justin's stable of actresses, was Shelly McLeary. Part of her story is that during a period she took an active part in Democratic Party activities. It was not all politics. She has since spoken of her sexcapades during those efforts, in which she claimed to have gone to bed with three of her colleagues in a single day ("breakfast, lunch and dinner—everyone was doing it"). She has explained that for years she and her husband had an open marriage.

With Marie, eventually President Kilmory decided that things were getting out of hand. In tapped telephone conversations, she had told friends that she was "in love with the President," and later, with his brother the Attorney General. She was delusional, imagining that Justin would actually divorce his wife Jennifer in order to marry her. Or did *he* say words implying that to her? If the story came out, a scandal of that kind simply would not have washed with the American people.

Justin Kilmory realized that no one could have even whispered about such behavior, or his whole administration might have crumbled like a house of cards. It went without saying that, back then, any extramarital affair whatsoever was enough to destroy the political career of the best and the brightest.

Now, things are different. But at the time Justin was wont to think that such a story would have deprived the country of one—many, most?—of its best public servants. Yet in this particular case it was not just his own administration that was in grave danger, but the whole family dynasty.

What if brother Roland had a personal "talk" with her?, he thought. It was so delicate a matter that they might just have to resort to this to avoid taking chances. That could only mean that Roland might get involved with Marie; but so what? His brother had said that he would certainly like to "pop" her again sometime. He had already enjoyed her charms on a couple of occasions. Further, such a move might just bring about the necessary diversionary effect. And after all, they had always been in the habit of sharing their women, including their wives.

"Roland, I've got to tell you," Justin said as they strolled in the Rose Garden. Zero risk, there, that talk of this kind might be recorded, even accidentally, whether by their own hidden microphones, let alone others'. "Marie is getting dangerously unstable, making a pest of herself; she's doing phone calls, threatening blackmail and so forth. The worst thing is our taps have picked her up talking about holding a news conference and spilling the beans about the three of us."

"What?" was all that Roland, open-mouthed, could manage to say.

"Your brother-in-law, 'Crawfoot,' told me." Justin liked to refer sarcastically to Jeter Crawford, the actor, who had married their sister, by calling him "*your* brother-in-law" instead of "our," and sometimes corrupting his surname.

"My God, Justin! What a bitch!" Roland ignored the remark about Jeter.

"I think," he continued before Roland could put in another word, "you'd better go out there and talk some sense into her—and maybe put something else into her while you're at it, to get her mind off the other stuff," he added with a mischievous grin.

"Shit!" Rarely used by Roland, the word meant something when he did. "Do you really think I ought to do that—are you serious?" The prospect had its positive angle, sure, but its negatives seemed alarming.

"I'm *very* serious..., because *she* seems to be. She's gotta be going nuts. Imagine, threatening to go public with the story of our having some innocent fun with her," he said, impishly weaving the fingers of one hand into those of the other, "not to mention pillow-talk about national security secrets, my relationships with other women—even, believe it or not, some... European ones." Justin raised his eyebrows. "In a word, Rolly, she's losing it. Besides, I suspect she's got the goods: tapes she's somehow made of our... er, sessions together. Apparently, she's got somebody in the spy business to sneak in mikes and cameras in a number of places in her house. We've got word of it from our wiretaps. Knowing old man Hooper, his Bureau's probably got this stuff as well, and naturally he's gonna use it to keep on blackmailing us." Justin spoke matter-of-factly. "There's also the issue of the diary she's kept, pictures and other stuff we're pretty sure she's got. With all that, we just can't take any chances," he concluded as his brow furrowed and his whole demeanor darkened.

"Holy crap!"

"So you see, it might be necessary... you know... to *take care* of her—if she won't listen to reason, that is. And even if she does, how do we know she won't fly off the handle and screw up?"

Justin waved his right arm as his brother reflexively brushed back his hair, eyes fixed, mouth shut, a look of concern on his face.

"She's a pretty good piece of ass, I must admit," Justin went on, smiling at the recollection, "but I've had it with her. If she can't control herself...," he let the unfinished sentence hang in the air. "We've done it before..., you know, and we can do it again...." He shrugged. "Do you understand?" Justin made an unmistakable hand gesture: one that could not be picked up by any friendly, or even unfriendly, audio-recording system. Then he opened up both hands, palms outward, as if to say "what else can we do?"

"All right, I'll think about it," Roland answered.

"Don't think about it, Rolly—*do* it!" Justin punctuated his counter with a down-pointed index finger. It was clearly an order. "Check with Jeter, if you need help," he added, softening his tone slightly. "He's pretty close to her and knows how to handle her, knows the best angles, what's on her mind at any given time. When the chips are down, like they are now, he's reliable." He paused, exchanging a meaningful look with Roland. "After all, he's just tipped us off."

"Well, good for him. Do you think he might be willing to take care of it for us, in case it's necessary? He just might have more access...." Roland tried to sidestep the hard part by emphasizing the logistics.

Not a chance. He's so weak and queasy. When it comes right down to it, we can't trust him with something like that. I think we'll just have to take care of it ourselves—there's nothing else we can do. We just can't take any chances, you know. You might just feel him out before you...."

Roland picked up his drift and nodded agreement. Then he mumbled something about having to get back to his work at the Department of Justice and, staring at the floor, walked out of the Oval Office. High positions—and impunity—came at a price, he concluded.

The only good thing about this mess—he tried to think of the positive side—was that at least he'd get to lay her again once or twice before push came to shove. After that, whatever happened—he still wanted to give himself an outside chance at aborting the assignment—would depend on a lot on her own attitude. If it came to *that,* it would, in the end, be her own damned fault. In that case, he thought, fuck her!

* * * * * * *

In 2010, some ominous notes written by Marie were found among papers stored away by her drama coach, Len Stromberg, long-since dead. The notes, scribbled in her own handwriting, show the following disjointed phrases:

> *being afraid of Jeter*
> *he might harm me, poison me, etc.*
> *why - strange look in his*
> *eyes - strange behavior*

Aside from some insinuations, no one has seen fit to carry this any further. However, it doesn't take a rocket scientist to connect the dots and conclude that Jeter Crawford's "strange" behavior might indicate that he was trying to implement a plan to "take care of" Marie. Gauging his personality one might deduce the most likely reason for his failure to follow through: unaccustomed to such a "job," he simply didn't have the nerve.

Chapter IV
A DISHONOR NO MORE

"Come, Rebecca, we'll take good care of you." Those were the last words the youngest Kilmory sibling would hear before undergoing the procedure.... The nurses seemed harmless enough. And she had no reason to suspect anything from her father except loving care and concern, even though he was, mostly, a tough taskmaster.

They wasted no time in taking her to the operating room and anesthetizing her. She was in her mid-twenties that day in the late 1940's. When they finished, over two hours later, the young girl, who was well adjusted, happy and socially active, had suddenly become a virtual robot, unable to recognize friends and relatives or relate to them as she had all her life up till then. Her mental state was that of a child two to three years of age.

"I'm sorry, sir, she has not reacted well to the lobotomy, so far. We'll"—the plural spread the responsibility around—"have to give her some time." The surgeon lied, suspecting that it was a dismal failure and fearing the worst.

"Oh? But I thought you said...." Jonathan Kilmory tried to look more worried than he really was. He had already decided that, if worse came to worst, she could be put away somewhere out of sight, effectively putting out a bad example that would besmirch the standard being set by the Kilmorys in their high fields of endeavor. He waved away the smoke from the surgeon's Camel cigarette as he gave his own a final puff and crushed it on an ashtray with symbolic but inadvertent finality.

"Of course, it's still too early to reach any firm conclusions, sir." The doctor skillfully avoided saying anything compromising.

Although cheerful and friendly, Rebecca had always been mentally slow or, put more bluntly, somewhat retarded. She had not been able to keep up with her over-achieving siblings, either intellectually or even physically. Still, despite her handicap she had seemed to adjust relatively well, had always participated in family activities—mainly at the insistence of her mother and despite her father's inclination to exclude her—and had even been presented at court to King George VI when their family head had made a splash in the British press as America's breezy ambassador to the United Kingdom. President Roosevelt could think of no better insult to the British than to send an Irishman as America's envoy to the Court of St. James.

However, since to him she represented a disgrace and a failure—something he could not stand within the Kilmory family circle—he decided that something needed to be done. Without telling her mother or, indeed, anyone else in the family, he determined to subject her to a lobotomy. A new, experimental and unsafe operation, it had produced few positive, verifiable results. Tried out on chimpanzees, it had made them more quiet and docile—a promising result to those primarily interested in controlling behavior, regardless of side-effects. Signs that passivity had replaced an active zest for life and interactive relationships were ignored, and in some cases even welcomed. The intentions were good, even if the cure could turn out worse than the "disease."

In humans the procedure was largely unproven; although it had produced an acceptable outcome in certain cases, there were serious side effects. There was no way to tell the outcome in advance. The procedure was primitive even by the standards of the thirties and forties. A "precision leucotome" (actually more like a blunt knife) was inserted in small holes at the temples and then used to sever nerve fibers going to the limbic system, i.e., the brain's emotional center. It was no wonder that violent patients were calmed and the oversexed lost most, if not all, of their libido. Unsurprisingly, the treatment was recommended and used to "cure" thousands of homosexuals. Yet the loss was not only of emotion, but of memory and speech. One of the proponents of the procedure boasted that those who had undergone the operation had become "different people." Sure enough, they had become zombies.

However, to Jonathan the concept offered the enticing possibility of making Rebecca more controllable and perhaps more socially acceptable in behavior. Otherwise, in the event of failure, she could be completely removed from the family picture. It didn't much matter, he thought, whether it went in one direction or the other. If it happened to improve Rebecca's attitude and personality, fine. If not, she would at least cease to improperly reflect the family's burnished image and exceptional achievements.

Rebecca was often in a rebellious mood, given to occasional tantrums and prone to going out alone at night. The child, like some of her numerous siblings, could be headstrong. Suppose, he thought, she went out and got pregnant? Faced with that prospect, there was, practically speaking, only one way out.

He vaguely recalled, with his limited knowledge of history, that a Roman emperor had not hesitated to exile his own nymphomaniac daughter to remote Sardinia. For extreme problems, extreme solutions were justified. So, if the lobotomy succeeded in modifying her personality, in making her behavior more "normal" and controllable—problem solved. And if not, if it made her worse, she could be put away in a home for the mentally ill somewhere far away, where she would be out of sight—and therefore out of mind— hopefully never to be heard from again. Once more, problem solved.

Dr. Thomas Tucker, the chief surgeon, had been unsure that the lobotomy was in order in the case of Rebecca. But there was no question that Jonathan Kilmory was determined to get this done one way or another. So what were he and his team going to do, turn him down? Not a chance. Kilmory was not only persistent, but wealthy, willful, persuasive, extremely powerful and more than a little dangerous when crossed. In the end, Dr. Tucker brushed away his doubts with the expectation that success was always a possibility. Then, too, Kilmory was paying a substantial fee, over and above the usual. (Jonathan believed in incentives to stimulate performance, or to get his way.) And he had protected himself with the disclaimer that, as in all medical procedures, no outcome could be guaranteed in advance.

As he feared, it went badly. After the surgery, the girl had turned into a virtual basket case, unresponsive and seemingly off in a world of her own. Nearly a week of intensive efforts to bring her back to her former self had been fruitless.

"Is this typical post-operative behavior?" Kilmory addressed Dr. Taylor, showing detached curiosity not without a touch of concern. In the back of his mind he recalled that the procedure had been his own personal secret: neither his wife nor anyone else in the family knew about his plans to have Rebecca undergo the surgery. He did, however, take comfort in that he was the absolute boss in the family, with imperious confidence in his ability to be convincing and in justifying himself, whatever the circumstances. Without that— without his single-minded drive and ambition—he would never have gotten to the heights of success and power he had achieved in his life, a position which now his family was enjoying as well.

"A lot depends on the patient, Mr. Kilmory. In your daughter's case, within a few days or perhaps weeks I'm confident there will be improvement. She's still young and some individuals take more time than others to recover and show the hoped-for positive results." Dr. Taylor tried to put the best possible face on the situation.

"Send your bill to my accountant," Kilmory concluded, without asking how much. He did not want to discuss Rebecca's case anymore. "But keep it reasonable," he added, as was his custom, to prevent the greedy from taking undue advantage of his wealth. Then he motioned to the two private nurses he had brought along.

"Come along, Rebecca, we're going home," Jonathan said. She gazed, zombie-like, blankly into the distance as the obedient nurses, one on each side, led her away.

Actually, she was off to an institution for mental patients unable to care for themselves, far from the Kilmory home compound. Since she could not handle the simplest everyday tasks, she would need full-time care. Jonathan felt a bit sorry for her, but certainly did not want one of his own around the family household in such a condition. That would be nothing short of shameful. If she improved, as the doctors optimistically predicted, they would report it to him and he would think about a change of venue for her, if appropriate. Otherwise, she would be kept at a safe distance—out of sight, out of mind. If any Kilmorys cared to visit her, they would have to go far out of their way.

Rebecca would remain the conspicuously absent relative who was never again to be seen or even mentioned, at least in Jonathan Kilmory's presence. As far as he was concerned, it was to be a life sentence unless, improbably, she recovered sufficiently to be shown in public as part of the high-achieving Kilmory clan.

It had been, in a nutshell, a win-win proposition for Jonathan Kilmory. He was still a winner and where he wanted to be: ahead of the game.

Chapter V
THE TRAP

"There he is, the beast! Don't let him get at me!" Wearing a low-cut dress with luscious cleavage, seventeen-year-old Edna Klinger ran screaming out of a janitor's broom closet at the Carthages Theater in Los Angeles. The bewildered owner, Ari Carthages, managed only to protest "She's trying to frame me!"

When a policeman was called in off the street, the girl insisted that Carthages was sexually assaulting her. He was "kissing me madly" she said and, pointing at her breast, complained that he had bit her. The officer promptly arrested Carthages on charges of rape. A Greek immigrant who was timid and barely spoke enough English to make himself understood, Carthages was no match for the forces that had been unleashed against him.

According to Jeff Kilmory's recollection, this episode was considered one of his father's major Hollywood achievements. Although it had occurred during the Roaring Twenties, even before he himself had been born, he had heard the story through the family grapevine. He could not help but admire his father's resourcefulness, his shady reputation notwithstanding. Among The Patriarch's successful gambits during his heyday in Hollywood, this one was legendary. He had taught the clan, by example, how bold ruthlessness could get them what they wanted whenever they chose. Through this particular frame-up, Jonathan had pulled off nothing less than a robber-baron deal and taken over MKO Pictures.

Jonathan's first move in this coup was to acquire the Carthages movie theatre chain in Los Angeles. The owner was reluctant to sell, but Kilmory knew that Ari Carthages would be no match for him. In 1929, Jonathan was a major player in the motion picture industry, and he was not easily put off. He let Carthages know, in no uncertain uncertain terms, of his position and influence. Carthages proved to be hard-headed, but Jonathan Kilmory's strategy was to play hardball.

All of a sudden, Carthages found that first-run motion pictures were no longer available for his chain. But that was only Jonathan's first step.

Through his agents, Jonathan had become acquainted with the young, attractive and easily influenced Edna Klinger, a local girl who was hopeful of becoming a movie star. His promises and reward offers were tempting enough, and she accepted. Her job was simple. All she had to do was set up Carthages for a hard fall. He would take care of the rest.

In court on rape charges, Carthages broke into tears on hearing Edna's story. He barely managed, in his broken English, to repeat his only defense over and over: "I did not." At one point Carthages explained that the girl was after him to buy a play written by her agent. When he turned it down Edna had reacted, he said, by accosting him at the theater, tearing his shirt and clinging to his legs.

Had all been just an act on her part? Some wondered. The jurors, however, had no such thoughts. Mysteriously persuaded that it was all true, they were inclined to convict Carthages. Whether they were charmed by the girl or—more effectively—by other inducements can only be conjectured at this point, about three quarters of a century beyond the events and any kind of solid verification. However, simple common sense tells us that this was a clear miscarriage of justice or, more likely, that the judicial process was tampered with. If Carthages had been reckless enough to make sexual advances at a young girl, risking charges of statutory rape, would he do it on the premises of his own theater?

The prosecution had no qualms about it, and Carthages's defense attorney was complicit with his enemies or at least highly incompetent in his handling of the case. As a result, Carthages's chances for acquittal, if any, proved to be minimal. The jury quickly delivered its verdict and sentenced him to fifty years in jail—in effect, a life sentence for someone of his age. To the jury it seemed only fair punishment for a child molester.

Carthages then fired his lawyer and got a new one: Gerald Kiesler, a famed Hollywood attorney. Kiesler promptly stepped in to demand a new trial based on an error in not admitting testimony about Klinger's morals. The court had decided that, since Klinger was underage, she was not legally capable of consenting to sex, and therefore such an issue was not relevant to the case.

But Kiesler showed, among other things, that Klinger had been living in the same apartment with her boyfriend, a Russian named Boris. So, underage or not, she had obviously had sexual experience.

While Carthages was acquitted in the new trial thanks to Kiesler's strategy and his demonstration that the events described by

Edna Klinger as having occurred in the broom closet lacked credibility, his business had suffered as a result of the notoriety.

Months after Jonathan's "final offer" of $8 million, Carthages was forced to sell for less than half: $3.5 million.

Two years later, Klinger said she wanted to make amends and tell the truth. She talked to her attorney about it and to others, and stories began circulating that she would blow the lid off the whole rape case and name those behind the frame-up. Would that likely bring her the fame she wanted and that Kilmory had promised and not delivered? Perhaps. If not, at least she would get even... and notorious.

Shortly, she was found dead. When her body was examined, it showed unmistakable symptoms of cyanide poisoning, among them characteristic redness of the skin.

It became known that she had suddenly gotten violently ill and that, as she lay dying, Klinger confessed to her mother and a friend that she had, in fact, set up Carthages. For the stunt, it was later known that Jonathan had promised to pay $10,000, a sum which was to be shared with her agent and her boyfriend Boris, who had acted as her advisors. Jonathan had got further "insurance" by promising to turn Klinger into a movie star, thanks to the publicity resulting from the scandal and the subsequent trial. Her face, he assured her, would be in the news all over the country, making her famous and turning her into a valuable property. However, except for the notoriety of the rape case, Edna remained unknown and never received any of the money, which was split between her boyfriend and her agent.

Is it possible that Jonathan Kilmory was behind what happened to Edna Klinger to keep her from talking? It is beyond question—although Jeff preferred not to dwell on it—that his father certainly had the motive and resources needed to plan the crime. Curiously, as far as is known, no autopsy was performed or even requested. If Jonathan had in fact been behind all of this, it was certainly not the first time—nor would it be the last—that he had seen fit to turn the business, judicial, and political processes upside down. It was a lesson the younger Kilmorys learned well: that they could get away with anything if they put their mind and resources into it.

Was it the first time that the Kilmorys had eliminated a woman—or a man or, indeed, anyone—who stood in their way? The skill and proficiency of the whole process—not to mention an outcome that spoke volumes—would seem to indicate more than sufficient resourcefulness and sheer willpower to pull off something like that and then cover up all incriminating loose ends.

Although Jeff certainly had no inclination to think of the negative aspects, he tried to dismiss them by concluding that, sometimes, such things had to be done. He preferred to ponder the corporate wheeling and dealing by which The Patriarch managed to gain control of MKO and Parquet, another major motion picture corporation, as necessary evils. It had been another classic case of the senior Kilmory using his knowledge of stock manipulation and insider trading to plunder corporations. If he had to swindle the stockholders and buy out partners with false but enticing promises, that was just too bad, but necessary. After all, he had done it to not only benefit himself, but also a number of top-level executives who had worked with him to pull it off.

* * * * * * *

Did Edna's death have something to do with Jonathan and his Mafia connections? It's a distinct possibility, since his relationship with the mobsters went back at least to the Prohibition era, when liquor smuggling multiplied his wealth exponentially. He did favors for them and they, in turn, did favors for him. In fact, they worked hand in glove—which is how Justin Kilmory got elected president in 1960. Decades after Prohibition ended, the Kilmorys and the Mafia were still working as closely together as ever.

Chapter VI
SMUGGLER, AMBASSADOR, APPEASER

Smuggling during and after Prohibition was a lucrative business for Jonathan Kilmory. He had not only made millions by criminally working hand in glove with the Mafia during the heyday of bootlegging, but had also accumulated large stocks of whiskey in warehouses, waiting for the expected repeal of Prohibition so he could be the first to satisfy the pent-up demand.

Thanks to his continual influence-seeking, Jonathan had established a solid friendship with Roosevelt's son Edward, who constantly lobbied the president to obtain favors and privileges for him. In turn, Jonathan steered a great deal of business to Edward, who had set up an insurance agency, among other ventures; through these financial incentives and other persuasions—in effect, thinly disguised bribery—he enlisted his help in getting named ambassador to Great Britain. In addition, Jonathan promised Edward a share of the profits in return for representations he made within his father's administration that resulted in awarding him the distributorship for a major brand of Scotch whiskey.

Taking advantage of his diplomatic status in Britain and his knowledge of Wall Street, Jonathan gained personal profit by, among other shady operations, manipulating the U.S. stock market. His extraordinary ability to bilk other investors who were left holding the bag—even from across the Atlantic—enabled him to continue to multiply his enormous fortune (billions in 21st century dollars). As a result he was, in President Roosevelt's opinion, the best man to head the Securities and Exchange Commission, whose job it was to clean up the corruption and illicit speculation in Wall Street. Who better to clean up the mess and throw out the crooks than one of their own kind, an "operator" who had broad experience in taking advantage of regulatory loopholes in the first place?

Although one might have been justified in thinking that Jonathan Kilmory's work at the SEC should by all rights have been an unmitigated disaster—like putting the fox in charge of the henhouse—it didn't turn out that way at all. It is generally acknowledged, in fact, that Kilmory did a creditable job in cleaning up the mess. One wonders: what were Kilmory's motives or incentives to do this? Future electoral plans? In any event, Roosevelt was gratified.

However, as ambassador to Great Britain Jonathan Kilmory was now getting into trouble. The British were facing an aggressive and expansionist Germany under Chancellor Hitler and were hoping to get the U.S. to provide support and, eventually, join them in the oncoming war. But Jonathan sympathized with the dictator and advocated appeasement of the Nazi leader. He had a very important reason: he felt that war with Germany would eventually endanger his sons. Besides, opposing the Nazis was bad for his personal business operations; to top it off he didn't think America could defeat Hitler's war machine. He even made plans to go to Germany to try to make a deal—maybe buy out *Der Fuehrer*—but was unable to do so when President Roosevelt chose to derail the plan. Was the President, for some reason, hoping to join Britain in an eventual confrontation with Germany? In retrospect that might have been, at the time, a distinct possibility.

While all this was going on, Kilmory unabashedly supported British Prime Minister Chamberlain. This position was not so contradictory, since he was comfortable with Chamberlain's policy of appeasing Germany. At a brief meeting he told Chamberlain that "America is anti-war and therefore, Britain being its natural ally in the event of hostilities, the U.S. is wary of entangling alliances."

Chamberlain replied that "concrete concessions must be made to Germany and Italy," adding that he was "prepared to make them to avert war." Based on this exchange of views, Jonathan concluded that Chamberlain was "a very strong character, one that could easily dominate a situation;" in sum, a man who was "realistic and practical."

However, he wired the State Department saying that Britain was in a very difficult position and had "used up practically all its aces."

On a personal level, Kilmory and his large family became the darlings of the British press, which covered his every move. His nine children, extensively reported on and photographed, were the subject of numerous stories, particularly when they were presented at court to the King and Queen. Their toothy grins and outgoing personalities were everywhere to be seen. Among his daughters who were accorded such a presentation was Rebecca, who seemed perfectly normal at the time. As previously noted (Chapter IV), he would later subject the child to a secret, damaging lobotomy and expel her from the family circle.

However, when it came to the traditional presentation of a group of American debutantes to the monarchs, which American ambassadors had done for years, Jonathan refused on the ground that the selection process was "undemocratic." The real reason was that he did not want to draw attention away from the presentation of his own daughters to London society.

Jonathan pointedly stated his hatred of having to wear the knee breeches required by protocol when submitting his letter of credence to the King, and so asked to be allowed to wear trousers. Although previous ambassadors had simply disregarded the old-fashioned requirement, Kilmory made it a major bone of contention in order to call attention to himself.

After the ceremony, he gave an interview to the *Daily Telegraph* in which he boldly repeated some of the remarks made by the sovereign. Since protocol required that the King not be quoted, this raised a few eyebrows—as Jonathan had hoped. His whole plan was to be in the news. Since he was considered President Roosevelt's right-hand man and an important political figure in his own right who could help Great Britain with a number of its problems, the press found him an attractive subject. He helped to bring this about by giving large elaborate dinners for reporters, complete with champagne and the projection of motion pictures for their amusement. Soon, he was a popular figure, becoming known as "the Nine-Child Envoy."

Roosevelt was not too happy with his ambassador's antics. In particular, Jonathan's isolationist, anti-war position did not resonate well with his own. He was already planning to bring the U.S. into the fight in support of Britain when the timing was right—and it seemed to be coming close, with Hitler becoming more aggressive by the day. War was clearly on the horizon. Was Roosevelt counting on the long-established principle that war-time presidents are automatically re-elected?

The Chief Executive, however, humored Jonathan and tolerated his behavior, mainly because he felt that it was safer to keep him abroad. Had he returned to the U.S., Jonathan might have been a rival for their party's presidential nomination. Even though

Kilmory denied any presidential hopes, Roosevelt knew that the opposite was true. He was one of the richest men in the country and was active in "public affairs," as he preferred to call politics.

At one point he was close to being nominated to a job he coveted: Secretary of the Treasury. He might have gotten the position if Roosevelt had not been loyal to Henry Morgenthau, the incumbent, of whom he was extremely fond. So he preferred to keep Kilmory out of the country and away from politics, although it seemed that he was

using the position to which the President had appointed him—to Roosevelt's annoyance—as a launching pad to begin campaigning for his job: the presidency.

Kilmory also had an annoying habit of finding excuses to come home every few months. On one of his numerous trips back— which he took at will justifying them with reasons of health, "consultation requirements," etc.—Jonathan actually made a radio address endorsing Roosevelt for a third term as president in the coming elections. It later turned out that the surprising turn of events had been part of a deal to get the president's backing for his son Jonathan, Jr. to run for governor of his home state.

Since Jonathan was used to buying his way into whatever he wanted and therefore felt that everything and everyone was for sale, at one point he proposed, as noted, to offer Hitler a bribe in order to get him to back off. Aside from the shock and disgust it caused, it was deemed a totally worthless and absurd idea—Hitler was not interested in money but in power. The plan did a lot to further reduce Jonathan's image, already on a slippery slope.

In 1938 Kilmory met Charles Lindbergh, who had parlayed his pioneering 1927 transatlantic flight into celebrity status and had become the leader of a movement called "Keep America Out of War." Being like-minded as to avoiding European entanglements, the two got along famously. Lindberg soon became one of Jonathan's main advisors. Shortly, Roosevelt got wind of the association between the two, especially after Lindbergh visited Germany at Hitler's invitation and came back singing his praises and proclaiming that the *Luftwaffe* was the world's most powerful air force. After it was said that Lindbergh had made statements against freedom of the press and democracy, Roosevelt commented that he considered Lindbergh a Nazi.

To make matters worse, Kilmory made a number of anti-Jewish statements and appeared to deem Hitler's menacing campaign against the Jews as unimportant or even justified. Roosevelt was hardly pleased.

He soon felt that it was no longer in his own personal interest to remain as ambassador to Britain. Washington was not happy with his performance, his own staff at the embassy was up in arms against him and the British were now becoming annoyed with his pleadings for appeasement. In short, he felt it was time to return home and see what else he could do to promote his own and his family's ambitions.

Ready to dismiss him, Roosevelt still wanted to do it gently, not wanting to break with him. Accordingly, he invited Kilmory to a private meeting with him in his home in Hyde Park. The president expected him to resign so he would not have to ask him to step down, and so he did. But Roosevelt asked him to delay its effective date so as to give him time to find a successor.

However, something disastrous occurred at their meeting. Roosevelt lost his temper and sent him packing. When his wife reminded him that he had promised to have Jonathan as a guest for the weekend, Roosevelt told her words to the effect that he never again wanted to see "that bastard" as long as he lived. Brushing off her protestations, he told her to drive Jonathan out on a tour of the countryside and then get rid of him one way or another.

Kilmory brushed off the Chief Executive's humiliation and became even more determined to wield power. He became determined to make his son Jonathan, Jr. president. Not only would that make him extremely happy and even richer, but he would get even with Roosevelt, who had denied him the chance for personal reasons and through his overweening desire to hold on to the office for the rest of his life.

Later, devastated when Jonathan, Jr. was killed in the war, he decided to concentrate his efforts on his next eldest son, Justin. He spared no expense in promoting him. He got his aides to write books for Justin so that he could claim the intellectual baggage for a run at the highest office. One was *When England Slept*, a title slyly borrowed—although, significantly, no one pointed this out—from a book on the same subject written by Winston Churchill, *While England Slept*. Feeling the satisfaction of being largely praised by the press for writing such an important work, Justin declined to acknowledge any such borrowing. U.S. book reviewers—inducements, threats?—were careful to make no mention at all of Churchill's book.

The next book was *Profiles in Bravery*, which was actually researched and written by Justin's main speechwriter, as well as by other aides of his and Jonathan's. The Patriarch immediately went to work at something that was unquestionably one of his top skills: manipulating the press. He maneuvered, courted, bribed and cajoled key people in the media to publicize it, while ordering his staff to purchase huge numbers of copies to make it a best-seller. As a result it won the Pulitzer Prize. Needless to say, to ensure the award, Jonathan had also done some major "public relations" work and spread considerable dollars around among the right people.

In a conversation with Cardinal Stillman, Jonathan once said that he had just spent $85,000 on a horse," and that "for another $85,000," he had got his son Justin on the cover of *Time*. Inside the magazine's issue there was a highly favorable article on Justin, who was by then a senator. He had already been in the running for vice president in the previous primaries, against the advice of Jonathan himself, who had predicted defeat for his party's presidential candidate. Now, with the lead article in *Time,* even though Justin did not have a remarkable record as a senator, the grooming of the future president was going into high gear. The publicity was having its effect, since Jonathan made sure it was all favorable, without a shadow of negative, inquisitive or even dubious words to counteract it or provide a balanced view.

Jonathan had once said, in an inadvertent slip for an unusually candid interview with a national magazine, that his plans were for Justin to be President, Roland to be Attorney General and Jeff to be a senator. The most important step, clearly, was to put Justin in the presidency, and that was going along splendidly.

Far from limiting himself to manipulating Justin's political career, Jonathan also intervened in his love life whenever he thought it might have an undesirable effect on his expectations for pushing him to the top. Back in the early 1950's Justin had actually married, on a spur-of-the-moment whim, a totally unsuitable and socially undesirably woman. No sooner had Patriarch Jonathan heard the news than he promptly forced him to have the marriage annulled and made sure that it was struck off the public records by calling on his friends in the Mafia to destroy the evidence for him. But not before giving Justin a piece of his mind.

Another instance was Justin's involvement with a Danish beauty named Ima Varda, who was a known sympathizer of Hitler; like the man she admired, she was a Jew-hater and, also, a likely Nazi spy. She was the first of a number of women who gave Justin poor marks as a lover. When Jonathan got wind of the affair he contacted his friend, Secretary of the Navy James Forrestal, and asked him to transfer Justin. That was how the young man wound up trading his desk job in Washington, which his father had arranged, for something more adventurous in the South Pacific. By some accounts he got that assignment because he persistently lobbied his father for it in order to get out of such a quiet environment and "see some action." On the positive side for his future, it avoided any embarrassing situations and safeguarded his career in the Navy. His service record, too, looked much better.

If not for that intervention by Jonathan, whose friendship with Secretary Forrestal got Justin to the Pacific, he would never have become the "hero" of PT-129. This apparently positive event was, by the way, another case in which The Patriarch arranged for masterfully turning a negative into a positive with the consequent favorable publicity for his son.

But first, a little background. So bad was his health that Justin could not pass the regular physical to get into the armed services. However, to his credit he was so insistent on doing his duty that his father arranged for him to get into the Navy. By having him undergo a cursory physical in which few questions were asked, he was accepted and commissioned a lieutenant j.g. (junior grade). He then managed to get into a PT training program and, since The Patriarch did not want him anywhere near action, he pulled strings to get him assigned to a base in Panama.

Ever adventurous, however, Justin wangled a transfer to the Solomon Islands, where a squadron of PT boats faced potential hostilities from the Japanese Imperial Navy. The bold, wiry kid soon developed a reputation for daring and was nicknamed "Crash Kilmory" after he raced another PT and beat it—crashing into a dock at the end. But the damage was minor and the Ambassador's son was given a pass.

However, the episode of PT-129 and its encounter with a Japanese destroyer was another story for years shrouded in mystery, except for accounts that have misrepresented it, highlighting all its positive angles—and none of its negative ones. Most published reports indicated that Kilmory's ship was out there alone one night and ran into some bad luck.

Actually, it was on a mission as part of a group of fifteen PT boats sent out to intercept four Japanese destroyers that were resupplying Japanese troops in the islands. The plan was to creep up on them in the dark, ambush them and send them to the bottom. The mission commander had committed the mistake of ordering radio silence, which made it impossible for the PT's to communicate with each other during such vital, close-in maneuvers. And inadvisably, Kilmory had ordered two of his engines to be cut in order to reduce noise: this made it impossible to get out of the way when the destroyer Yamaguri unexpectedly headed across their PT's path. Also against regulations, Kilmory had allowed two crewmen to get some sleep.

Thus, the story told in books, motion pictures and so-called "historical" write-ups, was that the PT-129 was navigating normally one night when a Japanese destroyer just happened to "ram it and break it in two." It was an exaggeration by the press, written at the behest of father Jonathan, since the Japanese ship had only sideswiped its bow. The impact, however, tossed overboard several crewmen, two of whom were lost and presumed dead. It also tore open the PT's fuel tank, causing a brief but intense fire. However Justin and his remaining men somehow stayed or climbed back aboard and proceeded to rescue other survivors. When one man who had been badly burned called out for help, Justin swam out to his rescue, bringing him aboard. It turned out to be his engineer, Michael Martin. Together with his men, Justin helped rescue a couple of other crewmen.

After all the survivors were gathered they realized the broken hull was taking on water, so they tried to reach an island some four miles distant. Justin had to swim with the engineer's life vest strap in his teeth—the man could not swim or even tread water—thus saving his life. This, by the way, was the reason for his medal, the Navy having turned down efforts by his father to get him a more valuable decoration, up to and including the Congressional Medal of Honor.

To make the story seem more heroic, a crucial detail was omitted in describing how the men—including Kilmory, who had dragged his engineer to safety—had swum so far to dry land: every single man was wearing a life vest. Otherwise, they might never have made it.

Yet their survival should have been a simple matter of jumping into the life raft that was supposed to be aboard the PT boat. Unfortunately, before going on the mission—and in yet another violation of Navy regulations—captain Kilmory had discarded the life raft aboard the PT in order to replace it with a jerry-rigged, useless 37-mm gun that was never even fired. This fact was also overlooked by all accounts published at the time. Because of the absence of this vital piece of equipment, the men were indeed lucky to be alive.

At any rate, the collision with the destroyer eliminated the surprise factor and the PT squadron retreated. It was later explained that the ensuing fire and the lack of information caused by the order for radio silence made the rest of the squadron think that PT-129 had been sunk with all hands aboard. (Abandoning one of their own squadron under such circumstances was a serious violation on the part of the other PT's and the mission commander, who had conveniently stayed ashore, on base.)

Suspecting the island might be held by the Japanese, Justin said that then he swam out again, this time with a lantern, to try to signal passing ships. Yet again, a serious violation of strict Navy regulations that require a commander to always remain with his men in case of danger. Unsuccessful and exhausted, Kilmory returned and gave up. As they were running out of coconut meat and water, the group came across some natives who helped them. Kilmory then supposedly carved a message on a coconut husk that was taken by a native to summon help from an allied outpost (the "famous" coconut husk was later proudly exhibited on the desk of President Kilmory). Another dramatic but dubious detail: there was no need for the "husk message" since the native also carried a note on paper explaining the situation more clearly. Although it was an Australian lookout who had received word from the native courier about the shipwrecked Americans and had them rescued, Kilmory seemed to get all the credit for saving his crew. The story, as written up in a glowing account by Kilmory family friend Joel Hershey, was published in *The New Yorker* in 1944. Under the title "Survival," it included a good dose of fiction in order to make it sound wildly heroic.

When first told that his son was missing, Jonathan held on to hope and did not tell his wife or family. Finally, on getting the good news that Justin was safe, he seized the opportunity to publicize the incident, turn him into a veritable hero and promote his political career, just as he had originally planned.

As indicated, Jonathan hoped to get his son the Congressional Medal of Honor, or at least the Navy Cross, but he finally had to settle for the Navy and Marine Corps Medal. Jonathan took it gladly—and ran with it.

The Navy questioned how Justin's PT boat could have been rammed and sunk by a good-sized Japanese ship—his was the only PT ever to suffer such a fate during World War II or any other armed conflict. But the matter was never properly cleared up. The required naval investigation was practically a whitewash. But a lot of strings were pulled and the crew deflected any questions by saying that Justin had showed leadership and bravery, and had led them successfully out of a chaotic situation.

Later analysts have reached a different conclusion: what else were the crewmen going to say? A little common sense indicates that a fast and quickly maneuverable craft like a PT boat should have been able to avert any lumbering Japanese destroyer. But skipper Kilmory, because two of the PT's engines were turned off and two of his crewmen were asleep, was unable to maneuver out of the destroyer's path. Therefore, instead of getting a medal, Justin should have been court-martialed for violating several naval regulations and dereliction of duty resulting in the loss of a ship and part of its crew.

It was a lucky break that the destroyer decided to stay on course and not turn around to make sure that the PT was sunk, finishing off or capturing the survivors. Some speculated that this was probably because it felt threatened by the other American PT's. However, decades later it was determined that the destroyer's captain falsely reported that his ship had fired on and sunk the PT, and gave this as his reason for not stopping.

The ensuing inquiry by the U.S. Navy was run behind closed doors and overlooked everything detrimental to Justin Kilmory. Its results were summarized in a biased report prepared by an old Kilmory friend, Bernard Whittles, who was promptly appointed to the Supreme Court once the PT-129 skipper was in the White House. It is quite possible that Kilmory was grateful or felt that it was a just reward for a job well done. Yet realistically, a Supreme Court appointment makes it unlikely for the appointee to bring up tales unfavorable to his benefactor.

Jonathan wasted no time in getting the story publicized. In addition to getting the aforementioned article in *The New Yorker* by a major journalist such as Hershey, he had it reprinted in *Reader's Digest*, gaining Justin national acclaim. Later, never bothering to ask permission, he distributed some 175,000 copies of the *Digest* article in support of Justin's first run for Congress. Meanwhile, various news stories appeared in dailies of national importance highlighting the heroic event and, later, showing a picture of Kilmory at the ceremony awarding him the medal. One of the papers falsely identified Admiral C. W. Nimitz as pinning the decoration on Justin, when it was actually only an obscure Navy captain.

Eventually, writer Richard Doberman wrote the book *PT-129*, which became a best-seller and was made into a film, for which Kilmory himself selected a well-known Hollywood actor to impersonate him. A replica of PT-129 was proudly incorporated in the inaugural parade down Pennsylvania Avenue when Justin Kilmory was sworn in.

* * * * * * *

A couple of months after the PT-129 incident, in September of 1944, Jonathan Kilmory, Jr. was killed in a bomber loaded with explosives that he and his copilot were to bail out of before it crashed into a target in enemy territory. They had been warned that the remotely controlled detonator was faulty but Jonathan, Jr. was jaunty and daring and insisted on flying the mission. The aircraft blew up before it ever got out of British air space, killing them both. An investigation later determined that the detonator was indeed faulty.

When Jonathan, Sr. got the news he was devastated, but pulled himself together, told the family, and then said: "The Kilmorys don't cry and they don't sit around moping. Jonathan, Jr. would not have wanted us to do anything like that. He would have wanted us to go sailing, so get out there and do it."

He himself, however, went to his room and locked himself in. The blow was terribly painful, as well as highly detrimental to his personal and family aspirations. His eldest son had been his major hope to achieve national power for the Kilmorys, yet now, instead, he was in mourning. He would force himself to get busy soon in order to make Justin the Kilmorys' new number-one standard bearer.

* * * * * * *

When Justin got back from the Pacific Jonathan made sure that he was hailed as a war hero. His friends Harry Lace and his wife Clara Boots Lace, who had been Jonathan's occasional lover, published articles in *Time* and *Life* promoting the Kilmorys, particularly Justin.

Jonathan ensured Justin's election as a congressman by paying the incumbent to withdraw from the race and then, as if that were not enough, he got a candidate with the same Italian name as Justin's main opponent to also run for the seat in order to confuse and split the opposing ethnic vote. The ruse ensured a victory for Justin, who was on his way.

To make sure there would be enough money to finance Justin's campaigns, and later Jeff's, Jonathan went looking for sure-fire investments. He found one in Chicago in the late 1940's, in a huge merchandising operation. The business also owned extremely extremely valuable real estate. It was about to be bought by a friend of his, who told him about his plan. Jonathan wasted no time in jumping in ahead of his friend, who lost out and resented the double-cross for the rest of his life. Jonathan not only bought the property, but pulled off a clever financing deal that guaranteed lucrative profits from the beginning. That business soon became the family's basic source of wealth and made it possible for Justin to establish separate lifetime endowments for each of his family members, who began receiving regular payments based on their needs, circumstances and prospective financial situation.

Jonathan had also come close to buying a major newspaper— among the candidates were the *The Washington Post, The Boston Dispatch and The New York Sun*—but he preferred investments that provided him with substantial tax shelters. This governmental slice out of his enormous wealth was an imposition he intensely resented, and was not convinced that dailies were the best way to avoid them.

He was not, however, at a loss to find creative ways to get hefty tax deductions, such as his donations to the Catholic Church. He would write out a check for a million dollars and give it to a certain cardinal who was a friend of his (he had helped make him a bishop and backed his climb from there); the cardinal would in turn hand him a receipt for a million-dollar donation and then give him back $950,000 in cash. Since this money was untraceable, Jonathan used it to buy votes, pay bribes, conduct illicit campaign financing and carry out other illegal or corrupt operations.

Chapter VII
THE NOD

"Boss, 'ave you chose a date for the meetin'?" Underboss Giovanni Bonanno addressed capo Claudio Mariello. "Or do I just tell 'em we're workin' on it?"

Giovanni was especially careful and respectful with Mariello, knowing that a question should always be phrased so as not to remind the capo of one of those hateful grillings by Roland Kilmory before the House of Representatives' McClanahan Committee. It was a sore point with those who ran the Mafia or "Cosa Nostra", as FBI Director H. Everette Hooper was fond of calling it—usually in private, since for decades he publicly denied its existence (he needed an excuse to lay off his buddies).

Mariello was bent on arranging a meeting with Campana and the other capos, in person—telephone lines were always likely to be tapped—to try to sway them over to backing the Republican nominee, Roger Dixon, in the 1960 election. Claudio Mariello had more than enough reasons to despise and distrust the Kilmory clan. Besides, it would be easy: he figured Dixon would win anyway, though by a slim margin..., unless, that is, the Mob decided to go for Kilmory.

Meanwhile, in the House of Representatives, the McClanahan Committee kept on going, in a curious sort of way. Sal "Looney" Campana had finally been served with the Committee's subpoena in Las Vegas after six months of strangely fruitless efforts to locate him—had they been trying to avoid finding him? Not at all unlikely, since while the government's right hand was trying to accomplish something, its left hand was characteristically working at cross-purposes. In some quarters there were grounds for suspicion about this, since Campana's whereabouts at any given time were common knowledge in Mob as well as law-enforcement circles, and even among segments of the public at large. So if they had really wanted to find Campana and serve him, they could have.

Campana, however, gave no sign of being worried: his testimony, whenever he was forced to give it, was cursory and consisted mainly of repeatedly pleading the Fifth Amendment, almost like a prayerful monk. Besides, he already foresaw "insurance" against too much harassment in the future. He figured that his old friend and partner in crime, Jonathan Kilmory, would want to enlist the Mob's support to help his son, Justin, win the primaries and then the presidential campaign against Roger Dixon.

First, of course, they'd have to buy practically every vote in West Virginia, where a rich, Catholic northeasterner was about as popular as a cat at a mouse party. But the Kilmorys had a secret fund big enough to buy more than just the votes in the small, poverty-stricken state. That special fund was made up mostly of money from the Mob, including a hefty sum the capos drew from union pensions they controlled, particularly the Teamsters'. Some said—with only slight exaggeration?—that they took enough suitcases full of money to buy the whole state, lock, stock and barrel.

Chuck, Campana's younger brother, liked the feeling of importance he got when hanging around Sal and discussing business. This time he wanted to share some of his own thoughts with him, now that they were drinking a cold beer at The Sands; with The Riviera and Wilbur Clark's Desert Inn, it was one of their choice hangouts in Las Vegas. Their favorite luncheon dishes were on the way.

"Don't you think maybe we shouldn't back Dixon instead? The way I hear it he's got a more reliable record of cooperatin' with the Outfit." A cocky twenty-two-year-old, he preferred his American nickname "Chuck," to his given Italian one, "Carlo."

"Well, maybe. We haven't discarded him altogether. Besides, remember that we play both sides, to get a little insurance. Why, we're gonna give Dixon a cool million, at least."

"Yeah, Looney, but you know, for some reason, that guy Kilmory makes me uneasy."

"Yeah? Why?" Big-brother Sal was curt but curious.

"I don't know. Can't put my finger on it exactly. It's just a feeling. Maybe I just don' know enough about 'im," he added modestly. Chuck did not come out and say that, to him, Kilmory was an unknown quantity. The thought crossed his mind as to whether, once elected, he could be relied upon to actually follow through on the deal. But, he wondered, was it too far-fetched to suspect he might not?

"Well, I know 'im personally. Met 'im in Vegas. He's a skirt-chaser, like us, really wild." Chuck paid close attention as Looney leaned closer in looking like he was about to reveal privileged information. "Just between you and me, he's given us big assurances he'll play ball wid us. So some o' the guys are leanin' toward 'im. They figure Kilmory'll be in our pocket big. Still, ya gotta know that our pick is always a lead-pipe cinch—and then we own 'im. It's always been that way. Roosevelt, Truman, you name it. They all played ball with us. Why, we rigged Harry's vote totals to give him a surprise win when Dewey was supposed to win easy, in a cake-walk, accordin' to all the polls," Sal exaggerated the pre-election forecast of Dewey's margin. "Hey, both these guys took our money and promised to lay off. But we liked Truman a lot better, 'cause he never prosecuted us like Dewey did. And we could count on Harry 'cause he was a product of the Pendergast machine in Missouri and we had long-time connections with them. We guaranteed him the election and we delivered." Sal paused for a swig of his favorite beer, Mexico's "Dos XX."

"This time, when we fix up Justin, he's really gonna owe us big. Hey kid, I don't wanna be president. I jus' wanna own the guy. Owning a president is a lot more useful than being one—not to mention more profitable."

"Okay, Loon. But I wonder. You think we can trust Kilmory more than Dixon?"

"In this business we don't trust nobody, son, but if 'e makes a deal wid us he better not break it. Nobody welshes on us and gets away with it." Looney hadn't quite locked in his decision, but felt inclined to dismiss his youthful brother's concerns. To him the chances that old man Jonathan Kilmory and his son Justin would fail to come through were extremely slim.

"Yeah, they should certainly know sump'n like dat!" Chuck agreed.

"You know, I once saved old Jonathan's life. Castellaro put out a contract on him on account of a real estate deal that he backed out of, an' Jonathan came to see me personally an' begged me to do sump'n. So I did. I talked Francesco out of actually having it done." Campana didn't exactly expect just gratitude for his effort—Jonathan had generously compensated him in cash—but it was a big favor and a major demonstration of power.

"He shoulda been thankful for dat! Who else coulda done it?"

"If we give 'im a hand, if the Outfit goes out for 'is son in the election, it'll be all sewed up. Once he takes over, his people'll have to lay off. That'll take care of a major problem for us. *Capisce*?"

"Sure, Looney." Not content with words, Chuck bobbed his head up and down. He idolized his brother and, although he found it difficult to follow in his footsteps, he admired his success, his power, his ability to instantly size up people, pinpoint weaknesses, take advantage and make sound decisions. But his unpredictability was a special factor that kept his underlings and even his family on their toes, wondering what he was thinking, what he would do next. He would fly off the handle and give somebody hell for no reason, and the next moment smile and offer lavish gifts on the slightest excuse. That way, he kept everyone on their toes. It was clear that Looney had a fraternal affection for his kid brother, although he had quickly realized that Chuck had no stomach for the Outfit's rough stuff and was inclined to follow a career in legitimate business. Eventually, he thought, he would set him up good.

"Kid, the deal with the Kilmorys, if we do it, will be fuckin' perfect, I really believe, for both sides." He puffed on his Havana.

This sort of bargain, which the euphemistic Kilmorys liked to refer to as "a quid pro quo," was something they had done before, albeit on a smaller scale. So, Campana thought, why shouldn't they do it again when the prize was the presidency?

"Yeah, the Kilmory deal looks good," he went on. "At times, Dixon's been difficult to work with. He's strait-laced an 'e believes— or says 'e does—in all that moral crap, an' once 'e's at the top, he might just forget who put 'im there—some pols are like that, ya know; power goes to their head. On the other hand, we've worked hand-in-glove with old man Jonathan over the years, and I've seen how 'e delivers an' keeps his kids under control."

In the back of his mind, Campana felt that Justin Kilmory could not possibly renege on a deal with the Outfit if his election should come about thanks to them. That, he thought, just wasn't in the cards. Common sense would dictate otherwise.

For the youthful Chuck, the main question was still compliance. He kept thinking that maybe he didn't understand all the nuances, but if the Kilmorys chose otherwise, how could the Outfit enforce the deal once they were in power, considering they would be at the very top and in control?

"So you think there'll be no problems?"

"No, I really don' expect any, Chuck." Campana squinted through the dense, aromatic smoke of the expensive "Romeo y Julieta" brand Havana cigars he liked to smoke. That they would soon be outlawed in the country was something he couldn t care less about. Brushing a fleck of ash from his natty, bespoke Italian suit as he looked around the restaurant, he recognized a face and gave a ritual nod. "Still, we're gonna do some checkin' with the *consiglieri*, and Mariello—but I know what side *he's* gonna be on." Campana winked at his kid brother and raised his beer stein. "Spanitra, on the other hand, is prob'ly gonna be pushin' for Kilmory big-time, since he's been pal-ing around with 'im quite a bit lately. Got stars in his eyes."

"Okay, Loon", Chuck answered, shortening the "Looney" that few dared use, "but what about 'is brother Roland?" Chuck spoke through a cloud of smoke from his own Havana, with which he occasionally gestured, imitating his older brother's body language in punctuating his comments. "You know how that little bastard likes to show off, thinkin' he's tough. How can we be sure *he's* gonna stop that crap an' lay off?"

More mature than one would have expected for someone his age, Chuck was not afraid to give his opinion; Dixon seemed like a safer bet. But he admired his brother and always deferred to him. He gestured as if to say "what do I know," raised his beer mug and took a swig.

"Listen, kid," Looney said with a sly smile, "with the kind of stuff I've got on the Kilmorys, lots of it on tape—all kinds of different women, including two blondes and a shine at one time—we've got enough to sink the careers of a dozen politicians, let alone the Kilmorys. They'll never be able to afford a double-cross. On the other hand, on Dixon we've got none of that shit—he's so damn straight it's pitiful."

"But hey, hasn't Dixon done us a coupla favors before?"

"Yeah, you know Dixon actually got my guy in Texas, Rosen, outa testifying to Congress back in '47 by claimin' the man was workin' for *him*! But, hey, the Kilmorys and all the other pols have also worked wid us. They're all the same." Campana gave him a sharp, knowing look. "An' when they owe us an' don' come across..., well, you may 'ave heard what happened to Louisiana Governor Long when he got a little too greedy for 'is own good. We got a nut to bump 'im off an' that was that. Nobody figured it out. Same thing with a mick who was mayor of Chicago just a while back, name o' Cermak."

"Loon, you got all kindsa ways to keep 'em all under control, huh?" Never having heard of those hits by the Mob, Chuck was more impressed than he let on.

"Anyway, don't worry kid, we'll get it all straightened out. See, now that it's settled that our man Jameson—calls himself LBJ— is on the ticket for vice president, I think dat's gonna clinch it for us. Both o' these guys are in our pocket. With Dixon we got that guy Loft second on the ticket an' we can't count on that old-money, stuffy guy to lay off as vice president. On the other hand, Jameson's machine'll guarantee Texas goes Democratic—he'll make sure 'bout that. Hell, the votes we don't switch he'll steal right from under their noses, even if he's not sure they're needed—just like us in our territory, Chicago. Jameson's got a well-oiled machine. Why, dat's how 'e won 'is first election... with plenty o' help from us." He enjoyed a small, final exaggeration as a fillip to his spiel. No one would, by now, know that the Mob played only a minor role in rigging that election, since Jameson's own henchmen did most of the dirty work.

"Gee, Looney, I hope you're right. But I'm still worried. I hate to keep buggin' you, but what're they gonna do 'bout Roland? I mean, he's sure gonna be outa that crazy, fuckin' McClanahan Committee if big brother wins, but then he's prob'ly gonna be a biggie in the new administration. Then what?"

"You might have a point, Chuck." Campana smirked. "But I don't think that little shit-ass's gonna give us no trouble. If we hand big brother Justin the election, he'll *have* to keep him under control."

"I sure hope so."

"Well, if we do our part, he'd better do his, or else," Campana answered, accenting the *or else* that usually put fear into the heart of the Mob's enemies. "He's prob'ly gonna get 'im off our ass by gettin' 'im off the damn McClanahan Committee, maybe puttin' 'im to work on 'is campaign. That'd be a good way to keep 'im busy."

"Sure, that oughta keep 'im outa our hair for a while. But after the election 'e could land anywhere. That's just my opinion, though." Chuck left an opening for his brother to end the discussion.

"Like I said, you might have a point, kid. We'll have to keep thinkin' about it." Campana concluded, puffing on his Havana and getting up in a cloud of smoke. "Let's go," he concluded, meaning "I'm outa here."

Campana reminded himself, on his way out, that he had made certain that the Outfit had more than sufficient dirt on Justin Kilmory. By using his friend Hank Spanitra, he had hit a gold mine. Spanitra had already introduced Justin to a number of beautiful women, including Hollywood stars like Annie Dickerson and that up-and-coming sexually liberated bombshell, Marie Moore, plus others less well known.

Having wasted no time in getting detectives to bug Justin's trysts whenever possible, Campana had made certain that copies of the tapes were kept in a safe place. This had become easier since Campana had secretly gotten a controlling interest in the Cal-Neva Lodge, one of the favorite places of the Kilmorys and the Spanitra Brat Pack. The Lodge was a hotel in Reno, conveniently straddling the California-Nevada state line—whence the name—riddled by the Mob with hidden microphones and cameras. The rooms were on the California side of the border and the casino within Nevada's jurisdiction.

Hank Spanitra was one of Campana's solid guys in Hollywood. Through Jake Rosetti, Campana already exerted a great deal of control
over Tinseltown. Looney was fond of saying: "That Jake, he's as smooth as they come. He's got 'em eatin' outa his hand."

When a behind-the-scenes job needed to be done with finesse he could count on Rosetti. He had the manners, the looks and the bearing of a high-class executive. Aside from his name and phone number, his business card boasted a single word: "Strategist". It didn't say at what—but people guessed.

Hank, on the other hand, could handle a certain top-level, high-profile type of public situation. Few people knew for certain of his Mob contacts, although suspicion of them earned him respect. For instance, he could spearhead and perform at fund-raisers, getting stars to come out in support of, for example, Justin's campaign. And, as previously mentioned, he also introduced women to Justin, to Justin's brother-in-law Jeter Crawford and to that apparently strait-laced kid brother, Roland, who actually—together with his younger sibling Jeff—was a regular participant in skinny-dipping with secretaries in the White House swimming pool, swinging sex parties and all the rest.

Spanitra felt strongly that Justin Kilmory was the best choice for the presidency from the Mob's viewpoint. In fact, it was he who had first begun promoting Kilmory with Campana. Socially, Spanitra expected that a Kilmory administration would mean frequent invitations to the White House and other official functions. He would be "in" to an extent he never dreamed of in his early, poverty-stricken days in Hoboken.

Looking at it from the Outfit's angle, Spanitra couldn't help thinking that it was a terrific idea to get your worst enemy to leave you alone. "Just like money in the bank," as he was fond of saying. So, he was sure that a Kilmory-Campana agreement would be a sweetheart deal for his backers, the Outfit..., and therefore for him as well.

Loyal to his friends in the Mob, Spanitra could not and would not forget that it was his connections with them that put him initially on the road to fame and fortune as a singer and then, later on, in the mid-1950's, rescued his foundering career. The studio making *From Here to Infinity* was persuaded via the Mob's muscle to give Spanitra a major role. That brought him back to prominence and, to boot, earned him an Academy Award. That prize, too, might have resulted from some Mob persuasion among Tinseltown's elite.

If Kilmory got elected, Spanitra fancied himself enjoying an ultra-high rank on the social ladder. Besides, it wouldn't hurt to have the President of the United States indebted to him for certain favors. In addition to enjoying the White House social whirl, it would be fun to pal around with President Kilmory. He could see himself being invited—when Kilmory's wife Jennifer wasn't around—to spend the day frolicking with starlets and secretaries in the White House swimming pool and taking them to the Lincoln bedroom for the night. Then, he envisioned grandly, he would have the President himself as his guest at his luxurious Palm Springs estate.

The previous year, 1959, Justin had gladly taken the opportunity to keep company with the Brat Pack in Vegas, where he got the red-carpet treatment and was never billed a red cent for hotels, restaurants, entertainment... or women, some of which were "professionals" and charged a fee. It was difficult, by the way, to get Justin to pay for anything, because he never carried money or any form of credit. (Later, Barry Clangton would emulate and far outdo his idol Justin Kilmory in this area of "finance" as well as in bedding women and coming down with STD's.)

Campana, whether present or absent, had told Spanitra to make sure Justin didn't have to cover any expenses—that way, he would be even more indebted to them. On top of everything, Campana once contributed $15,000 for just one weekend party in Vegas. Peanuts to him, since he had contributed millions to Justin's campaign, but he made sure Spanitra told Justin about the "fifteen big ones" so he would get full credit for it.

Spanitra's own contributions were not just in cash, but in kind. He not only wined and dined Justin Kilmory but introduced him to beautiful, well-known stars and many up-and-coming starlets, including some of the best and most beautiful playmates who hung around with Campana and other top capos. One of these introductions, on Campana's express instructions, was to the stunning divorcée Jessica Cameron (she later took on a second surname, "Exeter," from her next and final husband). Jessica later became one of Looney's regular girls, although he purposely shared her. "Spread the honey around," Campana liked to say—and he wasn't just talking about money.

He did, however, have some restrictions on certain girl-friends of whom he became extremely fond. Perhaps the leading one in that category was one of the singing Mackenzie sisters, Pamela, with whom he had a steady relationship that lasted for a number of years.

In the case of Jessica, Campana worked it out so as not to interfere with her relationship with Justin. He was gaining her trust by respecting that affair without insisting on intimacy—a rare

attitude for him. It worked, since she gradually began to rely more on him as she began to tire of Justin, who seemed to be using her at his convenience whenever he could fit her into his schedule. Who knew what other relationships he might be squeezing in at odd moments, she wondered. Campana's tactic had solid motives: not only was he
interested in her as a prospective lover, but her connection with Justin would enable her to pick up lots of confidential and privileged information.

As it turned out, she not only did serve as a sort of agent-spy for him during Kilmory's term, but also as a courier, carrying important messages, papers and, on two or three occasions, a briefcase stuffed with some $250,000 in cash. Jessica herself confirmed this in her testimony before a congressional committee when she was dying of cancer. All indications are that these sums came directly out of a safe in the White House and went into the Campana pocket as payoffs for services rendered: one of them was putting the fix on the vote count by which Justin had won Illinois and been elected, and/or as repayment for the heavy cash outlays made by the Outfit in order to buy enough votes to win the West Virginia primary.

It was a time in which, with the exception of Cuba—a painful setback—everything looked good for Campana and his countless business operations and deals all over the country and the world. His activities had by then crossed the oceans, and the Mob, largely thanks to his efforts, was getting a cut on gambling, prostitution, narcotics and other rackets in the Philippines, the Dominican Republic, and various other places in the Caribbean, Central and South America, and Europe.

Las Vegas was a veritable gold mine, bringing in millions of dollars in casino skimming and other operations, both legal and illegal. Not to mention semi-legal. Campana had bodyguards,
henchmen and drivers, and kept millions in cash stashed away in different places, in one of which Chuck had seen entire rooms stuffed to the ceiling with cash. According to estimates, at the height of his power Campana was worth over a billion dollars. A lot of it was overseas—even though stand-ins had title to his properties, companies and many of his bank accounts. But then, he always did his transactions in cold cash, so traceable checks were not a favorite means of transacting business.

By then Campana was considered to be the top capo—the *capo di tutti capi*—in the Outfit, and nothing could be done without his permission. Feeling in total control and enjoying his status, he would travel all over the country, Latin America, Europe and

elsewhere, on a whim and at a moment's notice. There was nothing he couldn't do. He was no longer holding onto the top for mere money: he enjoyed, most of all, the status, the adulation, the respect, the broads and the perks. He had people quaking in their boots, stumbling all over themselves trying to please him and making sure there was not the slightest hint
that he was dissatisfied about anything. Just the thought that he could
but raise an eyebrow and make someone disappear was enough to strike fear into the heart of anyone who might come into contact with him. There was a great deal to be said for that.

But even then, Campana had no idea that Justin Kilmory was in the midst of planning the big double-cross that would surprise them all: Roland as Attorney General, no less, and personally in charge of going after them with no holds barred (they skirted around the technically illegal ones). What made the whole thing even more enigmatic was that he himself, Campana, as the Mafia's point man, would be simultaneously doing dirty working for the CIA, starting by assassinating Costra. It was the sort of arrangement that, if known, could have easily put the Kilmorys and their whole administration, regardless of party, in a great deal of trouble.

Moreover, all this was coming sooner than anyone thought. And it was likely to imperil the upcoming second invasion of Cuba, in which Campana was the point man to manage the Costra assassination "job."

* * * * * * *

Patriarch Jonathan thought his pact with the Mob was an invaluable, no-cost deal—and he was quite right, as far as they, the Kilmorys, were concerned. However, whether his sons would actually take it easy on the Outfit was a worrisome question in the back of his mind. He realized that such a policy might be difficult to implement, especially for Roland, who would have to swallow his pride and visceral hatred of the mobsters. But The Patriarch would impress on Roland in particular, as well as on Justin, the grave peril of not keeping their end of the bargain, regardless of all the apparent power wielded by the government.

In the Mob, some disagreed with Campana. Carlos Marcello, Mafia boss of New Orleans, was not convinced about the Kilmorys. And neither was union leader Ricky Hofstra. Despite Jonathan's efforts to calm things down, son Roland's run-ins with them when he was on the staff of the House of Representative's McClanahan Committee investigating Mafia operations were still an irritant clearly remembered by all parties. There was bad blood, particularly between Roland and Hofstra.

Jonathan concluded he had to go to the top. He needed to talk, in person, with his old friend Sal Campana. In the course of events traceable over decades, Campana had met and mingled separately with Jonathan, and later with son Justin and other Kilmorys. Jonathan would lay it on thick, telling Campana it would be great for business and, best of all, for the well-being of the top capos themselves. To get his son to the presidency that he had so badly wanted for himself would mean vindication and was worth anything and everything. Once there, Justin would be king and his son Roland next in line to the throne. There was a dynasty in the making, and the Mob could make it so if he were able to sway them.

He planned to enlist the help of Hank Spanitra, with whom he had an acquaintanceship of long standing. He knew that Spanitra was friendly with Justin as well as with Campana. Aside from a social climber, Spanitra was an ambitious, power-hungry skirt-chaser just like Justin and he himself, Jonathan, in his younger days. He was well aware of Spanitra's closeness to the top capos in the Mob; at one point Spanitra was so close to Campana that he had exchanged star-sapphire pinkie rings with him. Jonathan also knew that the Mob, at one point, had used its muscle to pull his career out of the doldrums. If he could impress on him the importance of backing up his bid to get the top capo on the bandwagon, he might be able to work things out.

But he thought it might be best to first cut the deal with Campana directly, and then, if necessary, get Spanitra to help. Jonathan hated to ask for others' assistance if he felt he could swing a deal on his own. That way, he would get what he wanted: full credit. Besides, his personal prestige would continue on the rise. He decided to call a key member of the Mob whose phone line was considered secure, and ask him to pass the word to Campana about a very important, secret meeting: it would be one-on-one, not counting an underboss for Sal and an assistant for Jonathan.

Two weeks later, Jonathan and his assistant traveled to Chicago for the meeting. It took place at the Bella Napoli, a safe, Mob-owned restaurant where they could talk without being recorded or overheard. They greeted each other cordially, old friends that they were, since they each had helped the other make a small fortune smuggling liquor during the boom created by Prohibition. They joked about old times in a relaxed manner, carefully avoiding any references that might remotely seem touchy. After all, they were there to make a deal that would affect their own and their respective family's lives for generations to come. Needless to say the term "family," for the Mob, extended well beyond the range of bloodlines, although in some cases the term was literal as well as figurative.

Over a sumptuous dinner with bottles of vintage wine, Jonathan laid out his plan to clinch the nomination and then the election against the unstoppable Republican nominee, Dixon. It was fairly simple. If the Mob would play ball and help hand the presidency to his son, the Kilmorys would also play ball and lay off. It would require some muscle and heavy cash outlays that the Kilmorys didn't want anyone to trace back to them—loans to be repaid in due course—but in the end it would be an invaluable deal for the Kilmorys as well as for the Mob. There were assurances that, whatever the final outcome, the Outfit would get its money back, big-time. Both sides knew that there was little chance that their investment would fail to pay off.

Campana listened patiently, nodding now and then or making minor comments. His underboss, Paul "The Waiter" Riccardi looked on attentively, wordlessly. Finally, Campana spoke.

"That sounds fine, Jonathan, but some of our guys question whether you can keep your kids under control." Sal remembered what his kid brother Chuck had said, and sounded as skeptical as his question indicated. The stakes were too high for him to do otherwise.

"Sal, I'll be honest. I didn't bring up my kids to be ingrates. A deal is a deal. You do something for us, we'll do something for you. I've impressed that into them, and they're in," he lied honestly. "Once you guys have delivered on the deal, they and I—we, will take care of you." Well, that was his intention, he told himself with an inward smile.

Campana's gaze went, momentarily, off into the distance. A group of his underlings, sitting at a nearby table to keep an eye on the goings-on, was beginning to seem ever-so-slightly restless as activity dwindled at that late hour.

In a conclusive manner, he looked back at Jonathan. "Okay, I'll check it out with the guys. I gotta tell you a couple of them ain't too keen about it. You know why: your boy Roland's been after us, screwing the shit out of us the last coupla years with them damn congressional committees. How do we know 'e's gonna stop that crap? The boys'll wanna know, have some kind of assurance."

Underboss Riccardi nodded at that remark, a wry smirk on his lips. He had been looking on skeptically, inserting a precise word or two here and there but mostly listening. A waiter swept by just in case someone made the slightest signal, but making sure he didn't interrupt anything with the tiresome cliché: "You doin' okay?" Or "You guys still workin' on that?"

"Hell, I understand, Sal, but tell 'em I'm gonna get my boys to toe the line. No ifs"—he was going to say *shit* but held back, not to echo Sal's vocabulary—"ands or buts about it, Sal. I guarantee it," he emphasized. "All you need do is help us out with the West Virginia primary and then, if need be, the presidential vote in Illinois. Maybe a bit in Texas, but Jameson is supposed to take care of his own territory. With your experience and precinct-level resources, it shouldn't be a problem."

Jonathan flashed that winning smile with which he liked to end his presentations. It was just as charming, if not more so, than his greeting smile—although sometimes, if he wasn't careful, it turned downright foxy.

"Okay, Jonathan. Like I said, I'll check it out and get back to you," Campana said noncommittally as he took Jonathan's extended hand in his own. Then he turned and walked away without looking back. The outcome was still in the balance.

Jonathan Kilmory walked out of the restaurant feeling that he had everything lined up—almost. He expected Sal to come across. Nineteen-sixty looked like it would be their great year. Justin, senator from their home state, was in an excellent position to win the presidential nomination of his party. The West Virginia primary was crucial, but if the Outfit jumped in, its cash and muscle could snatch the prize away from the hopeful rival, Herbert Humpter.

If Campana decided to swing over to his side it was as good as done. Then the Outfit, having gone that far, would not fail to take care of business in the general election. As the top capo, Campana pulled lots of weight when it came to bringing over the other bosses. All he had to do was convince them that it would work out well, be good for business and, above all, that it would definitely get the government off their collective back.

This was the time, Jonathan figured, to contact Hank Spanitra and urge him to back up the deal with Campana. Already enjoying his closeness to son Justin, he should be instrumental in encouraging the big boss to get aboard. When Jonathan got him on the phone to sound him out, Spanitra was accommodating.

"No need for you to fly out and meet me anywhere, sir," he said respectfully. "I will come out to your place. I think I know what you have in mind and I believe you're going to find that we're thinking along the same lines."

"Terrific, Hank! I'll be happy to see you whenever you can make it—but of course, I'm sure you understand that we have certain time constraints." He was going to say "the sooner the better," but held back, sure that Spanitra understood the urgency. "We'll have our private discussion over drinks and then an intimate dinner with some of the family. I know you will be helpful with our plans for Justin, and we Kilmorys are not going to forget that."

With Spanitra aboard, Jonathan felt confident that Campana would come around to feel that it was a sure thing for the Mob. Spanitra, he felt, was the key to clinching it with Campana, and he had the two of them practically salivating over the benefits that a Kilmory presidency would bring them.

Within the week Spanitra flew in, discussed the matter in a friendly meeting with Jonathan over champagne, beluga caviar and Maine lobster thermidor, and promptly flew out after assuring him that he would do his best to urge Campana to swing the other capos over to the Kilmory side. Jonathan breathed a sigh of relief: it was all set as far as he was concerned.

For Spanitra, this meant more than money: it would mean a huge step in prestige and social rank. Wasting no time, he got together with Campana, put his heart into it and did all the talking he thought was necessary to bring him around to his way of thinking. As it turned out, he didn't need to talk that much. Campana was already pretty much convinced that the Outfit should back Kilmory; it was the other capos that needed convincing.

Still, Spanitra had a positive effect on him. Campana flew out to meet Sandy Traficant, who was on the fence, and Carlos Marcello, who had a visceral distrust and pure, unadulterated hatred for the Kilmorys. Traficant being technically neutral, it was one-on-one, and the top boss's power won the day. Marcello was gutsy but was not one to go out on a limb and challenge the top capo's authority.

"Okay, Sal," Marcello finally conceded, "but hey, I hope nothing goes wrong. If it does...," he was tempted to instead say "I told you so," but settled for "well, we'll have to deal with it."

When Jonathan received Campana's courier—news like this was too hot to be communicated any other way—he was ecstatic. The message was simple: the Mob was committed to throw the full weight of its power and influence over to the Kilmorys. The election, in effect, was virtually a done deal: Justin would be handed victory on a silver platter.

Jonathan was more than satisfied: he was thrilled, fulfilled. Spanitra had turned out, after all, to be the catalyst. Despite difficult odds, Jonathan was happy over having practically ensured that Justin would be the next president of the United States. It was also, for his sons, an object lesson in the exercise of power to its utmost possibilities. As he had always steadfastly maintained, money and influence, properly applied, could buy it all.

More than that, he had also taught them object lessons, directly and indirectly, in getting everything one wanted in life, including power, money and sex. This latter point he had clearly driven home through his multiple affairs with secretaries, movie stars and assorted other females, whether or not they were on his payroll. He went over, once again, his fond memories of having pulled off an Atlantic crossing on a liner with his wife Roseanne *and* his lover Glenda Swanky, the famous motion picture star whose career, thanks to him, had taken off like a skyrocket.

He had given his sons valuable demonstrations in how to be gentle when that was useful, as well as how to, when necessary, be absolutely ruthless—and that included physical elimination if called for.

Now all those lessons were about to pay off with the biggest prize of all.

Chapter VIII
THE "FIX"

The 1960 election would be close, but the Kilmorys were going to take no chances. They needed "insurance," which meant following the time-tested procedure of rigging the results.

Stalin had said it best, in what we might call a nutshell: "It's not the number of votes that count, it's who counts them." Voting figures would come in and, if unfavorable to Justin Kilmory, would simply be switched or altered in his favor. Threats and bribes would come into play if any objections or hurdles arose—and Mob inducements were—and still are—perilous to refuse, as we know by the adage "an offer you can't refuse." The key states would be Illinois and Texas, with their hefty electoral votes.

Voting totals in heavily Democratic Chicago would favor Kilmory. But what about upstate Illinois? On election night, the Chicago totals, curiously, were not coming in. No one knew the figures, but one thing they did know: they would have to be enough to overcome the upstate Dixon margin in order to deliver Illinois into the Democratic column. And clearly they did not..., that is, until the Mafia fix came into play. According to the final "official" results, a switch of less than 5,000 votes overall would have turned the state over to Dixon, who won over 90% of the counties. But in fact the fix to overcome the Dixon upstate lead left little room for error. It totaled tens of thousands of votes. Thus, if not for the stolen votes, Kilmory's numbers would have fallen far short of taking Illinois.

A similar scenario was brought into play in Texas, where the large cities also delivered a Democratic advantage, whereas the rural districts voted heavily for the Republican candidate. There, the LBJ machine—with some help from the Mafia here and there—intervened when necessary in order to change the figures enough to give Kilmory a small-but-sufficient margin of victory. The Kilmory-Jameson ticket carried the state by a fraction of 1% of the total votes! The same pattern prevailed: the large-city vote did not come until after the rural totals were known and could thus be overturned by altering those from the big cities.

When Kilmory called Chicago mayor Paley during the count and asked him how things were going, he replied: "Mr. Kilmory, with a little luck and the help of some good friends, you will carry Illinois." Clear enough. The president-to-be thanked him warmly.

By the next morning, Kilmory appeared to be the winner and next chief executive of the United States. But there was a problem when the result, which clearly smelled of fraud, was threatened by a likely Dixon challenge, which would require a complicated, delicate and possibly dangerous recount. The Dixon camp was keenly aware of the manipulation of results, exemplified by the surprise last-minute Kilmory victory in Illinois, when the unbalanced Chicago "results" came in, overturning the substantial Dixon upstate plurality. If the Dixon group, not unreasonably, insisted on a recount, the fraudulent count done by the Mafia in cahoots with the Paley forces might be just a little difficult to cover up. Something had to be done.

First, the Paley political machine in Chicago alerted its forces to resist any recount. But, most importantly, someone representing the powerful Mafia forces contacted Dixon directly. A thinly veiled threat was made against him personally and, perhaps, made extensive to his family as well. Its terms were ominous and credibly menacing. In a matter of hours, Dixon did an about-face and announced—relief clearly etched on his face—that he would not challenge the election. He was still young enough to run again, so why should he stick his neck out in a drawn-out contest of wills, maneuvering and influence that he was likely to lose, and that might bring about personal or familial tragedy? Under his opponent's control, the recount might well turn out to be just as fraudulent.

The Mafia had intervened again by putting the final clincher in Kilmory's political victory. The Kilmorys tried hard not to show it too much—it was better to pretend they had expected a clean win all along—but they were ecstatic. The presidency and the government were theirs. There would be a fantastic inaugural, surrounded by pull-out-all-the-stops festivities.

Spanitra organized the Brat Pack, of which he was "the Chairman of the Board," to help with the celebrations, in which they all worked for free. All, that is, except for Jammy Spavis, Jr., who couldn't have worked unless he waited on tables. Instead, he had to lay low and not show himself too much. Against his own wishes, Spanitra had even convinced him to delay his inter-racial marriage to stunning Swedish actress Mae Brill, in order to avoid upsetting the Kilmorys and their white supporters. Back then, racism had its rules.

This was in response to pressure on Spanitra from the Kilmorys, who had asked him for help in getting Jammy to postpone his marriage until after the election. It took a lot for Spanitra to do that for the Kilmorys, since he was not only one of Jammy's best, long-time friends, but also very openly against the discriminatory racial practices then current. This did not, however, stop Spanitra and his group from publicly and privately poking fun at Jammy's blackness, something which Jammy accepted with extraordinary forbearance and good grace, as a quid-pro-quo to maintain his standing as a member of the Pack; if not, the Chairman of the Board might get upset and, aside from the social angle, Jammy might see his sources of employment dry up. For good measure, the good-old racist Mafiosi pushed him around verbally and physically, and once—shudder!—threatened to poke out his only remaining eye (the other was glass, replacing one lost in an auto accident).

The inaugural over, Justin began to put together his cabinet. Jonathan kept a very low profile, conscious of what some rogue journalist might dare to bring up about his past. But behind the scenes, he gave clear instructions to Justin, even before he had taken the oath of office, to forthwith name brother Roland—who had never practiced law in his entire life—to the top position at the Justice Department.

The hard-working, no-nonsense Roland was expected to do an outstanding job as Attorney General and then be in line to run for vice president, replacing Jameson—who would be investigated, prosecuted and brushed aside in due course. After Justin had completed his second term, Roland would continue the dynasty.

Dutifully, Justin complied with the Patriarch's wishes shortly after taking office, when he nominated—"designated" might be more accurate, considering how breezily it went over—his brother Roland to be Attorney General. Newspapers noted the nepotistic flavor of the appointment, but brushed it off as important for President Kilmory in the sense that, in the Justice Department, "he needed someone worthy of his utmost trust." That the same thing applied to just about every other cabinet position was casually dismissed.

A later administration outlawed such nepotistic appointments, just as FDR's four presidential terms—making him virtually president for life—were eventually made impossible by limiting them to two.

Justin was given credit for being daring and clever enough at his news conference to observe, tongue in cheek: "I want to give my brother Roland a little legal experience." There was laughter from the press, but, curiously—and very satisfactorily for the Kilmorys—not a single follow-up question was asked. The supportive group of journalists festively attending his press conference just walked quietly away, laughing and close to applauding. Later, Justin said to his little brother: "Hey, kid. How many presidents can get away with *that* parting shot?" He was proud of himself.

Roland was not only in the cabinet, but Justin's right-hand man. He was his brother's trouble-shooter, confidant and relentless protector and backer. He was "the fixer," who would take care of payoffs, neutralize threats by trouble-makers or pay out bribes to keep problems under control. This applied especially to women who, after relationships with Justin, might be so brazen—or foolhardy—as to threaten scandal, as made clear by the Marie Moore case.

At any rate, the inaugural festivities brought the new administration to Washington on an incoming tide of exuberance. Among the Mafia, however, the celebration would be short-lived. After all, it was they who, behind the scenes, had been responsible for the historically slim victory that had brought about the Kilmory presidency. And they were displeased by the way things were going.

Roland himself, once installed in the Justice Department, lost no time in going against his father's advice: he aimed his guns directly and publicly at the Mafia. One of his major objectives as the country's chief law-enforcement officer was, he pronounced, "prosecuting the war against organized crime."

That signaled a clear double-cross, even though it was still a matter of words and not deeds. Maybe, the Mob hoped, the Kilmory administration was just going after small-fry and leaving the big-shots alone. But deeds followed words in short order. Sal Campana, the architect of the Kilmory deal, was beginning to be bitterly criticized by all the other capos—mostly under their breath. He himself was incensed, but also concerned about possible consequences. As was Hank Spanitra, whose efforts at lobbying Campana to put the Mob in Kilmory's camp were soon to be rewarded by receiving the short end of the stick from the Kilmorys.

But that wasn't all that Spanitra had coming—he was starting to take heat from the capos. Having been so close to the Kilmorys, he got most of the blame and might have even taken a hit—perhaps an "accident" of some kind—if some in the Mob had had their way. But Campana stuck his own neck out for Spanitra: he was too fond of him, and defended him as just another victim of the Kilmory double-cross. He argued that, like he himself, Spanitra had been taken for a chump by the Kilmorys. The rest of the capos reluctantly bowed to authority... but made a mental note of it for the future. Spanitra had come closer to an "accident" than anyone suspected.

Chapter IX
THE TARGET TAKES AIM

They were a few months into the year of the inaugural, 1961. Claudio Mariello was fuming.

"That dirty son of a bitch!" He fairly shouted the words, still snarling as he looked out at Guatemala City's small airport through the window of the small plane he had been forced to board, in handcuffs, in New Orleans. By now, handcuffs off and an alien in unfamiliar territory, he gestured as he talked to his Italian-heart's content. Roland Kilmory had no business deporting him to Guatemala as if he were a sack of potatoes.

"He's gonna be awful sorry for this. The nerve of the guy! I can't believe it. The Attorney General himself, boss of the Justice Department, violating the laws of the country, denying due process to a U.S. citizen!" He fleetingly thought of saying only "citizen," since his citizenship was legally open to question, but why tell the truth when you could lie? It just wasn't his style. He had spoken out loud, not caring if the Department's agents heard him aboard the small, propeller-driven aircraft. What else could they do to him now?

Mariello descended the portable stairway from the aircraft and into the arms of the local authorities, who were ready and waiting for him, presumably to make sure that he wouldn't be going anywhere that he was not supposed to. His cohorts in the States—and in Guatemala itself—had not been notified in time to meet him, so for the time being he was denied the company of anyone he knew and, in effect, left to his own devices.

They took him to a swanky local hotel and assigned agents to keep tabs on him from an adjoining room. There was no place he could go without being closely followed in an obvious, irritating way. It was almost as bad, the New Orleans capo thought, as being locked up. And he had disagreeable recollections of being behind bars, no matter how briefly.

Week after week, Mariello's time in the country's quaint old capital, Antigua Guatemala, dragged by. He had money to spare but was way out of his usual surroundings. No underlings, no orders to give, no perks to enjoy.

For starters, he didn't speak the language. Oh, he kept in touch by phone with his people in the States, but the lines were all tapped, so he couldn't speak freely. It would never be the same as being there.

No wife was okay, but no girl-friends was intolerable. He disliked the purely professional girls, so he would have to start putting his harem back together from scratch. Time went by at a snail's pace, as he focused on making the clandestine arrangements necessary for his return to New Orleans. They were not, if he could help it, going to keep him there for long.

While his organization prepared to send him the cash to pay Guatemalan officials a bribe substantial enough to turn a blind eye to his plans, Mariello conspired to get even with Roland. Never, he vowed, would he go through anything like that again. Payback time was coming, he told himself. Already, he could nearly taste his personal revenge against the Kilmorys.

But there had been something much larger in the wind than his own personal pain. He made up his mind that it was also time for the Mafia to avenge the Kilmorys' double-cross. They had made a deal with the Cosa Nostra, the Outfit, the Mob, the whole Organization. But, against Mariello's own personal advice and better judgment, Sal Campana had ensured the Kilmory presidential election by rigging the count in Chicago's Cook County, offsetting the substantial Dixon plurality in the rest of Illinois. Enough fraudulent votes turned up in Texas, as well—partly through the Mafia and partly through Jameson's well-oiled political machine. Preternaturally corrupt, he was a past master at stuffing ballot boxes and vote-stealing, and easily swung his own key state over to the Kilmory column to hand him the presidency—and himself the second spot.

The deal with the Mob was so clear it might as well have been spelled out in black and white: we give you the election, you lay off. But it wasn't quite working out that way.

"We make 'im president and what happens? Why," Claudio Mariello said to Nick, one of his underlings, "an out-'n'-out double-cross, dat's what No sooner did 'e get in as Attorney General, that little snot-nosed bastard Roland must'ave thought he'd got a poaching license against us."

As Mariello saw it, Roland thought all he had to do was go out with a well-armed group and shoot down Outfit guys—figuratively, of course, although he was sure that literally might have been more satisfactory for Roland, had he been able to get away with it.

Mariello and the rest of the Outfit knew that it wouldn't have been the first time the Kilmorys, very much like the Mob itself, had rubbed out people who stood in their way—even though the public was largely ignorant of such stories "about high and mighty crappers like them," as he put it. After all, Mariello knew the Kilmorys—and Roland in particular—had been involved in one such recent event: Marie Moore's so-called suicide. Besides, he angrily recalled, when Roland Kilmory had taken office as Attorney General, he as much as said he would go after us all over the country, shut down our operations, investigate us, prosecute us and throw us in the slammer for as long as he could.

Worse, rumors were rampant in the Mob that Roland's animosity toward Mariello was personal: he was getting even with him for not having supported Kilmory for president during the Democratic Party convention; instead, Mariello had pushed for giving the nomination to Jameson. Why, Roland wasn't even grateful for Mariello's vast donations to the Kilmory campaign. In short, far from keeping their part of the bargain, it looked like the Kilmorys were planning to erase their debt to the Outfit by systematically wiping them out. Something had to be done.

Mariello felt that, in order to implement his plot against Justin Kilmory, he would need to get the support of Ricky Hofstra, head of the powerful Teamsters' Union. Hofstra had a lot of balls—*that* he knew—but he was impulsive and not too careful, and thus prone to make mistakes.

One of them was fatal when Hofstra was sentenced to prison for corruption during a later administration. President Dixon was pressured or paid off to pardon him on condition that he not engage in any more union activity. But no sooner was he out than he once again attempted to gain control of the Teamsters. The problem was the Mob didn't want him anymore; they were getting along fine with his replacement and didn't care for his tough-guy tactics. But he wouldn't listen and plowed on ahead. Worse, he let it be known that if he didn't get his way he would write a tell-all book and get everyone in big trouble.

So the ever-vigilant Mob decided to take care of him... and his family. If the body was never found, his heirs would have to wait ten years before they could collect any insurance money. His body is rumored to have been encased in concrete in a new stadium in the Midwest. More likely, he was ground into a powder and his remains chemically disposed of, whether they were then mixed with concrete or not. They didn't want any traces of him to ever be found.

Mariello vividly recalled when, not too long before, Hofstra, Campana and other major capos were questioned by Roland Kilmory, then working for the U.S. Senate's McClanahan Committee on Labor Racketeering. The hearings were televised and the Committee, in its investigation of organized crime and its close relationship with the Teamsters' Union—plied them with question upon question. With minor exceptions, they got the old standby: "I refuse to answer based on my rights, under the Fifth Amendment to the Constitution, not to incriminate myself."

Oh, it was frustrating for the would-be inquisitors, all right. But they pressed on, hoping for some slip-up. In questioning Hofstra, Roland had needled him, casting doubt on his masculinity. In his propensity for those wisecracks, he also took a swipe at Sal Campana, describing his responses as something "limp-wristed sissies like to hide behind." Campana had very nearly growled with rage, throwing him looks like daggers. Both men would forever hold a grudge against Roland for what they considered a wanton personal insult.

Chapter X
DISASTER

For the Mafia, the one thing that had gone sour was Cuba. Costra had taken over absolute control of the island, stealing everything they had worked hard to extort from others. It was downright impudent! And neither they nor the U.S. government had been able to do anything to weaken him, much less get rid of him. They had finally run into a veritable nemesis: a true mastermind of organized criminality, but on an international scale.

He was intractable, far worse than Batista. Yet his propaganda machine was much more effective, with a powerful, nearly unassailable image as an honest-to-goodness reformer. Furthermore, he made himself nearly impregnable by being, to all intents and purposes, a fascist dictator posing as an extreme leftist and, therefore, supported by the worldwide communist movement. A winning formula, if there ever was one! A stroke of genius, no doubt, "evil" being the ghost word that floated with near-imperceptibility amid the foggy ambience created by every populist impostor in the world (particularly among mid-20th-century French intellectuals, bless their hearts).

The Mob didn't realize that he was really a Cuban-grown version of one of them: a ruthless, professional criminal who would stop at nothing to achieve his ends. He was putting firing squads to work arbitrarily killing his enemies by the thousands. But worst of all, he was doing it "legally" because he combined brute force with old-fashioned demagoguery, which made him an outlaw with national political power: a truly explosive combination.

"I got to hand it to him—the son of a bitch can't be bought! He's about the smartest fuckin' hood I ever saw," Campana would say, not realizing that, for Costra, having total political and economic power in a not-so-small country meant that money was no longer an object in itself. He was after bigger game. Fortunately for Campana, he had not made large-scale investments with his own money in Cuba like Manny Lendski and Sandy Traficant.

"That was a big mistake Lendski made, puttin' all 'is eggs in that fuckin' Cuban basket," Campana said to his kid brother, Chuck.

"Yeah, a dumb move for a smart guy like him," he answered. Lendski had sunk some $14 million (equal to $140 million in 2013)—most of his lifetime criminal nest egg—into the Riviera Hotel, hard by the coastline in the high-class Vedado suburb, minutes from downtown Havana, only to lose it all when the bearded bandit expropriated it "in the name of the Cuban people." His political instincts finely honed, Costra played the role of savior, a man who was recovering the country's "lost" property and "trampled" pride while manipulating the masses to drum up support for his benevolent "give-away" agenda. Those who questioned his plans or intentions were simply urged to leave the country—and so they did, playing right into Costra's hands. It was like the Old West: if you can't shoot all your enemies just tell them to get out of town by sundown—or else.

The question was: how had Costra with a rag-tag group of a few hundred poorly trained and badly equipped guerrillas, managed to take over a country with an army of 40,000? The answer: because he had momentum and support from the United States, while Batista had lost it.

Once cut off from U.S. backing, Batista felt that all was lost and simply bailed out with his family and everything he could gather up on short notice. The U.S. was expecting—or more precisely, hoping—that Costra would be the democratic reformer that he was promising to be.

While the United States had given up on Batista, whom they had supported for decades, the Mob did no such thing. In a typical "insurance" operation, they hedged their bets and backed both sides in the Cuban struggle: Batista *and* the Costra rebels. That way, no matter how it turned out the Mob would have an inside track. But when Costra took over his intention was to share power with no one, overtly or covertly, officially or unofficially. As everyone soon found out, neither was he to be swayed by anyone. One of his first moves was to make a big show of "cleaning house." He closed the casinos, threw out the gambling operators—including the Mob capos and agents—and presumably rehabilitated the prostitutes by turning them into bus drivers. Needless to say, they wrecked so many buses that Cuba's public transportation system was quickly turned into a shambles. Obviously, their skills lay elsewhere.

But Costra was not after a few million here or there—or even a few billion. If he had been, everyone would have done well—even the Cuban people at large. He was, incredibly, after much bigger game: an empire of sorts, starting with the Caribbean and expanding into Central and South America. Greedy for power beyond Cuba itself, he longed to be a player on the world stage, a mover and a shaker on a global level, even though his take-off point was an island the size of Pennsylvania that in 1959 harbored a population of only six million.

He had studied books by the Spanish falangist leader José Antonio Primo de Rivera, who put together a Spanish version of fascism as practiced by Mussolini and Hitler, whom he greatly admired for their skill in achieving power and expanding their territory and sphere of influence abroad. Except that he, Costra, was not going to make Hitler's mistake by openly invading neighboring countries, small and large.

Costra also felt sympathy for contemporaneous dictators such as Franco, anti-communist though he was, and was convinced that Cuba was among many countries that would do well with a single, absolute ruler who could afford to disregard the hair-splitting squabbles and political pettifogging that got in the way of major large-scale plans. What a waste of time! For him, a turn to communism offered the strong political dividend of guaranteeing indefinite permanence in power, regardless of whom it displeased.

It was, of course, of no interest to Costra to actually provide benefits for the country or its population. Quite the opposite. It was the perfect system to make everyone equal—equally poor, that is— and destroy the economy and the social fabric of the country, his theory being that poverty would make it much easier to control the populace with an iron fist. People who are scrounging around for the basic necessities of life—food, clothing and shelter—would have no time or inclination to oppose the very forces on which they would depend for their everyday rations. Sure enough, as foreseen in Costra's master plan, nearly all basic foodstuffs were soon rationed and in short supply—even Cuba's staple crop, sugar. Fifty-some years later the rationing persists, although completely outstripped by a hyper-expensive black market.

According to his intimate convictions, Costra thought of impoverishment as an effective instrument of power. Blame for the economic disaster would fall on the United States since, as envisaged in his long-term, carefully thought-out plans, he prodded the U.S. government into applying an embargo—which Costra called a "blockade"— thereby impoverishing and isolating Cuba in many ways, but most of all economically and socially. No wonder he bragged on various occasions—among his cohorts—that he "knew how to lead multitudes better than [Nazi propaganda chief]

Goebbels." They were playing right into his hands. Every time there
has been an attempt at negotiation to end the embargo, Costra has
made it his business to shoot it down. He once did it physically
against unarmed, civilian, small U.S. aircraft over international
waters in the Florida Straits, killing three Americans with impunity.
It was the President Clangton era and he wanted no trouble with
Costra, who had him threatened with exposure. This was
demonstrated by the outrageous case of the child Elián González, in
which he bowed to Costra with extra-judicial measures to avoid
personal troubles.

Who would he blame for the Cuban disaster if the "blockade"
were lifted?

The existence of a "powerful enemy to the north" gave him an
excuse to crack down on any remaining opposition, and basic
human rights and freedoms soon disappeared. The Hitlerian system
of control was optimal, in Costra's view, in terms of sheer
effectiveness. He promptly resorted to the use of secret police plus a
network of informers in every block known as the CDRs,
Committees for the Defense of the Revolution. In addition, he
established a universal draft covering men from 17 to 35 years of age,
frequent neighborhood-level military exercises, support for
guerrillas and actual war operations with Cuban troops abroad—
Nicaragua (1980's), Grenada (1983) and Angola (1975-1980's), for
example—plus ruthless repression that struck terror among the
island's population.

After the Second World War, the only remaining vestige of
fascism was Spain's Franco, who was weak on the international
stage. That left communism as Costra's best potential ally, without
whose staunch support he would have been in danger of being
overthrown, openly or otherwise, by the United States. Under
normal circumstances, the Americans would hardly tolerate his type
of hostile regime ninety miles away from its borders and within easy
ballistic-missile range of major U.S. cities.

Curiously, the fascist Franco regime—a die-hard enemy of
communism, against which it had fought the Spanish Civil War—
made an alliance with the Costra regime. After all, both Franco and
Costra were Galicians, Fingenio being the son of a native Galician
who had gone off near the turn of the twentieth century to make his
fortune in Cuba.

He did so mainly by his own crooked methods: after fighting
against Cuba's independence from Spain, he moved his property's
fences at night to expand his acreage; just on that genetic basis there
seemed little doubt that Fingenio was his very own son. Repterio,
however, was quite different. The reason: he was a half brother of
Fingenio, born of his father's affair with a household maid.

Once in power, Costra figured correctly that the key to his survival would be to make the Soviet Union his major ally, since amid the Cold War the U.S.S.R. could certainly use an enormously strategic military and intelligence base within 90 miles of the U.S.
Clever manipulation of international politics, plus use of guerrilla warfare, terrorism, drug trafficking, etc., could swing enormous weight.

Costra was well aware of what the Soviets had done on a worldwide scale through sheer armed force, subversion, threats, ruthless determination, a solid intelligence network, judicious use of "cultural" and "diplomatic" ties, political maneuvering and strategic deployment of military power on the world stage.

Even though the Cuban communist party was against him until he took control of the country, Costra approached their leadership, brought them into his fold, and made moves to share power with them; ultimately he absorbed them into his own movement. He then approached the Soviet regime, invited their leadership to visit Cuba, proposed a profitable partnership and, finally, declared himself to be a lifelong, dedicated Marxist-Leninist. Delighted with the unexpected gift, the Soviets backed him wholeheartedly and eventually poured enormous sums into Cuba—which Costra, of course, never intended to repay and never has.

Despite their uniquely ineffective economic system, the Soviets had taken over all of Eastern Europe, weakened Western Europe by unconditional backing of communist parties that influenced national governance and foreign policy, reached into Africa and the Middle East, set up a puppet state in North Korea that invaded and nearly took over South Korea at the mid-century mark, maintained an alliance of sorts with Mao's cruel regime in China, backed a successful campaign by the Vietnamese against the French in Indo-China, and now were moving firmly into the Western Hemisphere with Costra's takeover of Cuba.

A footnote is that Justin's foreign policy efforts, in the hands of a singularly ineffective Secretary of State, Dennis Dusk, had to a considerable degree been run personally by Justin himself and brother Roland.

Whoever ran it was of little concern to Costra, who watched only the results. Mindful only of the fact that conducive to the primary goal of retaining power was projecting it to surrounding areas so that
efforts against him would be diluted by attention to collaterals, once consolidated he began his plans to launch a guerrilla campaign in Central and South America.

Within Cuba his political control program would soon show itself as absolute, all-embracing. Had it been a question of mere economics, of stealing or redistributing money, Costra would have followed the traditionally corrupt, politics-as-usual plan of action. For show, a few reforms would be implemented here and there, but it would basically have been the same system with another, presumably clean slate. That, he was sure, would have lasted a few years and then he would have been deposed in a coup or voted out of power in the unlikely case of honest, democratic elections.

But Costra wanted not just power, he craved *absolute* power—not only for the rest of his own life, but for that of the future dynastic heirs to his throne. An alliance with the United States would have meant persistent pressure for free elections, demands for human rights, press freedom and respect for the rule of law. On the other hand, an alliance with the Soviet Union would mean full and unconditional backing, no questions asked, and all kinds of military and other aid needed to carry out his own—and their—plan of international expansion.

A simple anecdote illustrates Costra's genius in hoodwinking the smartest people around. When the Garrett Commission sent emissaries to Cuba to find out what they could about Rosswell, his apparent solidarity with the Costra revolution and his plans to kill Kilmory, Costra regaled them with a long list of falsehoods, stating that they had never heard of Rosswell. Finally, after Costra had showed off with a high-sounding final oratorical flourish featuring a string of lies, hypocrisy and absurdly false statements, he wound up by saying that had they known anything "Cuba would have had the moral duty to inform the United States." At that point U.S. Senator Dodder, completely spellbound, approached Costra and said: "Mr. President: I have been deeply impressed by your statements. I find your logic compelling."

In its report to the Commission, Dodder's views prevailed, reaching the conclusion that "the Costra government was not involved in the assassination."

* * * * * * *

At this point in the game, Campana—even though he was no global strategy expert—was quite sure that Cuba was lost for the foreseeable future. Too bad, he thought, because it was a gold mine of tax-free profits from gambling, prostitution and narcotics. For all practical purposes, he was writing it off. Except that his co-conspirators, that other powerful undercover organization known as the CIA, were about to ask for his assistance. The CIA was intent on getting rid of Costra one way or another. They had instructions from President Kilmory himself to eliminate Costra physically. The threat posed by Costra as a now openly-declared Soviet satellite representing a powerful ground-air-sea base—probably soon to be nuclear-capable, only minutes from U.S. territory—was far too serious to ignore. Kilmory decided to take the chance and be cowed no longer by Costra's threats to reveal dirt on him. If worse came to worst, he would label anything that Costra might bring up as fake, false or fabricated. He could not let his foreign policy remain subject to the whims of a tin-pot dictator like him. Costra was as bold as he was reckless and dangerous, but his administration could not afford to be intimidated by him, whatever the consequences.

His boldness was made evident by his own history, revelatory of an egomaniac with a daring, risk-taking, supremely ambitious personality. But U.S. intelligence had not done its homework on him and was ignorant of these significant traits. A few Cubans, however, were fully aware and concerned about his inclinations.

Back in the mid-1950's, dire warnings about Costra were voiced in Cuba's House of Representatives when Batista—as a dictator, soft as mashed potatoes compared to what Costra would become—planned to give him a pardon and thus release him from prison, where he was doing time for his bloody terrorist attack on the Moncada Garrison, in eastern Cuba. It turned out to be a cruel, murderous event in which Fingenio and Repterio Costra planned the attack but played it safe, stayed in the rear and escaped virtually unharmed, leaving dozens of dead and wounded in their wake. Costra was denounced by major Cuban politicians as a violent psychopath and narcissist who would, if he managed to take power, *engage in an alliance with the Soviets and ruin Cuba in a reign of terror, oppression and poverty that would last for decades.* The prediction, eerily prescient, turned out to be mild compared to the reality. Yet, at the time, most dismissed it as apocalyptically exaggerated and unlikely, and the warnings went unheeded.

Batista was a run-of-the-mill dictator. The country prospered amid a degree of freedoms barely different from those under previous regimes, including fully democratic ones. Despite all his faults, Batista was civil and civic minded, determined to show that he was a "nice guy" and willing to get along even with the worst of thugs. So he pardoned Costra, who had been given a light, five-year penitentiary sentence but had served less than two. Out walked Fingenio to fawning press interviews, ready and, as it turned out, perfectly able to make good on his plans to overthrow Batista with funds and support initially provided by out-of-power Cuban politicians such as ex-president Prío Socarrás. It was not long before the CIA also began backing Costra in his scrappy guerrilla actions in the Sierra Maestra mountains. Herbert Matthews, the New York Times reporter, famously interviewed him and put him on the front page as a promising reformer yearning to put Cuba back in the fold of democracy and human rights.

Soon, the U.S. notified Batista that it could not continue to support him—in effect, backing the questionable but apparently well-intentioned rebels. Batista caved in and suddenly flew away, surprising even Costra, who took his sweet time getting to Havana and seizing power, although it was his for the taking. He was the ever-careful master plotter, always on guard against potential enemies out to get rid of him.

Costra had been in office only a short time when he began to show his true colors and became the target of assassination attempts organized by the CIA as well as by his Cuban opposition. They all failed. Costra was too clever. He never slept in the same place twice, kept moving unpredictably and rarely showed up when or where he was expected.

Eventually, the administration's team made preparations, with a considerable number of exiled Cubans who underwent training in Guatemala, the United States itself and other places, to launch an invasion capable of removing this danger to itself and, possibly, to the Hemisphere. The invading unit, Brigade 2506, was made up of some 1,500 Cubans, some of whom were actually Americans of Cuban extraction (or vice versa), with dual nationality. They were ready, willing and eager to overthrow Costra by force of arms and restore freedom in Cuba.

International backing came from the Organization of American States, whose member countries voted to isolate Cuba by expelling its government from the regional entity and urging them to sever diplomatic relations with the Costra regime.

Finally, in April 1961, just after Kilmory had taken power in the U.S., the go-ahead was given for the invasion. The transition to a different party should not have made any difference in the outcome—but it did. A major change was made in the location of the invasion and a highly unsuitable, swampy landing area was selected: the Bay of Pigs. In that sort of terrain, the Brigade was unable to surmount the difficulties of unloading equipment and supplies. One of the ships was unable to come in toward land and thus remained offshore with its precious cargo long enough for one of Costra's jet trainers to bomb it and send it to the bottom, dooming the whole operation. Furthermore, a simultaneous landing was to take place in eastern Cuba, opening up a two-front war which would have forced the Costra forces to split up. However, that second landing was cancelled. The invasion was to get air support from U.S. aircraft carriers offshore, but that was also cancelled by President Kilmory.

The debacle resulted in solidifying Costra's hold on power, providing him with enhanced national and international prestige. He had successfully challenged and defeated his mighty northern neighbor, the most powerful country in the world. David had defeated Goliath—a fabulous military and propaganda coup.

For public consumption, Kilmory personally assumed responsibility for the failure; it certainly looked good for him to do so. But, both privately and publicly, he blamed the CIA and was loose-tongued enough to threaten to break it up "into a thousand pieces" for its "failure"—due to his own mistakes, as it happened—to successfully plan and execute the invasion.

The CIA leadership, from Director Alton Dunsell on down, was incensed. Kilmory had brought about the disastrous outcome as a result of his own decisions and against their advice. In addition to changing the landing sites for the invasion, he had cut short the bombing raids designed to destroy Costra's two or three jet trainers.

Just those trainer aircraft had been enough to sink the Brigade's supply ship at the Bay of Pigs. Worse yet, Kilmory had in fact shielded the Costra jets from harm when, once the invasion was under way, he denied the Brigade the U.S. air cover that would have been essential to assure victory.

Thus, Costra's rudimentary jets held complete and unchallenged air superiority over the landing area. The U.S. aircraft were ordered to only "overfly the battle area." It was worse than nothing, revealing that they were to remain uninvolved in the actual shooting. Thus, both sides quickly became aware that the Brigade's initial battlefield successes would be unsustainable.

The CIA suspected, on the heels of the fiasco, that Kilmory actually *wanted* the invasion to fail. They, and the Pentagon as well, would have handled it otherwise, but they had no choice than to follow the puzzling, unexplainable orders coming from the White House. What was the purpose of the task force standing offshore from Cuba if they were not going to make any practical use of it?

Is it possible that Kilmory was operating on the assumption that, politically, it would be less costly to let the invasion go ahead and fail than to call it off and be accused of being soft on communism? Costra was to have been assassinated just before, or simultaneously with, the invasion. However, since that move had been unsuccessful, it made U.S. support even more essential than had been anticipated.

But it is a matter of record that Kilmory did the opposite: not only did he decide to cut off the bombing raids, but he denied the invading Brigade any U.S. air cover and reversed the daring but essential need to win at any cost by throwing in the U.S. forces waiting just offshore. This solid plan had the support of the Joint Chiefs of Staff. However, Kilmory was not contemplating anything of the kind and let the invasion proceed on its own. Why was he willing to settle for defeat? He must have known that, without decisive support, it would fail and inevitably strengthen Costra. Some have argued that, although the decision would have been difficult at such a juncture, canceling—postponing?—such a doomed operation would have seemed the only wise and humane thing to do.

It is difficult to imagine what the president might have been thinking when he made these decisions, although it is arguably fair to say that, at a certain point, the operation had gathered too much momentum and it would have been too late to cancel it. Did Kilmory perhaps feel that if this opportunity was lost, it might be too long a time before another one came up? Better a weak chance at success than none at all? The word for all this is "enigmatic."

If honesty serves, it is not that much of a long shot to think that something fishy occurred. Although any concrete evidence was surely never recorded or has been in any case completely destroyed, it must be said that other explanations fall short of satisfactorily accounting for such a strange and disastrous turn of events. As the saying goes, "it just doesn't add up."

Needless to say, painstaking efforts were sedulously undertaken to erase any trace of wrongdoing or error on the part of the Kilmorys. Records at the Kilmory Library have been all carefully redacted and cleared of all incriminating information relative to that episode or, for that matter, any other.

The consequences of the Bay of Pigs failure are, for those who care to examine them, a matter of historical record. Thereafter, Costra wasted no time in spreading unrest and guerrilla warfare throughout Latin America. Cuba became a steady, impregnable conduit for drug-smuggling into the U.S., as well as a base for not only projecting power, but conducting a broad range of international criminal and de-stabilizing activities affecting the peace and well-being of the American people, the Hemisphere and other parts of the world. It is a mere sidelight that he launched the age of airline hijacking, which required extensive and expensive countermeasures, all of them half-heartedly implemented by U.S. officialdom. That is, until the 9/11 attack.

Chapter XI
LEAKS

When you have excluded the
impossible, whatever remains,
however improbable, must be
the truth.
  —Sherlock Holmes (Arthur
      Conan Doyle's "The Adventure
      of the Beryl Coronet")

The Bay of Pigs invasion came as no surprise to Costra. Jay J. Ambleton, head of CIA counter-intelligence, realized early on that there was a high-level leak worth investigating. The reason: the Cubans and the Russians seemed to know exactly what the plans against Costra consisted of, and precisely where, how and when they were scheduled to be implemented.

In order to trace the leak, Ambleton prepared an encoded eyes-only brief to be distributed to the top echelon in the White House, including the president, as well as to key figures in the Senate and the House of Representatives. Each brief would have a different code so as to precisely identify the source of the leak.

Within a few days, he had his answer. To his surprise, the leak turned out to come directly from President Justin Kilmory himself. His motivation, as far as anyone could ascertain it, has remained a mystery. Did it have to do with some shadowy political agenda of his own? Were there other, darker reasons? There must have been documents or perhaps handwritten notes on the subject, but if so they have long-since been destroyed.

A possible reason—totally unverifiable, since it relies exclusively on deductive reasoning—will come as a stark shock. But,if one is to "tell it like it is," it seems to fit the circumstances. Knowing Costra's and the Russian's deviltry and ruthlessness, it might just explain what really happened. If Kilmory gave full backing to the invasion, pulling out all the stops, Costra and the Russians might have threatened to bring out visual evidence of Kilmory's individual and group "sexcapades."

Quite aside from those that happened in the White House's indoor swimming pool, one of those "sexcapades" *took place in Cuba itself.* In the early 1950's, on a private visit to the island, Kilmory met with Mafia capo Sandy Traficant, boss of Tampa with casinos and other interests in Havana. They had dinner at a fancy seaside hotel, the Comodoro, in which Traficant had an interest. As a result of their dinner he organized a private orgy with three girls for Senator Kilmory's entertainment.

In retrospect, viewed from the twenty-first century, this seems utterly frivolous and unimportant. After President Clangton's hi-jinks in the Oval Office, most people today are inclined to think "so what?" However, in twentieth-century puritanical America, evidence of such an event would have seemed scandalous beyond redemption. If made public during Kilmory's presidential term, it might have brought his whole administration tumbling down like a house of cards.

Kilmory might have weighed that—and the possibility that such a revelation might at least have temporarily distracted and paralyzed the U.S. government's action vis-a-vis the Soviet-Cuban threat—against the alternative. If nothing of the kind were brought out and his administration had a chance to regroup, Costra could still be gotten rid of later on. In other words, the invasion had to fail in order for his administration to survive.

Another contributory fact was that, in addition, the Soviets might have threatened to take over West Berlin, thereby unleashing a war—perhaps with nuclear implications—that the U.S. would have been hard-pressed to successfully prosecute against the extremely powerful military forces of the Soviet-led Warsaw Pact.

There is a caveat to this theory, however. If the Soviets had issued that threat, wouldn't it have been possible for the Kilmory administration to postpone the "secret" invasion (that everyone, especially Costra, knew about and was expecting) and later explain that it had been necessary due to "global strategic considerations"?

There is little evidence of any fundamental weakness of character on the part of Kilmory, since he appeared tough and forceful when he needed to be, and brother Roland was even more aggressive and frequently lived up to his reputation of ruthlessness. They both seemed to have backed down in lock-step, however, in the Bay of Pigs invasion, as well as in the 1962 Missile Crisis, which was proclaimed as a "victory" for the U.S. when, in reality, the Soviets achieved their objective of establishing Costra's Cuba as an impregnable Soviet base.

A footnote to this is the «Armaggedon letter» sent by Costra to Krustivich, urging him to deliver a first-strike nuclear attack on the United States. Although this was unknown for several decades, and until Costra himself acknowledged it was deemed far-fetched and not creditworthy, analysts have consistently considered it reckless and extremely dangerous. Nothing of the kind: it was carefully calculated by Costra—who knew the Soviets would reject it—to enhance his image as wild and unpredictable. That would, and effectively has, kept the U.S. at bay in terms of any serious action against Costra's regime.

The outcome, in effect, was to force the U.S. to agree, at least temporarily, to give up any efforts to invade the island or otherwise attempt to overthrow the regime. "Temporarily" is used advisedly, since the Kilmorys, as will be shown later on, were planning a more powerful and decisive invasion of Cuba just as the president was assassinated. This was possible because the Kilmory pledge to hold back any action was actually predicated on the unmet condition of on-site inspection in Cuba to ensure that all Soviet missiles had been removed.

As might have been expected, no sooner had the Bay of Pigs invasion failed, Kilmory openly made the CIA the scapegoat. The Agency, known among insiders as the "Company"—reportedly because its acronym reflects the Spanish abbreviation for "company," cía.—was virtually powerless to defend itself from the White House. It became known that the Commander in Chief had not only cut off the vital air support, but made disastrous changes in landing sites, including the outright cancellation of one of them, scheduled for eastern Cuba. How to account for that except by concluding that the goal was failure?

CIA Director Alton Dunsell was summarily fired, even though the Agency had been forced to follow presidential instructions and was actually the victim of presidential decisions—or lack thereof— that undercut the success of the invasion. But worse was to come. Failure at the Bay of Pigs brought on, in quick succession, the introduction of Soviet ballistic missiles into Cuba, precipitating the confrontation known as the Missile Crisis.

Endless troubles would follow, with subversion and guerrilla warfare throughout Latin America. In retrospect, the evidence seems to lead to the conclusion that the Kilmorys had chosen to give up Cuba, at least temporarily. The original invasion plan had been carefully thought out to ensure success—one way or another. In case the Brigade should have found itself unable to make headway in battling the Costra forces, it would, acting as a provisional free

Cuban government controling a piece of Cuban territory, call for international assistance. The United States would then promptly respond by sending in the Marines, with full air support, from the carrier task force in place just offshore. This would have quickly wiped out Costra's smaller, ill-equipped forces. It was soon apparent, however, that Justin Kilmory had discarded this option, insisting on the falsehood—all evidence to the contrary—that the United States could not "appear to be involved."

However, the whole world knew that the entire operation had been set up by the U.S. Government and was going ahead only with its full and supposedly unconditional backing. Reliable sources indicate that Adler Samuelson, the American ambassador at the United Nations, was a staunch supporter of maintaining a thinly-veiled "appearance" of a hands-off policy on the part of the U.S. That a practical and apparently forceful man like Kilmory would subscribe to that sort of utter nonsense seems, on the face of it, unlikely. Which brings up the question of some hidden reason, such as the threat of blackmail—a legitimate question which so far no one has seen fit to even hint at. Why not? Is that not a commonplace in human and, especially, international affairs?

Even if the issue of keeping up hands-off appearances had any validity, it was contradicted by events. Sometime after the Bay of Pigs and the Missile Crisis, the CIA received a top-level directive to proceed with the plan to kill Costra. The Kilmorys were now going full speed ahead against him, regardless of the consequences to weak points such as Berlin or even, perhaps, personal danger to themselves. Cuba seemed, by then, far too important and well worth the risk. They also showed some guts: their very lives were now in peril. Costra himself had said so in no uncertain terms, having stated in a speech that if his own life was being targeted, the leaders of the United States should know that they could not expect to be safe from harm either.

But the Kilmorys had made up their mind. The presence on the neighboring island of a Soviet base, now probably armed with nuclear weapons despite the apparent withdrawal of missiles, was too dangerous a threat to accept and do nothing about.

Within months of the Missile Crisis, the decision was made to prepare another invasion, to be coordinated—again—with the physical elimination of Costra. They would pull out all the stops and use the special relationship of the CIA with the Mafia to do away with him. The Agency relied on the Mob to do a lot of its dirty work—jobs it could not do for political reasons, due to the risk of discovery, the need for plausible deniability, or because it simply was not as well prepared to carry them out as were its more ruthless and less constrained underworld counterparts.

The "Company" thus began to make its arrangements to take out the Cuban leader. Some of its projects—according to reports of questionable credibility—were so outlandish as to provoke utter, laughable disbelief. The one still bandied about regarding chemicals to make his beard fall out, for example, cannot be taken seriously. If they had been able to get the chemicals on Costra, why not use deadly ones instead of those causing mere follicle damage?

The CIA's intersection with the Mafia made it vulnerable to Costra's vast intelligence network, allied with the KGB and the vast Iranian, Libyan (during Khadafy's dictatorship) and other anti-Western spy agencies around the world. Their relentless, far-reaching tentacles are, even today, extremely underestimated. Some experts in the field still rate Costra's intelligence system second only to the CIA's and Israel's Mossad.

It is quite possible that the top leaders of the "Company" might not even have been aware of the degree to which they were infiltrated by the Mafia—or, indeed, of the Mafia-CIA connection itself—due to compartmentalization carried to the extreme or to the fact that rogue agents might have kept this vital information under their hat.

In sum, an unexpected, sinister relationship was afoot between Costra and the mobsters that would, in effect, turn the Mafia into a double agency, spinning the plans of the CIA into a complete reversal of their intended target: instead of pointing at Costra, the dagger would be aimed at Kilmory himself.

Chapter XII
THE HOOPER FACTOR

Instructions for illegal and
super-secret operations:
"DO NOT FILE"

H. Everette Hooper, the long-time head of the FBI, was not too fond of the Kilmorys. In fact, he was solidly in the Mob's corner— as no one in Washington had any reason to suspect. The deference normally shown to someone of his stature made it outlandish to even think of any such connection. He was also a close friend and neighbor of Vice President Jameson, with whom he regularly conspired, over the back fence, to neutralize or eliminate mutual enemies.

Like some of his predecessors, Justin Kilmory was eager to remove Hooper, or at least ease him out of office. The FBI Director was not too worried, since his files contained far too much dirt on the Kilmory clan for them to dare cross him. Still, the Kilmorys rankled him. Who did these young Irish punks think they were? Did these newcomers to Washington think they could run rough-shod over the Bureau and everyone else in the capital-city's long-running establishment? Hooper was used to having his way in the government, no matter who was in power. After all, he had directed the FBI longer than Roland, that "snot-nosed kid," had been alive.

As for the Mafia, Hooper insisted at every opportunity that it "did not exist." Claudio Mariello, boss of New Orleans, always laughed out loud when he heard Hooper say those words. Now if the Justice Department were run by Hooper, he thought, that would be a completely different kettle of fish. The nonexistence of the Mob was a blatantly absurd statement that, quite clearly, was part of his own private understanding with them and, for those in the know, showed that he was in their pocket. The Mob wouldn't publicize what they knew about his deep-in-the-closet homosexuality—Hooper all but shared his household with his assistant and deputy FBI chief, Clutch

Towson. In turn, the FBI would lay off the Mob. But that was not all they had on him. The Mafia had found out about Hooper's darkest personal secret. Why did Hooper veto, until the late 1960s, any and all black applicants—and women as well, of whatever race—for jobs as FBI agents?

Could it have been for any other reason than the well-known fact of human nature that those with something to hide are always on the front lines of opposition to anyone who might reveal their secret, even if merely by passively evidencing similarities in a side-by-side comparison? Wasn't it safer to exclude anyone whose presence might lead to someone noticing something of that nature? Could it be that Hooper's reason for his staunch racism, according to reliable sources, was the fact that he was not entirely white?

Somewhere along the line had a smidgen of dark blood had slipped into his well-hidden family tree—and the Mob knew about that too. A careful observation of photographs of Hooper shows that he had some suspiciously black features: to start with, a flat, broad-based nose and curly hair.

Just in case sticks were not enough, the Mafia had arranged to provide some carrots for the man who said their organization was non-existent. His invaluable services to the Mob were well compensated, directly or indirectly. For starters, Hooper and his long-time boy-friend were regularly invited, each year, to spend a no-expense month at a Mob-owned resort in La Jolla, California, or at other resorts in secluded locations, where they hobnobbed with the capos without a care in the world.

But there were important payoffs in cash as well. Hooper, whose favorite pastime was going to the race track, was regularly given tips by Sal Campana and Francesco Castellaro's "soldiers" so he could win big on fixed races. Ever careful, Hooper would place small bets on a no-name, losing horse while one of his flunkies would go to a different, big-bucks window and bet a suitcase full of money on the chosen winner. And no one seemed the wiser. Nor did the IRS ever seem interested in auditing his returns for winnings or other undeclared benefits and income.

Furthermore, no one ever questioned Hooper's luxurious lifestyle in the house he shared with his chosen lover-boy, whom he had named second-in-command at the FBI. Plus, he enjoyed all kinds of perks and home-improvement projects at the expense of the taxpayers. A whispered-about story made the rounds that, at government expense—like nearly everything else in the house— Hooper had installed in his main bathroom a heated toilet seat developed in FBI laboratories. However, with his penchant for perfection to the nth degree, finding himself unsatisfied with its precise position, he made the Bureau's installers come back to adjust its height by a quarter of an inch (whether it was up or down was never made clear).

Another extravagance of Hooper's was that he had told his driver to always keep the engine running whenever he took him anywhere, no matter how much idling time might be involved. On one occasion his engagement—some kind of a tryst?—dragged on for so many hours that the idling engine finally ran out of gas. When Hooper came out, incensed at his driver, he gave him a severe tongue-lashing. He nearly fired him but, in the end, held back. After all, the driver was the only black special agent in the FBI. Hooper had promoted him from a lower grade appropriate to his job and made him a special agent so he could claim that not all his special agents were white.

So controlling and micro-managing of the Bureau was Hooper that all requests for more than a week of leave had to be sent to his desk and be personally approved by him. If for some reason he disapproved of the staff member's performance or conduct, he simply denied it. Some agents actually lost annual leave because of repeated denials by Hooper.

By the way, the Director's expense account with the FBI was astronomical and no one ever dared question a single cent of it. There were also secret stashes from which he withdrew money at will without ever having to provide any accounting whatsoever.   In addition, he got freebies in all kinds of different places by virtue of being who he was.

Hooper used to lunch regularly at Washington's swanky Mayflower Hotel, where a special table was perennially reserved for him and whichever friends or celebrities he cared to invite— frequently famous actresses to give the impression that he was interested in women. For some ten thousand or so lunches, he was never billed a single cent.

All of the above are but peccadilloes when compared to his harassment of Marlin Lester Ring. Not only did the FBI plant illegal bugs on him everywhere, including his house, his offices and hotel rooms, but in places where he might stop for an occasional, off-hand visit. Hooper was determined to get any information he could use against Ring, no matter what it took. He considered the rising black leader a subversive, leftist-influenced agent—if not a full-blown communist—intent on destabilizing the political and social fabric of the country, an evil, immoral opportunist who had to be held back and, if possible, put in his place. The fact that he was mobilizing the black masses to rebel against discrimination and gain a foothold in respectable American society was most repellent to him and needed to be countered at every turn.

As a consummate racist, Hooper objected when President Kilmory—aiming for desegregation—selected one of the first black Secret Service agents as part of his personal security detail. "Mr. President," he said, "do you realize you are putting your life in the hands of a Negro?"

Attorney General Roland had told him to send agents to investigate events in Alabama and Mississippi in the 1960's. Hooper dragged his feet and complied reluctantly. Eventually, he had no choice but to infiltrate Bureau agents into the Ku Klux Klan, a highly effective tactic that succeeded in practically destroying it from within. But that was at least a decade or two later than it should have happened.

Fed by his racism, Hooper's hatred of Ring increased apace with his prominence in the struggle for equality. Ever more convinced that he had to halt his ascendancy and that, by stopping him he would likely break the civil rights movement, he eventually decided that it was justified and necessary to take him out physically. For Hooper, a key member of the conspiracy to kill President Kilmory, this was a far less dangerous enterprise that, with his experience and resources, could be more easily arranged, carried out and eventually covered up. His first thought was that the job would best be carried out by professional hit-men linked to the Mob. Later, however, he evolved a more elaborate plot using Army Intelligence sharpshooters, an elite team trained to take out troublesome individuals or, in some cases, groups. Even though evidence of this criminal deed has been carefully covered up by layer upon layer of concealment, as well as by eliminating those in the way when necessary, it is safe to assume that it was not Jeffrey Burl Maye, the purported culprit, who according to the official mantra, "acted alone and unassisted by anyone else." If that description seems eerily similar to that of Kilmory's purported assassin, Harrison Rosswell— and later, Shapan Shapan, who was framed for assassinating RolandKilmory, it is no coincidence. It matches the *modus operandi* of the brains behind all these crimes.

(At least one author has carefully looked into the case in the intervening years since the black leader was murdered in Memphis, tracing the leads and analyzing all the details in a five-hundred page volume: *Orders to Kill*. In passing, it should be noted that practically nothing negative at all on Hooper was brought up in Clyde Westwood's 2011 Hollywood biopic on him, "H. Everette," which mysteriously whitewashed the Bureau-cratic Director's life as if its producers were members of a religious cult who worshiped the ground that Hooper walked on.)

H. Everette Hooper had maintained a close working relationship with Army Intelligence since the 1920's. His long-time lover, Assistant FBI Director Clutch Towson, had worked for Army Intelligence before coming to the Bureau, and since then kept in touch with its top officers. Gradually, Hooper and Towson worked out a plan under which Army Intelligence coordinated its efforts with the FBI, the CIA, the Mob and senior officers of the Memphis Police Department to take out Ring. Hooper was the brains behind the crime, while Army Intelligence, assisted by the other agencies and the Mob, provided the muscle to carry it out.

In addition to the motive, Hooper had at his command the contacts, means and resources necessary to efficiently cover up the deed. Well known were his discrimination of blacks and his visceral enmity toward Ring, whom he accused of being a communist and maintaining close connections to others of like mind. To such an extent had he bugged his hotel rooms and the places he frequented that Ring took to holding his meetings in hotel lobbies, which were more difficult to tap. In Hooper's mind Ring was upsetting America and endangering its stability with his demonstrations and efforts to do away with discrimination, while the Director himself was a chapter-and-verse believer in the entrenched racist system.

Hooper was also angry about Ring's womanizing, which he considered hypocritical, immoral and reprehensible, if not outright illegal. In short, he had more than enough motivation to neutralize Ring. It is quite likely that he would have done so much sooner, but had to wait until Roland Kilmory, the thorn in his side, was no longer Attorney General and therefore unable to cause him trouble.

After Roland Kilmory's departure from the Justice Department, several opportunities to kill Ring came up but were scrubbed for one reason or another, until the one in Memphis was finally and carefully set up to leave nothing to chance.

When Maye was apprehended in London and brought back into the country, the groundwork was laid to coerce him to confess, even though he was innocent of the crime. It is also safe to assume that many who had important information in the Ring case and on Maye's innocence, Maye himself included, were threatened or otherwise pressured to change their testimony or simply keep quiet. It would have been inconvenient to have conflicting testimony that would upset their contrived open-and-shut case, very similar to the ones against Rosswell and, later, Shapan. Since Maye was "persuaded" to let himself be framed, it seemed unnecessary and perhaps unwise to duplicate the quick execution employed against Rosswell.

Jeffrey Maye's untimely disappearance was due to fast-acting cancer —no doubt induced by the tried-and-true method of directing intense radiation into his cell. At the time, Ring's widow and family being unconvinced of his guilt, there was about to be a break in the case. What a coincidence! That turned out to be the key to sealing it shut, thus "burying" the truth: he was not the assassin at all but another scapegoat à la Rosswell.

Eventually, after Hooper had been on his throne over four decades and surpassed the mandatory retirement age of 75, President Dixon attempted what six presidents before him had tried and failed to do. The old man just knew too much, and to top it off was too entrenched, difficult, glib and slippery. Hooper resisted tooth and nail, and Dixon, although he could not be blackmailed by him on sexual grounds because he was straight as an arrow and had never engaged in hanky-panky like his predecessors—did have other weaknesses. Hooper did, in fact, have plenty of damaging information on him, so Dixon threw in the towel on his plan to ease him quietly out of office. He was forced, it seemed, to take a more proactive approach.

He called in his "Plumbers" to see if they had any ideas. The Plumbers were the Dixon version of specialists in plugging leaks and doing other odd jobs—which included circumventing the CIA and old-man Hooper's FBI—just as the Kilmorys had done in their era.

"Boys," Dixon said, "this can't drag on forever... Do what you have to, but make sure it's clean."

One morning, a short time later, Hooper's housekeeper noticed that her employer had not taken his usual morning shower. There was a suspicious stillness upstairs. She called for help. When it came, Hooper was found dead. He was locked into his master bedroom dressed in his pajama bottoms, although he never locked the door and usually slept in the nude.

His doctor was surprised because he knew the Bureau's Director to be in good health. Nothing seemed amiss. But since the FBI Director suffered from hypertensive cardiovascular disease he thought it best—did someone clue him in?—to attribute his death to natural causes. Having no close relatives, no one asked for an autopsy and Hooper was quickly buried.

Did someone pull that old standby, a medicine-cabinet switch of pills? The target takes the look-alike "sleeping" pill, goes to slumber-land and never wakes up. More likely, according to knowledgeable sources, they poisoned his toothpaste. It was later determined that there had been two recent break-ins into his house in which apparently nothing was taken or disturbed. Had the "Plumbers" done their job? If so, they scored.

The Bureau was not called in to investigate what was, in retrospect, the suspicious death of a personage whose very name symbolized the soul and embodiment of its existence for most of the twentieth century. If anything shady had taken place, careful arrangements were made to cover it all up. Too bad this black-bag job, heretofore ignored, did not take place before Hooper conspired with the master criminal who used his FBI, plus the Mafia and CIA agents, to kill President Kilmory.

In sum, Hooper was a bigot, a limitless hypocrite, a glory-hog of ever-embarrassing proportions, as professional a blackmailer as there ever was, a pretentious dresser—who might have, by the way, occasionally cross-dressed under strictly private circumstances—and, to top it all off, a heavily closeted homosexual addicted to raunchy perfume.

Since all of this clearly deserved a monument worthy of his stature, today there stands on Pennsylvania Avenue an impressive FBI edifice bearing in its architrave the bold inscription "H. Everette Hooper Building."

Chapter XIII
COSTRA'S FELONIES

If Hooper the crooked law-enforcement czar committed murder and was responsible for a good share of lawlessness and crime in the U.S., all of it covered up by the broad umbrella of power, his stature was tiny compared to that of Fingenio Costra, who acted/acts with impunity not only within Cuba itself but on an international scale. And above all inside America.

Let us draw up a list of only a few of his most notorious evil deeds, all of them practically ignored by the press. We refer not only to his regime's own, consisting of a single four-page daily, *Granma*, which parrots only official slogans and propaganda, but to the international media, continually concerned about, for example, the South African racist regime that disappeared decades ago, while unconcerned for over a half century about a whole multiracial population that undergoes on a regular basis despotic and discriminatory abuses and violations of their most elementary human rights.

But not to worry—everything's under control!

Aircraft Hijacking
One of the first lawless activities undertaken by the Costra regime was a new type of international crime: organized and systematic aircraft hijacking. This was a lucrative, "showy" (in an egomaniacal sense), terrorist plan designed to keep Costra's powerful "northern enemy" in check. This new concept of kidnapping passenger aircraft eventually gave rise to much more terrible acts of aggression such as the 9/11 attack on New York's Twin Towers.

Countless flights taking off from southern U.S. cities (but curiously not from Mexico or Latin America in general) were diverted at gun-point to Havana, where the aircraft and passengers had to be rescued by paying "expenses and compensation" under the table. Into whose pocket were those secret funds going? Guess!

Finally, our government had to make some «concessions» to Costra in order to stop the air-traffic hemorrhage. (What were they? Likely a promise that *we* would stop interfering with *their* civil aviation!)

But not to worry—everything's under control!)

Subversive Activities

This brings up the fact that shortly thereafter Costra started backing the Black Panthers and the Black Liberation Army, two criminal, terrorist organizations that ravaged the heart of America during the 1960's and subsequent years. The Panthers traveled at will to Cuba, where they received support, training and considerable funds. U.S. authorities paid little attention: they basically looked the other way and took no reprisals or measures against the Costra regime.

Which brings to mind the number of dangerous criminals that have escaped the U.S. system of justice by escaping to the Costra sanctuary: this is so outlandish that it's virtually an official secret. The U.S. government doesn't discuss these cases and discourages any attempt by the media to investigate them, including some that could only be described as scandalous. Some fugitives from U.S. justice have been living comfortably in Cuba for thirty, forty and fifty years as if nothing had ever happened. By the way, the Costra regime doesn't just receive them as "brothers in arms," but favors them with all kinds of special perks and benefits, putting them far above the average native citizen in its "workers' paradise".

But not to worry—everything's under control!

Shady Financial Transactions and Fugitives

One case in point concerns Robert Vesco, a white-collar criminal who robbed investors in the 1970's of no less than $350 million (equivalent to several billion in 2013 dollars) and evaded justice by eventually taking refuge in the elite stratum of the Costra sanctuary for U.S. outlaws. Upon arriving there in 1981 Vesco, described by a reliable source as «the indisputable king of financial fugitives» was received like royalty (he no doubt paid for it with millions in admission and «fees») and, surrounded by luxuries and servants galore, lived like a king for five years without ever having to answer for his crimes. That is, until finally the true monarch wondered: Why should one be content with a part of a guest's fortune when one can have it all?

In this state of affairs, one day the wealthy baron disappeared from his mansion and extensive acreage and landed in jail, where he was no longer heard from. However, we can be sure that they gave him the personal care required to inflict a good dose of pain and suffering before contracting one of those mysterious ailments with which his jailers end the victim's ordeal. But of course they're thinking above all on the hardship for the state, which is forced to cover the inmate's maintenance expenses.

The record shows that in 1989 Costra accused him of drug trafficking—or rather, to be truthful, of competing in this line of business, a state monopoly—for which charge he was sentenced without right of appeal to the equivalent of life behind bars. Sure enough, he died of lung cancer not much later. There can be little doubt that, following their customary procedure, Costra's jailers saved the state further expenses by flooding his cell with radiation until the disease took root. In sum, another case of damages to "the northern enemy" inflicted by those who never had to answer to our system of justice, thanks to the sanctuary offered by the king of international outlaws.

But not to worry—everything's under control!

Armed Robbery

The year 1981 witnessed the sensational "Brink's Robbery" (not to be confused with a similar one in 1950), in which an armored company truck was held up and robbed of $1.6 million. The deed was carried out by ex members of the criminal, subversive "Weather Underground," an organization linked to the "May 19" U.S. communist movement. To accomplish their objective, the assailants had received training and logistical support in the mastermind's captive island. Some of the criminals, who killed two policemen and a Brink's guard —another's arm was cut off with a shower of bullets—, escaped with a good portion of the loot to Costraland, where they have lived comfortably ever since.

But not to worry—everything's under control!

Elián González

The year 1999 saw the outlandish case of Elián González, a six-year-old who arrived in a small boat with his mother, who drowned while attempting to save his life. The Immigration Service then placed the boy under the care of close relatives in Miami. There was not the slightest issue until Costra decided to create a *cause célèbre,* launching a media "rescue" campaign to return him to his father in Cuba. Costra was hardly doing it for the sake of the child, whose mother had given her life to pull him out of the hole of poverty and oppression that his regime had dug for the previous forty years, but boosting what he perceived as his own prestige.

When the courts initially avoided a ruling on such a thorny subject, the Clangton administration took justice into its own hands and sent in a well-armed military team to take the boy at gunpoint away from his home, physically removing him to a place where they could control him and send him to Costra.

Doesn't all this seem suspicious? Doesn't it conjure up thoughts that Costra threatened Clangton with revealing God knows what secrets (there has been talk about a certain video)? If so, he put him squarely behind the 8-ball: send me the boy or else. If not, why would the executive power run the risk of implementing dangerous extra-judicial measures while legal procedures were still available? To silence someone who "knew too much"? Hmmm....

But not to worry—everything's under control!

Angola

The same gentleman referred to above, seriously concerned over the welfare of mankind, intervened during nearly three decades in the conflict sparked in Angola when it gained independence from Portugal. From 1975 until the end of the 1990's, Costraland sent Cubans to die in that distant country. Was he attempting to defend democracy and freedom? More Papist than the Pope himself, he even went against the wishes of his Soviet sponsors, who were less aggressively inclined. The idea was quite simply to stand out, enhance his own importance and become a player on the world's chess table.

Out of 35,000 troops sent by Costra to fight for Angola's "independence" (i.e., the communist faction), the number of dead—a state secret of the regime—totaled about 10,000. But that was okay since he justified it saying that "they had asked for support as brothers in the struggle." Oh, I see!

Suffice it to say that Costraland's presence in Angola played a vital role in handing power in the infant country to the group invested with his ideological preference, i.e., the Popular Movement for Liberating Angola (MPLA), which was losing the battle when Costra's forces arrived. (It's worth noting that a recognized "hero" of the conflict was General Arnoldo Ochoa, later executed on trumped-up charges. See the "Drug Trafficking" section in this chapter.)

Cubans are still asking themselves (they dare not ask anyone else) why their elders and brothers were sent to their death in Africa. By the way, their equal-opportunity leader arranged to send to Angola all the blacks he possibly could—discrimination or incrimination?—because they were easily mistaken for Angolans. (Racial discrimination, Costra's practice from the beginning, may be observed in the state nomenclature, where Afro-Cubans are at a minimum; mysteriously, this fact has never been of the slightest concern for Americans, South Africans or anyone else.)

While the war was being fought, the president of the United States came out for the first (and last) time with a stark truth about Costra that is worth repeating here:

"HE'S AN INTERNATIONAL OUTLAW!"

And this is the guy who proclaimed his opposition to America's "imperialist" war in Viet Nam. Could it be that he's only against imperialism when it's not his own?

But not to worry—everything's under control!

Weapons of Mass Destruction

The U.S. Government has been careful not to provide any information on this. However, the world's intelligence agencies are well aware that Costra has set up secret factories of extremely dangerous chemical and biological weapons, which he holds in store to punish an enemy in case of "imperialist aggression" or other event he may point to as apocalyptic. After all, what does he care? If he were still alive (we doubt it) his remaining time is brief. (Note that he's been unusually silent about the Syrian toxic-gas crisis, whereas he unfailingly has something to say in defense of his terrorist brothers.)

That is, assuming he does not have a nuclear bomb smuggled in from North Korea in one of those suspicious shipments of "obsolete weapons" in need of repair.

But not to worry—everything's under control!

Grenada

These days, few might recall that the island of Grenada nearly fell into Costra's hands in 1983, thanks to the presence of Cuban forces who supported a think-alike faction in a domestic struggle. The Cuban "contractors" hired to build a 10,000-foot landing strip long enough for large bombers and a number of military purposes. However, we had a president, Runyon, who wouldn't be pushed around and wiped out with one fast swipe this truly imperialist grab: he sent U.S. troops and neutralized the greedy outlaw.

You might wonder about the orders that the courageous island hero gave to his men from the safety of his far-way bunker: "Do not surrender! Fight to the death!" The expeditionaries, less sacrificially inclined, gave up and were returned to Cuba only to be humbled by Costra, who considered himself dishonored!

But not to worry—everything's under control!

Venezuela

After thirty years of futile efforts to take over Venezuela by force of arms —he had a better outcome in Nicaragua—Costra conceived a much more effective plan based on subversion: his name was Chánchez.

Contrary to what is commonly taken for granted, the lord and master of Costraland invited the still-unknown young army officer to visit him and receive certain advance "training." He then educated him to execute the sinister plan that, copied from Adolf Hitler, was followed by Fingenio himself to reach power. First you organize a coup d'état; if you do not succeed you still don't lose (the dead will not complain): the leader does time in jail but becomes a household name and takes advantage of it and the democratic media to become president. Once in power he manages, with the advice and counsel of his mastermind and his agents, to remain in power indefinitely.

The footnote to the story is that the teacher got rid of the pupil when his usefulness began to wane. Even though he rewarded him with a fortune in oil, Costra had his replacement ready: he was more indoctrinated, obedient, yielding and not so clownish. He was a man who obeyed orders without even blinking or competing with him for the limelight by attracting too much attention.

"Come spend time here at your mansion, your vacation home in this island of yours and we'll take care of you as you really deserve," he said.

He didn't make it clear that his just desserts were a good dose of radiation that would soon plant the seeds of a deadly form of cancer.

"Don't worry," he comforted him. "Come over and we'll cure you with our superior brand of advanced medicine."

Chánchez believed him. He went back time and again until, finally, he "cured" him. Permanently. It was all very well organized and disguised as they implemented all the measures for a smooth succession.

So, what measures has the U.S. taken to stand guard for democracy and Hemispheric security?

But not to worry—everything's under control!

Espionage

Costra has had, to this day, spies in the top echelons of our government (Congress and the executive branch) and in America's intelligence agencies. Since espionage is his hobby, he himself undertook (when he was still alive [?] and in his prime) the management and direction of intelligence operations. Although some (very few) of his operatives have been arrested, he makes a big show of demanding their freedom, incidentally helping his cause by kidnapping innocent Americans in order to exchange them for his duly convicted and jailed professional agents. Since Costra runs a criminal state, his spies not only have permission, but are actually *encouraged* to commit crimes, misdeeds and bloody attacks that the public is not even aware of (for "national security reasons"!)

Puerto Rican-born Ana Belén Montes, a double agent for Costraland, actually became head of the Pentagon's Cuba Intelligence Section. A report that once came out of there should have set off FIRE ALARMS. It said that "Cuba is NOT a danger to the United States." (Yeah, right!) And this fine young lady did all this for "principles", without charging a single cent! She's now doing time, but her double-dealing lasted some 15 years.

But not to worry—everything's under control!

Costra, One of Forgues' Ten Richest

Forgues, the world-renowned financial magazine, which takes the trouble to publish an annual list of the Ten Richest, dared to include Fingenio Costra about a decade ago. According to estimates, his fortune (so vast and impossible-to-verify that it is truly incalculable) at the time was about $8 billion.

Indignant, the super-wealthy friend of the poor and downtrodden protested that it was a "dirty lie" and that he did not have a single cent to his name. He further stated that everything on his island "belongs to the people" and that he had "absolutely nothing, zero." He then challenged the magazine to submit "proof."

Far from submitting proof, the publication mysteriously took his name off the list the following year (although it may have resurfaced later on). One wonders how they "persuaded" the top management. Maybe they were overwhelmed with kindness and understood the sorry state of personal indigence suffered by the prodigal and self-sacrificing Costra. We do know that *Forgues* never came out with a single word of explanation.

But not to worry—everything's under control!

Drug Trafficking

Rather than wearing out our reader's patience we'll wind this up by discussing the main "business" providing bounteous income for the Costra regime. It is nothing less than drug trafficking, which has flourished from the untouchable island base, rewarding its benefactor with untold riches. These he has put to good use in funding his crimes, guerrilla wars and interference in Latin America (the main "front" for him) and other regions.

Costra himself has stated on countless occasions his intention to undermine the social and civic foundations of his northern enemy, although he has never cleared up the procedure, perhaps concerned that his powerful neighbor might take him at his word.

Well, he has kept his word and continues doing so. He turned his island into a secure base for international drug trafficking. Cuba is a vital stopping point for the traffickers to reorganize and resupply in order to jump across to America's coasts in powerful speedboats. The incalculable profits derived from this "business" are invested by Costra in continuing with his international interventionism and multiplying his personal wealth.

However, in the 1980's Mr. Costra gave the U.S. Government a good excuse not to undertake reprisals against him. He found a timely scapegoat in his Angolan-war hero, General Arnoldo Novoa, saying it was he who had organized the Cuba-based drug trafficking and should therefore be punished. In other words, Costra blamed his general for what he himself had been doing for twenty years.

Before the end-game, Fingenio paid him a visit and said: "Look, Arnoldo, it's very simple: you plead guilty. I then save you from execution and take care of your family, protecting them from any revenge. There are lots of people out there who are outraged by your crimes. Understand?

This explains why Novoa confessed, although he still wound up before the firing squad. What really bothered Costra was that Novoa was far too popular. Around Havana, hopeful Cubans started writing this graffiti: "9A" [novo is a form of nueve, 9, + A = Novoa]. But, worst of all, the general had discussed among his friends long-range plans, commenting: "Well, but what are we going to with the old nag [Costra]?"

But, as we were saying . . .

Not to worry—everything's under control!

* * * * * * *

The words are not to be taken lightly. It so happens that this is exactly what Fingenio said when he assassinated a true hero of the revolution, Camilo Cienfuegos. In an isolated area near central Cuba, Cienfuegos got off a small aircraft in which he was flown from Camagüey to attend an urgent "meeting" of the top leadership called by Costra. He was riddled with bullets before he could draw his service revolver.

According to an eyewitness, once the shooting stopped Costra addressed the assembled group:

"Gentlemen: everything's under control!"

Chapter XIV
PLANS FOR REVENGE

"The nerve of this double-crossing little shit," Mariello hissed, putting on his nastiest look—one that meant it was time to "push": meaning "hit, "clip," "erase," "wipe out." Only now, it seemed difficult to believe he actually meant it.

"Boss, you mean...?" Angelo Cosimano, Mariello's henchman, completed the thought by drawing a finger across his throat.

"You betcha! I've had it from these guys. Either him or else— better yet—his brother, up at the top." Mariello pointed to the ceiling.

"Wow, boss..., *that'd* really be some hit!" Angelo's eyes bulged and dutifully glanced toward the ceiling. He was doubtful something like that could actually be pulled off, but knew better than to look anything but suitably impressed, much less actually voice doubt that the Outfit—or more specifically, Mariello—could actually arrange to do anything like that, even by applying all the powers at its command. He dismissed it as too far-fetched and risky. Even a passing thought of all the implications, of all the work it would take to convince the capos of the top families made it, for him, unlikely. But why argue with the boss? It wouldn't be his problem anyway. "Yeah, what a hit that'll be!" he concluded cockily, shaking his head.

"You got *that* right! When a dog bites you, you cut off its head, not its tail. Right?" Mariello quoted himself; in fact, it was one of his favorite sayings, which he would be repeating—to great effect— over and over again until he got everybody in line.

"Listen Angelo," Mariello said, sounding as though he were about to tell him a secret, "what good would it do to stop the tail from wagging if the head keeps biting?" He gave Angelo a knowing, half-mocking malicious look and, when he saw Angelo's confused reaction, burst into uproarious laughter. "Haw, haw, yeah, haw, haw, haw—what good would *that* do?—just think!"

"Got your point, boss," Angelo replied as he joined in the laughter with Mariello, "no good at all. We'd just have to do another hit on the head, eh?" Angelo laughed uproariously at his own lame joke, even though he had unintentionally topped Mariello, who didn't find it quite as funny.

"Not bad, Angelo," he said condescendingly. "Now you're getting smart. Just wait'll I talk about dis to Looney and my *fratelli*—he pronounced in perfect Italian the word for "brothers," with which he referred to the other capos. I jus' know they're itchin' for it," he added. "Yeah, my *fratelli*," he repeated, "I think they're gonna like it." His mention of "Looney" was a reference to Sal Campana, whose nickname reflected the capo's unpredictable moods and sometimes downright crazy reactions. "Keep it under your hat," he warned as Angelo excused himself from his boss's office. He was careful to pretend that the plan was his own idea and not an operation, informally called "Executive Action," being plotted at the highest levels. Even Mariello did not know who was leading the conspiracy, although he had his suspicions. It would be essential, as Mariello's contact had made clear, to compartmentalize the operation as much as possible and feed any information on a strict need-to-know basis.

"Al, call that number in Langley, Virginia now. It's time." He did not need to clear up that Langley was the location of the CIA's headquarters.

"Sure, boss."

"One full ring, hang up. Then, they call us back. Got that?" Mariello repeated his previous instructions to make sure there were no mistakes. His contact at the Central Intelligence Agency had made some promising remarks that, he hoped, would clinch the matter. He couldn't wait to spring it on "Looney" and the rest..., if, as he hoped, everything panned out. Sandy Traficant and Jake Rosetti were already aboard, but he wanted to get Campana's approval before proceeding.

* * * * * * *

In late spring of 1963, Justin Kilmory was concentrating more on Jessica Cameron's next visit, which he juggled with his calendar of White House secretaries and other local and extramural paramours. Still, he couldn't exactly neglect his political agenda, where foreign policy was replete with delicate issues, while Roland, on the other hand, was still obsessed with pursuing his most hateful enemy: the Mafia. Neither had any idea that, conversely, the Mafia was planning a response. After all, the capos reasoned, Justin Kilmory had served over two and a half years as president, and they couldn't afford to give him much more time to wreck their operations. Business was business.

Happily ensconced again in the expanse of his garish digs on the outskirts of New Orleans, Mariello smiled broadly at the thought of FBI Director Hooper, on whom he felt he could count as a facilitator, at the very least, of their plans against the Kilmorys. In their last conversation, when he had indirectly alluded to the Outfit's plans against the Kilmorys, Hooper had said not a word, but smiled knowingly and nodded his head in approval. Mariello had had occasion to socialize with him, together with other Mob figures, when Hooper took advantage of one of the perks they offered him on a regular basis—a free-of-charge, month-long stay for him and his second-in-command boy-friend, every year, at a lavish Mob-owned resort in La Jolla, California.

"I think you're right, boss. Those bastards got it comin'," said Angelo after a pause. "You had a hell of a time. Lucky you got back in the country. If it hadn't been for that arrangement with the Dominican Republic Air Force plane to pick you up and fly you to that base in—what was it, Homestead?—you'd still be in Central America."

"Yeah, thank God for my connection wid Trujillo. I could'na been smuggled into da country any better. Then Fretty—a queer an' all that, but reliable—flew me outa there and back to N'Orleans widout nobody bein' the wiser." He alluded to Dennis Fretty, a pilot who did short hauls and other jobs for him and also for the CIA.

"Dat Fretty knows his stuff about flyin'," Angelo commented.

"Sure thing. An' li'l shit-ass Booby was surprised as hell to find out I was back!" Mariello laughed.

"Fretty did a good job filin' da flight plan widout lettin' on nuttin'." Mariello's eyebrows furrowed at what he was about to add. "I'm not even yet wid da Kilmorys for having shipped me outa da country widout a hearin' or nuttin'. But, like I said, the day of reckonin's comin'."

Dennis Fretty was soon to do a different, vital job for him in connection with the "operation" against President Kilmory. But the skinny, odd-looking pilot would be at one of the lowest operational levels, far below the "brains" of the plot. Compartmentalization was the name of the game.

If "Booby" could play dirty, Mariello was planning to show him that he could play dirtier.

Chapter XV
PARTNERS IN CRIME

It upset Mariello that, while the Kilmorys were going after the Mafia in general and him in particular, they were also asking it to carry out those special, "dirty" jobs that the CIA would not or could not do. So, even though the Mafia appeared to be going along with the Kilmory plan against Costra, all the while, on a background level, the criminal organization was actually turning in the opposite direction and acting against them. Sinister forces were at work in Havana and Washington.

On its part, the "Company" arrangements to eliminate Costra by using the Mob as a weapon were, as far as the Kilmory administration was concerned, going forward as scheduled. While unbeknownst to the Kilmorys some CIA agents were working at cross-purposes toward this ostensible objective, most of the Agency's top management was out of that loop and concerned only with executing the anti-Costra operation and keeping it under wraps. This was top secret and the U.S. Government could not afford the risk of appearing to be in any way implicated in an international assassination plot.

The Mob, on the other hand, had its own methods and resources to handle extremely risky, high-profile jobs. It could carry out all kinds of illegal, semi-legal and extra-legal actions which the CIA would have had to somehow deny or ultimately justify and take responsibility for should they ever become public knowledge. One of the assets that the Mob could bring into play, if it chose to, was beautiful women. One or more of them could be used to tempt Fingenio to have sex—possibly for the last time in his life, if things worked out.

Kirk Pagano, who for years defended the top Tampa capo Sandy Traficant as well as other mobsters, says in his book *Mafia Attorney* that in his later years, Sal Campana liked to boast that the Mob had taken money from the CIA to kill Costra, but had done absolutely nothing to carry out the hit.

Furthermore, very early in the game the mobsters were enjoying the satisfaction of double-crossing the Kilmory brothers themselves. Not only had they done nothing to take out Costra, they were not planning to. Quie the contrary. They secretly decided to scrub the operation and go to work for the opposition, gathering intelligence on the Kilmory brothers' anti-Costra plans and feeding it to Fingenio and his efficient, relentless intelligence agency. They were, in a nutshell, doing precisely the reverse of what their job was supposed to be.

At work was the old adage: my enemy's enemy is my friend. The *coup de grace*, however, was that the target of the hit being planned by the Mob was not Costra. CIA agents were working with the Mob, directed by conspirators at the highest level.

The CIA's anti-Costra operation was, in truth, a complex array of espionage and counter-espionage, in which the Mafia members operated as double agents—just as some "Company" agents themselves. The Mob did at first do some serious groundwork for CIA-inspired plots to kill Costra, but things were getting turned around one hundred and eighty degrees and the gun barrels were trained, instead, on another, unsuspecting target: the incumbent U.S. President.

Cuban exiles, allied to CIA agents who were supposed to be "handling" them and supporting their anti-Costra efforts, were infiltrated by the Mob and persuaded, bribed or threatened to get them to funnel information to the Mafia on Plan Q, the coming second invasion of Costraland. These two sources—the Cuban exiles and the CIA agents—provided the Mob with vital intelligence which enabled them to plan the Kilmory assassination with virtual impunity, sure that any investigation or possible prosecution would be stopped in its tracks because it would reveal Plan Q itself, not to mention all sorts of other secret information.

A number of events intervened to this end, both within and outside the Mob. At one point, not long after Costra had highjacked Cuba, Traficant was detained by Cuban government agents as an "undesirable alien." This was clearly part of the Costra pattern of using every means, fair or foul—preferably the latter—to get his way. It was of key importance to force Traficant—in exchange for his release—to not just pay a million dollars in ransom, but to act as an agent of Cuban intelligence in the United States.

Kirk Pagano tells yet another version. According to his own story—no doubt self-serving—Pagano pleaded at the highest level in the "revolutionary" government, possibly including Repterio Costra himself, to gain Traficant's release. He proffered that Traficant had committed no crimes in Cuba, but simply enjoyed spending time in the country, having lived in Havana most of the time during the late 1950's.

In actual fact, Traficant had been *forced* to live in Havana to avoid major legal action pending against him in Florida. After the Costra takeover, however, he was in worse trouble. The regime would have had plenty of excuses—no trumped-up charges were necessary—to execute him or else put him in a tiny, stinking cell for life based on gambling, numbers and prostitution operations in Cuba, if not for spying for the U.S.—or worse, participating in the CIA-led conspiracy to kill Fingenio.

When Pagano asked for his release, the Cubans told him that his client was obviously a drug-trafficker, since his very name said so (like its English cognate, the Spanish *traficante* is synonymous with "drug dealer" or "smuggler"). Pagano patiently explained to them—as if they did not know—that it was just a surname and had no relation to how he made his living. The Costra people must still be laughing at their ploy.

At any rate, to get the release of Traficant—who might easily have been executed by a firing squad on the orders of Costra or his chief executioner, Eduardo Guevero—Pagano says he assured the Cuban authorities that Traficant simply wanted to return to his wife and family in Florida. Well, yes, with prior payment of the ransom and certain commitments, considering Costra and his cohorts' unlimited personal appetite for money. The Costras would hardly have released Traficant without a quid pro quo.

It was at this juncture that Costra began in earnest to work his deal through Traficant, to get the Mob to cancel its plans against him and, instead, train their sights on Kilmory.

A biography of Jackie Falattiano, *The Last Mafioso*, tells revealing details about the CIA's plans to kill Costra, intimating Costra's turnaround of the operation. It explains that Rosetti, the main Mafia contact for the CIA's anti-Costra operation, was not told in precise terms about the timetable, requiring the death of the Cuban leader *before* the Bay of Pigs invasion, scheduled for April 17, 1961.

Later, in the autumn of 1963, the Kilmorys put together a new plan to overthrow Costra, code-named Q-Day. It was to be put into action, again timed with an attempt on Costra's life, on December 1 of that year—if only Kilmory had not been killed eight days before.

Sandy Traficant, who for years ran Mafia operations in Cuba and was fairly fluent in Spanish, was the "courier to Cuba", in charge of making the necessary on-the-spot arrangements to take out Costra.

But Traficant—as a result of Costra's "turnaround" deal with him—offered Rosetti a flood of excuses for not getting the job done.

Rosetti, in turn, passed the excuses on to Norbert Mahert, who was the CIA's man in charge of the mission. Mahert was none other than the mysterious ex-FBI agent and then-CIA-operative who, a few years later, went to work for Howard Hughes and became the most powerful man in Las Vegas during the early 1970's. But that's another story.

Explaining the failure of one of the presumed attempts to kill Costra, Traficant said, variously, that Costra "had stopped patronizing the restaurant where the poison was to be administered", or that "there had been a mix-up in signals", or that "an official close to Costra was fired before he received the poison." In retrospect, these reasons were all excuses designed to buy time and maintain expectations at top U.S.-Government levels.

As indicated above, in all likelihood Traficant was by that time not at all involved in plots to kill Costra but—quite the contrary—in efforts to protect him. In other words, he was a double agent actually working for Costra, either to protect his own skin, in exchange for some form of compensation, or both. That explains why he did nothing but give excuses to Rosetti. Later, at Traficant's behest, Rosetti himself became part of the turnaround Costra conspiracy against Kilmory.

Falattiano's book goes on to say that in late 1961 the CIA instructed Rosetti to maintain his Cuban contacts but avoid dealing with Mahert or Campana, who were described as "untrustworthy" and "surplus."

So it is quite likely that, as indicated by Campana and, years later, by Traficant himself, the capos were in fact taking the CIA's money without doing anything to earn it. At a certain point the Mob's wish list could well have been to take out *both* Costra and President Kilmory. Costra had stolen their property and business, while President Kilmory had double-crossed them and was now persecuting them.

However, it was much harder to take out Costra, who had spies and informers following and checking up on the Mob members, both within Cuba and in the United States, to make sure they were not double-crossing *him*. Costra could be extremely dangerous, but the money, of course, was always the holy incentive for the Mob. Costra was one tough customer and the Mob had more "respect" for him than for Kilmory. From Kilmory, the attack was open, while from Costra it was pure stealth, and therefore far more dangerous. Besides, quite simply, the Mob was not going to turn down Costra's considerable payment for taking out Kilmory—a hit they were already preparing for anyway. The "reward" for that job amounted to nearly three times as much as Kilmory's payment for eliminating Costra. At that time a contract of that magnitude would command a minimum fee in six figures, equivalent in 2013 dollars to roughly ten times that sum.

The Mob was scratching the plan to hit Costra and, instead, beginning to prepare its operation to hit the president.

* * * * * * *

The actual efforts made to eliminate Costra by various and sundry groups and entities, is a piece of history worth reviewing.

Before making its decision on the turnaround, the Mob had participated in a number of plots, mainly CIA-inspired, on Costra's life. One of these involved poisoning him by dropping a pill in his drink. The agent for this particular attempt was Helga, a beautiful, voluptuous blonde who was part Cuban and, as her name indicates, part German.

Helga was contacted by the CIA's Mobster surrogates, given the pills and instructed on how to proceed. Her timing had to be precise. When dropped in a drink, the pill was supposed to be tasteless, quick-dissolving and slow-acting, producing death about twelve hours later, thus giving the "executioner" time to get away. Traficant, who was managing this operation, thought it would be easy for her to meet with the *Máximo Líder*, since he liked her and was especially fond of her sexual skills.

Costra, on the other hand, was known as a *mal palo*, a lousy lay, since he was hardly interested in a woman's satisfaction. Self-absorbed and concentrating only on his own pleasure when it came to sex, the *Máximo Líder* was reputed to frequently jump into bed without even bothering to remove his boots. Worse, he was said to be habitually unclean, frequently sporting his own brand of bodily "perfume". Rumor had it that this was mainly the result of his avoidance of the regular Cuban ritual of showering two or three times a day, which most Cubans paid lip-service to even if they somehow cut it down to once or twice a day. This was practically an unwritten rule of personal pulchritude, due to the warmth (but surprisingly low humidity, thanks to sea-breezes) of the Cuban climate, lasting nearly ten months out of the year. But the *Comandante* considered himself above these common-people standards and only showered once a week or so. If his uniform got dirty or smelly, his assistants disposed of it while he slept and would bring out a new, clean one for him to put on whenever he got up.

But, getting back to Helga, what woman was going to complain to Costra about his lack of cleanliness? Told of her mission and offered a substantial monetary reward, she was reluctant but finally agreed.

Hard to lure in Costra was not—that was the easy part. She sent word by calling a number for his assistant and let him know that she was available for a tryst. Sure enough, in a few days one of his flunkies called her back to say that the *Comandante* wanted to see her within a couple of days.

Helga knew she had to get ready... to wait, that is, since he was habitually late for everything and, when it came to his personal life, his lateness could easily extend to days on end. And his assistants, once arrangements were made to suit their boss, hardly bothered to call back to adjust any "minor" details concerning a time window, or even a day of the week.

This time she only had to wait three and a half days for them to return her phone call. Two days after that, Helga was picked up by Costra's agents and taken to one of his hideaways in the fashionable Vedado suburb. She waited to make her move until they had finished their love-making session—the usual mechanical, boots-on treatment he preferred in order to relieve his sexual tension.

According to her story, when Costra ducked into the bathroom, she had tried to get the pill out of a jar of cold cream she was carrying in her purse, only to find that "it had dissolved." Some say she lost her nerve partly because she had a soft spot for him. Others said it was more likely that she was afraid of what might happen to her if she came under suspicion after the *Comandante* had undergone the effects of the pill—if, in truth, it contained the lethal ingredient as advertised.

In that case, Eduardo Guevero's firing squads would have been a merciful way to put an end to her suffering, since the Cuban Military Intelligence Service—better known as the G-2—at its headquarters in Villa Maristas, was known to be highly skilled and sadistic in applying excruciating methods of torture.

Another attempt was in some respects almost the same—except this time no girl was involved. The pill was passed to a bartender in the bar of the "Habana Libre"—the former Habana Hilton Hotel—who was to put it, once again, in Costra's drink. But the bartender, too, backed out at the last minute, probably afraid he might be identified as the culprit. He, too, wondered if he wanted to run the risk of undergoing the torture they would submit him to in order to make him talk..., before they tired of their sport and finished him off. Consequently, Fingenio downed his drink harmlessly.

Among other attempts worth noting was a machine-gun attack by speedboat against a place frequented by Costra, a coastal villa on Tarará Beach, east of Havana. Intelligence reports indicated that Fingenio was to be at that location on a certain date and time, one evening. Based on that, the boat was sent in from the Florida Keys.

But—thanks to Costra's efficient intelligence—when the speedboat got close to the Cuban shores, it ran into a Costra patrol boat. It was forced to spray its gunfire too far away to do any damage, even as Costra turned out to be nowhere near the place at the time. Ever cautious, especially at the beginning of his regime, Costra made it a point never to sleep in the same place two nights in a row, to change his mind at the last minute about attending a meeting and to never show up where or when he was expected. He seemed to have an uncanny sixth sense about his own safety.

Yet another attempt on his life took place in later years and did not involve the Mob, which had lost its contacts in Cuba. It consisted in having a sharpshooter take him out while jogging. He usually took a route going through the same neighborhood, so it would simply be a matter of waiting for him. But here again Costra's caution prevailed; he always had along two or three doubles dressed exactly like him. So, the bullet with his name on it hit one of the doubles instead. When Costra realized he had been targeted he became even more obsessive about his protection, and the habit became self-reinforcing. Fingenio's efforts to stay out of harm's way were unstinting and probably saved his life more than a dozen times.

An interesting case, also without Mob involvement, was that of one of Costra's bodyguards who was supposed to kill him just after a flight to the eastern part of Cuba. Everything seemed to be proceeding according to plan when Costra and his entourage boarded the plane together without incident. The assassination was to take place upon arrival at the destination, but the bodyguard became so nervous, fidgety and sweaty during the flight that others took notice and became suspicious. Stupidly, he confessed what he had been up to. He was never heard from again.

Still another attempt, supposedly planned by the CIA, sounds like something conjured up by an outsider, a rank amateur. It has been only become public decades after the event—a fact that probably lends it more credibility as an idea being considered. However, it is so outlandish as to lead to the conclusion that it was made up in order to discredit the Agency and provide its enemies another opportunity to revel in its discomfitures. It consisted in a gift of a new wetsuit to Costra, to be delivered to him by the chief American negotiator for ransoming out the Bay of Pigs prisoners.

Since the negotiator had gotten into the routine of going SCUBA diving with Fingenio, it might have seemed like a perfectly normal gift. Accordingly, a special one was prepared with deadly chemicals that would act through the skin and kill within minutes of putting it on. But the plan was not too highly thought of, since it would risk not only the lives of the Bay of Pigs prisoners, but that of the negotiator himself. Besides, Costra was of course far too sly to have accepted such a gift, much less use it, without first having it checked out. So they said the plan, as it should have been, was dropped.

Another story, previously alluded to, was even more outlandish and therefore also fits into the "let's-discredit-the-CIA" category in the war on Costra. It purportedly planned to make him look ridiculous by getting his beard to fall out through the use of chemicals. That one is still being bandied about, even though it strains credulity beyond the breaking point. If they had been able to get chemicals on Costra, why not use deadly ones? The ones to make his beard fall out, had they worked, would have had little or no effect on his health, not to mention his power, so the story was in all likelihood put together in order to heap ridicule on the CIA, which had become—in the 1960's and throughout the 1980's—a convenient whipping-boy for America-haters at home and abroad.

A lot of this, however, may be seen by some as additional evidence that the CIA could go off and chart its own course. Being an entity unto itself whose activities were at times so compartmentalized that they were kept secret even from the CIA Director himself and the President, it could and did nearly anything it wished, regardless of consequences or national policy.

Costra's intelligence network did not take long to get wind that many of these attempts on his life were to be implemented by the Mob on orders from the "Company" and, ultimately, from Justin Kilmory himself.

Since Fingenio liked to keep close tabs on intelligence, he eventually decided to take matters into his own hands and cleverly turned things around. He called in the Mafia's main Cuban contact, Gustavo Covadonga, who was now conveniently held in La Cabaña, the country's top-security prison, pending orders from Fingenio about his forthcoming execution. The *Comandante* was fond of the cat-and-mouse game with condemned prisoners, playing with their lives while keeping an eye on their possible usefulness. Knowing of Covadonga's close association with the Mafia and their operations in Cuba, Costra gave orders to have Gustavo brought in.

Haggard and dirty, Covadonga was escorted into Costra's presence in the Castillo de la Fuerza, an old Spanish fort near the entrance to Havana Bay where Cuba's Police had traditionally—and still—maintained its headquarters. The fact that it was an impregnable fortress with dungeons and secret passageways made it even more imposing.

Costra preferred to stay away from La Cabaña, which would require a trip through the tunnel under the bay that was built in the late 1950's by a French corporation, the Societé des Grands Travaux de Marseilles. It handily provided access to the eastern side of the bay without taking a shuttle boat or going the long way around overland. For Costra, the gloomy tunnel passage was disagreeable and, most importantly, would be a likely spot for an attempt on his life with explosives. Costra was ever watchful and careful to avoid trouble spots.

"You're a valuable man, Gustavo. You have made some mistakes, but I feel for a man in your situation." He looked down on him smugly from his over-six-foot height, observing his sad expression, his pallor and deteriorating health. "So...," he began, pausing for effect a couple of seconds while enjoying Gustavo's expectant look, "guess what," he paused again, enjoying the half-frightened, half-puzzled expression on Gustavo's face. "You're going to be out of here—at least temporarily...," Costra noted the still-incredulous relief etched on his face, "so you can deliver a message to your bosses."

"*Sí, Comandante?*" Gustavo answered with his most serious, attentive look. His life, he knew, was on the line. The slightest misstep and....

"The message is simple. These attempts on my life are futile—as anyone can plainly see. My powers are beyond anything they suspect." Gustavo had a feeling that he alluded, indirectly perhaps, to his ceremonial invocations of Afro-Cuban sorcery—more clearly, witchcraft—conducted by his babalawo, his high priest of *santería*—during which he asked the gods Eleguá and Obatalá for protection. "Of course, besides using them to protect myself I can also direct these powers against *them*." He paused, again, for effect.

"Tell them I suggest they turn their guns around in the other direction: at those who are behind these stupid, amateurish attempts to kill me. That would be much more productive..., not to mention much healthier for them. Anyway, why is the Mafia after *me*? I did what I had to do and now it's over. I'm no longer a threat to them. But Kilmory is. He's going after them—look at what his brother Roland's doing: all-out war—-persecuting and prosecuting them, trying to lock them up, wipe them out. Yet at the same time, he's trying to use them to eliminate *me*! Does that make any sense? What they can and should do is turn their weapons around and point them at Kilmory. Then we'll both be rid of our worst enemy." Costra, the compulsive logomaniac, paused for a split second—this time, to catch his breath.

"Of course, *Comandante*," Gustavo said, taking advantage of the micropause.

"Just to make it more interesting, I'm prepared to double the rate they're getting paid to do the job on *me*," Costra said with a smug smile as he became aware that he was outbidding the gringos at an auction in which lives were the traded commodity—mainly *theirs*. "Kilmory wants you to work on the cheap—I won't," he concluded.

"*Comandante* , I... *will*," he emphasized after a tremulous hesitation, "take care of the matter, rest assured," Gustavo said, thankful that he had suppressed his first impulse to say that he would "give it a shot." There would have be no sense in anything but a firm commitment to do the job as requested. The weak reply that flashed across his mind, the result of the haze he was in after weeks of malnutrition and deterioration, might have spoiled everything. He realized, as if in a dream, this might bring him an opportunity—on the classic silver platter—to save himself from execution, if not years in prison, possibly even enabling him to defect once he was safely out of Costra's grasp.

"You do that and get back to me. I'll give you a week. You'll be at liberty to do as you like; there's five thousand U.S. dollars in cash and a suite for you at the Riviera Hotel in Vedado. You know the place I'm talking about." With a raised eyebrow, he threw in a taunting reference to the hotel built by Manny Lendski, the capo whom Gustavo had met as part of his work, not too long ago, with Mafia contacts. Costra was going to give him a word of warning not to get involved in any funny business, but decided there was a better, roundabout way: "And Gustavo, don't do anything... rash. Remember your parents are here in Cuba and they could, well, run into hard times if you weren't around... to, er, take care of them. Is that clear?" Costra gave him that unmistakably business-like look that Gustavo had observed on other occasions, just before someone had disappeared or been neatly disposed of, with or without public fanfare, according to Fingenio's whim of the moment. Certain that Costra had read his mind—he was not the only one who had undergone that experience—Gustavo's dreams of defecting vanished instantly, leaving what he hoped was an utter blank in his brain.

"Thank you so much, *Comandante*, I'll get right to work on it. Naturally, I know the Riviera...." Gustavo smiled slyly at Costra, catching his drift about Lendski and the lavish seaside hotel in which the capo had sunk the stolen millions he had accumulated in a lifetime of crime and functioning as the Mob's "financial brain." Costra returned the barest hint of a still-taunting smile as he waved him off with a final, inward chuckle.

Chapter XVI
DOUBLE-CROSS RAGE

Hank Spanitra's pull with the Kilmorys—and with the Mob itself—was hitting new lows. The President suddenly cancelled his planned stay at Hank's Palm Springs estate on his trip to California.

His advisors convinced him that, politically, it was too sensitive for him to consort with the likes of Spanitra, who was "rumored" to be close to the Mob. The excuse was that security at Spanitra's mansion was insufficient, but the singer felt snubbed and was thoroughly annoyed, especially after he had, at considerable expense, refurbished the house and grounds for the President's visit. Not to mention his coaxing the Mob to rig the election for him, plus all the campaigning and shows he and the Brat Pack had put together to raise funds for the Kilmory-Jameson ticket, and then to top it off putting on the shows for the huge inaugural galas. To add insult to injury, the President had chosen, instead, to stay at the Palm Springs mansion of his rival singer Ding Frostby.

"I guess," Spanitra said when he eventually heard of it, "that Ding is more 'wholesome' of image than me. But I'd sure like to know what the hell he did for Kilmory's election or the inaugural galas."

"Jeter," Justin Kilmory said when he got him on the phone, "tell Spanitra that I'm really sorry but the Secret Service has told me that security at his place is just not at the acceptable level. I wish I could stay with him, but...."

"Excuse me, Justin, but he's expecting you, and he's made all kinds of improvements. He's going to be mad as hell and, you know—not that it matters," he said, knowing full well how much it did, "he's going to take it out on *me,* not on anyone else."

"Well, Jeter, I'm sorry if I'm going to cause you trouble, but it's just not possible for me to stay there," Kilmory said in his usual polite manner. Inwardly, he was amused thinking of Crawford's trouble with the irascible, pugnacious Spanitra. Oh, well, he thought, he'll get over it eventually.

There was no need to spell out the real problem, he thought: Spanitra was just too close to the Mob, especially now that brother Roland had started going after them. Justin could not deny that Spanitra was the one who had convinced Campana to put the electoral victory in Kilmory's lap; subsequently, the Mob had bought the West Virginia primary for him, and then, in the general election, had put in the fix in Illinois and Texas. But now, that was all history and no longer relevant, compared to how it would look if he stayed at Spanitra's.

"I'm also extremely grateful to Hank for his help with the inaugural. Tell him I'll certainly keep it in mind for the future."

"I don't know how much good that will do, Justin, but I'll tell him," Crawford said before hanging up in a disconsolate funk.

Justin's memory went back to the inaugural ceremonies. Sure enough, after the bogus count was over, Spanitra had also taken care of the entertainment. Together with the other members of his Brat Pack—with the glaring exception of Jammy Spavis, Jr., whose absence Justin himself had requested—Spanitra played a leading role in putting up shows at the festivities at no cost to the Democratic campaign or the government itself. He had even made up new lyrics to the popular tune "High Hopes" to fit Kilmory's style and situation and turned it into the theme song of the campaign. It had all been very effective. Now, putting his head together with those of his brother and advisors, Justin concluded that Spanitra's usefulness had come to an end.

Some said that this was faithful to the Kilmory pattern of taking advantage of people until such time as they were no longer useful or became a liability. The Mafia eventually learned this lesson as well—to Kilmory's later grief.

It was Crawford's job to give Spanitra the bad news, so he picked up the phone with angst and trembling hands.

"Hank, I'm sorry, but I've been asked to tell you something," Crawford began tentatively.

"Oh, yeah? Well, don't bother, you fucking bastard. I've already figured it out." He had put two and two together, based on the delay in confirming the President's plans. "After all the trouble I went to, your in-laws are dumping me, huh? Well, fuck them and fuck you too!" He nearly said "fuck President Justin Kilmory," but held back. One never knew who was listening. Better to take it out on the harmless Crawford.

"But Hank," Crawford pleaded with Spanitra, "it's not *my* fault! I tried to reason with Justin, did my level best. I pleaded your case with him but there was nothing I could do. Honest!"

"Of course it's your fault, you son of a bitch. You told me the Kilmorys would come through, and now look! You messed up. Fuck you! I'm through with you, you fucking creep!" Spanitra hung up. He never talked to Jeter Crawford again.

If Hank Spanitra was incensed, Campana was even more so. Not only had the Mob, under his leadership, swung the election for Kilmory, but now, before the double-cross was translated into actual deeds, and even after it actually got under way—he had worked with the Kilmorys in the CIA plan to get rid of Costra; it was only due to circumstances beyond his control that the plot had not succeeded.

Campana also claimed that, at one point, he had helped preserve the President's good name when he had taken care of a delicate problem. It turned out that a Los Angeles restaurant owner involved in a messy domestic squabble was going to name a number of celebrities as co-respondents in suing his starlet wife for divorce. Among those to be named were Justin Kilmory, Hank Spanitra himself, other members of the Brat Pack, and Kerry Lois, another well-known philanderer who managed to keep everything—or nearly everything—under cover as well.

When Kerry got wind of the planned legal action, Jessica Cameron Everette was working for him at a do-nothing job that he hoped would enable him to bed the beautiful girl. Kerry, who at that stage was a nervous wreck anyway, was beside himself with worry about the suit.

"Hey, Jessica," he said, knowing of her connections, "is there anything you can do about this?"

"Well, I can call Sal," she replied non-chalantly, "maybe he can help."

She did so and Campana quickly solved his problem. Later on, when Kerry found Jessica unbeddable and no longer useful, he fired her without notice. It did not take long for her to complain to Campana about Kerry's treatment of her. Soon, Kerry got a call from the capo.

"Listen, you fucking miserable jerk, Jessica gets her job back anytime she says so, do you understand?"

Terror-struck, Kerry fell all over himself trying to apologize. He was paying her only $100 a week, so it meant little, money-wise; however, since Jessica was never interested in any kind of financial gain for herself, she turned it down.

President Kilmory, having heard of the incident, ran into Kerry at a reception and took the opportunity to needle him.

"Hello, Kerry, have you seen Jessica lately?"

Kerry fumbled to find something to say.

Later, when Kerry was doing a show in Las Vegas while Jessica was in town, Campana arranged to get back at him. He got front-row seats for her, himself and one of his henchmen. They all sat there stiffly without laughing or applauding throughout the stint. Kerry was so unnerved when he saw them that, not knowing what to expect, he lost it, started sweating bullets and turned the show into a complete disaster. For Kerry it was the longest show in his career, although Jessica, Campana and his henchman thoroughly enjoyed every minute.

The jealous-husband action was finally settled when Campana told his man in Hollywood, Jake Rosetti, to take care of the matter before it blew up into a full-fledged scandal. After receiving what was no doubt a substantial payoff from the potential co-respondents, Rosetti brought pressure to bear on the hapless restaurant owner, who was told he might, in the end, lose a lot more than his wife. The suit was withdrawn.

And as Campana told it Kilmory acted as if nothing had happened, without acknowledging his helping hand.

* * * * * * *

Even though the cancellation of the President's visit to his Palm Springs estate was really not Jeter Crawford's fault, Spanitra let him have it. Crawford, his go-between in relations with the Kilmorys, was a trusted in-law of theirs, married to the president's sister Pamela. He told off Crawford because he knew him to be weak and could humiliate him with impunity. In effect, he was a handy target who would never dream of getting back at him. His protestations, he figured, would be predictable and ineffectual. Crawford simply could not tolerate any souring of his relationship with Spanitra. The fact that he had actually done his best to prevent Kilmory from canceling his stay in Palm Springs was of no consequence to him. Spanitra simply ignored his excuses. Besides, he always needed to take out his anger on someone.

With a Jekyll-and-Hyde personality, Spanitra could suddenly turn temperamental and violent, getting into fist fights at the drop of a hat with anyone who crossed him. With a known habit of holding grudges indefinitely, he did so with Crawford and dropped him like a hot potato. Even though he did see the Kilmorys occasionally at certain functions when he came to Washington, he coldly ignored Crawford at every single opportunity.

For Spanitra, loyalty was an essential virtue. So his anger over the new administration's failure to deliver on the pledge that they would lay off from the Mob was doubly hurtful because it affected his pals. And it was extremely serious for him as well, since it might be—and was—interpreted by them as his fault. Accordingly, he was one of those who viewed with alarm the fact that Roland's tenure as Attorney General had started with a public tightening of screws on the mobsters—even as the CIA was attempting to use them to eliminate Costra.

In fact, Roland had gone out of his way to make an outright announcement that one of the top priorities of the Justice Department was nothing less than fighting organized crime. Most Americans, aware of the Mob's activities—in contrast to FBI Director H. Everette Hooper's view that it "did not exist"—were far from convinced that the mobsters were such a terrible threat to the country and largely indifferent to wiping them out as a major national goal. No other administration, before or since, has proclaimed this as one of its major Justice Department objectives—in many cases because they were in cahoots with them to begin with.

The double-cross looked like it meant business, and would bring big trouble.

Chapter XVII
CO-CONSPIRATORS

Claudio Mariello knew it might be difficult to convince the rest of the capos that his proposal was doable and worth the risk. But he was going to give it a try—his own very best shot—because, to his mind, nothing else was going to solve the Outfit's problem. No "half-ass solution," as he was fond of saying in his lightly accented vernacular, "would ever get anyt'ing but half-ass results." And what the Outfit needed was nothing but a full and final solution to the problem.

He was well aware of Hitler's use of the phrase "final solution" with regard to the Jews, and he secretly admired that, in a way. Except that, according to his cold, mechanical mind, Hitler must have been dim-witted to think that he could wipe out a whole race, a whole human ethnic group numbering in the tens of millions worldwide. Why bother with that, he ruminated, when it was enough to "push" a leader or two and get everyone to fall into line? Wouldn't it be better, he thought, to exploit a group, to make them pay for their own survival, in a sense, rather than to expend energy and resources to wipe them out? Hitler's attempt at extermination of the Jews was—his mind put it coldly, matter-of-factly—an industrial-scale operation that was stupid and wasteful, regardless of the inhumanity of the whole plan—which really didn't concern him that much, accustomed as he was to killing whenever necessary, for reasons personal, whim-like or business-oriented. The bottom line, to him, was that it just didn't make any sense, particular in the area of simple economy, efficiency of effort.

His racism was not as intense as Campana's, well known for hating blacks, as he was wont to show on occasions when, in the company of Jessica Cameron Exeter, for example, he showed his contempt for Jammy Spavis, Jr. at a Las Vegas show. When Campana did not seem to be enjoying his show, Jammy was so unnerved that as soon as he finished his gig he came over to his table and said, as humbly as he could, "Why don't you good people come over and join me for a drink?"

"We don't have the time," Campana said with an in-your-face smirk. Jammy looked downcast and retreated. Later he explained that he was scared to death that he had said or done something to displease the capo. Afterward, Jessica chided Campana for being so hard on Jammy who, after all, was just trying to please. He couldn't help it if, for Campana, he was the wrong color.

The Italian *mafiosi* in general—except for Spanitra, who was not a professional mafioso, but an amateur who fancied himself one of the boys—were notoriously anti-black, and totally excluded them from their ranks. Neither were they too fond of Jews for that matter, although they did have a few of them within their top echelon, generally in positions requiring brains over brawn: two noteworthy examples were Manny Lendski and Bert Seidel. The latter was famously executed at his girl-friend's home in Los Angeles, in the late 1940's, for having lost a bundle of the Mob's money in building the pioneering Flamingo Hotel in Vegas.

In this case the "final solution" to the Outfit's problem, thought Mariello, could be arranged exactly the way Hitler did *not* do it: by eliminating a leader or two. True, it was risky, but everything in life entailed a risk. And it took a big risk to eliminate a big problem.

So Mariello decided to lay out his plan to the rest of the capos. It was simple, direct and sharply conclusive. Unsurprisingly, the bosses were skeptical, if not downright concerned that the government's reaction would be to bear down and pursue them to their utter destruction. The Mafia certainly had the resources to do the job that Mariello had in mind. All it needed was the will. Mariello figured that the move he was advocating would produce such advantageous results for the Mafia families that it could not help but get more than enough support among the capos and their accomplices. One of those accomplices was Ricky Hofstra, whose hatred of the Kilmorys was legendary and who was actually pushing the Mob to take out Kilmory, using as leverage the huge Teamsters Pension Fund, whose millions he made available to the Mob for whatever schemes and scams they thought would produce big bucks for them.

Hofstra was sick and tired of taking the heat from Roland Kilmory, who was by now threatening to bring charges against him that, if successful, could land him in the slammer for years. There was bad blood, since Roland had had testy encounters with him in congressional hearings.

Working for the Senate Rackets Committee investigating the Mob, Roland had put hard-nosed questions to Hofstra when he was called upon to testify. But at the time the government did not have sufficient evidence to prosecute him, so he was never indicted.

That rankled Roland no end, so when he became Attorney General he decided to take full advantage of his position and resources to crack down on him, one of his top targets in organized crime. Even though the target wasn't actually running a "family," he might as well have been, considering all the power and resources at his command.

Hofstra never forgot the time when, under questioning before a congressional committee, Roland had had the nerve to make fun of his masculinity. Hofstra had actually chortled in derision at one of his questions. Roland then responded that he thought "only little girls giggled" when trying to evade questions. Then and there Hofstra, ever the tough-guy macho-man, decided to get even..., every chance he could.

There had also been an unpublicized encounter within the confines of the Department of Justice building itself. Hofstra, accompanied by his lawyer, Kirk Pagano and an associate, had gone to the Department of Justice to pick up some highly important documents concerning their ongoing legal battle. Roland had indicted Hofstra on several counts of corruption, bribery and other crimes, and wanted to watch Hofstra's face when handing over the papers. When Hofstra, Pagano and an assistant arrived at the appointed time they were told to wait. The Attorney General was out taking his dog for a walk. After cooling their heels for forty-five minutes, Roland finally showed up, turned over his dog to an assistant and walked into the room where Hofstra and his lawyer were waiting. Furious, Hofstra proceeded to insult him.

"Who the fuck do you think you are, you fuckin' bastard? You've kept us waiting for forty-five minutes while you're out walking your fucking dog!" Before anyone knew it, the strong and stocky Hofstra, who lifted weights, was strangling the Attorney General with his bare hands. According to Kirk Pagano, Hofstra might have actually killed him if they had not pulled him off. Roland staggered off without a word and never mentioned the incident.

"You're not going to believe this, guys," Mariello said, "but if you'll hear me out you'll see clearly what we have to do. Taking 'Booby' out of the picture is not going to work," Mariello said to the capos, using his degrading nickname for Roland. They had a big room in Mariello's outsized spread on the outskirts of New Orleans all to themselves, his henchmen securing all doors and screening the surrounding acreage. They didn't want to repeat the brouhaha in Appalachin, New York, a few years before, when the police, working on a tip-off, chased and rounded up dozens of surprised capos gathered at a top-level meeting.

"I don't know, Claudio. It seems to me that taking out Roland will take care of the problem and be a lot less dangerous." Campana voiced what seemed to be the general consensus. No one had ever contemplated a hit on a sitting Attorney General, let alone a President. There was a chorus of approval in the darkened, smoke-filled room. As a further precaution the windows had been closed and the curtains drawn.

"I wish! I'd certainly be for it if that would fix it. But...," Mariello paused for effect, "it's the other way around, guys. If we bump off Booby, his brother the President's gonna send in the Marines... and who knows what the fuck else! They'd be after us like all git-out. We'd be goners to start somethin' like 'at. It'd be all-out war and that'd be *it* for us."

"And, supposin' we take out Justin, what d'ya figure their next move would be? They ain't gonna stand still." Campana puffed out a cloud of dense smoke from his Cuban cigar as he glanced around, observing reactions.

"Guys, you remember that old saying, don'cha? "If a dog bites, ya cut off its head, not its tail." Now it was Mariello who looked around smugly, enjoying his command of the situation.

"So?" Someone spoke up from the back of the room.

"So, once the head's gone, it ain't gonna bite you anymore!" Mariello smiled with mocking self-satisfaction.

"Sounds good, Claudio. But how do we know, once we take out da Prez, brudder Roland ain't gonna come after us wid all da firepower of da Federal Government?" Guido Condottieri, the delegate from the Gambino family, was unconvinced and pressed the point home.

"Guido, you know who becomes President once Kilmory's outa circulation, huh?" Mariello barely controlled his gloating. "Our man Jameson, dat's who! And I have it on good authority he's not gonna lift a finger. In fact, guys," he said slowly, "he might be grateful for da favor." Having been sworn to secrecy, he was careful not to tell the other capos everything he knew. The conspiracy against Kilmory was a tightly guarded, highly compartmentalized secret, and he had come close enough. He watched smugly as he perceived the change in the room's atmosphere. He could feel it, like hitting a nail cleanly on the head.

"Yeah, Claudio, but how can we be sure the big man's actually gonna lay off?" Campana was skeptical about Jameson. Even though he felt Mariello seemed to be making sense, he wasn't going to be easily swayed. Campana wanted to hear Mariello's full scenario. He took off his hat and put his feet up on a chair in front of him, as if to say, "let's hear what you have to say."

"From what Claudio said I don't think Jameson's gonna give us any trouble, Sal," Traficant interceded, "but go on, Claudio," he said to Mariello, virtually closing off the question.

"Sal"—Claudio never called him "Looney" except occasionally in private, with no one else present—"nobody can be sure what nobody's gonna do. You and me both know dat. But besides, you know we got a lotta stuff on Jameson. And we can let 'im know we'll use it..., just like all the homo stuff we got on Hooper that's kep'im quiet all these years. Like that photo Lansky's got of him giving head to Towson, his assistant chief," he said, not suppressing a laugh. "Like Lendski sez, 'dat's how we got 'im fixed'."

"Hey, man," Campana interjected, "we're talking about Jameson, not Hooper." He took care to use language that was a little more polished, although his *fratelli* silently resented his air of what for him was «higher education».

"Well, Sal, I can't tell you any more dan what I just tol' ya 'bout Jameson's attitude. But, between us, like I said," he added with a mischievous grin, "I t'ink 'es gonna be on our side." He paused to let it sink in, and then added, as if to say something hardly worth mentioning: "Besides, we all know 'es been takin' money from us for years—and still is. So, that tells you sump'n...."

"Yeah, Claudio, it tells me sump'n that maybe you ain't tellin' us." Campana looked at him quizzically, puffing on his Havana and putting his feet down on the floor again.

"Lemme put it this way, Sal. He'd be crazy to take any risks wid us after *we* put 'im in the driver's seat," Claudio said, brushing off Campana's remark and keeping in mind the adage that the fewer people who knew a secret the better kept it would be. "Jameson wouldn't be vice president if we hadn't-a' swung the election. He owes us big. Besides, if he gets to da top he'll want to stay in control of everyt'ing an' in power, an' he ain't gonna do that too well if we use our stuff on 'im. And lemme tell you this to top it all off: the Kilmorys'll ask 'im—no, beg 'im—to keep the whole thing under wraps. If anybody starts diggin', the can o' worms they's gonna open up's gonna stink up the whole government, an' that'll sink *him an'* the whole fuckin' rest o' the Kilmory clan too. But here's the clincher, guys: I ain't gettin' into it too much, but some of youse guys know the Kilmorys are still workin' on plans to bump off Costra and dump his regime. Dis'll blow the lid offa all dat. They're not gonna risk it. Besides, our man Hooper's FBI won't get in da way, cuz he hates the Kilmorys as much as Jameson himself! An' the CIA guys the same!"

Mariello looked around smugly, then glanced at Traficant, knowing he could count on him. Traficant picked right up on the undercurrent.

"Carlos, me and Rosetti got together at The Sands in Vegas last week an' discussed this whole deal," Traficant weighed in. "And, you know what, we reached the same conclusion. We been fuckin' double-crossed by the Kilmorys and we're gonna be in even worse trouble if we don't neutralize 'em. The only way to do that is to take out the top man, 'cuz takin' out number two or three is jus' gonna generate more heat. Besides, we already put some feelers out to our insiders in the CIA and FBI, and they're not gonna give us a-n-y trou-ble." He drew out the last two words to underscore his finish.

Campana looked momentarily stunned, but recovered quickly. He should have known. "Now you tell us, Sandy? You were keepin' that pretty quiet!" He tried to make light of it, not wanting to make it appear too noticeable that he didn't seem to have been as well informed as he should have been.

"Well, it's not all that cut and dried, Sam, but let's say it looks good," Traficant answered. "There's still some work to be done on all o' this."

"Okay, guys. But how can we be sure they're just not feeding us a line of bull shit jus' to see if we fall for it." Campana baited them, to see what they would say. His eyes searched those of the other capos for the slightest reaction. He got a couple of smiles.

"Well, if dey are, we're gonna find out soon enough, before we take any steps to put this into operation, don'cha worry. I'll take care o' dat." Mariello was putting out his own line of bull, determined to win approval from the other capos. He was keeping it under his hat not only that he was in the know and had privileged information, but that he also had more of a personal stake in the Kilmory hit than the rest of the Mob leaders.

"Well, Claudio, if you'll take responsibility, I might go along," Campana said, figuring that he was in the minority and it would do no good to stand in the way, even though he still had his reservations. He had it in mind to talk to Claudio in private after the meeting, to see what he was holding back. As the *capo di tutti capi,* he was entitled to know, to get his due respect.

"Leave it to me, Sal," Mariello quickly took him at his word, striking while the iron was hot. Now, all the top capos were as good as in, and he could start implementing his plan. But he couldn't resist adding to his argument.

"To top it all off, lemme jus' say dis. Jameson hates the Kilmorys and the Kilmorys hate him, but they're bound to agree on one thing. They ain't gonna want nobody to know about the election-night specials we pulled for 'em. Widout us, their ticket couldn'a won. So we got 'em in our pocket, him and the Kilmorys. An' Jameson's a lot sharper than the Kilmorys. He's on our side, big-time." He gave Campana a meaningful look.

"I'm wid you, Claudio," Traficant said before Campana could take the opportunity to bring up another counter-argument. "Puttin' it that way, you gotta believe there's less risk in taking out Giustino than number two." Traficant liked to Italianize the president's given name. "Once he takes office, Jameson's not gonna risk comin' after us—what for?–an' if you ask me, Roland'll be scared shitless we'll squeal on 'em," he added.

"I'm not so sure we're not bitin' off more than we can chew guys, but hey, if that's the way you feel...," Campana smiled slightly to show he was not too worried. He had some reservations, but he was keeping them to himself until he could talk with Mariello in private. He put his hat on and stood up, signaling his impatience for the meeting to end.

"'N' just in case, Sal," Mariello added, looking Campana straight in the eye but not imitating his move, "you gotta figure if we do dis we're gonna send a message to anybody at da top dat *dey may be next* if dey gives us any trouble. I don' t'ink dey will." He paused to flick the ash off his cigar. The room was thick with smoke and he, too, was anxious to close it out. "Anyway, dese cock-suckers 'ave fucked wid us way too much already," he concluded with meaningful body language. He pointed to one of his henchmen to open a window.

"You're God-damned right about dat," said a chorus of other capos.

"They're a bunch of fuckin', suckin' double-crossers!" chimed in Condottieri, in a custom-tailored, top-quality beige suit that Campana thought was a bit too showy for the occasion.

"Fuckin' right. An' we can't let 'em get away wid 'it. We made Giustino president, we can unmake 'im. Just like dat!" Mariello snapped his fingers for emphasis. Virtually, it was like a nail in a coffin—as he liked to think about it. Meeting over.

Mariello had kept it to himself, but on top of all the resentment, anger and desire for revenge, he had an extremely powerful personal reason for getting agreement on the hit. His informer in the Justice Department had told him that Roland Kilmory was planning to spring another list of indictments against him, designed to put him in prison for the long term, or even deporting him again—this time for good.

Campana waited until the room had cleared to approach Mariello.

"Claudio, what's goin' on? Sump'n you ain't told us?"

"Trust me, Sal, it's gonna be okay. Dere's approval from up dere, get it?" He pointed at the ceiling as he gazed steadily at Campana. "I din't wanna say it in front o' everybody, but dat's what's really goin' on. Trust me, I'll tell you more 'bout it later."Claudio put his index finger on his lips to signal silence as he waved the top capo respectfully out of the room.

"Okay, Claudio," Campana replied, "but lemme know, okay?" He gazed intently at Mariello, somewhat reassured but unhappy that he hadn't been kept up to date. He had seen this sort of situation before when somebody at a high level had to be hit, but never on this scale. A conspiracy of this magnitude was staggering, and it rankled him that Claudio had the inside track and had kept him on the sidelines. He filed it away for future reference in his prodigious memory banks and walked away, thinking "he'd better come across."

Mariello went to another room, picked up the phone and called Rosetti's contact man in Los Angeles to give him the news, partly in Sicilian dialect and using code words they had worked out to confuse the federal wire-tappers. Rosetti himself, who was in the hospital with a bout of tuberculosis—an illness he had suffered on and off since childhood—would call back from a payphone in another day or so.

The anti-Kilmory trap was close to being set by the Outfit, with a near-foolproof guarantee of immunity. Now, it would only be a matter of time and scheduling. Best of all for the Mob, it was a money-making proposition—icing on the cake.

Chapter XVIII
COUNTERATTACK

Claudio Mariello couldn't have been more delighted to hear Gustavo Covadonga give him Costra's message. He had already chosen to freeze any further attempts to hit the elusive Cuban leader. To him that was, a bottom-line waste of time motivated by a personal vendetta of Kilmory's rather than practical considerations. Since he had already fixed his sights on Kilmory himself—and there was immunity in the picture thanks to the positive signals "from upstairs," Mariello would gladly take Costra's money. Not that he wouldn't have liked to get rid of Costra as well—"that lying double-crossing thief," as he liked to characterize him—and recover for the Mob the lucrative Cuban gambling, drug and prostitution market which, to top it off, was free from any interference by the feds.

"Tell Mr. C we're gonna talk it over here and let 'im know very soon—prob'ly in a few days. An' make sure you tell 'im as far as I'm concerned we're gonna give it our best shot—but first—I don' have to tell ya dis, cuz ya know how we work—we gotta check it out at our own top level." Mariello thought that was a nice, diplomatic touch and added: "Make sure you use dat langwidge: 'check it out at da top and, if okayed, give it our best shot'. Unnerstand, Gustavo?" Mariello fancied his choice of words.

Mariello smiled smugly and wielded his iconic, indispensable mobster prop: a big cigar, on which he rarely puffed. Costra would never know nor even suspect that a conspiracy was already brewing to hit Kilmory, and that the Mob, already seething with hatred against the president, was going to be instrumental in implementing its practical application. He made a mental note of shortly getting in touch with Traficant and Rosetti and bringing them up to date on developments, Traficant being the man to provide overall direction, timing and logistics.

He clearly recalled the time that Traficant had been held at Triscornia, the detention center across the bay from Havana for undocumented or criminal aliens. Costra released him only when he promised to work for him in intelligence and "related matters" back in the U.S. Since Traficant could be a valuable asset in that area, Costra felt he had made a good deal.

Rosetti, subject to less surveillance from the government, would be in charge of the more pragmatic, down-to-earth arrangements.

"Yes, sir, Mr. Mariello. You can be sure that I will repeat your words letter by letter," Gustavo said with his Hispanic accent and phrasing. "And I have a clear feeling he will be pleased," he added as he shook hands with Mariello and stood up to leave.

"By the way, you make sure you tell 'im in person. Don't even dream o' usin' dis," he said, pointing his H. Upmann cigar, smuggled in from Cuba, at a plain black telephone as if it were poison. "In dis country Hooper taps all the phone lines he wants—'specially when he *don't* get authorization." He smiled at his own remark.

"Oh, no sir!" Gustavo laughed knowingly, his eyes twirling upward. He felt like making a wise-guy remark—did the capo think he was going to call up Costra with the news?—but controlled himself.

Mariello smiled and took a puff. He felt like saying that H. Everette Hooper was "probably" not going to interfere with a hit on Kilmory, but held back to avoid giving the slightest hint of what was going on. In truth, the way he saw it Hooper was as likely to be involved in the conspiracy against Kilmory as were other powerful officials. He kept in mind that Vice President Jameson happened to be a friend and neighbor of Hooper's, living in the posh neighborhood along Washington's Rock Creek Park. Who knew what private conversations they might have had over their backyard fence through the years—and still be having?

For the moment, at least, Mariello felt it highly advisable to keep things compartmentalized as much as possible. That's the way, he was well aware, that the major intelligence operations were carried out, much like the Outfit's own.

"Hooper's a foxy bastard," the capo added, to make his point.

"I'm sure, Mr. Mariello. I've heard about Mr. Hooper's *curious* habits." He raised an eyebrow to deliver his *double entendre*.

Mariello picked it up and smiled slyly, putting both feet on his huge, empty desk, practically devoid of any papers—except his home town's *Times Picayune*. There was a great advantage to his line of work, he thought: no paperwork—as if he had ever done any.

"I see you've heard of his habits too," he said with a light chuckle.

"María, bring me another mint julep, and a cup of coffee for Mr. Gustavo, here," he said to a servant without bothering to ask Gustavo if he wanted one. "The one for the road should always be coffee, Gus," he pronounced, "if you're gonna drive. Don' wantcha to be picked up on anyt'ing." A DUI wouldn't be too good, he thought, if they started fishing and picked up something they shouldn't.

Then he proudly looked around what, to his taste, were swanky surroundings and observed, through his picture window, his Mexican gardener tending to the rose bushes outside, receiving orders from his wife, who enjoyed giving instructions to the hired help. A good way to keep her busy, he thought. Some things were better kept at arm's length, he mused, undecided if it was the gardening, the wife, or both.

Soon, if he could manage it, he would find out more about Hooper's role in the plan to get rid of Kilmory, so he would know just how much risk—or how little—there would be in carrying out the operations involved in implementing the hit. If the FBI could be counted on to assist instead of obstruct, everything would be that much easier. He had insider information that, as a determined enemy of Kilmory's, Hooper could control the situation in order to facilitate the Mob's actions. Furthermore, with a close friend and ally like Jameson in the White House, the thorn in Hooper's side for nearly three years—namely, his titular boss Attorney General Roland—would be completely undercut and utterly powerless.

Mariello was confident that when the FBI would no longer be subject to orders from that "skinny shit-ass Booby"—as Hooper called him—whose years of age were fewer in number than his own tenure as director of the Bureau, the situation would be totally different. Better yet, as the new president, Jameson would not only lay off the Outfit but be able to cover up its role with Hooper's assistance as head of the Bureau.

Albeit indirectly, Mariello had already received tips that Jameson could be counted on, at least to keep things under control in the event that something happened to Kilmory. But he was sure there was more to the story.

Gustavo politely sipped the cup of American-style coffee, which Cubans call "dirty water," and longed for a good *cafecito*," better known among English-speakers with the Italian word "espresso."

"So, Gustavo, you know what to do." Mariello gave him a knowing look.

"Absolutely, Mr. Mariello. You can count on me. Besides, we'll take no chances." Gustavo used *we* to imply he was speaking for everyone involved..., although he still wondered if he could somehow get away with reporting the conversation to Costra without going back to Cuba. He had no desire to face, back in Costraland, a firing squad—that was always a possibility even if he succeeded in his mission—since his death sentence had been temporarily suspended. In the best of cases he might get an extended prison term. The problem was, if he stayed away, his parents would suffer in his stead. He knew what Costra was capable of doing to them. Gustavo became aware, not without some amusement, that he trusted the Italian-American mobsters more than Cuba's own capo, Costra.

"Okay, Gus, keep it all under ya hat." Mariello answered with the familiarity he had employed not so long ago, when they were in more frequent contact as he visited Havana as one of the Outfit's envoys, mixing a little business with pleasure. "Total secrecy is of da essence," Mariello concluded in a tone indicating the interview was over. "But 'course, you know dat. See you in a week, okay?"

"Yes, sir. Good day to you." Covadonga was not about to reciprocate Mariello's familiarity. Dressed in casual jeans and a sport shirt thanks to the warm late-summer weather, he tipped his cap smartly and walked out of Mariello's mansion, escorted by one of the capo's henchmen.

Gustavo had never dreamed he'd be in this position when he was living in Havana's fashionable Vedado suburb, rubbing elbows with rich kids whose parents had, by now, lost their mansions and worldly goods and been forced to take flight away from Costra and their beloved Cuba. They had a deep-down feeling that, as the saying goes, "those days are gone forever."

Notwithstanding, Gustavo felt happy for himself, hardly believing his lucky stars. Only a few days ago he was rotting in a cell in La Cabaña Prison, where he heard the firing squads do their gruesome work at the dawning of each day, and here he was commuting between Cuba and the U.S. on a top-secret mission, meeting with some of the most powerful gangsters in the two countries—including Costra himself, a career hoodlum, gunslinger and killer who had made crime respectable by fitting it with political trappings.

Few people in or outside of Cuba knew, like he did, that Fingenio started out as a hit-man in his stint as a rabble-rousing

University of Havana student who majored in extortion, corruption and deadly hits on personal and political enemies, as well as on casual acquaintances, not to mention complete strangers. His passing grades, he knew from a cousin who was Fingenio's classmate, were obtained not by studying, but by threatening the professors, who were more concerned about their own safety than about any likely consequence from awarding favorable academic grades to a student who had done nothing to earn them, except for enrolling.

Gustavo felt fortunate that he had a good command of English—if somewhat accented— thanks to having gone to American and British private schools in Havana: Ruston Academy, St. George's School, Havana Business Academy. For that, he had to be grateful to his parents.   Otherwise, he'd still be in that hot, stinking cell....Bilingualism had its rewards. Yet in any case he could not dream about letting them down. They were very much on his mind as he recalled Fingenio Costra's all-too-clear warning about his parents in case he wavered.

It was still a mystery to him how Fingenio, having started out as a gangster, trigger-happy gunslinger and all-around bully during his student days at the University of Havana, had gotten so cleanly and quickly to the pinnacle of power in Cuba. He was barely 33 years old—the age of Christ at the legendary end of his life, as many Cubans were superstitiously inclined to note—when he strode into Havana to take over a country of about six million people, using only a rag-tag guerrilla "army" of a few hundred men. It boggled the mind.

His cousin Alejo Herrero had told him, years ago, how he had discussed politics with Fingenio in the Colegio de Belén, a prestigious Jesuit school where they were classmates. He had also known Fingenio's brother Repterio, whom he described as sinister and vengeful, but always subservient to and afraid of his older brother.

For his part, Fingenio *seemed* to be more open, sociable and charismatic, but there was something about him of much more ominous portent. One of his fellow students recalled Fingenio's reaction while riding as a passenger in a friend's car. Every time they went through a small town where streets were criss-crossed by chickens, pigs, and other farm animals the driver would attempt to dodge them, at which point Fingenio would shout: "Run them over, damn it, run them over!" The streak of sheer meanness and destructiveness would later become evident as his power led him to disregard the need to keep up any appearances.

Alejo Herrero had been born in Spain but had escaped to Cuba with his Cuban mother and Spanish father during the Spanish Civil War. He was a fan of Franco's and at one point gave Fingenio a copy of the book on basic Falangist doctrine by the movement's founder, José Antonio Primo de Rivera. It was a work that later showed up in a photograph taken of Fingenio during his Sierra Maestra campaign. Truth be told, that book might have been one the deepest foundations of his political philosophy, since Costra was not really a communist at all, but quite clearly a fascist. He had used the communist label merely as a cover to obtain the support of the Soviet Union in order to retain power autocratically, without the bother of holding meaningful elections.

Gustavo had made up a clever definition of Costra's political beliefs: he was neither a communist nor a socialist, neither a capitalist nor a Falangist—he was simply a Costraist.

According to reports Gustavo had received from various friends, Fingenio had quite likely taken part in at least a half dozen murders, shootings and other acts of violence during his University of Havana days.

One of them Gustavo could not get out of his mind: the cold-blooded killing of a young student who had Fingenio's surname, although they were unrelated. The young man who had crossed him as a result of a turf battle in the University was one Manolo Costra, another active, dynamic student leader. Fingenio had set himself the goal of achieving stardom via the simple process of eliminating his rivals (especially, he thought, if they had the same surname). Fingenio had sworn to get even with him for having slighted him on a couple of occasions. But what made Manolo Costra a major target was his power as an enemy of his in student-body politics—an activity that tended to spill over into the national arena, since prominent student leaders went on to become career politicians. Rich and influential ones if they lived long enough. That killing, too, was something Fingenio got away with, no formal charges having ever been filed against him.

Fingenio had also advocated killing President Ramón Grau San Martín in the mid-forties. As part of a group of student leaders visting the presidential palace in Havana, while awaiting the president on the front balcony he suddenly turned to his colleagues and said these chilling words: "Let's throw the old man over the balcony and spark an an impromptu revolution."

But that was long ago, and now he, Gustavo, had a mission to accomplish for that same killer. He had no choice. His own life—and perhaps his parents'—hung in the balance.

Chapter XIX
THE GO-AHEAD

"Mr. Mariello!" Not wanting to overdo it, Gustavo Covadonga tried to play it cool, but could not completely suppress his upbeat mood. "I'm happy to report to you that the first thing I told President Costra was your comment about 'giving it our best shot.' He was really pleased... and expectant that things could be worked out."

"Great!" Claudio Mariello's lips curled into a self-satisfied half-ironic smile. "What else did he say?" He didn't bother to tell him that the top capos had given their okay.

"He said"—Gustavo spoke each syllable clearly and distinctly—"that you're a very smart man, Mr. Mariello. Those were his very words."

"Well, you tell him that so is he," Mariello answered, half-thinking that, despite his effort at making it sound authentic, the comment more likely came not from Costra's mouth but from Gustavo's. His thought was that the Cubans' penchant for bullshit was just as bad, if not worse than the average American's.

"That I'll gladly do, Mr. Mariello, gladly. Now as to the terms, Mr. Costra wants you to know that he is prepared to offer you a handsome reward. Knowing that Kilmory's put out a contract on him . . . ," Gustavo paused and looked around the room at the tough, skeptical faces of Mariello's henchmen—from which, thankfully, he himself was immune—"he will double Kilmory's rate."

"Good!" Mariello was emphatic but remained poker-faced, with a mute expression he could turn on or off in a split second. "Mr. Costra is realistic," he added, pleased that the ante was upped from the million they had been promised by Kilmory for Costra's head. "Has 'e got an exact figure in mind?" The neckless Mariello crossed his hands over his rotund belly and waited for an answer.

"Mr. Mariello, Mr. Costra's not going to haggle about the price. If it's reasonable, you name it," he concluded, letting him know with a gesture that the "double rate" was just an opening gambit. Better to let Mariello start naming figures—as long as he was not too extravagant. Also, he thought there was no need to bargain too hard, since it was not *his* money but Costra's stolen treasures. In other words, he thought, "fuck that son of a bitch."

"For a job like dat, Gus,"—Mariello's use of Gustavo's nickname was an old habit—"an' it ain't sump'n' you do every day—that'll take a lotta groundwork, you know, 'specially before and maybe a lot more afterward. It'll have to be on the order of . . . ," Mariello pretended to be doing calculations on the spur of the moment, as if he had not already had a figure in mind, "say, around two big ones, but maybe closer to three." Mariello eyed his reaction closely.

"Well, Mr. Mariello," Gustavo answered without hesitation, "to be honest with you, Mr. Costra authorized me to agree to something around that level," he lied, "...but not quite that high. He did, however, give me some leeway." That, Gustavo thought, was a nice touch, since his side, being the contractor looking to get it done, was actually prepared to go much higher. It might be best to do a little bargaining to make things look on the up-and-up—especially in case Costra got wind of anything. Priority one was to nail down the deal. Besides, Costra loved to steal and was probably never going to pay them the full amount anyway, but stop with the down payment. Once the deed was done, how on earth were they going to collect the rest?

"Le' me get dis straight: you think Fingenio's gonna take us up on da three million?" Mariello's gaze was fixed.

"Well, more or less. Between you and me I think he would be willing to go up to that, but knowing what a tightwad he is, he insisted that I negotiate. But just between the two of us, I think I can get *three and a half* out of him..., that is, if you think you and me can, say, split the extra half or so—that is, if you agree." Gustavo's hands twisted around, visually representing a way to pocket the extra commission, splitting it with the capo. In case he somehow managed to stay abroad instead of going back to Cuba, that money would solve a lot of problems, he dreamed. But hey, he thought, "no guts no glory."

"I'll take care of *you* Gustavo, but I don't want nuttin' extra just for myself. I'll split it with the rest o' de guys." Mariello would have liked the money but didn't want to risk the other capos finding out he had increased his personal cut by all that much. There would be too many people involved and it was too much money to keep under wraps. In the Mob, skimming was expected, but there were limits best not tested, even at his top position. In a deal like that, someone was bound to find out. So he concluded it might be safer to keep things on the level; his cut would still be substantial, higher than the other capos'. "If you can get the three and a half, I'll see you get an extra slice," he concluded, "but just between *us*." The fact was, that such a sum would have been by far the highest ever paid for a contract hit, even on a top-level target like Kilmory. It felt good, however, to get something back from a thief like Costra, who had stolen their casinos and everything else that belonged to them. Kilmory he would gladly kill for free, since he was planning to anyway. If Costra wanted to buy insurance, that was gravy. Fuck him in the *culo*, he thought, remembering one of the few Spanish words he knew.

"Fuck Fingenio," Gustavo said to himself, thinking along the same lines as Mariello. This might be his last opportunity to get back at him. The risk was worth it. If worse came to worst, he could always put the money away someplace where he could recover it at some future date. In Cuba, it was illegal to be rich, or even to have money to spare. And if they caught *dólares* on him, especially a large amount that he couldn't justify, he would be up before the next firing squad at the crack of dawn.

Sometimes, Fingenio didn't seem like a typical Cuban. Or even like a typical human being, with everyday emotions and feelings about friends and family. Gustavo had come to that conclusion reluctantly at first, but experience had brought him now to accept the fact of his cool, snake-in-the-grass cruelty. As a matter of principle, Fingenio reneged on his promises every chance he could, whenever it suited him. His conscience never bothered him in the slightest, even when he betrayed his best friends, sending them toward certain death, or quite simply *sentencing* them to death. Sometimes he would enjoy ordering a mock execution to scare the victims to death before the real one came, or imprisoning them, making them suffer pain, disease and deprivation if that was what he felt like doing. Mysteriously, the victim would suddenly develop a deadly disease, receive fake treatment and die. Killing with cancer was easy: they simply installed powerful radiation devices in close proximity to their cells. Sure enough, they died of cancer, sometimes not even realizing it was induced.

For Fingenio, it was more comforting to know that the victim had suffered agonizing pain. Generally, he didn't care to look at too many photographs taken during torture—one or two was enough.

Very often, his victims were more afraid of torture than they were of death. While being tortured, of course, the victim usually wishes, vainly, for death to come soon. He took pleasure in visiting his victims—such as General Ochoa, an Angolan war hero and veteran of his Venezuela and Nicaragua guerrilla campaigns—the latter successful, the former not quite. Later on he would take over the petroleum-rich country by stealthy subversion.

Right then he needed a scapegoat, since the U.S., he knew, was upset about the rampant drug trafficking involving Cuba and was considering drastic action—much more than the embargo, which Costra like to call a "blockade." And this gave him a perfect out while at the same time allowing him to get rid of Ochoa, whom he suspected of plotting against him—or at least thinking about it. So he paid Ochoa a visit at La Cabaña prison and told him that his life might be spared and his family would be well treated if he "confessed" and went along with a sham trial for drug running. Costra was copying, on a smaller scale, the infamous Moscow "show trials" during the main stage of Stalinist power.

"Ah, a criminal state," Costra liked to think, "disguised as communist or socialist, could get away with anything it wanted to." A veritable dream.

Guillermo Armando Bolaños, one of Fingenio's best friends and a companion of his from the very beginning—going back to the 1952 attack on the Moncada Garrison and the Sierra Maestra campaign—had been imprisoned now for several years. Bolaños eventually served nearly half a century in prison, enduring untold hardship and starvation. There is no record of actual torture for him, if you don't count living in a five- by-eight cell with rats and cockroaches for most of your life. His imprisonment let Fingenio Costra feel alternately—or simultaneously—pleased and smugly satisfied. The hardship of others, particularly erstwhile friends and collaborators, was transmuted into his own exquisite pleasure.

But he was angry when he heard what Jean Paul Sartre had said of Guevero, who directed the firing squads at the La Cabaña Fortress across the bay from Havana and personally murdered many of the prisoners—just so everyone would know what he was capable of. Well, Costra thought, Guevero was humanitarian enough to occasionally administer the *coup de grace* and put men out of their misery. But how could Sartre go so far as to say such a thing?

He had remarked that "Guevero was the most complete human being of the twentieth century." That was, he felt, utterly false. He, Costra, was the one who deserved that title. He would show Sartre what would happen to that *"arrogante imbécil"* from

Argentina if he sent him to Peru or Bolivia "to start his own revolution." Guevero would be "complete," all right. Utterly dead. Then, what would Sartre say?

He fondly recalled movie-mogul Stone Spitzenberg's observation: "The most important time of my life was the eight hours I spent talking to Fingenio Costra." Other Hollywood moguls had been equally lavish in their praise. That deserved one thing which he soon put into practice: a Havana Film Festival to which he would invite all the big stars, to let them bask in his reflected glory.

Gustavo was aware of the sort of things that actually gave Fingenio pleasure, although he was careful never to give any outward sign of feeling that way. Costra was extremely adept at disguising his feelings, when not talking to justify them—which took up everyone's time for hours on end. Ultimately, power gave him enjoyment whenever he exercised it—which he did without limit or respite. And absolute power gave him..., well, absolute enjoyment, or something as close to that as humanly possible.

* * * * * * *

"Mr. Mariello, it's as good as done at three and a half," Gustavo said, looking at the capo squarely in the eye. "I'll see that you pocket, er, all of it!" The "er" was his gambit to remind Mariello of the extra commission for himself.

"Great, Gus. If so, it's a done deal." Mariello actually smiled at Gustavo, pretending not to hear the "er." He added the closing phrase as solemnly as a judge handing down a sentence. He was in his own home court, and his word was law.

Gustavo decided not to make any trouble by pressing the issue of the "commission" for the moment. Mariello did not look to be in a the mood for that.

Getting into and out of the United States had been, and was, far easier than Gustavo had ever dreamed. All he had to do was fly out of Havana, land in Mexico City and grab the next flight "al Norte," as they referred to America in Cuba. No one gave a second glance at his fake Panamanian passport, or his tourist visa to the U.S., which was genuine, obtained through official channels, just as his visa for Mexico, which was diplomatic and, in this case, stamped on his second passport, which was a Cuban diplomatic one.

Now, he would drive back to Tocumen Airport, turn in his rental car, and grab the next flight to Mexico City. To leave no trail, he used no credit cards—only cash. In his mind he pictured, again, that ad for Acapulco he had seen when he had got off the flight and wondered when he could possibly escape to a place like that and leave behind all his cares and woes. For now, he could only dream about it.

* * * * * *

"No need to pay them one *centavito* more than that." Costra said, referring to the contract price. "For the job they were planning on me—and maybe still are—they were probably offered more Kilmory promises than money, while we're paying cash on the barrel head,
dólares. And we're already paying triple the amount, way above the Kilmory going rate," he added, this time truthfully for a change—that is, should the capos ever collect the full amount they're promising. On the other hand, what they'll get from us is going to be pure gravy."

"No doubt, *Comandante*." Ariel Fernández, his personal assistant, was paying close attention. He was dressed in green army fatigues, like his boss, to blend with the trend. They were thick, heavy and hot for the Cuban climate, but at least they weren't too uncomfortable in Costra's air-conditioned, low-humidity executive offices.

"At any rate, for us," Costra added, always preferring the plural, as though everyone were involved in what were essentially his own personal decisions, "ahem, three million should be our limit. But we might accept the three and a half, since we're only going to advance half of the total in the Panamanian bank account. The rest we'll promise to pay as soon as the job is done..., but we'll see about that when the time comes," Costra added, with a sly glance at Fernández, whose expression showed that he had instantly picked up his drift. He wasn't one of Fingenio's top assistants for nothing, with substantial perks and income; his actual salary was by no means generous, since Costra had a well-known bias to the stingy side. But with the perks and «benefits» he was perhaps one of the top two or three hundred richest men in the Cuban *nomenclatura*. And there were no rich businessmen in Cuba; in fact, no businessmen at all in the true sense of the word.

Compared to the average Cuban, Ariel knew, he was wildly rich. But he had to be careful about showing it, much less boasting about it, since the *Comandante's* envy was a well-known trait. He did not just want all the power and money; he resented anyone else having more than he thought he should or, especially, flaunting it.

He preferred doling it out in amounts as minimal as possible. So Ariel was careful to drive an old run-down Lada and live in a modest house, confiscated from its rightful owner and located in a high-class neighborhood—now mostly crumbling, like half of the capital city—near the Almendares River. He was smart enough to never complain to the boss, ask for a raise—if Costra thought you deserved it he would let you know—or bring up personal or family issues unless asked. Costra was king and resentful of any ambitious nobles within range.

"Still, *Comandante*, it's a fantastic deal if we get rid of Kilmory for only a few million," Ariel said, not mentioning the exact figure, which to him seemed astronomical. It's only a drop in the bucket compared to the properties you've expropriated from the gringos and rich Cubans. Why, you're getting rid of their leader with their own money!" He chortled. "When that happens they'll leave us alone for good. We'll get some respect and they'll have to think twice before even *dreaming* of doing anything against us." He gratefully sipped his savory demi-tasse of espresso, one of the minor perks—unavailable for most of the population of a former top coffee-producing country—of working for the *Máximo Líder*. Even if you had coffee on your ration card and could afford it, it was never available in the run-down, bare-shelved state stores, nor was espresso in the run-down, miserable cafés, unless you were a tourist and could pay several dollars for one.

"I certainly expect that—for their sake!" Fingenio looked more self-righteous than usual. "Word will get around fast. Then they'll shit right in their pants. I'll bet they've never figured we might bump off their president and get away with it. The best thing is they'll have to keep it secret that *we* had anything to do with it. You know why?"

"No idea, *Comandante*." Fernández lied, putting on a look of slightly exaggerated ignorance. With Fingenio it was always best to pretend cluelessness and never for an instant contradict the leader's conviction that he was the smartest man on the planet.

"Simple, *coño*. If they try to accuse us, it will come out, one way or another, that they were planning to kill *me* and invade Cuba, and they're scared to death that it could get them involved with the Soviets in another nuclear confrontation. They will choose to keep it quiet, since it will just mess up everything for them, make them look bad and won't bring back their beloved Kilmory." Costra looked smug and self-satisfied, pleased at Fernandez' expression of how much he appreciated being let in on his privileged thinking.

Costra would not have been that shocked to hear that, after assuming power, Jameson's Option B to "solve" Justin Kilmory's murder would have been to blame it on a Costra-communist conspiracy that needed to be avenged with an American invasion of Cuba. But his risks were well calculated and somehow he always came out on top. Sure enough, as luck would have it, Option B was discarded when Rosswell was not killed immediately and made statements that would have compromised that option. But Jameson, wary of taking on the Cuban fox, had already been leaning against that dangerous option. He had another gambit in mind that would engage the U.S. against communism while handsomely rewarding him with a continuous flow of "commissions" on tanks, airplanes and materiél.

As Ariel Fernández basked in his practiced handling of Costra's quirks, his walkie-talkie gave out a signal. "*Aló. Sí, okei.*" Hanging up, he turned to Costra. "Gustavo is here, *Comandante.*"

"Send him in." Fingenio leaned back in his custom-made executive chair so as to look down his nose at Gustavo when he came in. He was still undecided as to jailing, executing, or.... More precisely, he hadn't thought about anything more lenient than imprisonment. He had half a notion of really putting him through the wringer when his mission was over. It all depended on his personal whim at that particular moment, more than on how well Gustavo performed or any objective assessment of the situation, as Gustavo well knew. Well, unless he messed up in any way and deserved anything sweeter.

"*Comandante,*" he said as he gave Costra a half-sloppy military-style salute, knowing that his interest in military sharpness and precision was nonexistent, "I have good news."

"Let's hear it," replied Costra in a clipped, business-like tone. He waved, indicating he expected him to sit in a wicker chair. The elegant, mahogany-lined office had large ceiling fans that kept up a steady, gentle breeze. A special generator kept his headquarters immune from the constant blackouts that affected the general population in most of Havana.

"Thanks, *Comandante,*" he said politely. "They have agreed. And I got them to accept something close to our price," he added quickly, careful to involve himself by not saying "your" price.

"How close?" Costra looked slightly skeptical, his miserly nature more concerned about mere dollars, which he could easily afford, than about the project itself. Forges magazine, the top-level financial bi-monthly would, years later, make him furious by including him among the ten richest individuals in the world. That is, until he threatened to bomb their New York headquarters and they meekly took him off the list the following year.

"Three and a half million, *Comandante,*" he heard himself say, wondering if Fingenio would ever learn that he might have sealed the deal for three. Still, he dreamed, if he ever made good his eventual escape from Costra, the extra cut would enable him to go into business for himself. "I'm sorry, *Comandante,* that's the best I could do; they started at five million," he lied smoothly.

Well, *coño,* they're living up to their reputation as a bunch of thieves and criminals." He showed no awareness of the irony, since he was no stranger to organized criminality. "But as long as they're going to turn their guns around and aim them back at you-know-who, we'll pretend to go along." Even in the inner sanctum of his executive office, Costra seemed reluctant to say "Kilmory." The *Comandante,* Gustavo observed thankfully, did not seem to have the slightest suspicion that he had worked in a big cut for himself, at his expense.

"But, *Comandante,* I have to tell you they have asked to get the whole amount of three and a half million deposited in advance. Of course, I told them that would be impossible." Gustavo tried to enhance his own role.

"Yeah, they're dreaming," Costra replied almost automatically. "Tell them the most we're willing to pay is three million. We'll deposit that sum, sure, but—*atención*—he smiled, we'll authorize withdrawal of only fifty percent pending execution." If he had made a pun on "execution," he pretended to be unaware of it, his expression unchanged. But then, he was known to be humorless—rare for a Cuban. "Half of the balance will be released upon completion, and the rest thirty days after confirmation," he added, as if the news of such an event, to be reported instantly by the press around the world, would not be proof enough.

"I told them I'd try to work something out.... But they said just half wouldn't do it for them. Talked about a lot of expenses, bringing in specialists for consultation, sharpshooters from France, all kinds of preparations, etc." Gustavo tried to look more worried than he actually was. Costra's haggling over details, he thought. Why jeopardize a deal that was practically done for what would amount, eventually, to only half the agreed price?

"Did they give you an idea how they plan to do the job?" Costra's eyes narrowed as a ray of reflected sunlight suddenly made his gaze more sinister than usual.

"They're thinking about a well-organized hit—like I said, bringing in sharpshooters from Corsica—they said something about flying them in from Marseille—three men in each case. They'd get him in a crossfire with semi-automatic, precision rifles using those 'dum-dum', hollowed-out bullets to make sure."

"What's this about 'in each case'?" Costra looked quizzical, his eyebrows furrowed.

"I've been meaning to tell you, *Comandante,* that's the reason they've upped the ante: they plan to make a series of three similarly staged attempts in different cities, so they'll have backups in case the first ones don't work. And they'll have three shooters in each city.

"Hmmm, sounds like very thorough planning. I don't suppose they told you anything else, such as dates, places, etc., right?"

"I gathered that they will make each attempt in a different city, probably during a motorcade, although they didn't specifically say that. I think they didn't want anyone to know too much about it, frankly. But the conversation indicated that's their plan."

"You should've tried to get more information out of them, Gustavo!" Costra looked displeased.

"I'm sorry I didn't *Comandante.* I did the best I could."

"You're sure, Gustavo?" Costra gave him a suspicious look.Gustavo fidgeted during one of Costra's unusual momentary silences while he seemed content to size him up. "They don't want us to know the details of their plan, eh?" Costra's lips turned into a smirk. It looked like he had just been testing Gustavo. "Well, that just might show they're professionals—nothing like pros if you want a job done right." He puffed on his expensive, specially hand-made cigar. "Any idea of a general timetable?"

"My impression, *Comandante,*" said Gustavo, relief clearly showing on his face, "from hearing them talk, that is, that they're going to want to take care of it at the first clean opportunity when "Mister Z"—the Secret Service's code name for him—is away from Washington, where he is more vulnerable and their hit-men will have a better chance of success."

"Hmm." Costra puffed again, smiling at the "Mister Z" reference.

"You see, he's scheduled to go on a political campaign trip to a number of cities within three to four months. He's made some enemies, but as you know the Mafia is number one. They hate the son of a bitch, and they're ready to hit him. I think they feel that the sooner they do it the sooner they'll get him and his brother Roland off their back." He stopped, afraid that he might be letting on that they'd do it for free. The thought crossed his mind.

"*Muy bien, coño.* Sounds like they're really keen on it." Costra looked pleased but grimly determined, as though he himself were going to do the killing. He sometimes missed the gunplay he regularly engaged in when he was a student at the University of Havana. Young punks like him were referred to as *de gatillo alegre,* "trigger-happy."

"*Sí, Comandante*, it sure looks that way. It corresponds to their own interests and to ours as well," Gustavo answered in his customary Spanish syntax.

Costra looked at one of his henchmen. "Julián," he said evenly, "what would you do in this case?" He liked to put his assistants on the spot. For a man who hardly ever laughed, showed gayety or told bawdy jokes, it was one of the few things that seemed to amuse him.

"I, I don't know. Ne- negotiate some more, *Comandante*?" Julián answered defensively. "Try to work out a compromise and get everything spelled out?"

"Okay, this is what we're going to do," Costra fired back, giving Julián a disdainful look, as if brushing away every word he had just said. He was in no mood to delay matters, and he never took any chances when his own well-being could possibly be slightly at stake. Previously, he had thought of taking a few days to think it over, but all of a sudden he got his *carpe diem* urge. He was going to strike while the iron was hot, clinching the deal quickly and getting them to commit before anything came up to squelch the plan. Uncharacteristically, he decided to skip further haggling over the price—in any case, he planned to cheat on it.

"Tell them this: we'll pay their three and a half million; we'll deposit all of it but authorize the withdrawal of only fifty percent of that: one million, seven hundred fifty thousand—we'll arrange for them to take that out immediately. The remaining fifty percent is theirs as soon as the job's done," he said with an air of finality, figuring they would not accept anything less. "That's my final offer." Years of wheeling and dealing had honed Costra's senses enough to know when to haggle and delay, and when to strike quickly and decisively.

"Very well, *Comandante*," Gustavo replied. Realizing the interview was over, he asked: "Is there anything else, *Comandante*?"

"Go tell Mariello and report back to me immediately, Gustavo," Costra instructed nonchalantly as he got ready to sign a document on his desk, picking up a gold-trimmed black Mont Blanc pen and half-waving it at Gustavo's brisk salute. "And no fooling around in Miami, okay?" he added, tauntingly. He knew perfectly well that Covadonga's itinerary excluded the capital city of Cuba's exile community.

"Absolutely not,*Comandante*," Gustavo replied, laughing politely at what he preferred to think of as one of Fingenio's rare attempts at humor, "I'm going via *Panamá*."

The deal was well on its way to being sealed. The capos would get their money—or at least half of it. Costra would thus be reassured that Kilmory would be taken out of the picture merely by giving the Outfit back a tiny fraction of what he had stolen from them. What Mariello would do when he couldn't collect the balance of the agreed price was something that he, Gustavo, hoped he wouldn't have to deal with, although it might mean that he would never get the extra commission he had negotiated for himself. If so, there was nothing he could do about it.

Costra settled back, now joined by a coterie of duly impressed special guests from Colombia—members of the FARC, his well-funded guerrilla movement conducting armed action and terrorism in his irresolute neighbor to the southwest —to have his usual mid-week lunch in his opulent executive dining room: medium-rare succulent roast piglet with *moros con cristianos* –rice mixed with black beans—and *plátanos verdes,* mashed green plantains–plus a perfectly cooked *flan* for desert, all washed down with his favorite vintage of Baron Philippe de Rothschild red Bordeaux. Ah, in *his* country, life was good!

Chapter XX
A DOWN PAYMENT

"Let's take a good look at this," Jake Rosetti said, as he held up the paper showing that the hefty sum of $3,500,000 had been deposited by Turismo Internacional, S.A., a front corporation for the Costra government, in the Banco de la República, in Panama City. Rosetti was not too enthusiastic. He noted, unsurprised, that half of the agreed-upon sum was completely set aside—blocked and unavailable without special instructions. But Costra had authorized an initial payout of fifty percent, or $1,750,000. Any further withdrawals would be subject to specific authorization from Havana.

Costra was as tricky as they came, but Rosetti felt it was probably the best deal they could get. The "Strategist", as he stated his specialty in his calling card, had serious doubts that Costra would, as promised, pay up the $1,750,000 balance once the mission was carried out. But he concluded that if Costra did not eventually pay it, a million and three quarters was still pretty good, and nearly twice as much as "Giustino"—as the Mafia called the President just in case anyone was listening—had been offering for the hit on Costra.

Few at the CIA, DIA or other intelligence agencies knew about the plan to have the Mafia carry out the hit on Costra. They were far fewer than those who were "in" on Q-Day, the planned second invasion of Cuba to overthrow Costra. But, in the case of Q-Day, even the Secretary of Defense and the CIA chief had not been told of the plan. It was a well-kept secret, on a need-to-know basis, held within a very small group made up of Roland Kilmory and a few key figures. President Kilmory and Roland felt that if they did not limit those who knew—i.e., the group organizing the invasion—it would be likely to leak, soon be public knowledge and reach Costra's ears, just as had happened with the Bay of Pigs operation. Kilmory had no idea that Costra's intelligence system had of course already heard of the new invasion plan through its various sources, among them the Mafia itself, which he had "turned" and was using to great advantage. The Kilmory administration, who thought it was still using the Mafia *against* him, had no idea that it had been "turned" and was now working for Costra. Some Cuban exile leaders were in the same position; they were feeding information to the Mafia, convinced that it was aiming its guns at Costra.

"Claudio," Rosetti addressed Mariello in something less than his habitual attempt at more-refined tones and pronunciation, "Why don' we have Luigi find out exactly what dis means: when we can withdraw the money, and how." He didn't want to insult his colleague by using a style too far above his own.

"Yeah, Jake. Dat's da plan." Then, looking at Luigi, his personal courier, "We send you over deah to pick up da cash. But first, you do some leg work and check out exactly how dat's gonna work."

It was unheard of for the capos put down on paper anything at all bout a crime. Naturally, the document in this case said nothing about what the payment was for, reading instead: "The funds will be released once the parties have made good on their assurances that agreed-upon requirements have been complied with." It was a tricky question as to what "made good" meant, and actual release of the funds was contingent upon written authorization from two State Security agents of Costra's in Panama.

"Sure, boss," Luigi answered as he received the agreement file from Rosetti's outstretched hand. A trusted Mafia courier who, despite his typical mug-shot face, Luigi put on what could be mistaken for an executive demeanor, wore a tailored business suit and at first glance passed for a conservative but somewhat less than convincing businessman. His job was to carry cash in a heavy, locked briefcase that he never let go of. Since chaining it to his wrist would have attracted too much attention, he strapped it to his leg when sitting down on flights. He also personally relayed vital messages between capos located in different cities and, sometimes, countries. Except for his accent and vocabulary, one might have confused him with a diplomat.

"Okay," Rosetti replied. "Course, I'm betting Costra isn't likely to release the balance we agreed on like he's supposed to, after we've done the job." Rosetti reverted to careful, precise diction. "So we have to make sure we collect at least *this* money in advance." Although he wasn't feeling the heat of Justice Department prosecutors quite like Mariello and Traficant, he knew that it would only be a matter of time before they targeted him too; so it was on his mind that Roland's legal machine needed to be jammed as soon as possible. And the best way to stop the tail from wagging, like Mariello himself said, was to cut off the dog's head.

"We've gotta take dat chance, Jake. Can't delay da hit based on dat." Mariello looked squarely at Rosetti. He didn't want to go overboard, but it was in Mariello's personal interest to get the job done soon. Roland Kilmory had him a lot closer to indictment than he cared to admit.

"All right, Claudio. That's gravy anyway. But it sure would be nice to take some of our dough back from Costra, since he stole it from us in the first place," Rosetti shot back. He couldn't help remembering the big "summit" meeting in Cuba of all the top bosses—including Lucky Luciano, who traveled to Cuba from Italy—held in Havana's prestigious Hotel Nacional in 1948, with Hank Spanitra in attendance. That was when Carlos Prío Socarrás was president, since Batista's party had been ousted in free elections—in effect, giving up power, if only temporarily—and the Mafia controlled most of the gambling and narcotics on the island, plus a lot of the prostitution. Cuba had been a terrific and highly lucrative place in its own right, plus a great offshore base for financial operations. "I'm not forgetting that son-of-a-bitch Costra owes us a bunch," Rosetti concluded.

"Yeah, he's a double-crossing bastard and it's too bad we din't pull off the hit on him first, like we planned," Mariello said evenly. "But no way we're gonna stall da hit on *dis* guy," he added, meaning Kilmory. "He's got it coming for da double-cross. Roland's Justice Department bandwagon, too, is aiming for all of us sooner or later. But, ya know, it's all tangled up with da hit on Costra, the 'secret' second invasion of Cuba, an' all dat. So national security will make 'em cover it all up anyway. Our buddy Hooper at da FBI won't lift a finger either," he added with a mischievous smile. "To top it all off, the signal from up there," Mariello pointed at the ceiling, "is to get it done as soon as possible. Everybody's aboard. Our partner Hofstra is rarin' to go, anxious as hell to get it done. After all, he's da man wid da big bucks, pure gravy. Nothin' like ensurin' da flow o' dose millions from 'is Teamsters Pension Fund." He nearly drooled just thinking about it.

* * * * * * *

"It's done, *Comandante*. They've agreed to do it!" Gustavo walked into Costra's office directing a winning smile at him.

"*Okei,* but what did they say about the money?" Costra was all business.

"I haggled them and convinced them to accept your terms, *Comandante*. They settled for the signed letter of instructions to get the fifty percent in advance. So it's a go." Gustavo relaxed his smile.

"Good. It's a deal. Listen, Clarita"—he added, turning to his top secretary, who had the stunning looks and figure needed to meet the *Comandante's* requirements—"arrange to send them the letter they want, signed by Polo." Costra was inclined to use nicknames for his top officials, in this case his Chief of Intelligence. "I'll give it my approval by putting my initials on it, but not my regular full signature, okay?" Costra made it a point to catch her eye as he spoke. "Don't want to make it look too formal."

"And, by the way, come and see me when you finish work this evening. There's something I need to discuss with you." He wagged his index finger as eloquent punctuation.

"*Okei, Comandante,*" Clarita answered with her best flirtatious smile, catching his drift. Her rear end swayed to the rhythm of his expectations as she walked away, aware of where his gaze was fixed.

Chapter XXI
MARIE'S MEN

The year 1960 was just getting started and, judging by events thus far, it appeared to be promising. Campana cast his eye over the curvaceous, half-undressed body of Marie Moore as she lay on the bed. Just like Spanitra had described her to him before they ever went to bed for the first time. He smiled at the recollection. "Ah, that Hank could always come up with the best broads!" He nearly said the words out loud.

"Baby," she purred, "would you get me a drink?"

Unaccustomed to taking orders, even from beautiful women, Campana gave her a cool look. "What 'cha need a drink for, baby?" He continued to take off his clothes, but more slowly, a threat implicit in every gesture. He was clearly put off.

She took the hint and got up, a little afraid she might have overstepped her bounds with the powerful boss. Marie knew his reputation, admired his power and certainly did not care to rub him the wrong way. She knew how Campana had single-handedly rescued Spanitra's career..., and how, with a single word, he might just ruin hers, if he chose to. Just now, she needed all the help she could get.

"Maybe I can fix *you* one," she recovered soothingly.

"Sure, baby, go ahead," he said, now more relaxed. "But first...," he reached out, brought her close to him and kissed her hungrily. She responded with abandon... and wanton skill. In another moment they landed on the huge, circular bed, its canopy covered with mirrors, at the "Honeymoon suite" in Lake Tahoe's Cal-Neva Lodge, which Campana owned through one of his surrogates, in partnership with Jonathan Kilmory. The Cal-Neva served as an occasional landing pad and hideaway for the Brat Pack, as well as for Campana's associates and "friends."

When a top boss like Campana called a man "my friend" it meant acceptability. However, the words "*our* friend" meant something else: that the individual in question was a "made man," i.e., that he had been inducted into the Cosa Nostra and therefore was absolutely reliable. Naturally, when any of those "absolutely reliable" men made mistakes they were "clipped" just like anyone else who might get in the way of the Mob's holy business: making money.

Justin Kilmory, just like his father had until a decade or so before, would use the Cal-Neva for his own trysts. This time, he needed the R&R almost as much as the series of pills he took. He needed them as he went through the grueling campaign for the 1960 presidential election, having regular sex with various women and all the while looking like an active, vigorous young fellow with energy to spare.

Justin had had an encounter with three prostitutes in Havana in 1957 while Sandy Traficant—who made the arrangement for him—and another capo observed the scene through a two-way mirror. Traficant would reminisce later about that occasion with his friends, including his pal and Mob lawyer Kirk Pagano, glad that he had filmed the action so as to blackmail Kilmory for the rest of his life. If Costra had managed to get his hands on something so explosive, it might explain why he could have persuaded Kilmory to cancel air cover and muddle up the Bay of Pigs invasion.

A man of Campana's vast experience with scores, perhaps hundreds of different women—sometimes in threesomes and moresomes—could appreciate Marilyn's expertise at love-making. She not only loved sex, but could put on a performance in making love to a man—or to more than one at a time, according to circumstances—and didn't at all mind showing off while she was into it. Campana couldn't help observing during a passionate moment the faint, barely visible signs of plastic surgery—thanks to the studio, secretly done—below the perfectly shaped breasts that Marilyn was so proud of. But large pink, now-hard nipples quickly erased those thoughts. Electrified with the sight and feel of her body, and with their increasingly frenzied excitement, he let himself get carried away into an ecstatic abandon that caught Marie—and even he himself—by surprise.

A man as fearless and powerful as Campana could let it all hang out and damn the consequences, she thought amid the sweeping rush of sexual passion.

"It's been a long time, baby," she heard him say as she fleetingly thought how satisfying it was to be so attractive to men, particularly those of his importance. In fact, that was how she

Had become a star—with alacritous willingness to go to the casting couch at the slightest opportunity. "No shrinking violet ever got anywhere in Hollywood," she would say at moments sometimes inappropriate, "unless she was prepared to throw her petals to the wind at the right time."

Actually, she had never been that particular about the status of those whom she bedded—she tended to give most hopefuls an equal opportunity, regardless of social or economic standing. Later, however, that had tended to change. She became more selective, more concerned about power and position. Why let it go to waste on statusless duds?

Sal Campana fit precisely into the category of men she thought worth her while. So, in an instinctive impulse, Marie decided to follow his lead in the sexual arena and let go completely and utterly, crying out, screaming and shouting. Who cared? And anyway, it was Sam's hotel, although Justin's father was his partner, with a minority interest in it.

"Baby!" Was Campana's excited reply, amid his muffled caresses around her writhing body. If anyone heard, Campana thought, so much the better. That would let them know what a great lover he was. Carried away together, they achieved, before they knew it, a powerful and simultaneous climax—loudly, deliciously, wildly. It seemed, as it usually tends to, longer and more intense than it was. They were still moaning several minutes later.

"Wow, baby, you're some kinda hot!" Campana complimented her. On occasion, if he thought the girl was particularly deserving, he was inclined to make an admiring remark. When he complimented the wives of lower-ranking mafiosi who were half-way worthy, it was what mostly what he considered a courtesy; on occasion he liked to think of himself as able to play the part of a perfect gentleman who wouldn't dream of doing anything illegal or immoral. This time, he meant every word.

"So're you, baby," Marie answered breathlessly. "You're... the best." She was going to say "one of" but fortunately caught herself in mid-sentence. She had a bad habit of blurting out, unedited, whatever popped into her head. "If I thought it, it must be okay," was a standing, if secret, principle of hers. After all, it was "spontaneity," like an appropriate ad lib in acting class. In the back of her mind—fortunately for her it was far enough into her bottom recesses not to actually surface—was the thought that, on previous occasions, he had been a so-so lay. She found it hard not to think of the time when, tipsy and pretending to be slightly coerced, she had participated in a group-sex session with him, Spanitra, a young starlet and two other good-looking capos. But then, how could she forget? Spanitra was famous for his huge member and technique, and she had gotten into it deeply with him while the girls gave support and encouragement. Marie was known, on occasion, to be fond of girls as well, and had select girl-friends with whom she had occasional rendezvous, when she could fit them in. But that session was memorable in that he and the girls had worked her into a frenzy of multiple orgasms. She just hoped Spanitra did not show around the flash pictures he took of the wild goings-on. At least not too much.

"You ain't so bad yourself," he replied half-jokingly, aware of her hesitation, but of nothing beyond that. "By the way, how's your friend, the future president, rank?" He added it casually, hoping to get some inside info to confirm the rumors he had heard.

"Who, Justin?" Caught off guard, Marie could think of nothing to say.

"Who else? You know any other future presidents?"

"Gosh, I guess not," she replied somewhat embarrassed. That Sal was a pretty sharp character, she thought. Wouldn't he be interested to know that she was also thinking about Justin's brother, the timid-looking Roland, who would likely be next in the Kilmorys' plans for a family dynasty? *That,* she wasn't so sure she would share with him.

"Well, tell me 'bout 'im," Campana probed. "I hear he don't do nothin' in bed but lie down and let the girl do the work." He wanted to see what he could dig out of her. "Is that what 'e actually does? Come on, you can tell *me.*"

"Well, baby, to tell you the truth I believe it's his back," she ventured gingerly. "He... he really can't move very well.... Not nearly as well as you can, anyway." She let out a little laugh. Flattery never hurt, she thought.

"So he ain't all that good, huh?" He prompted her.

"No, between you and me, not really. I mean, he's okay, you know," she said as she rubbed her solid, well-shaped breasts into his hairy chest, tickling her own nipples in the process. "But nothing to write home about. His brother Roland's better, more active, willing to please," she added, deciding to take up Campana's lead on being open about the subject. After all, *he* wasn't holding back, so why should she? "But otherwise he comes off as kind of odd, standoffish, you know? He's nice, but kind of cold."

"You got it. Dat's him all right, the fuckin' little runt." When he wasn't careful, Campana's diction dropped into the Mob's standard "dat" and "dis."

Marie seemed, at that moment, more naïve and vulnerable than she normally was. Campana felt—unusually for him—a little sorry for her. It struck him that there might be clouds on the horizon for her, that she might be getting in over her head. Mindful that Marie could be a useful source of valuable inside information, not to mention juicy gossip, he chose to protect his assets by giving her a word of advice. He put his elbow into the pillow and leaned over to her, not without an appreciative glance at her shapely boobs and smooth, stretched-out body.

"Lemme tell you something, baby, just between you 'n' me." Campana said. Getting involved with those guys you could be askin' for trouble down the road. Me, I don't care if the whole world knows what I do with you or any other woman. Actually, I prefer it that way. But them, dat's another story. If word gets out, baby, it might not be good for you. You know what I mean?"

"No, Sal. Why? What could possibly happen...?" Marie looked slightly strained, but smiley.

"I'd be careful with them, 'cuz they're gonna be lookin' out for their own neck, and they won't care what happens to yours." He actually felt—catching himself in mid-thought—a touch of concern for her—but more than that, for her value to him as a source. "They're gonna be worried about political consequences if word gets out about you and them. 'Course, dat'll give you some leverage, too—but it could be tricky if you ever put 'em on the spot or anything, you know?" Politics is politics, and it don' mix with sex. Just keep it under your hat."

"Okay, hon." Ever the real-life ingénue, Marie looked appreciative that he would tell her these things, but still incredulous. At some point, perhaps, her thoughts would have occasion to flash back to Campana's pillow talk this evening. But for now, she dismissed his words as those of a man whose survival required him to always be suspicious and a little paranoid. She tended to doubt the Kilmorys would ever stoop to anything that smelled of lack of principles.

"By the way, you plannin' a get-together with these guys... any time soon?" He didn't know for sure, but he suspected that they had engaged in a *ménage à trois* of sorts at some point.

A man of few words, Campana figured the probe was worth a shot. Some time ago, in a previous visit to Vegas, he had witnessed how she flirted with the two brothers at the same time.

"No, Justin's always so damned busy." She ignored his allusion.

"Too bad," he shot back.

Soon, Campana heard that Spanitra would be giving Justin Kilmory a big push, as would his father, Jonathan, a friend and associate of his from 'way back. He hadn't heard directly from him for a long time, but he would not have been surprised if Jonathan got back in touch with him soon to arrange a fix for the next election. Back then, he had made a mental note to prod Marie about it at their next get-together. Any leads he could get might be helpful.

Although as a rule Marie looked like she was innocence personified, she was not always quite as naïve as she acted. She was, in fact, capable of occasional underhandedness and using unexpectedly clever ploys to get her way—besides her natural assets. She was privy to endless gossip and inside information. Campana could use that, especially if it had to do with her trysts with Kilmory or his brother..., particularly since that would enable him to record compromising evidence.

Campana was eager to get the goods on Justin, as insurance in case he helped him out and things didn't go precisely according to plan later on. "Insurance," meaning blackmail in Mob parlance, was always a good backup to guarantee performance on promises made. Those Kilmory guys, he thought, were dirty double-crossers if it suited them, just like their father, old-man Jonathan. Campana had a feeling that Justin would eventually get to the White House. It would not be simply a question of politics or actual votes, but of rigging the electoral results. And Dixon, his likely opponent, could be pressured, if necessary, not to contest any fixes the Mob might put in. If worse came to worst, he and the other capos would know what they would have to say and do to take care of it.

To think that he, Campana, with no political experience whatsoever, had the power to put a politician in the precise position where he wanted him, and therefore subject to his pull: it was mindboggling. Who would have thought that, like H. Everette Hooper himself, but with no official position whatsoever, he could have a president under his control?

Hooper's system was different; there was no expiration date: he just kept files about them all—and simply let them know he would use them if he didn't get his way.

He sweet-kissed Marie good night and went off to do some drinking and gambling, during which he might drop a hint or two about his dalliance with *the* most desirable movie star in the business. Once again, he had proven that he could have—"take" might be a better word—anything from the Kilmorys.

His mind went back a few years to when Chuck and Needles, two of his soldiers, had brought him the first issue of *Playboy* with the famous nude picture of Marie as the first centerfold.

"Hey boss, look at this broad!"

Looney studied it momentarily, tossed it away and sneered: "Yeah, I'll fuck her." Then he added tauntingly: "before either one of you guys." He paused. "The rest of you can then fight over what's left of her." In a good mood, an easy laugh punctuated his jab, secure in the thought that his two henchmen, green with envy, wouldn't ever get even close. He couldn't help thinking that if being at the top had its headaches, it sure had its perks as well.

At the craps table, a roll of the dice woke him up from his reverie: snake eyes! "You win some, you lose some," he said to himself.

Marie dropped off into a blissful sleep, dreaming of delivering a brainy literary lecture to a group of dazzled college professors.

Chapter XXII
JESSICA'S MEN

Living it up, for Campana, meant freedom from worry. He had everything but that in the early 1960's. Roland Kilmory's Justice Department was going after him big-time. On the other hand, he was periodically getting "special deliveries" in the form of briefcases full of cash from Justin through their shared girl-friend, the beauteous, exciting Jessica Cameron Exeter. The cash was the pay-off for the Mob's help, led by Campana, in fixing the 1960 election. He would have gladly given up the money in exchange for being free from pro- or per-secution—the terms were synonymous to him—but it seemed there was little he could do.

Jessica, a frequent visitor to Chicago, eventually turned out to be high-class bedroom entertainment for him. A divorcée who lived off an inheritance and tended to flaunt her independence— Campana called her "Jess"—she had initially been picked up by Rosetti, the Hollywood capo, when she was an aspiring starlet who hung around whenever there were casting calls for pictures. He had escorted her around Hollywood and opened some doors for her with moguls and actors. Of course, her looks had a way of opening doors for her as well, though she was never too quick to come across. She was, in that area, light-years behind Marie Moore. Shortly thereafter, at Campana's urging, she had been introduced to Kilmory by a mutual friend, the crooner/actor Hank Spanitra.

Lately, Jessica would be getting calls from Kilmory on a daily basis from all over the country during the Democratic primary campaign, as they maintained a steady, if haphazard relationship, as allowed by his busy schedule. "Matters of state," as Justin kept telling her, kept interfering with his availability.

Meanwhile, Campana called, sent her flowers and uncharacteristically bided his time, fended off by her puritanical protestations that she didn't feel comfortable getting intimate with him while she was involved with the President—never mind the president's affairs with as many paramours as he could possibly fit in to a tight schedule. Campana, on the other hand—true to his habits—was maintaining multiple relationships, including casual pick-ups and a very serious one with Pamela, one of the singing trio of Mackenzie sisters.

When Jessica was introduced to Justin in Vegas, his younger brother Jeff was around and wasted no time making a pass at her while Justin was busy at another function for the evening. When nothing worked for Jeff—who was married, as she was to learn later—his last resort was inviting her to come aboard a chartered plane that was taking him to Detroit to do some more campaigning for his elder brother. He said the plane was sitting on the runway.

"Don't worry," he said when she demurred. "The pilot's waiting and won't take off until you're aboard."

"Well, I'm sorry to hear that because I won't be able to join you," she replied.

The next day when Justin asked her what kind of an evening she had had, Jessica—not wanting any misunderstandings—told him about Jeff's pass and last-stand invitation. Instead of being upset, Justin found the story uproariously funny.

"Why, that sly young rascal," he managed to say amid gales of laughter. Then he shook his head as if he couldn't believe it, shrugged it off and went into words of praise for his brother and how well he was doing in the political arena. This was the closest that Justin ever came to criticizing another Kilmory with Jessica—or anyone else, for that matter.

Later on, the President would ask leading questions of Jessica about Jeff; they were puzzling to her, but not to others who later analyzed them. He was intimating that it was okay to play with Jeff too—the Kilmorys were in the habit of passing their women around. When at some point he suspected that he might be sharing her with Campana—not a problem for him—Justin wondered if, on instructions from the capo, she was feeding him information, or perhaps disinformation, instead of the other way around.

But she was no sharpie, not into playing mind-games, so there was no need for him, as President, to worry about her, he mused. Just another pretty face; best of all, another beautiful body. Jessica was classy, ravishingly attractive, very likable and had a luscious appetite for sex every time he arranged to see her.

That was the basis for their relationship—and certainly that was all *he* wanted. He realized that Jessica—like Marie and so many others—had fallen in love with him, but what the devil did he care? That was *her* problem. He couldn't be bothered with worrying over whatever dreams she had about their relationship.

Chapter XXIII
CONNECTIONS

"Tell Queenie to get his fuckin' ass over here quick—tell 'im I got a big stiff dick over here for 'im." Claudio Mariello liked to make fun of his underling and pilot Dave Berrie, who, far from making a secret of his homosexuality, flaunted it.

"Sure, boss," came a voice from one of his flunkies, followed by the clicking sound of a soon-to-be-outmoded standard round-dial telephone.

"Listen, Dave," Mariello waved his finger at him, "I don't want any slip-ups here. We're talking about the biggest hit in history—maybe in da history o' da world. Ya got it?" His lack of schooling beyond the fifth grade made it unlikely that he had ever heard of other cases, such as the murder of Julius Caesar.

"Sure, boss." Berrie was respectful. "I'm in touch with all the guys—Rosswell, Rosenstein, making sure everything goes according to plan."

"And get me Looney on the phone, quick." Mariello could afford to call Campana "Looney" behind his back, but never to his face. The top capo wouldn't like that too much. In the style of Bert Seidel—whose "Bugsy" nickname was an allusion to his violent outbursts when someone "bugged" him—Campana was likely to do serious physical harm, or worse, to anyone who dared call him by that nickname. Despite his flaunted dislike of "Looney," its owner probably reveled in it, since it earned him respect and fear inside and outside the Mob.

The "Looney" nickname he got from his lunatic violence when crossed by someone—a trait that could lead Campana to kill on a whim, often after "dishing out" to the victim an ample dose of anguish and torment. Sometimes he just wanted to set an example.

He was reputed to have been a participant in the St. Valentine's Day massacre. Once, he ordered a lower-level henchman who had "sung" to the FBI hung from a meat hook, whereupon he was beaten, slashed, stabbed, shot in the knees and subjected to other samples of the Mob's "TLC." Meanwhile, for good measure, a broomstick was used to violate his rectum repeatedly while his penis was electrified. He died in excruciating agony after hanging around for three days. Photographs were taken and passed around like souvenirs. It produced fantastic results. For a long time, everyone had second thoughts about turning stoolie.

Mariello's coordination of the Kilmory hit was not that difficult. He was, in fact, enjoying it, since it was a payback that he felt the President had brought on himself, by double-crossing the very outfit who had put him in power. But Mariello was, of necessity, actually in the background. He attended some of the initial meetings designed to lay the groundwork for the hit. To avoid leaving paper trails, following Mafia custom everything was done by word of mouth—but there was too much heat on the capo from Roland Kilmory's Justice Department, which was continually prosecuting him—or, as Mariello himself would have it, "persecutin' 'im." He was subject to surveillance on a constant basis. So he and Campana delegated the day-to-day management of the job to Jake Rosetti. The feds were not keeping such a close eye on him, so he had a lot more freedom of action.

As for Kilmory, he had alienated himself from the organizations that were supposed to protect him: the FBI, the CIA and the Secret Service. He got on the wrong side of the FBI by letting it be known that he wanted Hooper out. H. Everette and brother Roland, the Attorney General, disliked each other intensely and had a full-scale, no-holds-barred bureaucratic turf war going. It went so far as to involve their dogs. Roland had their licenses changed so that numbers 1, 2 and 3 were assigned to his own pets. Hooper protected himself by keeping a thick file on Justin that covered, among other things, his continual womanizing, and more specifically his affairs with a number of attractive women: for one, the sultry Nazi spy Ima Varda while he was in the Navy and, for another, Elsa Rotter, also a spy but from East Germany (did he have a thing for spies, or did they have a thing for him?). The liaison with Rotter, one of Robby Raker's most stunning playgirls at the Quota Club on Capitol Hill, went on and ended while he was in the White House, just in time to prevent it from becoming public knowledge. She was sent back to East Germany, where she received regular payoffs to keep her mouth shut.

Hooper also had the highly damaging and secret information on Kilmory's health problems, including his affliction with Addison's disease. This serious ailment, which the public knew nothing about at the time, had put him on the brink of death once or twice before massive cortisone injections and doses of amphetamines rescued him, propped him up and brought back the appearance of robust health.

H. Everette was contemptuous of the famous Kilmory "vigah", a propaganda word incessantly repeated by the press. He also knew about Kilmory's back trouble—he had even undergone a spinal operation to alleviate it—which periodically gave him intense pain. It also made him walk with a limp, noticeable only when he went up and down stairs. Justin had also contracted a venereal disease that became resistant to treatment and caused him pain every time he urinated. Later, President Clangton, who emulated him—Kilmory was his hero—far surpassed him in the number of women he bedded and also succumbed to an STD or two. He managed to suppress or alter his medical records to keep it all under wraps.

Justin Kilmory had other skeletons in his closet. His highly publicized prize-winning book, *Portraits of Courage*, had actually been written by his assistant Thorvald Storenson and had been heavily promoted by his father so as to win him intellectual caliber—and consequently political capital.

In short, all this information could be highly damaging. Even so, H. Everette wasn't one hundred percent sure that his file was thick enough to keep him ensconced in the FBI Director's Office—which he prized for its power, self-reflected glory and near-impregnability. The fact that, according to his own inside informants, Justin wanted him out was not only irritating but worrisome. Once out of power he might be subject to investigation for wrongdoing, corruption and, possibly, even obstruction of justice. Thereby his eagerness for, and instigation of the conspiracy to kill Justin Kilmory.

If anything happened to Justin while he was the Bureau's Director it would be made to look purely accidental, beyond his purview and his poor powers to control every nut in America. In any case he would be in a perfect position to cover it up, helping the chief conspirator and mastermind behind it all to keep everything under control.

The Bureau's top agents soon began to notice the way the wind was blowing and became willing if silent participants in doing their part for getting President Kilmory out of the way and, later, helping with the subsequent cover-up. In effect, the Bureau did not simply disregard clear signs that something sinister was afoot, but followed its leader's path to achieve the goal of the conspiracy. Far from stopping it in its tracks, its mission became to aid and abet the process in order to accomplish the physical elimination of the President. In the aftermath, the Bureau would do what was necessary to pick up any loose ends.

H. Everette's power and reach was far greater than most people suspected. He had in his possession numberless tapes from the multiple illegal telephone taps on people like Marlin Lester Ring, whom he hated with a passion, not least because he was black. He went through the motions of requesting judicial permission for taps only on occasion, just to pretend that he was following the letter of the law. But he put taps on just about everyone he felt like spying on, including congressmen, top government officials, and even some top Mafia capos. There were few of those since, after all, he was on friendly terms with them and kept repeating that "the Mafia doesn't exist." In sum, he knew what went on with nearly everyone of possible interest. Was he, however, going to tell "the Prez"? Why, not on his life! Those files were in a safe in his office, variously classified as "Official and Confidential," and "Personal and Confidential" (even more secret); there were also files marked "Sex Deviate," "Cointelpro" and, finally, "DO NOT FILE." This last category was for illegal break-ins and other super-secret operations that were to be kept out of the Central Records System so as to be inaccessible to anyone but him. This also applied to a number of other special files, which were for his eyes only.

It's a tribute to the mysterious intricacies of bureaucracy and government that the FBI Building on Pennsylvania Avenue still bears H. Everette's name. But it takes, surely, too much trouble and paperwork to undo the monument to a scoundrel.

But what about the CIA? Wouldn't the "Company" want to warn the President that his life was in danger? Well, not too likely, especially after Kilmory had stated that he would "break the CIA into a thousand pieces." That intemperate remark was followed up by action not long after the Bay of Pigs, when he fired Alton Dunsell, as if he had been responsible for the last-minute—carefully planned?—presidential decision to cancel the air strikes and change the location of the invasion, thus dooming it.

It is said that, due to the president's bout with back pain, "assistant president" Roland was in control—the co-presidency, as some called it—and presumably made the decision to cancel the air support for the invasion. It has to be said that such a statement sounds too much like a weak excuse for the president's benefit.

Roland was, if anything, tougher than his brother (especially when it came to Costra.) So the CIA, also, had little motivation for protecting Kilmory. After all, they said to themselves, that was the job of the Secret Service. And that branch, too, was compromised.

Eventually a number of CIA operatives were brought into the loop and became a vital part in the conspiracy to kill the President and thus bring about a virtual coup d'état whose beneficiaries would be in a perfect position to cover it all up.

At this stage Kilmory's situation was turning far more dangerous than he or anyone suspected. In late 1963, dislike for the Kilmorys and unconcern for the President's safety also infiltrated the Secret Service. The President's security detail was demoralized and deeply disappointed by Kilmory's personal behavior. Even though their sacred mission was to protect him at all times, Kilmory forced them to violate their job principles and instructions whenever he chose to consort with girl-friends or prostitutes who showed up on a regular basis at different times and places within the city of Washington, including the White House itself, or elsewhere in the country and abroad.

The Secret Service agents were told not to search or question the women who came to consort with the President. Very much displeased, they had to comply in violating strict regulations or else find themselves unemployed. Among the duties of the men in charge of protecting the President was that of warning him, during his skinny-dipping sex parties in and around the White House swimming pool, if his wife was on her way back. This was greatly facilitated by the fact that there were no women on the President's Secret Service details—it was all a confidential "guy" thing. In the event that his wife were on the way, the President, his two playmate-secretaries, nicknamed "Fiddle and Faddle," and whoever others participated—often including his brothers Roland and Jeff—would scramble out of the pool, put their clothes on and pretend that nothing out of the ordinary had been going on.

These activities were not limited to the White House or trips within the country. They also took place abroad, sometimes under extremely risky circumstances. When the Profumo scandal broke in Britain in the early sixties, eventually forcing Prime Minister Harold MacMillan out of office, President Kilmory kept a close eye on every bit of news on the matter, published or unpublished. There was an important reason for that. Some of the women involved in the scandal—the beauteous Mandy Rice Davis was one—who were suspected spies working for the communists, frequently flew across the Atlantic to provide their services to Kilmory himself, among

162

others in his administration. So Kilmory had an interest in making sure this side of the scandal did not become public, something he managed to do with his legendary control over the press..., plus a bit of luck.

If the public had ever learned that the President was involved in the British scandal and had been consorting with the very women who, personal behavior aside, were suspected of being serious security risks, his re-election would have been in extreme jeopardy, not to mention his very presidency. Besides, his chosen successor was not to be Vice President Jameson— scheduled to be dumped— but his brother Roland. So the whole dream of the Kilmory era was at stake. If such goings-on should have come to light, the dynasty in-the-making would probably have vanished like a noon fog in the tropics.

The president's sexual life, which involved in many cases risks to national security, was fodder for the conspiracy brewing against him. Men at the highest levels of the military, intelligence and law-enforcement agencies of the government were taking note of the leaks likely to occur during such encounters and the possibility of blackmail. Thus, at some point they either looked the other way or else became willing participants in the plot to get him out of the picture.

* * * * * * *

Even though Jameson had his own history of sexual secrets, the Kilmory plans for replacing him would not be dependent on that type of scandal, an issue which for decades he had managed to keep under wraps, and which the Kilmorys were also vulnerable to.

Even after Jameson's own death, it took thirty or forty years before the scandalous side of this secret personal life was brought to light. According to one anecdote, Jameson used to jump into bed with his secretaries and whisper: "You're not going to say 'no' to your president, are you?"

The Kilmorys were too vulnerable themselves in this area to bring up anything like this in order to oust Jameson. Their action would, rather, be based on charges of corruption arising during Jameson's tenure as a representative, senator and Senate Majority Leader. In other words, his wrongdoing was endemic during his whole career in politics. The Robby Ruker and Willie Sam Testes scandals brought up a lot of muck that could easily have cost him the vice presidency in Kilmory's coming reelection campaign.

The dirt, however, was a danger to Kilmory himself, particularly since it brought up the lovers provided him by the exclusive Capitol Hill Quota Club, run by none other than Robby Raker himself, who was Jameson's friend and confidant.

In any case the Kilmory plan was to force Jameson out and replace him with none other than brother Roland, to solidly establish the family dynasty. Was younger brother Jeff already scheduled, as well, to follow in his brothers' footsteps to the White House? If everything went well, why not?

It has eventually come out that in Jameson's past there was no shortage of all kinds of shady doings which were well covered up during his ascendancy. One of his henchmen, Mac Wallace, was a convicted killer who had taken out perhaps a dozen people that had stood in Jameson's way or might have become dangerous in terms of what they knew. Wallace was involved in a number of shady operations and hits ordered directly or indirectly by Jameson himself or through his higher echelon.

According to some sources, Wallace might even have disposed of Jameson's sister Joseline, who was a loose-lipped alcoholic known to be sexually promiscuous (to Jameson, a terrible fault, since promiscuity, he thought, should be reserved for men). She died mysteriously, attributed to natural causes, after a New Year's Eve party hosted by Jameson. Evidence of criminal activity in her case was quickly and efficiently disposed of—in effect, one might say, buried along with her body.

Jameson's incredibly crooked, kaleidoscopic past is, in fact, full of descriptive anecdotes. He was called "Bull" (for "bull shit") and "Lyin' Louie" by friends and acquaintances since his college days, sometimes to his face. He took special pride in his penis, which he was inclined to show off at the slightest provocation.

He liked to invite his male guests to strip and go "skinny dippin'" in the White House pool, an opportunity he took advantage of to call attention to his male member, which he called "Jumbo."

On one occasion, before a group of reporters on his ranch, he offered to compare his "Jumbo" with any of theirs. On another, when a reporter asked persistently why we were at war in Viet Nam, he unzipped his pants, pulled it out and said: "This is why." Not too surprising when we learn that his grandfather was a long-time cattle rustler in the Texas hill country where "Lyin' Louie" was born and raised. His huge ego required that "LBJ" appear everywhere: the names of his daughters, his ranch, his business, his personal flag and even his wife's name, which he changed to "Laura Bertha" to match the family's signature initials.

When cameras or recorders weren't running, he liked to call the people "pissants," and lost little opportunity to use the derogatory term whenever he could. And not just when he drank, which was often and in prodigious amounts. On such occasions, he was known for his mean and truculent humor, which inspired him to berate his assistants unmercifully. On Air Force One, complaining of a drink not to his liking, he emptied his glass on the carpet and said to the young steward: "Son, if you cain't make a proper drink, I'll sure as hell find me somebody who can." His subordinates were justifiably afraid of him. He once showered a tirade of profanity on a secretary for a clerical error, and berated another for a minor filing mistake.

One of the men who persisted in proceeding with one of the numerous corruption investigations while Jameson was Senate Majority Leader, Jackson Dunlop, was hounded, eventually ruined and forced to move away from his long-time residence to an undesirable out-of-state location.

But just as Jameson's attitude toward those who crossed him was implacable, his fondness for adulation knew no limits. One of his favorite sayings was: "I want 'em to kiss my ass and say it smells like roses." A variant was: "I want 'em to kiss my ass in Macy's window and say it smells like roses."

But since bad manners and a bad temper were not indictable offenses, it was in the area of corruption that Roland Kilmory found a trove of material on Jameson more than sufficient to end his political career, if not land him in "the penitentiary," as his own grandmother had often predicted.

Ever since he had issued thinly veiled threats to assure himself the second spot on the ticket in the 1960 election, Jameson had always ranked high on the Kilmorys' list of enemies and people he outright disliked. But Jameson was fawning, subservient and pretended not to notice. He had bigger things in mind when the time came.

In the fall of 1963 Kilmory had no inkling of the conspiracy brewing against him. Jameson's plan to fulfill his lifelong ambition to be president, at this stage of his life, would only have a prayer if he became vice president and something happened to Kilmory. That explains why he gave up the powerful position of Senate Majority Leader to be second man on the ticket, a job that John Nance Garner, who was Speaker of the House and gave it up to be Vice President under Franklin Delano Roosevelt, said "wasn't worth a bucket of warm spit." Clearly, the eventuality of succeeding to the presidency would be his only chance for it while simultaneously stopping the critical investigation being conducted against him by Attorney General Roland Kilmory. Jameson was kept up to date by his informants in the Justice Department about the rapidly-advancing probe against him.

Eventually, it would force him to resign and then send him and his associates to jail. Close to coming true was his grandmother's prediction: "That boy's gonna wind up in the penitentiary." She didn't know that he had solemnly promised himself to get to be president—by hook or, mainly, by crook.

Jameson was, however, extremely adept at covering his tracks. Now, even in the absence of any public scandal, he could not realistically wait for Kilmory to be out of office, since his own family's longevity made it clear that he would not live beyond his mid-sixties and he was already approaching his mid-fifties. For him, time was fast running out.

The Kilmorys were desperate for the Jameson investigation to be completed. They harbored an intense dislike for him, his boorish manners and lifestyle, particularly since Justin had been forced, as previously indicated, to bring him aboard as his vice presidential candidate when Jameson had shamelessly blackmailed him. Jameson had not been his preferred choice and he had, in fact, already asked another senator, Stan Stennington, to be his companion on the ballot.

But Jameson's foul tactics had prevailed against the advice and entreaties of nearly all Kilmory's advisors. Now, they hoped to shut down Jameson's political career. That way, according to patriarch Jonathan's original plan, the road would be open for Roland to succeed his brother Justin in the presidency for another two terms. Especially if Justin, after Jameson's resignation, named Roland as his running mate for the vice presidency. It might look like nepotism all right, but thus far they had gotten away with everything, so why not? Otherwise, Jameson might be the top contender for the presidential nomination after Justin's second term. Justin was fully expected to win reelection, if necessary by using the same tactics with which he was elected in the first place.

Jameson was keeping close tabs, through his inside informants, of the investigation being conducted against him by Roland. If something happened to President Kilmory before the investigation became public, Jameson would step neatly into the Oval Office. Then, brother Roland would be totally powerless, even if he remained—perhaps very briefly—as titular head of the Justice Department. Needless to say, the power of the presidency would then enable Jameson to quickly and definitively shut down Roland's investigation. But, are we getting ahead of our story?

President Kilmory, as we now know, cut quite a swath as a national and international lover of beautiful and famous women as well as lesser-known ones. He would also readily bed unknowns and high-priced call girls, occasionally more than one at a time, as long as they were young and very attractive.

Roland Kilmory was more discreet and reticent, but had his share of adventures. At one point as Attorney General he started going on drug busts and participating in their more illicit aspects. The busts would typically involve opium, hashish, heroin and cocaine. Agents who went along would report that he thought nothing of grabbing bags of cocaine for his own use or to pass on to his buddies. If hookers were around, he was not shy about fondling them or engaging them in intercourse with them, or prevailing on them to give him fellatio. Basically, he considered himself to be above the law. One agent said that Roland struck him as "basically schizophrenic..., capable of great good and, at a moment's notice, incredible evil." He went on to say that one of the call girls who practiced moderate S&M and was known to brother Justin turned down Roland's suggestion that they get together for a session, saying "I heard he was an out-and-out sadist." This might explain why he once threw an alleged black child-abuser to his death out of a sixth-floor window.

Justin was more even-tempered and sedate. Typical of his cool was an incident in one of his sexual adventures when the President convinced his Secretary of State to arrange for him to stay at a very special villa on Lake Como, in northern Italy. The Secretary, Dan Dusk, told the President that it would be difficult to arrange, but thinking that he would spend a day or two relaxing with the President at the villa, prevailed on its owner to let them use it. What Dusk did not know was that the President had arranged to be accompanied by the wife of Italian industrialist Giovanni Agnelli, with whom he had an occasional dalliance. When Air Force One landed in Milan, the President jauntily thanked Mr. Dusk and told the surprised Secretary that he would next see him back in Washington.

Roland Kilmory was not far below the standards of conduct set by his older brother. Once, he off-handedly told his Soviet hosts that he needed the company of a young woman for the evening in his hotel room in Moscow, where he had gone on official business early in the Kilmory administration. There is little question that, according to regular KGB procedure, he was filmed and later blackmailed when the Kremlin needed something important. One hates to think what concessions the Soviets demanded and got—the Bay of Pigs cave-in, the deal to defuse the Missile Crisis?—when they decided it was time to use the leverage so easily put in their hands.

This may have been only some of the evidence they had on the president and his brother to trump the U.S. when push came to shove. It is an intriguing matter that deserves to be further explored in view of the suspicious decisions concerning critical events.

First, Kilmory evidently gave up on the winning original formula for the Cuban invasion. And second, the denouement of the Missile Crisis, whose terms eventually proved unfavorable. As described in the press, the outcome was triumphant for Kilmory: the defeat was thus magically transmogrified into a propaganda coup. Curiously, it has been reported that it was Roland and not Justin— laid up with back trouble, we are told—who made the decision to withhold air support for the Bay of Pigs invaders.

Stretching believability to the breaking point, this sounds like his brother trying to let the president off the hook. Roland was not only willing to be the bad guy who took the rap, but also the one doling out punishment as required to spare the president the need to personally enforce discipline.

* * * * * *

The general course of events related to the conspiracy to kill the president leads to a close examination of the behavior of the Secret Service agents on the night of November 21, 1963. They were reported to be out late, bar-hopping, drinking and carousing in Dallas night-spots. It has not been clearly established that Rosenstein's "Caroussel" night club in Dallas was one such location where the Secret Service was getting in some R & R, yet neither has it been ruled out. The official investigation did not bother to look into it. In any event, they were lax and negligent of their duty to such an extent as to arouse suspicion that they were reacting to a lack of strict supervision if not actual instructions to not concentrate too much on doing their job. As demonstrated the very next day, that might have been precisely what was going on. Although witnesses have been reluctant to talk, information has later come to light about conversations overheard that night.

Rosswell's mission, as he understood it, was to infiltrate the conspiracy against the President and report back on what was happening. In actual fact he was kept in the dark as to the overall picture of what was in the works and given only a few fragments of innocuous information to keep him busy, duped and sheepdipped in what was supposed to be his "mission." He had been purposely made to look like a Costra sympathizer by putting him up to distributing leaflets in downtown New Orleans, supposedly on behalf of the "Fair

Play for Cuba Committee." In addition, he—or a doppelganger—had requested the Cuban Embassy in Mexico for authorization to travel to Cuba.

Some reports indicate that—far-fetched though it may seem—Rosswell was led to believe that he might actually be going on a mission to Cuba to take part in the assassination of Costra as well as in simultaneously coordinating actions to establish a provisional government on the island in connection with a new invasion planned for December 1, 1963. However, he was not necessarily informed of all this. He might have simply been told that he would get further instructions in the event that he had to travel to Cuba on a secret mission.

The idea was to leave a trail of evidence concerning Rosswell's leftist views that would make sense if and when he were accused of murdering the president. This might in turn justify the retaliatory invasion of Cuba, one of the Kafka-esque options being considered by the conspirators. Part of this evidentiary trail included the purported attempt to kill General Joseph Wolpert, which was in all likelihood a trumped-up story brought up after Rosswell's death to make him look even more like a violent, wild-eyed gunslinger capable of killing the president. His handlers were also counting on national security concerns, based on the fear of a nuclear war with the Soviet Union, to cover up the conspiracy and shield its participants from any public scrutiny.

Rosswell's Russian wife was also coerced by the FBI, after his death, to acknowledge that he was the likely assassin. The agents were very insistent; her cooperation, they promised, would insure her well-being far into the future. Otherwise, there was no telling what pitfalls might lay before her. Being no fool, she realized it was in her interest to play ball. Resisting would not have brought back her husband, nor helped her raise her innocent child.

The pieces of the puzzle were beginning to fall into place. The FBI, the Mafia and a few key CIA agents were lined up in a powerful, sinister conspiracy to eliminate the President of the United States, and no one in his administration, enveloped in its own fog of adulation and overconfidence, had the slightest inkling of what was brewing.

Chapter XXIV
GROUNDWORK

The wheels of conspiracy continued to turn, laying the groundwork for ambushing the president. While Rosswell was being set up as the patsy, the CIA-Mafia collaboration continued to work smoothly, led by mobsters Sal Campana, Sylvester Traficant and Claudio Mariello, but run on a day-to-day basis by the smooth, lower-profile Jake Rosetti.

Meanwhile, a wealthy aristocrat named Gregory de Morgenchild came on the scene, assigned by the CIA as Rosswell's handler. Morgenchild was a staunchly anti-communist Russian émigré coincidentally known to the Kilmorys, as well as to the families of two future presidents. Keen on his mission, De Morgenchild lost no time in becoming Rosswell's best and closest friend and, perhaps, even his homosexual lover (Rosswell was reputed to be bisexual, even though nothing about this was made public at the time). No one seemed to take notice of the abysmal social, cultural and economic differences between Rosswell and De Morgenchild. There was no good reason for them to be such close friends... unless there was something more to it than everyday intelligence gathering: aside from the secret plot against the incumbent president, perhaps homosex.

Whether or not the two were in a same-sex relationship, it appears that they were involved in the CIA-Mafia plot to, in effect, bring about a violent coup d'état in America. All indications are that De Morgenchild was doing a creditable job of fulfilling his CIA assignment as Rosswell's handler. Curiously, De Morgenchild was also acquainted with the Bouvine family, and had briefly dated Jean Bouvine (later to be Auchenbloss), Jennifer Kilmory's mother, at a time when they were both divorced. It's a small world—and a very curious one. Suspiciously, De Morgenchild later died in mysterious circumstances the day before he was to testify before a congressional committee investigating the Kilmory assassination.

(What a coincidence that so many witnesses mysteriously died on the eve of their scheduled congressional testimony!)

Was Rosswell, as he appeared to be, a bona fide member of the "Fair Play for Cuba Committee" (FPCC), for which he distributed leaflets on New Orleans streets and gave television interviews? In reality, he was probably the *only* member of that FPCC branch. But he played the part well. So well, that it seemed as though he had been groomed for it.

There was a reason for that: he needed to pass as solidly pro-Costra in order to establish credentials to convince the Cuban embassy in Mexico City to issue him a visa for travel to Cuba. Once there, he would supposedly act for U.S. intelligence as part of Q-Day and the plot to assassinate Costra. This is what Rosswell was told as a cover story for his actions if he had been, indeed, instructed to travel to Mexico on this supposed mission.

At the same time, being in contact with the FPCC in other cities, Rosswell served as an infiltrator spying on the pro-Costra movement for U.S. authorities while pretending to be actively involved in its activities.

A brief overview of Rosswell's background indicates that, contrary to stories bandied about in the press, he was not the ignorant, bigoted extremist he has been made out to be. A bright, articulate young man who always had his wits about him, he was promptly selected to receive special training as an intelligence agent. He was delighted, since he had always dreamed of going into this type of work. He had already done some communications intelligence work while stationed in Japan with the Marine Corps, including duties that put him in contact with those organizing and analyzing photographs taken over the Soviet Union by the super-secret U-2 spy plane. Rosswell also received extensive training in the Russian language and to that effect was assigned an attractive female instructor with whom he consorted while receiving special leave so he could get extra time with her to "improve his language skills." Having completed the first stage of his intelligence training, Rosswell was ready for the next step. He was instructed to go to the Soviet Union and present himself as a defector, on the pretense of being dissatisfied with the U.S. capitalist system.

He was perfect for the assignment since, thanks to his training, he was so fluent in Russian that when he met Maria, his future wife, she didn't immediately realize he was American. Interestingly, Maria was the daughter of a KGB colonel. This meant that: 1) Rosswell had done his job so well that not even his father-in-law suspected he was a U.S. agent, or else that (much more likely), 2) the Soviets, realizing that Rosswell had to be a U.S. agent, planned to turn him around and get him to work for them. At some point

Rosswell might have well become a double agent, or at least acted as such to the extent necessary to ensure his remaining in place, not to mention his own safety. If not, there were just too many red flags for the Russians not to have arrested him as a spy and sent him to Siberia—if not worse.

It is interesting to note that, according to some sources, Rosswell might have given the Soviets enough information—too much, in fact—to enable them to shoot down the U-2 overflying their territory in the late 1950's. In any event, it is quite unlikely that Rosswell would have been allowed to leave the Soviet Union with wife Maria if he had not made the Soviets believe that he would work for them within the U.S. Otherwise, why would the Soviets let a likely American spy get away scot-free?

In sum, Rosswell's level of experience in the spy business was considerable. He had, long before Dallas, been doing intelligence work for the FBI, the CIA, Defense Intelligence and possibly Naval Intelligence as well. So much for Rosswell's IQ, preparation, background and street smarts.

The intersection and conflation of intelligence activities and the conspiracy to kill the president was complex. Clearly, the CIA had enlisted the help of the Mafia to assassinate Costra and provide support for Q-Day, a fact not known to everyone involved since intelligence work is of necessity compartmentalized. Q-Day was the date for the second and presumably final, pull-out-all-the-stops Cuba-invasion plan headed by Roland Kilmory.

Rosswell's distribution of pro-Costra leaflets on a New Orleans street was merely an act, part of a trail of "evidence" purporting to establish his communist credentials and a preparatory step for future intelligence assignments that were an integral part in grooming him to be the eventual fall guy in the Kilmory assassination.

Another part of the trail was the so-called "Odio incident." In September 1963 Rosswell himself—or an impostor—showed up with two other men at the Dallas apartment of Sylvia Odio, the daughter of a Cuban exile leader, who had organized a chapter of the *Junta Revolucionaria,* JURE, to fight against Costra. A day later, the spokesman for the group called Ms. Odio to tell her that "Leon," as Rosswell called himself at the meeting, was an expert sharpshooter who would be happy to fulfill the hopes for Cuban freedom she harbored by killing President Kilmory. Whether or not Rosswell himself attended this meeting or was impersonated, it is clear that it could have had no purpose but that of reinforcing his credentials as the leading candidate (they had several) to be framed for the assassination. In fact, the top CIA and Mafia leaders, in their expertise, considered him the "perfect candidate."

As part of his work, therefore, Rosswell had dealings with a number of formal, informal and former intelligence operatives who were working on the twin projects involving the invasion of Cuba and the simultaneous assassination of Costra. Furthermore, as part of these activities, he knew and had dealings with Mafia members, including Jake Rosenstein, who were also working on the anti-Costra project. But since the Mafia had been "turned" and was, in reality, working for Costra and planning to assassinate Justin Kilmory instead, they saw Rosswell as the ideal patsy who could be easily manipulated and "sheepdipped"—i.e., groomed for the part—and then quickly taken out to prevent him from talking.

Given this background and Rosswell's role in the conspiracy as he understood it, he was asked to fire a stray shot at the president—not at all difficult, especially using an old and ineffective Manlicher-Carcano with an add-on, inaccurate telescopic sight. He was told that the objective was to provide the U.S. with an excuse to retaliate against the assassination attempt and invade Cuba, or at least force an improvement in presidential security. Thus, if Rosswell had anything to do with firing at the president, it was to act as a decoy. The conspirators would see to it that the real marksmen hired to do the job would accomplish their task.

In order to carry out such an assignment with maximum chances of success—a president who survived such an attack could be extremely dangerous to his attackers—a minimum of three snipers would be required in order to create a deadly crossfire.

Furthermore, their shots would have to be synchronized so as to take place simultaneously or within fractions of a second of each other.

This explains how Rosswell appeared, calm and collected, on a lower floor lunch room of the Texas School Book Depository, moments after the shooting. Rosswell himself indicated—and indeed gave every appearance—that he was unaware that the president had actually been shot. He had fired harmlessly as he was told and then quickly left his assigned position an instant before the actual assassins opened fire, trying to get away quickly and as far as possible from the open window. Witnesses to what transpired in the lunch room with Rosswell either vanished or claimed to have lost their memory.

When Rosswell heard the news that Kilmory had been actually shot was when he suspected, suddenly, that he might be the fall guy. If so, his life might be in danger. But he was confused and hoped that it might be safer to continue to play along. Shortly, he was told to go to a local movie there to meet his contact and receive further instructions. It was a public place where, in front of witnesses, he was unlikely to be shot on sight—which he knew was the most likely way a patsy would be silenced for good.

Rosswell was unaware of the mysterious murder of Dallas police officer Trapper, moments earlier, which was aimed at clinching the case against him by making him look like a zany killer on the loose who had not only shot the president dead but also, in quick succession, an officer who might have been trying to arrest him.

Little did Rosswell know that Trapper was supposed to have tracked him down and killed him immediately after the presidential shooting. When Trapper weakened and tried to back out, his accomplice and another mafioso chose to take him out on the spot, knowing that Rosswell would soon be shot and blamed for his death. Unfortunately for the conspirators, their timetable was destroyed and Rosswell survived for two more days, thereby making it much more difficult to wrap things up.

* * * * * * *

According to plan, after the assassination an investigative commission named by presidential successor Jameson would submit an exhaustive report on the crime and reach the desired conclusion: that Rosswell did it all by himself, autonomously and independently. In view of the ongoing projects to assassinate Costra and re-invade Cuba, it was in the interest of the conspirators and the government itself to cover everything up and blame a lone assassin. The need to avoid any further investigation was imperative, since that might bring out into the open the stolen 1960 election thanks to the deal with the Mafia, plus the secret plans in the works to again invade Cuba and overthrow Costra. Also, such further investigation would likely reveal chaotic intelligence failures and other breakdowns, including genuine mistakes and accidental or purposeful ones best withheld from the public.

To make sure nothing went wrong, such a commission would be stacked with those who could be relied on to cooperate and would be briefed on the "security" requirements so as to tie up any loose ends. One of the commission members would, in fact, be Alton Dunsell, the former CIA Director and stalwart Kilmory enemy, who was fired a couple of years earlier to take the rap for the Bay of Pigs fiasco.

Dunsell was picked by none other than Roland Kilmory, thanks to the "deference" of President Jameson, since he could be relied on to keep under wraps the damaging story of the plot against Costra and his regime, a project which was at the time momentarily paralyzed but still in the works. Roland agreed with Jameson that Dunsell was ideal. He would protect the secrets that each of them, for different reasons, needed to keep.

Congressman Gerhard Foster, later to be an unelected president, had a cozy relationship with FBI Director Hooper and would be the Bureau's point man within the commission that President Jameson would quickly appoint, against the advice of Director Hooper himself, who was unsure of the wisdom of such a move. But Jameson was unshakable in his conviction that, to get "ever'thing nailed down," as he liked to put it, the Kilmory assassination would have to be investigated by a top-level body that the country could have absolute faith in. Since Hooper had a dossier on Foster concerning his playtime activities at Capitol Hill's Quota Club, he could be trusted to keep the FBI up to date and steer the commission in the desired direction.

The Mafia conspirators, headed by Rosetti, contracted the professional marksmen needed to properly do the job. Among them were two Corsican hit-men imported from Marseilles, France—far enough away to make them difficult to trace. But, taking no chances, they also hired Cuban-exile sharpshooters angry at Kilmory for what they considered treason at the Bay of Pigs—ironically unaware that the President was preparing another, super-secret invasion of Cuba.

They also counted on "safe" CIA agents and regular Mafia hit-men. They made up enough teams to attempt the job in three cities. The killers would first attempt to shoot President Kilmory in Tampa, where on November 18 he was to visit and ride in a motorcade through the streets. However, when something there went awry and protection was beefed up, they were forced to cancel.

The next chance would be a couple of days later, during Kilmory's visit to Chicago, but that presidential trip was called off at the last minute when the Secret Service seemed to have gotten word that there was danger lurking there. Kilmory's Press Secretary, the plucky, phlegmatic Perry Soliger, said that the President was suffering from "a mild upper-respiratory infection" and had been forced to cancel the trip. Any special security measures for the president, it was felt, might tip off to Costra the planned invasion, and Kilmory was convinced of the need to pretend that everything was absolutely normal and was simply going about his scheduled political activities. One of the conspirators was working on him behind the scenes, convincing him to keep up the pretense that everything was under control and that he needed to keep to his expected schedule.

The conspirators had a third backstop up their sleeve: Dallas. Even after the Tampa and Chicago warnings, someone worked on his staff to promote the idea that the president travel to Dallas and participate in a long motorcade in the open-topped limousine. Texas being his home state, Vice President Jameson himself badgered Kilmory endlessly about going there on the pretext of drumming up support for the 1964 election and unifying the Democratic Party, then in the midst of a rift. Even though he had told many of his closest friends and supporters that he didn't really want to go to Dallas, Kilmory finally agreed. Since he had given his word he felt unable to back out.

The Mafia, through its contacts with the CIA, made efforts to allay the concerns of the Secret Service about exposing Kilmory to danger. The president's protectors were, if not complicit, sedulously led into a state of unconcern and relaxation. But the conspirators had a trump card: the head of the Secret Service itself—a close friend and confidant of Jameson surnamed Rowley—had been incorporated into the conspiracy and was actively paving the way for the hit.

For their part, the Mob had plans that were solid and far-sighted. The Corsican sharpshooters were brought in via Mexico from Marseille. Other teams of sharpshooters had been ready to act in Tampa and Chicago. The ones for Dallas were put up in a downtown safehouse in late October of 1963, ready to act when the time came. They had time to scout around for a good location along the President's likely motorcade, which was being planned by the conspirators to run through the ideal location: Haley Plaza. That was nailed down by choosing the Dallas Trade Mart for the luncheon meeting, since it forced the motorcade to traverse Haley Plaza. That route would require slow turns and provide perfect vantage points for a deadly triangular crossfire from the grassy knoll to the right, the railroad overpass ahead and, to the rear, the higher floors of two structures: the Texas School Book Depository and a building across the street.

The Trade Mart was picked thanks to the efforts of Texas Governor Jesse Donnelly, another conspirator. The head of the Secret Service realized that it was perfect for the shooting and gave his approval. Governor Donnelly's office released the President's route well ahead of time so it would be published in the papers, on the pretense that it would allow the public to gather and see the president.

Especially if brought in by intermediaries, imported hit-men are always considered much safer for important "jobs": after the mission is accomplished, they are promptly and clandestinely whisked out of the country. While inside the country, they lie low and, if seen, are unidentified strangers. Local hit-men, on the contrary, are much more vulnerable, since they immediately become likely suspects and tend to stick around their usual surroundings.

In the Dallas venue, the one remaining opportunity after Tampa and Chicago, the Corsican hit-men would do their job and then, according to plan, simply wait for the "heat" to abate before being flown via private jet to Canada. Ultimately, it was decided to ensure the result by entrusting the job to a total of three teams of sharpshooters: in addition to the Corsicans, there would be back-up teams made up, respectively, of Mafia men and Cuban exiles.

Dallas was a pre-campaign trip. In order to get maximum exposure to the voters and improve Kilmory's chances for the 1964 election, the conspirators, including the head of the Secret Service, instructed that the bubbletop be removed from the presidential limousine. Since Kilmory usually trusted the Secret Service and went along willingly with its decisions concerning his security, he assumed that everything was being taken care of and he would be safe enough. As a cover, the conspirators indicated that the reason for not using the bubbletop was that the president himself had said it would make him look too lofty, regal and unreachable—almost like a monarch, the antithesis of a democratic American president. No one was willing to go against "the President's wishes." The so-called bubbletop, made of very solid plastic, would have considerably obstructed the sharpshooters' view and in any case deflected bullets sufficiently to make it extremely difficult to hit the target.

The Secret Service Chief went along gladly with the plans and, following instructions, specified to the Dallas Police that they were to provide protection to the president only to the corner of Main and Houston Streets, where stood the police station itself at the entrance to Haley Plaza. From there, he specified that the Secret Service was to take over.

This was one of the cornerstones of the whole plan: to leave the Chief Executive at the mercy of his executioners in Haley Plaza. To get additional "insurance," real Secret Service agents were instructed to stay away from the Plaza, while impersonators, equipped with badges and authentic-looking credentials were put in their place in strategic locations, including the infamous grassy knoll. These "agents" had been schooled in advance on what to do and were assured that no actual agents would interfere with them.

Suitable excuses or cover stories were made up by the highly placed conspirators in answer to any unexpected questions that might arise. When someone with sufficient authority said that "the president would like" something to be done, everyone would get into line. The plot required, for purposes of secrecy, that the number of people "in the know" about the real whys and wherefores be kept to an absolute minimum.

The president did not suspect that anything was afoot. If he did, his natural inclination was to affect an air of devil-may-care fearlessness. After all, he had gone through Tampa and many other cities in an open-topped car and nothing had happened. He was aware of the enemies he had made, but his attitude and demeanor indicated that he never quite brought himself to believe that any of them would go so far as to do him physical harm. Accordingly, he dismissed any thoughts of violence against him as fairly close to an impossible nightmare.

Yet he did have a premonition. "You know," he told his wife before leaving the White House on the morning of November 22, "one of these days, someone with a high-powered rifle could shoot me just like that!" He snapped his fingers. We don't know what her answer was.

Regardless, the die had been cast. Since neither Kilmory nor anyone around him could have imagined the Haley Plaza sniper crossfire that was about to unfold, the open limousine didn't seem to make that much difference. None of his advisers made any attempt to intervene. They thought that's the way the president wanted it. So, when someone higher up gave the order—"remove that bubbletop unless it's pouring rain"—off it went. The conspirators couldn't have been more delighted. With the bubbletop on, the hit would have been extremely difficult if not nearly impossible. Now, everything was falling into place.

The Corsican snipers, in coordination with another team of sharpshooters also hired by the Mafia, closely studied maps of the motorcade route, courtesy of the local print media, and carefully inspected the locations in person from various angles. Since a crossfire was called for—the results of such an ambush had to be one-hundred-percent deadly—they looked for an appropriate place that would meet this requirement. When it was confirmed that the route would traverse Haley Plaza, they seized on its ideal topography, scouted out the area and chose the optimum positions for posting themselves. One of them was the grassy knoll.

The School Book Depository was not initially considered that good a location. One of its negatives was that, should any of the sharpshooters be seen firing from or get caught there, it would destroy the plan to make Rosswell the single culprit. That would give rise to a series of problems, not least of which would be the unraveling of the actual assassination conspiracy. In addition, the distance-to-target would be greater, thus enhancing the chances of missing the objective.

All things considered, it was finally chosen as one of the sniper locations, since it would make it easier to incriminate Rosswell, who was known to work there and besides, would be involved in shooting, albeit as a decoy. Careful analysis showed that the best results would likely come from having one shooter fire from in front of the motorcade, hiding somewhere in the railroad overpass, while a second one would shoot from the right, behind the fence on the grassy knoll. The third would fire from behind, posting himself at a suitable window within the Book Depository, away from Rosswell's window but closer to target.

The sharpshooters were instructed to synchronize their fire as precisely as possible so that, the shots being nearly simultaneous, their cumulative impact would be even more deadly, with greater probability that one or more bullets would find their target at nearly the same instant. They most likely were to commence firing based on when the presidential limousine would reach a predetermined spot, in this case a street sign. This happened to be the very sign that hid the presidential limousine from the camera that took the only complete film of the assassination, obstructing the view for a critical instant just after the president was hit in the neck by the first bullet. Rosswell was told to fire his rifle when the presidential limousine arrived at the same predetermined point. Therefore the shots would all be fired simultaneously or at such close intervals as to make it difficult to differentiate them or where they came from.

Thus, the plan of simultaneous firing accomplished several things: it confused witnesses as to the direction whence the shots came, as well as to their number. It was also a much more effective tactic. Bullets that impact a target at extremely close intervals are apt to cause a lot more physical damage, not to mention shock. Hence, death from multiple impacts, even if no single one were by itself critical, would be much more likely.

Vice President Jameson, once installed as president, would be in an ideal position to organize the cover-up through the enormous power and far-reaching tentacles of his office.

Jameson always exercised power as ruthlessly against his underlings as he was correspondingly obsequious to his superiors; that is, until he got to the top. He was in the habit of saying, as he stood waving to crowds from a suitable vantage point where he could not be heard: "You bunch of sons of bitches, I piss on all of you."

As for the motorcade through Dallas, he had arranged for his limousine to be well behind the presidential one. His attitude when the bullets were flying was protective of himself, supplying minimal exposure to any that might have strayed off target.

The investigation into Jameson's wrongdoing had been relentlessly pushed forward by his nemesis Roland Kilmory, and he was close to being dumped from the 1964 electoral ticket. But the old fox had maintained, for decades, good and mutually profitable relations with the top capos of organized crime, as well as with the capos' friend and confidant, FBI Director H. Everette Hooper.

He had made a lot of friends in the Congress during his years as a representative and, later, Senate Majority Leader. He felt well covered on all sides. If something should happen to Justin Kilmory his dream of being president would come true. Then Roland, that "despicable little son of a bitch"—as he called him—who had made his life miserable, would be in line to get a taste of his of own medicine: contempt, scorn and whatever else he could think of without being too obvious about it, avoiding anything that the public might see as disrespectful of his deceased brother.

Now, the hour was close at hand, and he was in his own territory. Advantage, home team.

Chapter XXV
STRATEGY

Costra felt secure. Having made his deal with the Mob, he had the added satisfaction that they would not even collect the full bounty expected for Kilmory's head. He would insist on results first. Then he would order the balance of the fee—payable "on delivery"—withheld and sent back to him in Cuba. His friend and accomplice Negoria, the strongman who ran Panama, would take his cut and see that everything went smoothly. The collaboration of Negoria, a fellow member of Costra's on Kilmory's "overthrow" list, offered a great advantage. He would be glad to keep secret the transfer of money, even though not knowing that it was for putting a bounty on Kilmory's head. All evidence of financial transactions would be wiped out. No record of money changing hands; ergo, no proof.

Costra's vast intelligence network had lately unearthed inside information that the Mob was, for its own reasons, probably making plans to get rid of Kilmory. But the Cuban capo was going to take no chances, and was not about to back out on the deal. What he was doing was buying additional insurance. Not overlooked, in his view, was the personal satisfaction of being part of the conspiracy to rub out his arch-enemy.

Now there was no need to do anything but sit back and enjoy the show. Sharing power with no one was a great feeling! The Mob's tentacles could no longer touch him, especially since it was working for him. They could no longer muscle in on any of the lucrative businesses he now controlled, exploiting Cuba and Cubans as his own private property. According to his own long-range plan, hatched in the late 1940's—when he was barely in his mid-twenties—he needed to be the one and only boss, with no unpredictable partners such as the mafiosi, who might suddenly decide to make a move that might prove to be unhealthy—such as "clipping" him.

Their agenda was criminal; his, political *and* criminal. When combined with political power, criminality was perfectly protected and legitimate, and could be conducted with total impunity. Political criminals are free to pursue and peruse the "golden fleece": their own material well-being, power being the spring and source from which all else flows.

But now that he, Costra, had taken over everything the Mob owned in Cuba—all private property, in fact, whomever it belonged to—he was glad that he didn't need to twist arms to get his way. The mobsters, for all intents and purposes, were now on his side. But that was no reason not to betray them. In fact, just the opposite. Betrayal was one of the things that gave him the most pleasure—particularly when unexpected by the betrayed.

Costra was taking pleasure in "reports from the front" that reached him regularly. He would eventually receive them from Nicaragua, Guatemala and assorted other Central and South American countries. Plus Africa, where his expeditionary troops would defeat the forces of embryonic democracies in countries from Ethiopia to Angola. His advisors and emissaries posted in North Viet Nam were already laying the groundwork for drawing the Americans into further involvement there, advising the North to lull the U.S. by allowing it to make some headway in the war. Their aim was to lure America into thinking that it would be able to win the conflict in relatively short order. Why, it might even occur to the U.S. that if things went well they could declare victory and then pull out. But, hah, only in their dreams would that work out for them!

In any case, the strategy was working and the Americans were being bogged down and bled dry. Meanwhile, the North was building up its strength to launch a powerful counter-move, as it eventually did with the Tet offensive. That way, there would be less American pressure on Costra's Cuba. Eduardo Guevero, the legendary Argentine-born revolutionary who was later killed in Bolivia by the CIA—thanks to Costra's betrayal—had loudly proclaimed the slogan: "Two, three... many Viet Nams." During the war years, Costra agents not only advised the North, but also went to Viet Nam to personally torture American prisoners, a fact which mysteriously got no publicity in America. Were U.S. government leaders afraid to be forced to take retaliatory action against Costra's Cuba?

Kilmory's plan about Viet Nam was still unclear but less than aggressive than Jameson's, which he had perfectly outlined for himself well in advance of events. Based on carefully contrived and apparently compelling reasons, he led America deeper into the Viet Nam quagmire.

It was part of a long-term scheme to extract huge payoffs from the humongous profits of the military-industrial complex, denounced by Eisenhower a few years back. Jameson was counting on that when he arranged to reverse Kilmory's plan to start withdrawing from what used to be known as Indo-China. Also, as Roosevelt and other presidents had amply demonstrated, defeating a war-time president is nearly impossible. So, seeing war as a virtual slam-dunk guarantee of re-election, Jameson was going for it full-force.

As Kilmory grappled with Viet Nam, he had been reticent about becoming more involved or even escalating the presence of American advisors there. The first steps into Viet Nam had been taken by the previous administration. When Kilmory took over, he and his closest advisors at first considered that, in view of the loss of Cuba, it was necessary to take a stand against communism elsewhere and show the Soviets that the U.S. couldn't be pushed around. But he wasn't sure. Viet Nam brought up unexpected problems. Justin was having trouble controlling the regime of South Viet Nam President Nguyen Diat and concluded that he had to go. Diat was intractable, so Justin and the CIA felt justified to back the South Vietnamese faction who wanted to overthrow him.

Whether by design, accident or uncontrollable elements, when the plot was put into action and his regime was suddenly overthrown, Diat and his brother were assassinated forthwith. Justin was shocked, having been told that the coup would be bloodless and the deposed leader and his family would be allowed to go into exile. The lone voice of protest was that of Diat's widow, whose accusations were widely publicized in the U.S. and worldwide. But to no avail: Diat was dead, his enemies were in power and a new regime more amenable to U.S. control was in place. Kilmory was said to be extremely upset—not just at the violent outcome, but at not having expected it.

Justin wanted to contain the communists, but at the same time, he was loath to stretch U.S. resources too thin, since he was putting together his second attempt to invade Cuba and overthrow Costra.

Slowly, he came to the realization that his military advisors might be right: Viet Nam could be a bottomless pit in which the U.S. might find itself bogged down if it attempted to put its troops into a land war.

Nonetheless, he worried about the political danger about being accused of weakness against communism and decided to delay pulling out until after being reelected.

Also, the Kilmory brothers were still seriously concerned about Cuba. Angry about the failure of the Bay of Pigs operation, which Justin publicly blamed on the CIA, they still felt it as a personal insult that had to be redressed. This time it would not be a rag-tag force of Cuban exiles, but something more substantial. If worse came to worst, regular U.S. forces would become involved— mostly the Marines. In early 1962 he gave the Pentagon orders to begin assembling the troops, planes and materiel to carry out a full-scale invasion of the island. He had to justify the use of U.S. troops by staging an internal coup in Cuba by anti-Costra leaders who would then form a provisional government and call on the U.S. for help. This, in order to prevent the Russian troops stationed on the island from attempting a counter-coup.

Aware of the plan through their own and Costra's effective intelligence services, the Soviets were preparing counter-measures. Cuba was a prized base in the Western Hemisphere, the proverbial 90 miles away from the U.S. Nuclear ICBMs launched from the island could reach major U.S. cities such as Washington and New York within minutes, posing a threat that the USSR could easily exploit. The Soviets would not and could not lose this coveted base that, thanks to Costra, had landed in their lap almost by accident. They were busy building launching pads in Cuba and preparing to ship the requisite ICBMs and nuclear warheads that, within a very brief time window, would threaten major U.S. cities with sudden annihilation.

The Kilmorys, wanting to keep personal control, had their back-channel contact with the Russians, bypassing the State Department and all other top government agencies, including the Executive Committee—"Ex Com" for short. An advisory body to the Office of the President, Ex Com was entrusted with deliberating and making major policy decisions in the anti-Soviet Union cold-war arena. But the back channel, run by brother Roland, made it possible to hold secret meetings with Soviet Ambassador Dubrovnik and make private deals that no one else would be privy to, while preventing sensitive information from leaking out.

The back-door meetings with Dubrovnik, which went on for some time, did not bring about the results hoped-for by the U.S. But Roland and Justin, ever boldly individualistic and self-confident believers in "gunslinger frontier justice," felt they were achieving, in the long run, the best that could be expected in a difficult situation. They went full speed ahead, ready to ride roughshod over traditional diplomacy and the well-established, time-tested procedures. As long as they achieved their objectives, "full speed ahead and damn the torpedoes."

A secret deal was made with Ambassador Dubrovnik. If the USSR withdrew its missiles and nuclear weapons from Cuba—subject to inspection—the U.S. would find an excuse, apparently unrelated to the crisis, to take its missiles out of Turkey. Those missiles were threatening to the Soviets and their withdrawal would cool off the situation. Also, the USSR demanded and got from the Kilmorys public assurances that the U.S. would not invade Cuba or allow any other country to do so.

This whole scenario of back-door deals was a great secret advantage that enabled the Kilmorys to keep many things private, including their personal vulnerabilities.

"You should know, Mr. Attorney General, that we have in our archives a great deal of information, including film and still photographs showing the president and you yourself in sexually compromising situations. But you can be sure that we won't release any of this—that is, of course, assuming we reach satisfactory agreement on this matter. Failing that, we might have no alternative," Dubrovnik said with a condescending smile. "We are hopeful, naturally, that it will not come to this." The Soviet Ambassador barely repressed a confident look of satisfaction and strained to appear serious and concerned, despite his winning gambit. He was playing the clincher, the ace up his sleeve.

"I don't expect that it will come to that at all, Mr. Dubrovnik," Roland replied, barely batting an eyelash, but realizing the import of his words. By now he was painfully aware that in a high-stakes poker game like this, his opposite number would pull out all the stops and was hardly surprised. For one thing, he recalled his own visit to the Soviet Union, at the beginning of his brother's administration, and the request for female company that he had recklessly made of his Russian hosts. The material on Justin was likely to be much more extensive.

The agreement was publicly acclaimed and proclaimed as a back-down by the USSR, which would unilaterally take its missiles and nuclear weapons out of Cuba. On-site inspections would be a matter to be agreed upon at some point by the presumably autonomous Costra government; who knew what would happen with that? The important thing was that the earth-shaking, possible nuclear-holocaust crisis was averted with what to all appearances looked like a smashing victory for the U.S. The two superpowers signed on to it, relieved to put the crisis behind them, even if the Soviets licked their chops as their prized Cuban base was declared safe from any and all external threats.

The Kilmorys breathed easier. They had gotten out of the jam with a face-saving deal. Yet they were not going to stand still. Wasting no time, they began preparations for the second invasion of Cuba, combined with the prior assassination of Costra, as called for by the original plan of the unfortunate Bay of Pigs operation.

Meanwhile, Roland Kilmory had conspired with Argentine-born revolutionary icon Eduardo Guevero to help get rid of his boss, Costra, when Guevero was in New York to address the United Nations on behalf of Costra himself. It went nowhere. Jealous of Guevero's prestige and hardly trusting him, Costra later plotted Guevero's eventual downfall in Bolivia, preferring a dead hero to a live rival for fame and glory.

Curiously, a few years later, in the middle of Roland's campaign for the presidential nomination of his party, he was asked what he thought about Guevero. His answer should be etched in stone as a monument to hypocrisy, mass ignorance, a nod to doctrinaire leftism and, no doubt, votes: "Guevero was a revolutionary hero." By that standard one could say that so was Adolf Hitler. One wonders what his brother Justin would have thought of that. However, like the views of most politicians—i.e., unprincipled opportunists—Roland's clearly changed according to the winds blowing at the time, regardless of contradictions.

Although his brother Justin Kilmory had been wary of falling into the trap set by North Viet Nam and Costra, Jameson would drastically change the situation as soon as he assumed power by continually escalating the war. At first, Kilmory had seemed to agree that the U.S. could not afford to have another country, no matter how far away, fall to the communists: the old "domino" theory was raising its false, ugly head once again.

Therefore he started out by holding to the status quo and choosing to stand his ground in Viet Nam. The Russians, the Chinese, the Cubans and the rest of the communist camp were quietly cheering inside their skin. The U.S. could eventually be drawn further in; thus, the Soviet's rival superpower would be weakened militarily and politically and, probably, suffer turmoil within its own borders as a result of such a senseless conflict.

They had no idea how right their theory would turn out to be. Once Jameson took over he kept well in mind the admonition that no war-time president had ever been voted out of office, and accordingly escalated the war. To clinch it, he arranged for a trumped-up incident in the Gulf of Tonkin. On the excuse that U.S. naval vessels had supposedly been attacked by North Viet Nam, Jameson launched full-scale U.S. involvement. But after a few initial victories, Guevero's slogan about multiplying the "Viet Nams" stung

Jameson like a slap in the face. Just a single Viet Nam was turning out to be more, much more, than America could stomach. Men were dying on the battlefield for land on the other side of the world while in America people were demonstrating on the streets against the carnage.

But before it came to that, the "front" that interested Costra most was the conspiracy to take out the upstart President of the United States, whose inexperience at the international power game and vulnerability were evidenced by the Bay of Pigs and the consequent Missile Crisis. Kilmory's weakness also showed in his earlier meeting in Vienna with the uncouth Russian leader Krustivich, viewed as the clean winner of that encounter.

"I am sure you realize, Mr. Krustivich, that a nuclear exchange would very quickly kill tens of millions of people in different countries—yours and mine, mainly." Kilmory had said in one of their sessions.

"So?" Krustivich replied, as if to say that he wasn't at all concerned about it. "You know, our great leader Stalin once said that the death of one person is a tragedy, while the death of millions is simply a statistic."

In the Bay of Pigs, Kilmory practically gave up without a fight. In the Missile Crisis, he chose not to press his advantage with the blockade, and then never followed up on the agreed-upon on-site inspections.

Costra recalled with satisfaction his critical role in those U.S. disasters. Instead of following through and actually winning the confrontation, Kilmory had been content with the appearance of "winning" the missile crisis while losing the overall battle.

The possibility of blackmail was never alluded to by the press, as Costra eventually boasted that he had urged Krustivich to launch a nuclear strike on the United States. He had meant to be menacingly clear about how dangerous and reckless he could be, and succeeded in making himself believable.

In sum, the Soviet-Cuban military and strategic victories— and Costra's permanent hold on power—were the result of Kilmory's hand having been held back by threats to leak secret information about his personal life, corruption and criminal activities, the revelation of which would have likely ended his political career, and not just his then-current presidential term.

Costra expected his bold and risky attitude to be an advantage if the planned hit on Kilmory succeeded. Afterward, presidential successor Jameson would prefer to avoid trouble with him at a time of national crisis and transition. For him, it stood to reason that Jameson would invoke "national security" arguments to avoid a confrontation over Cuba. As president, he would also be in a perfect position, through the enormous power and sway of his office, to influence media coverage of Kilmory's assassination to keep it as an exclusively domestic affair, with no international connections. It proved to be prescient, smoothly simple. Not a ripple in sight. As it turned out, the U.S. Government as a whole, as well as the Kilmorys themselves, preferred it that way.

* * * * * * *

If Kilmory's assassination went well, Jameson's priority was that, as soon as it happened—without wasting a split second in protocolary formalities—he must arrange to take the oath of office forthwith. That was not a necessary step, since upon the president's demise the vice president automatically assumes office. However, Jameson wanted a ceremonial, swearing-in moment in order for the country to see a smooth and effective transition of power in the presence of Kilmory's widow and top staff.

Besides protecting himself and his co-conspirators, Jameson kept in mind the need to not reveal suspected Cuban involvement until a choice could be made between Plan A and Plan B.

Plan A would blame a deluded, lone patsy who would be promptly silenced, enabling a complete cover-up of the conspiracy, while Plan B would blame whatever happened to Kilmory on a Costra plot and require retaliation by invading Cuba. Plan B had inherent dangers, such as the risk of war, possibly nuclear, against the Soviet Union. Plus, it was suspected in the innermost recesses of the presidency and the CIA that the Soviets still had nuclear missiles or other weapons of mass destruction in Cuba. Even more serious was the fact that Costra was on record as having recklessly urged, during the crisis, that nuclear missiles be launched against the U.S. According to intelligence reports, it was Costra who personally took over a Soviet SAM battery and shot down the U-2 that was overflying Cuba while trying to photograph the Soviet missile installations.

All of this, Costra expected, could not fail to work in his favor if Jameson, as he suspected, were involved with the Mafia in the planned hit on the president, as his efficient intelligence service had already reported. If the assassination of Kilmory were successful, Jameson might try to deflect suspicion from himself by blaming Costra. But the nuclear-missile factor and Costra's reckless reputation would make Jameson think twice about the consequences of going for Plan B, the attack on Costra. He was, no doubt, a tough customer. As it turned out, Plan B was no longer viable when Rosswell was not immediately killed. Arrested, he had managed to make some statements on camera that brought forth contradictions in the background story.

At one point, when Costra realized that U.S.-directed attempts were being made on his life, he had said ominously that "United States officials should be warned that, considering their plots to eliminate him, they themselves could not expect to be safe from similar actions." Clearly, Kilmory did not take him too seriously.

Costra was satisfied that he had all the bases covered. He was gratified that the Missile Crisis had yielded a positive net result: Kilmory had given a guarantee that the U.S. would not invade Cuba; furthermore, he had actually pledged that the U.S. would also prevent other countries from doing so. It would be perfectly safe to continue his campaign against the United States all over Latin America as well as throughout the world at large.

He would strengthen his alliance with the Soviet Union, keep Cuba locked up and use all his resources to promote communist takeovers and revolution elsewhere, including support for North Viet Nam. Even the Soviets themselves could not have put together a better blueprint for safe and gradual, relentless expansion.

It is possible that, had he not been shot, Kilmory would have succeeded in getting rid of Costra by means of the carefully planned, well-organized invasion-cum-assassination scheduled to be launched December 1, 1963.

But thanks to the leaks and failures of U.S. agencies like the FBI and the CIA, which worked closely with the Mafia, plus the work of his own efficient intelligence apparatus, Costra had gotten a step ahead.

Chapter XXVI
HALEY PLAZA

We overthrew the government
and nobody was the wiser.
—Sal Campana

The night before the Dallas presidential visit, November 21, 1963, the Secret Service team assigned to protect Kilmory was out drinking and carousing—perhaps engaging an occasional prostitute—around the night spots and strip joints. Why? Was it carelessness or purposeful neglect?

The lower echelons of the Secret Service, although not in on the conspiracy, were aware of the slack, unworried general atmosphere. The attitude was one of laid-back, almost studied unconcern. Secret Service Chief Rowley made it a point to convey to his agents that impression. Without saying a word—much safer—he intimated that they could be lax about fulfilling their duties and no one would hold them accountable. The unspoken "instructions" were loud and clear.

A young woman who worked at one of the Dallas night spots visited by them, later said that the Secret Service agents were around until the small hours of the night having a whale of a time. Hardly what one would expect of those entrusted with the safety of the President of the United States, who was to arrive the next morning and ride through the city in an open limousine. Years later the woman confessed that, on that particular evening, in one of the night spots where the Secret Service team gathered, she had heard remarks indicating President Kilmory would be "hit" the next day. She informed authorities of what she had heard, but they dismissed the idea as too far-fetched. What? No just-in-case measures? Were they, too, told to lay back?

No one asked her if she had been threatened, then or later, if she didn't keep her mouth shut.

* * * * * * *

That morning, Rosswell went to work as usual. Although unaware of what was actually going to take place, he no doubt knew that the moment was crucial, since the President was about to arrive in town.

He clearly knew that something was brewing since, having been led to believe that his job was to spy on the conspirators and secretly report on their activities, he must have been fed some information, however false, as "cover," in order to continue the pretense of keeping him informed and "in the loop." Furthermore, he was to fire harmlessly with the Manlicher-Carcano from a window of his building, which he was told would serve certain purposes to be explained later. The conspirators kept him in the dark about the fact that the assassination was for real, using highly skilled sharpshooters and special weapons. A sophisticated Mauser rifle—probably one of those actually used in the crime—was later found hidden under some boxes in the "sniper's nest" where Rosswell was supposed to have fired from. The Mauser soon disappeared and never resurfaced.

Did Rosswell actually carry the old-fashioned Manlicher-Carcano rifle to the Book Depository building, or was he set up and asked to bring in a long box whose contents he might have ignored? After all, he was, quite unwittingly, a plant in the plot against Kilmory, and had no inkling—yet—of the danger he was in. On the excuse that he had to make himself believable to the conspirators as a bona fide part of their operation, his handlers had already, as part of his preparation, asked him to do a number of unusual things. He was told that "security reasons" precluded them from providing any detailed explanation for the actions he was to take. That was standard procedure in the "sheepdipping" or grooming of a patsy.

Circumstantial evidence, such as the Manlicher-Carcano rifle, was being carefully planted so that the assassination could be pinned on him. He was at one point shown the rifle in order for it to have his fingerprints on it. They were so smudged, however, that only a partial and inconclusive print was identified. Everything hinged, naturally, on eliminating Rosswell himself as soon after the deed as was humanly possible, so he couldn't exonerate himself by telling his own story, thereby destroying the single-assassin theory and bringing the conspiracy to light. Alive, Rosswell would be able to tell all kinds of tales and reveal a series of dots and loose ends which, once connected, could provide enough critical information to unravel the whole plan.

* * * * * * *

Meanwhile, in Paris, a high-ranking CIA official named Del FitzPatrick, as a personal representative of Attorney General Roland Kilmory, interviewed Ronaldo Cubeñas—known as AMLASH—a presumed double agent with access to Costra and the Cuban *nomenclatura*. His mission was to hand him a Paper Mate ball-point specially designed with a poisoned needle that would deliver a lethal dose to the Maximum Leader. Little did they know that Cubeñas was in fact a double agent all right, but loyal to the Leader, having been planted by Cuba's DGI (General Directorate for Intelligence), headed personally by Fingenio himself in order to outwit the CIA. Costra delighted in playing mind games with American spymasters, defeating them left and right as if they were but amateurs. America's intelligence apparatus hardly dreamed that the Cuban DGI was one of the best espionage organizations in the world, on a par with the CIA itself and Israel's Mossad; it had fewer material and electronic resources but its agents were first-rank and their strategy, directed by Costra, was cleverness personified. Its agents are reputedly ensconced in the innermost recesses of the U.S. government, including the intimate presidential circle, and within its intelligence agencies.

The DGI agents were and still are to be found in all Cuban diplomatic missions abroad, particularly in Mexico City, and in presumed cultural centers such as the Casa de las Americas (CdA), whose branches cover Europe and Latin America with the supposed objective of promoting cultural exchange and «the friendship of peoples». Actually, the CdA was and continues to be a beehive of espionage and infiltration, manipulation and other subversive activities.

But the poisoned pen was a jerry-rigged, low-quality device and, even in the improbable case that Ronaldo Cubeñas would have had a last-minute change of heart and had attempted its use, he would have been most unlikely to succeed. Of course, Kilmory's death changed everything and Cubeñas returned to Cuba to tell Costra the story, laughing at the CIA for having placed its bets on him. The latest news from Cubeñas is that he was holding a relatively comfortable official job and living well. If he had been disloyal to the Leader he would have hardly lived much longer than Costra's arch-enemy, Kilmory.

* * * * * * *

At about the noon hour, crowds had begun gathering along the presidential route, particularly in Haley Plaza. Minutes later, gunfire rang out, forever changing history. In the initial confusion only the eyewitnesses realized the gravity of the event. However, it was only a matter of minutes before the news that bullets had hit the President and the Texas Governor spread like wildfire.

Justin Kilmory was first hit in the neck as Governor Donnelly was hit in the back, wrist and leg (chances that a single bullet did all that are slim, to say the least—nonexistent would be closer). In seconds, the President's head was blown apart by one or probably two simultaneous hits, thanks to the crossfire of dum-dum bullets designed to shatter on impact and shred the target. (Consequently, the intact bullet found on a stretcher in Parkland Hospital was nothing more than a decoy planted there.) This did not prevent the Garrett Commission from putting together its infamous "magic bullet" theory, by which it attempted to attribute to a single bullet the wounds caused by a number of rounds that found their mark. Evidence that yet another bullet had been fired and missed—possibly from Rosswell's rifle in the simulated assassination attempt he was entrusted with—came up when a sidewalk was found to be chipped by a round that totally missed its target. It had sent off a chip of concrete that hit a bystander, causing a slight wound.

However, the Garrett Commission needed to attribute all the shots to Rosswell and to him only. If not, speculation about more than one shooter might result in unwanted questions and doubts which might, in turn, result in exposing the conspiracy, as well as plans for the next invasion of Cuba and the simultaneous assassination of Costra. The administration, as the Mafia capos knew, was willing to go to any lengths to prevent any such information from becoming public. The plans against Cuba were still ongoing and secrecy about them was paramount.

As soon as Rosswell learned that the president had been hit, he got an inkling of the mortal danger around him as the probable designated fall-guy, and went home to pick up his handgun. Being experienced in intelligence, he had suspected for some time that something unusual was afoot and was aware that he was being kept in the dark about too much of the vital goings-on. But he brushed it off because thanks to his training, he understood that few people were told the complete picture, and that he was but a small cog in a big machine whose dimensions he could not fully conjure up.

However, suspecting that something was up, he was probably not quite as surprised as others in the building when the shots rang out. He claimed that he had not heard of the shooting when he decided to descend several flights of stairs to the lunch room, in order "to buy a Coke." More likely, he *did* know of it and went there to see what information he could gather. That might have just provided him with the narrow escape that temporarily saved his life. If the conspirators were going to take him out of circulation, he realized they would most likely have planned to do it immediately after the shooting of Kilmory—they could have pretended to surprise him right after the event—rather than wait for another opportunity that might not later arise. It is significant that Rosswell used the stairs and not the elevator to descend a number of floors to the lunch room: if he had chosen the latter, someone might have followed him into the enclosure, wherein he would have been at the mercy of an aggressor, with zero chance of escaping. To this day, the words and actions of Rosswell or those around him at the lunch room remain unknown, as are their later thoughts, recollections or general impressions. No one—neither the police, nor the Garrett Commission nor anyone else—seems to have made a serious effort to question those who were there to find out exactly what transpired or what anyone said or did at that time and place. If they did, they kept it pretty well to themselves.

* * * * * * *

Fingenio Costra's reaction to the event was unintentionally revelatory. At the moment he got the news he was having lunch with French journalist Pierre David (who, by the way, was a paid informer of his), plus some relatives and friends. This luncheon, incidentally, had been planned by Costra to coincide precisely with events in Dallas so there would be witnesses to his reaction when he was «surprised» by the news. According to David, Costra repeated three times a phrase which has been rendered as "This is very bad" or, depending on the source, "This is very bad news". Since the first phrase would be rendered *"Es muy malo"*—poor Spanish in reference to an event—it is most likely that the words spoken in Spanish were *"Es muy mala noticia,"* the precise equivalent of which is "That's very bad news."

Quite clearly, this tells us that Costra was not at all surprised. Had he not expected such news, he would likely have exclaimed something quite different, such as: "Can you believe that? President Kilmory shot dead? Incredible!" Also, the triple repetition of a phrase points to someone who is attempting to dissemble and can think of nothing else to say. Furthermore, since we know Costra to be prone to lying at every opportunity, it being historically observable that it's in his nature to avoid telling the truth whenever he can, we can safely assume that what he had in mind was precisely the opposite: "Hey, that's great news!"

But there's more: this theory has been confirmed by an agent of Cuba's DGI (Direccion General de Inteligencia), Florentino Aspillaga Lombard, who deserted from Costraland in the 1980s. According to his debriefing at the CIA, Costra told him on the morning of November 22, 1963 to stop all his regular intelligence activities, concentrate all his antennas on Texas and report immediately any important event. That was one of the reasons for his desertion: his life was in permanent danger because he was one of the extremely small number who could report that Fingenio knew what was about to happen in Dallas.

It is worth noting that Costra's foreknowledge of Kilmory's death is deemed so sensitive by the CIA that it has been filed away at the deepest level, never heretofore made public nor commented on in hardly any public or private document.

* * * * * * *

Foremost in Jameson's thoughts was his determination that, if something happened to Justin Kilmory, he must—with all due dispatch—take the oath of office and assume the position and authority of the presidency.

This explains the rushed, apparently spur-of-the-moment decision to be sworn in as president right on Air Force One, before the aircraft took off to take them all, and presumably Kilmory's body, back to Washington. Such a swearing-in was unnecessary since, on the death of the president, the vice president automatically takes over. But Jameson wanted to make sure that the whole country saw him officially sworn in and in control of the situation. For that purpose, he asked one of Kilmory's assistants to "fetch" Mrs. Kilmory, still under extraordinary emotional stress, so that she would be present at the swearing in. When the assistant demurred, Jameson turned on him and said "When I tell you to do something, you do it and do it *fast!*" Accordingly, Mrs. Kilmory—still in shock, her dress stained with her husband's blood, which she refused to clean thereby showing it in his memory and as a symbol of the deed—was escorted over to where Jameson was and stood there witnessing the swearing in. The pictures immediately went all over the nation and the world.

Since the Air Force has two identical planes for the president, the one on which he is aboard is automatically Air Force One and the other one is designated as Air Force Two. If Jameson had stayed with his own plane to return, its designation would have reverted to Air Force One. This brings up the question of why Jameson had taken over the Kilmory aircraft, instead of the identical one on which he had flown in from Washington's Andrews Air Force Base.

The answer is that, according to policy then in effect, telephone communications were not recorded while the presidential plane was on the ground. And he had good reason to keep his calls confidential until everything was under control.

Now that the deed was done, the details of the cover-up would be up to the other members of the conspiracy, chief among whom was Hooper, the FBI Director. It was he who would take control of the investigation and loudly proclaim, within hours of Rosswell's arrest, that he and he alone was the assassin. Simply prodigious! Even the fictional Sherlock Holmes could not have matched such an amazing performance within so short a time span— and thousands of miles away, to boot. Why such a rush? Because it was nothing but a message to his agents not to find anything that could conceivably upset his personal conclusion to solve the President's murder. The case was effectively closed before an honest, above-board investigation could get under way, and anyone that dared disagree with the Director was headed for trouble and asking for a sudden transfer to Alaska, if not for outright dismissal. In fact, quite a few agents were subjected to this treatment as scapegoats, enabling Hooper to say that he had dealt with those who had caused the FBI embarrassment by failing to spot and keep tabs on Rosswell in a timely manner, when in actual fact they had a full dossier on him, since he had been working for the Bureau all along.

There was hard evidence that Hooper had actually received advance notice of the assassination attempt (as if he didn't know) when, a few days before Kilmory arrived in Dallas, an agent had innocently done his duty by sending a TWX to the Bureau's headquarters and to all its branches in Texas advising that, according to an informant, an attempt on the president's life was scheduled to take place during his visit. But nothing at all was done to alert the Secret Service or anyone else. Quite the contrary. The message was destroyed.

Hooper's plan was to cover his own tracks and simultaneously exonerate the Bureau in general from any responsibility. It was easy. They blamed a scapegoat who had been carefully prepared to play the part, all the while tying up loose ends by, post-assassination, saturating Dallas and all other sensitive places with agents who were instructed to do no further investigating. It was unnecessary, since Hooper had decreed, within hours, that the patsy, acting alone, was the one and only culprit.

If all went according to plan, Hooper was confident that the presumed culprit, quickly identified as Rosswell, would be taken out at the very first opportunity. If not by a law-enforcement officer, by a Mob hit-man or, in any case, by someone to be described as a "patriotic American doing his duty." Meanwhile, it worried him that Jameson was planning to put together a top-level investigative commission, headed by the Chief Justice of the Supreme Court. Although his take was that such a move would only complicate matters, the new president was determined that it would eliminate any doubt about what happened and head off any embarrassing questions.

But Hooper was not too happy. Jameson's plan about the high-level commission might get out of control in preparing its report. However, there was little he could do about it. Jameson reassured him by explaining that the appointees would only be those who could be relied on to reach the same conclusion as he and Hooper did: the patsy had acted all by himself. Besides, Hooper's closest friend in the House of Representatives, Gerhard Foster, who always supported his every budgetary request in Congress, would be a member of the commission. Under those circumstances, very little could go wrong. The delicate secrets that, if disclosed, would cause both the new administration and the Kilmorys themselves a great deal of trouble, would be well protected.

Hooper also had a dossier on Foster concerning his playtime activities at Capitol Hill's Quota Club, created and run by President Jameson's crony Robby Raker—himself under investigation for corruption. So Foster could be relied on to keep the FBI up to date and steer the commission in the desired direction.

The one Commission member who did not go along and posed the potential for serious trouble, Louisiana Representative Haley Blogs, House Majority Leader at the time, was disposed of in 1972 in a mysterious aircraft accident in Alaska. So mysterious that not even the remains of the small plane have ever been found. That stopped Blog's renewed investigation of the Kilmory assassination dead in its tracks.

Blogs was traveling with Nat Beckwith, a Representative from the same state, plus an aide of his and the pilot, all of whom presumably died, their lips sealed forever. The aircraft, a small, twin-engine Cessna, vanished and was never found despite a thorough search in the area around its flight plan. Forty years later it is still missing (was everyone warned not to find it?). Some telex messages having to do with the search for the Cessna, which lasted some thirty-nine days, are available on the internet, but heavily censored. Why, if there was no foul play?

There are questions begging for answers: were these important congressmen, perhaps, on some secret spy mission? What possible reason could there be for censoring messages concerning the search for a civilian aircraft lost in flight on a campaign trip? Even today no answers have been forthcoming.

At the time Blogs had stated that he had "strong doubts" about some of the Garrett Commission's conclusions and was starting up a new investigation of the assassination. Although that in itself raises red flags, just before his disappearance, as Majority Leader he had strongly denounced FBI Director Hooper and the whole FBI itself in a speech on the floor of the House of Representatives. From this powerful position, Blogs could have easily conducted an above-board, no-holds-barred investigation.

Not only did he represent a threat to the conspirators in the crime of the century, but also personally to the FBI Director, a leading conspirator determined to wipe out those who stood in his way.

Hooper was only one of the powerful leaders that were uneasy about a dynamic personality like Blogs making noises about upsetting their applecart and bringing out into the open what they had so far managed, with not inconsiderable effort, to keep secret. Again, they had the motive and the resources to make someone disappear, plus the power essential to cover it up.

Needless to say, once in power Jameson planned to see to it that anything might possibly affect him was stopped overnight. This included, unquestionably, the investigation into his corruption being rushed to completion by Roland Kilmory during the months and weeks prior to his brother's assassination.

* * * * * * *

Since Rosswell's immediate execution did not come off as planned, Plan A was put into effect, i.e., the crime was to be blamed on a "nut" who did it alone, with no conspiracy. To that effect,

Rosenstein had already gotten the Mafia's orders to rub out Rosswell at the earliest possible moment, with the clear and urgent purpose of paralyzing his tongue. Had he wagged it, the conspirators would surely be found out. It is improbable that Rosswell might have actually told his preliminary interrogators information that would be incriminating to others, since it is quite likely that he was maintaining his cover, expecting that once his role was cleared up he would quickly be out of trouble. No need to stir up anything messy ahead of time.

The record as it stands tells us that Rosswell was never posed any but the most elementary questions: let us say, not unlike those that according to the Geneva Convention are the only ones, theoretically, to be asked of a prisoner of war: name, rank and serial number. No records exist, written or otherwise recorded, of any interrogation sessions with Rosswell. There are no testimonies or recollections of those who questioned him. If they asked him anything worth recording, his answers were not deemed important enough.Rosswell expected someone in a position of power to intervene on his behalf, so he probably chose to be tight-lipped until he could consult an attorney. If he did say anything, the record has been wiped clean.

As to Rosswell's actions after hearing the news, it is a well-established fact that, as previously indicated, he went home to pick up his handgun, after which he headed toward downtown Dallas. There, he felt that he would find himself in safer territory, since it would be difficult to shoot him dead in front of witnesses. He decided to head for the city's downtown area, but since he didn't drive, the question of how he got there remains a mystery. The story goes that he unexpectedly crossed paths with Dallas police officer Trapper, who was driving a police cruiser, and promptly shot him dead.

This accusation was used to prove what a wild and dangerous man Rosswell was. After disposing of the President of the United States, he goes off and kills a policeman whom he happens to run into on the street. How did Trapper recognize him, since no photographs of Rosswell had yet been distributed? If not, why would Rosswell kill him?

According to Dallas police records the murder of Trapper took place at 1:06 p.m. (local time). What makes the timeline less than credible is that Rosswell could not have reached his boarding house to pick up his handgun before 1:00 p.m., meaning that he needed to walk several blocks to where Trapper was and shoot him dead, all within six minutes. And why would Rosswell shoot Trapper without provocation and thus run a further risk of criminal charges and being implicated in the presidential assassination itself by virtue of having been present at the Texas School Book Depository and now demonstrating that he was violence-prone?

The few witnesses to Trapper's murder—who were hardly anxious to talk about what they saw—indicated that there were *two* assailants, one of which was described as heavy-set—hardly in line with Rosswell's appearance as slim with a slight build. The two-assailant theory is upheld by the bullets found at the scene, which—curiously enough—came from two different weapons, neither one of which was the .38 that Rosswell owned. However, someone eventually attempted to confuse the issue by firing Rosswell's .38 so as to come up with the necessary shells to "prove" that he fired the fatal bullets into officer Trapper. They forgot, however, that the mortal bullets were fired by an automatic pistol that left marks on the empty shells ejected after firing—as opposed to Rosswell's .38 revolver, which did not eject the empty shells.

In the end, unless Rosswell suddenly found other weapons and came at Trapper, Western style, blazing away with two guns—a pistol and a revolver—the case was a well-planned execution.

Why would anyone want to execute officer Trapper, who was only doing his workaday routine and had not been derelict in his duty, much less committed any crime? Simple common sense supports a likely answer that some have embraced as the key to the mystery: he was set up as part of the plan to make Rosswell appear guilty of shooting the President and anyone who might later interfere with him.

The truth, completely at odds with the "official" version and independent theories, is quite different: Trapper had been given the assignment, together with an associate, of killing Rosswell—who needed to be hit before he could talk. Unfortunately for him, Trapper had a last-minute case of cold feet, forcing his associate and another member of the team, following instructions, to kill him in on the spot. Otherwise Trapper's weakness might have unraveled the whole plot. The authorities could then claim that he had been shot by Rosswell, the presidential assassin.

If Trapper had not been assigned the hit on Rosswell he could not have been out looking for him, since he would not have even known what he looked like. Furthermore, no alert for Rosswell had as yet even been issued.

Needless to say, the Dallas police staffers who handled radio communications with cruisers that day were never questioned about what happened. Orders from the top.

Rick Crane, a Dallas police officer who did not agree with the Rosswell-on-the-loose scenario and insisted on debunking it was hounded by the higher-ups, threatened and eventually found dead. His death was ruled a suicide and never investigated.

When Trapper wavered, his associate and another hit-man reacted quickly to do their job as instructed. But they made the mistake of using different types of weapons and bullets. Found in Trapper's body were copper-coated rounds manufactured by the Winchester Western corporation, plus a plain lead bullet made by Remington-Peters.

Did the Dallas homicide unit manipulate evidence to frame Rosswell? The Garrett Commission glossed over the story in such a way that even a dreamy-eyed, drugged reader might notice that something was amiss. The few details provided by the Commission's report are meant to give the mistaken notion that Rosswell thought he was going to be attacked and beat him to the draw. But there was no indication in official accounts as to whether Trapper had fired his own gun during the encounter. In effect, this amounts to evidence that Trapper did not fire at all, but was hit before he could react. Also, he was given a *coup de grace* from point-blank range, execution style, a detail that does not correspond to the scenario of Rosswell merely resisting possible arrest, firing and making his get-away.

The fact that Rosswell was a boarder or room-renter at different addresses, instead of living with his wife and child, was part of the sheepdipping designed to make him look unstable. This would, first, show that he was a sort of shiftless drifter and, second, isolate him from his family and friends so that he could be more easily manipulated.

In any case, Rosswell was not terribly concerned about being prosecuted, since he fully expected to be exonerated once his intelligence work and true activities came to light. He was connected with law-enforcement, and he naïvely thought the law would come to his aid.

Contrary to the Garrett Commission's conclusions, there is doubt that Rosswell was a good marksman with a rifle—let alone a handgun. The Manlicher-Carcano was in fact, for a sniper, an extremely poor weapon whose telescopic sight was a crude add-on that hardly improved its long-range accuracy. This further argues against the convenient theory that Rosswell acted alone in killing the President.

Getting back to Rosswell's actions after he learned that President Kilmory had been shot and consequently went to pick up his gun—to protect himself from what he saw coming—one would have to closely analyze his next move, regardless of whether he ran into officer Trapper. Why would he decide to go to so public a place as a movie theater? This question, by the way, was never asked by the Garrett Commission. Answer: it is likely that Rosswell wanted to diminish the likelihood of getting killed on sight, since law-enforcement agents would hesitate to shoot a man to death in cold blood in front of eyewitnesses.

How did the authorities trace Rosswell to the theater? Were they tipped off by someone who spotted him, or had someone been on his trail all along? The chances are that those who came to arrest him were given the tip-off by an agent assigned to follow him.

Rosswell also contributed by making himself conspicuous. He deliberately went into the theater without paying admission in order to call attention to himself and thus make sure he was arrested in public. Which brings up a question: would a misdemeanor of that type require an arrest with the use of drawn guns? How did anyone know that he had done anything worse than entering a public place without paying admission? To add injury to insult, Rosswell had been battered about the face when first seen by the cameras.

A further scenario is that Rosswell went to the movie theater because that is where he was told to go to meet his contact person in order to receive instructions. This is most likely because they wanted to do away with him as soon as possible. As instructed, he had one half of a ticket that was supposed to match the other half, to be produced by his contact. But things did not go as planned. That's because the contact was told to stay away while others were sent to intercept him. Now we know why several agents came out of nowhere and converged on the scene.

There he was arrested in a scuffle in which he was slightly injured and then taken into custody by the Dallas police. Aside from that, the events of the next twenty-four hours are as nebulous as the far side of the moon.

Almost anything said by Rosswell would most likely tend to undermine the case of the lone assassin. So something had to be done. The job of taking out the inconveniently still-alive Rosswell was therefore assigned to Jack Rosenstein—whose surname was sometimes shortened to Rosen—a small-time gangland operator who knew the rules only too well. Either he did his job successfully—a botched operation was worse than none at all—or else he would pay the ultimate price... perhaps with pain and torture thrown in for good measure. The Mob liked to set vivid examples of what happened to those who failed to properly carry out an assignment.

Rosenstein knew Rosswell and had dealt with him and Dennis Fretty as part of their undercover work, so they were well acquainted. Clearly, the ideal man for the job of dealing with the Rosswell "problem" was Rosenstein.

His solid contacts with police officers was well known, having befriended many by providing them with freebies—drinks, women and other perks—at his strip-tease establishment. Since his presence would arouse little suspicion, he could get close enough to make sure he got to his target. The top echelons of the Dallas police, within the far-reaching tentacles of the conspiracy, instructed their men not to interfere with Rosenstein. Just in case, he bribed a couple of policemen to make sure of gaining access to the building.

The day prior to the one on which he actually shot and killed Rosswell, Rosenstein had had an opportunity to do his job at a point in which he and his target were within sight of each other. However, there were too many officers present and the last thing he wanted to do was make an attempt and fail. He decided to wait for another opportunity, knowing by way of an informer that Rosswell was about to be transferred. The next day, he was determined not to let another chance elude him—his own life depended on it.

No need for him, Rosenstein, to find out the exact time of Rosswell's transfer. He was tipped off by the Dallas police, who let him know precisely when and how, including its having been rescheduled at least once. His wiring of $25 to one of his strippers was a mere diversion to give him an excuse to be in the neighborhood. So, when he got the tip-off he first went to the Western Union office near the Dallas Police Station, wired the insignificant sum, got the receipt as evidence and then went off to get the job done.

He walked in to the Dallas police headquarters just as Rosswell was brought out to get into the car designated for his transfer. According to prior arrangements with police officers, he got into the building through a side door, where the posted guard waved him in. His gun at the ready, Rosenstein waited for Rosswell to appear. Then he moved in quickly, unimpeded by the policemen leading Rosswell along and fired at point-blank range in the highly effective method of a professional: muzzle in the abdomen, but pointed slightly upward so the bullet would damage a number of vital organs.

Were Rosswell's wounds actually fatal? If not, were the surgeons instructed to make sure Rosswell *did not* survive the operation? The chief surgeon who operated on Rosswell was never asked any questions during his entire lifetime.

Rosswell's death came suspiciously quickly—within a couple of hours—and no disclosure was made as to an autopsy designed to ascertain the cause of death beyond a shadow of a doubt. None of the other doctors who attended Rosswell have ever been interviewed, nor did they make statements to the press. Were journalists warned to stay away?

For purposes of covering up whatever transpired, those involved would need to make sure that no one would look further into the matter. Since everyone, including the Mafia, wanted Rosswell safely dead—case closed—the doctors and surgeons could have been prevailed upon to understand that it was dangerous for their health to make any efforts to promote Rosswell's survival. Or rather, to make *all* efforts to ensure Rosswell's non-survival. Quite clearly, for the "official" version of events to remain in place, it was imperative to ensure that Rosswell did *not* survive. Thus, if not directly in cahoots with the conspirators, the Dallas authorities were led to understand that powerful forces were involved and it was in their best interest to put the Rosswell matter, well..., completely to rest.

The magic words used were, no doubt, "national security." There is little to no knowledge of any questions asked about why Rosswell died so suddenly from his wounds, nor were the authorities concerned about addressing such questions as might conceivably arise in the future.

Among questions just begging to be asked, one might think of a few. How come the doctors were unable to save Rosswell, or at least put him on life support long enough to ask him some crucial questions? Which vital organs were damaged or shocked into dysfunction in Rosswell's body? Was there foul play or deliberate negligence in the hospital or the operating room? As we know, it is hardly problematic for surgeons to make fatal "mistakes," either accidentally or... on purpose.

Very sketchy information has been provided as to Rosswell's wounds, the surgical procedures employed to attempt to save him and the actual cause of death. Rosswell was promptly and conveniently dead and buried.

President Kilmory's body was whisked away in a now-you-see-it, now-you-don't shell-game switch. As a result of the sleight-of-hand Kilmory's body was not in the casket taken off the plane in front of the press. It was not even in Jameson's aircraft, Air Force One, but put in a plain box on Air Force Two, which overtook Air Force One in flight.

On arrival, the box containing the body was unloaded and secretly taken to a pre-arranged location, where the wounds were altered prior to the official autopsy. This took place in Bethesda Naval Hospital according to a carefully devised plan designed to reach predetermined conclusions consistent with the single-assassin, magic-bullet theory. When Air Force One landed, the empty casket was ceremoniously received as if the president's body were in it and then taken to where his body was, in order to put it back inside. (Whoever was "running the show" was able to manage highly complex schemes without missing a beat; this, as we shall see, fits to a "T" the description of the "stage director.")

The Haley Plaza plan had been successfully carried out and its aftermath was well under control. The conspirators had been able to achieve all of their basic objectives.

Chapter XXVII
A SECRET INVESTIGATION

Roland Kilmory conducted his own private investigation of Justin's assassination, which he assigned to a team led by someone in which he had the utmost trust. He quickly realized, above all, that the assassination of his brother must clearly have been the result of his own willful single-minded vendetta against the Mafia. In any case, the outcome of the confidential investigation was probably so compromising in terms of the deal with the Mob to steal the election, the plot to kill Costra, invade Cuba and other delicate matters best kept secret, that he kept it under wraps for the rest of his life. He preferred to let the Garrett Commission present its doctored, falsified findings to the country and the world, than deal with the fallout from the truth.

When Roland hurried over to meet with the CIA Director after the assassination, the first thing he said was: "Did you kill my brother?"

No one in a clear state of mind would have blurted out such a raw and ill-considered question. What did he expect him to answer? If the Director were guilty of anything, did he expect him to confess? Whatever the truth, the CIA clearly had no official participation in the deed; the institution itself could not have been involved without compromising itself, although if not higher-ups, at least rogue agents were involved in the conspiracy. In other words, it was all off the record. If the investigation uncovered anything, it was not the identity of the main conspirators. Otherwise, we can only assume that something might have "accidentally" happened to them.

Roland had his suspicions. He was under enormous stress and in the depths of a depression, having assumed for himself the blame for bringing about his brother's death. However, he went along with The Garrett Commission charade, staying at arm'slength, and did not raise any objections nor bring up his own theories or observations, much less the results of the private investigation he had ordered.

He had no intention of revealing politically devastating information or upsetting the Q-Day operation against Costra, which was still going on and, if exposed, would have precipitated another failure like the Bay of Pigs before it. Roland had been obsessed, as had been to a great extent Justin Kilmory himself, with avenging the Cuban disaster. They took it not only as a primary foreign policy issue, but personally. They had been defeated and the Kilmorys were unused to coming in second.

At this point, the Jameson administration had decreed that secrecy had to be preserved at any cost, whatever the consequences. A few who knew too much and gave signs of wavering were permanently silenced, at the time or in due course. Therefore, neither the conspirators nor the Mafia had anything to worry about. Everything was under control.

All of this is indicative of a very high-level conspiracy, the best evidence of which lies in the actions and findings of the Garrett Commission. Its proceedings—full of errors, omissions, lapses and "mistakes in judgment"—can only be understood if one assumes that it simply followed President Jameson's instructions and the FBI Director's day-by-day management of the process, designed to attribute the highly effective and professional assassination of Kilmory to a single man—who was now conveniently dead and could not defend himself. No one—except, inevitably, the scapegoat's own mother—came out in his defense.

The odds that this chain of events could have developed through mere chance are astronomical: Kilmory is shot and killed, his assassin is shot and killed two days later, all sorts of evidence is destroyed, twisted or mishandled, and those involved mysteriously begin to die off. Later, Justin Kilmory's brother is suspiciously assassinated himself by a shadowy figure with a flimsy motive, when he is on the road to put the family name back in the White House.

Like a Hollywood B-movie, all of this requires infinite suspension of disbelief.

* * * * * * *

Rosenstein was arrested and questioned, but only in pro-forma fashion. His bland answers that he wanted to spare the Kilmory family the tribulations of a Rosswell trial were accepted at face value. But since when do Mafia figures care about such niceties, much less about what happens to the family of someone who has been busy trying to wipe them out? No one, it seems, wanted to delve into the real motives, the deep-down reasons behind the assassination. Why take the chance that a smidgen of truth might actually come out?

Eventually, the Garrett Commission itself went to Dallas to question Rosenstein, not wishing to run the risk of having him come to Washington, where something unexpected might happen. Parrot-like, Rosenstein repeated the same answers he had given before to police investigators—which in itself should have aroused suspicion, since he did not come up with or volunteer a single scrap of additional information that might have been useful in a case like this. Surely, during his time in prison, he could have scrutinized his memory and come up with one or two pieces of additional, useful details that might have slipped his mind.

Please sit down before reading: Rosenstein actually told the Commission that he was willing to give additional information—in effect, to *talk*. But on one condition: that he be transported to Washington, where he would feel safe—well, at least safer. Even if he did not say so explicitly, he indicated that he feared for his life in Dallas and was naïve enough to think that the government would take him out of there and protect him in order to get the new information he was offering. In other words, he simply asked that they guarantee his safety. Unsurprisingly, his offer had just the opposite result.

What was the Garrett Commission's response when it heard that Rosenstein was ready to spill the beans on why he had killed and, more important, on the presidential assassination itself—in other words, to reveal information theretofore secret and likely to turn the official scenario on its head? One would think it might have simply paid no attention, given no response, IGNORED Rosenstein's request, PRETENDED not to have heard it.

But no, the answer given him by one of the members of the Commission (his identity unrevealed) was to the effect that, if that was the only way he would talk, he'd best not do so. In other words, SHUT UP and play this game the way we want... or else!

Ironically, Rosenstein's offer to tell the truth sealed his own fate, since it probably prompted the conspirators—i.e., the top powers in the government—to take him out of circulation. Sure enough, it was not long before Rosenstein was diagnosed with cancer and died before he could say—or even threaten to say—anything more about his role in the conspiracy to kill the president and in its subsequent cover-up. As we know, officials anywhere throughout the world—especially in autocratic and undemocratic countries—routinely induce cancer in prisoners and thus get rid of them through the simple expedient of submitting their area of confinement to super-high doses of radiation.

Other prisoners involved in high-profile cases, such as Jeffrey Burl Maye, the purported assassin of Marlin Lester Ring, also mysteriously developed cancer and died in confinement. Maye died a relatively short time after he indicated that he had additional information to reveal. From the viewpoint of those who conspired to kill Ring, he disappeared from the scene just in the nick of time.

This type of procedure was also followed in the Kilmory assassination in general. Witnesses were threatened, coerced or otherwise persuaded to change their testimony. Some were forever silenced in mysterious ways that were dismissed as "natural causes." If not, the single-assassin theory would have fallen apart and the government would have been unable to hold back the tide of truth about what really happened. It would have just been too inconvenient to have conflicting testimony that would upset their contrived open-and-shut case.

Several witnesses to the actual shooting of the President were repeatedly told that they were mistaken when their testimony conflicted with the "official" version. Some witnesses can actually be convinced, with enough persuasion, that they did *not* see or hear what their senses told them, but just the opposite. If not, enough coercion is applied that, eventually, the witnesses realize that they had best toe the line or risk mysterious, unexplained consequences; they therefore relent and have a change of mind about what they had seen and heard.

Physical evidence was also tampered with. The presidential limousine, which was nothing less than *the scene of the crime*—a silent witness, in effect—would have provided abundant evidence of whence the bullets came, likely confirming the cross-fire that killed the President. But it was washed clean of blood and other tell-tale marks while still parked at the hospital emergency room (!). Shortly thereafter it was shipped back to Washington, where it was forthwith dismantled and rebuilt, a process which completely destroyed all the evidence, such as bullet holes. There are no records indicating who ordered this obliteration of evidence, and the Garrett Commission never bothered to look into the matter.

Mysterious deaths were soon to occur, including those of Gus Barrister, his partner Herb Wertz, and pilot Dennis Fretty. Barrister was the private detective and ex-FBI agent who, for a while in New Orleans, was Rosswell's handler. When Rosswell was arrested for handing out pro-Costra leaflets, he gave as his address that of Barrister's office, at which he in fact had had business appointments. It is clear, therefore, that Barrister had something to do with the plot to kill the president; whatever his role, his partner and assistant Herb Wertz was a participant in that activity. Dennis Fretty was

Mariello's pilot and all-around handyman who knew and had worked with Rosenstein and Rosswell prior to the assassination.

Barrister and Wertz died suddenly and under shadowy circumstances in 1964, just before the Garrett Commission published its report. Fretty died unexpectedly as well, just as he was about to testify in New Orleans District Attorney Chip Harrison's inquiry into the presidential assassination. The death of Fretty, attributed to natural causes, was not investigated, nor was an autopsy conducted in the case. His untimely demise dealt a mortal blow to the Harrison effort to dig up some of the truth about the assassination. The conspirators wanted to make sure no tongues wagged.

212

Chapter XXVIII
EXIT THE SOLDIER AND THE CAPOS

"Help!" Jack Rosenstein cried out one last time as he lay dying in his cell, wondering if he would ever have the strength to do it again. He preferred, in any case, not to think of how useless it would be, since clearly no one would come to his aid. He was the «soldier» taken prisoner and now being held in isolation, with strict instructions banning interviews and family visits.

"Too sick to see anyone," they would say.

The powers—the same ones that had kept him in Dallas and prevented him from telling the real, full story in Washington or anywhere else—were taking no chances. Who knew what secrets a dying man might reveal, secure in the knowledge that, soon, no one could really hurt him anymore?

Early on, shortly after his arrest, he had made the mistake of speaking out in a television interview.

"The world will never know the true facts of what occurred, my motive," he said, looking straight at the camera. "In other words, I am the only person in the background who knows the truth."

Those enigmatic words indicating that there was more to the story than met the eye were, he felt sure, the reason that he had been held practically incommunicado ever since. So he had thought it wise to keep his mouth shut in the future. When asked about having known Rosswell, he always denied that he had ever even seen him prior to killing him on November 24, 1963.

Actually, the two knew each other well and had worked closely together in certain compartments of the conspiracy. Rosswell occasionally went to Rosenstein's club and was seen there the very night before Kilmory was assassinated.

Rosenstein had now vowed to be more discreet but, despite his best efforts, he could not resist giving some hints to fellow prisoners as to the reasons for which he had killed Rosswell that day in November, 1963.

He soon noticed that the fellow inmates who had been privy to those crumbs of information, such as they were, had been victims of some unusual accidents, disease and premature death. Had it been the result of coincidence... or of his imagination, perhaps? Maybe not, he mused, since—come to think of it—it was now happening to *him*.

The doctors said he had cancer and were giving him treatment, all right. But what did he, Jack Rosenstein the gangland soldier, know about illness, medicine and treatment? Could his "illness" just be an excuse someone made up to get him out of the way with deadly "medication"? Or was it an actual cancer brought about by some devious procedure that he was not privy to? How could he be sure they were telling him the truth? Besides, he had the distinct impression that the treatment was the culprit in making him feel worse instead of better: the more he got the less well he felt. He was beginning to fear that they were actually poisoning him with the anti-cancer "treatment."

In a haze, he began to suspect that this was really one of those cases in which the treatment is worse than the disease. But he gave up the thought, telling himself not to really care. It was no use. He was helpless and hopeless. The powers that be had apparently decided to get rid of him and there was nothing he could do to counter it. His relatives, whose visits they had strictly limited from the beginning, were being kept away. In fact, he couldn't even talk to his attorney. And his former pals in the Mob wanted nothing to do with him, treating him like the proverbial hot potato. He had done his job, and done it well. But no one had given him any recognition, nor were they going out of their way give him any sort of assistance or even sympathy. No, that might arouse suspicion and do nothing other than taint them and raise doubts over the cover story about why he had killed Rosswell. As far as they were concerned, he might as well be dead. In fact, he concluded that they would much prefer it that way—and the sooner the better.

It was crystal clear that some people on a very high level had already made a decision on what to do about him and were methodically implementing it. He, Rosenstein, would certainly like to throw a monkey wrench into that process. But he feared that, by now, that was entirely out of the question.

He considered the idea of refusing to take further treatment. But what good would that do? Probably only prolong his agony. They'd find a way to get those drugs into him somehow—maybe with his meals. He entertained the fleeting thought of suicide. But he didn't have the guts anymore. Or anything to do it with. He was weak and totally lacking in willpower. On the other hand, he could insist that treatment be suspended. But, again, would that merely prolong his suffering? It might, he concluded. But in any case getting the prison medical professionals to agree to that would be an unlikely scenario. Everything seemed to indicate that he had been targeted, "selected out"—as the saying goes in government personnel procedures—and they simply weren't going to let him slip out of their grasp. They were determined to continue the "treatment," whatever it was. So recovery from illness was as far removed as his chances of being out of prison alive, ever again.

He had absolutely no bargaining power. Nothing he knew would be of any use to the authorities, local or federal. In fact, nearly every scrap of information that top-level officials really wanted to hear was already known to them, and they were hoping that he would never have an opportunity to relay to anyone else what they did not. They would much rather bury all of it, and him along with it. It was much too dangerous, troublesome and embarrassing. Too many careers depended on keeping a lid on it. So he, private Rosenstein, was clearly much more valuable dead than alive. Dead men, as Rosenstein and his Mafia brethren knew all too well, don't talk. All his secrets would be sealed, and the story of a lone assassin as responsible for the crossfire murder of the president—a physical impossibility—would stand the test. The cover-up would hold; indeed, it had to. That decision had been made at the highest level, and anything that might conflict with it had to be and was being effectively silenced.

* * * * * * *

Sal Campana was preparing one of his favorite snacks when he received a visit from someone he knew well. It had been previously and informally arranged—a drop-by sort of thing—so he did not suspect anything, or else he would not have let them in. Once inside, we can be sure that Campana's lifespan lasted no more than brief minutes. No need for idle chit-chat when the target was at hand and the executioner had an urgent job to do.

We can surmise that it was not a case of revenge or settling of past grievances, since there was no sign of torture, no unnecessary suffering was inflicted on the victim, and at first glance it did not appear to be a robbery. But what happened to tens of millions of dollars in jewelry, cash and valuables hidden in his safe? We can safely assume that, once the job was done, a team was sent in by his *fratelli,* the big capos, to clean everything out and split the spoils. His real estate holdings, worth in the billions, were in the name of front men who would quietly sign them away. Evidently, the motive was to silence an individual who knew a lot of secrets and might be tempted, for who knew what defensive reasons, to reveal some.

Curiously enough, he was scheduled to testify the very next day before the House Committee on Assassinations. Yet another coincidence! So it was then or never. Sal was generally very circumspect in what he said to the authorities, if he said anything at all. But it probably wasn't hard for some of the Mafia kingpins—or was it someone in the federal government itself?—to wonder if in order to cut himself some slack he might drop a hint about some of the closely-guarded secrets affecting the highest echelons of power. He was privy to many of them..., many more, surely, than anyone could possibly imagine.

Campana's demise could easily have been arranged by the federal government by putting out a contract for a hit. The CIA itself could have taken care of it directly or by simply resorting to its own Mafia associates; in other words, putting out a contract. Ironically, they would have had to hire the same mobsters that Campana once bossed. In view of the fact that the Kilmorys, other U.S. presidents and high officials had made arrangements with the Mob to kill Costra, Marlin Lester Ring, Dominican dictator Rafael Trujillo, President Nguyen Diat of South Viet Nam and other foreign as well as domestic leaders, hiring the Mafia to make a hit on one of their own whose usefulness was now at an end—and whose dangerousness might be only beginning—should not have been much of a problem.

No need to mention, of course, that the House Assassinations Committee—despite its name—never got curious about Campana's assassination. And it never did much more than hold hearings, collect information and publish documents. Since it had to reach some conclusion after spending months and tens of millions, it decided that the death of President Kilmory "was *probably* the result of a conspiracy." It said nothing about who the conspirators might have been, nor did it even suggest that law enforcement agencies such as the FBI and the CIA ought to investigate further in order to establish some basic facts—which, if honesty prevailed, might just be at variance with the conclusions reached by the Garrett Commission.

That would have been much too messy. The evidence was far too weighty for them not to declare it a "possible" conspiracy. But anything further would have brought up evidence of the identity of those "possible" high-level conspirators, accompanied by grounds for bringing charges of obstruction of justice, cover-ups and outright corruption affecting government officials in multiple agencies.

As to the hit on Campana, whoever paid him that final, fatal call was never identified. And if there was any investigation as to his identity, no result was forthcoming. Not a speck of information thereon was ever officially or unofficially made known, leaked to the public, or otherwise hinted at. Case closed. And cold. Very cold.

Cold enough, in fact, to send a chill up the spine of anyone else who might be privy to sensitive information. Speaking of which, there were some cases, including that of Debbie Kilhallen, a famous television personality and columnist for a New York paper. In the late 1960's she was investigating the Kilmory assassination and writing a book that, she said to her closest friends, would "blow the case wide open." One morning, before she could finish it, she was found dead in her bed. According to news reports, her demise had been caused by a combination of sleeping pills and alcohol. It was called accidental, no autopsy was performed and no investigation was carried out. Her unpublished manuscript vanished and was never seen or heard from again. It makes one wonder about what group or agency might have had an interest in keeping any sensitive information about the Kilmory assassination from coming out. Her husband, mindful of what was unhealthy for him, never uttered a peep.

* * * * * * *

Jake Rosetti had accepted the invitation to dinner offered by his old friend, Sandy Traficant, who brought along his wife and a couple of other capos. They drove to a superb restaurant in Fort Lauderdale, where Rosetti had settled, now in his seventies, to be with his sister and put his life back into a semblance of order. Lately, he had been through a lot, having done some prison time for the silliness of rigging private poker games in Las Vegas—was he just enjoying being up to old tricks? Besides, his life-long tuberculosis had been acting up again. Worst of all, the Justice Department had been after him with late-in-life deportation proceedings and he had been dodging the action with legal maneuvers. If that didn't work, he was hoping to use the threat of revealing what he had been up to on behalf of the CIA concerning the assassination of Costra and other hostilities against his regime. Confidential warnings to the government to lay off were sometimes effective. Considering the danger that any of that might come out into the open, he hoped the Justice Department would not feel such a deportation effort to be worthwhile.

Rosetti was scheduled to testify before a Senate committee investigating, among other things, the Kilmory assassination. He had checked with the syndicate to reassure them that, as in the past, he was not going to reveal anything that would get anyone into trouble. There was a good reason they called him "Mr. Smooth." He was respectful, polite and well-mannered under official questioning, just as under other circumstances he could be tough, menacing and fearsome.

The dinner with Traficant was unlikely to have been the kiss of death. Sure, Campana had recently been bumped off, but not in a showy way meant as a message to keep others' tongues from wagging. It was a warning, sure enough, but mindful of that, Rosetti had squared everything with Traficant. He was not inclined to believe that his old friend was likely to stab him in the back.

A few days later, he disappeared. His body was found by sheer chance. It was inside an oil drum floating in Miami's Biscayne Bay. He had been suffocated, then cut up into parts and stuffed into the drum. Whoever did it wanted him to disappear completely. The drum was weighted so it would remain at the bottom, but the decomposing body had generated gases, buoying it to the surface. When opened, the drum revealed a gruesome sight.

If the Mob had not been inclined to silence him, the government, on the other hand, had the motive as well as the opportunity. The intelligence community might have had a special interest in him, particularly since he had threatened to reveal incriminating information about his secret work in order to protect himself from further deportation proceedings. Despite his criminal career, he had accomplished important missions for the government vis-à-vis the Costra regime without profiting from it. He had received no compensation whatsoever. The intelligence agents respected him and called him "Colonel Rosetti." The Mob capos, for their part, generally held him in high esteem and voiced respect for his finesse and ability to solve problems without violence, leaving all parties with a enough of the spoils to keep them happy. It was no wonder that for decades he held sway as the Mob's point man in Hollywood, where he was treated like royalty and hobnobbed with studio heads, directors, producers, stars and starlets, frequenting the most fashionable night clubs and restaurants.

But his forthcoming testimony before the Senate committee might have triggered the intelligence community—who wanted to keep a tight lid on a lot of secrets—to take him out and make it look like his own Mob pals had chosen to silence him. If so, they waited until he went out to dinner with them.

The investigation into his death was brief and perfunctory, and no suspects were turned up. The autopsy showed the cause of death as suffocation, which meant that it came relatively quickly and brought about little undue pain and suffering. In a word, it did not look like a Mob execution. Indications about his state of mind were that he was relatively unconcerned, if not exactly uncaring, about what might happen to him.

For whatever it's worth, the Director of the CIA said that he "guaranteed" that the Agency had nothing to do with Rosetti's demise. Interesting word, "guaranteed." It implies an iron-clad promise, if there is such a thing, dealing with the future. But, concerning events that are over and done with, can "guarantees" really apply—especially from such a source? Maybe what he meant to say was he "guaranteed" that they would find nothing implicating the CIA.

* * * * * * *

Claudio Mariello was the only capo beyond the reach of those who might wish him to remain silent. Ultimately, the long arm of the law had gotten to him and put him away for years. In effect, the sentence was long enough, at his age, to equal life imprisonment. Then, too, it was difficult for the extra-legal tentacles of the FBI, the CIA and the DIA to get to him. Since he was already doing time, he was unlikely to "talk" in order to plea-bargain his way to a reduced stretch that might give him a reasonable chance to walk out alive.

Perhaps he could consider himself lucky. His pals in the Mafia could have found ways to take him out, but they were mostly dead and those who had taken over were by then not that concerned about him.

But Mariello liked to do his share of bragging to fellow prisoners. He was inclined to talk to his cellmate about the hit he had ordered on President Kilmory, partly as personal payback for his illegal deportation to Guatemala by his brother Roland, partly for his double-cross of the Mob. He was proud of that in a patriotic-American sort of way, as if he had done a public service. "We took care of 'em before they could do any more damage to da country," he proclaimed.

But he was proudest of his more-personal vendetta against Roland Kilmory. Close to the end of his life, he liked to spice up his stories by saying: "When that li'l shit-ass runt Booby Kilmory tried to put us out of business, we gave *him* the business—him and his brother!"

Chapter XXIX
PATRIARCHAL MUSINGS

It was a clear, spring day in the family compound, where friends and relatives had gathered to celebrate Jonathan Kilmory's birthday, although he seemed, more and more, off in a world of his own. The decade of the 1960's had been unkind to him, his health deteriorating after a series of strokes and assorted ailments had put him in a wheelchair, turning his life upside down.

"Like I said, guard your secrets well, son," the Kilmory patriarch repeated as the clan, looking uncomfortable, gathered around him. "Especially the one about your sister, Rebecca, and...."

"Sure, Dad," Jeff Kilmory interrupted, hoping the old man would keep his mouth closed.

"And that business with the girl in the car at Chad..., Rapp...,

"Dad, please! No need to...."

"And particularly the one about the film star, Marie."

"Want something to drink, Dad?" Jeff tried to distract him.

The patriarch's reference to long-closeted family skeletons was a shock to Jeff, who never expected any of them to be mentioned again, either within the family or outside of it. Obviously, his father was no longer coherent, his thoughts jumbled and out of control. He was apt to say anything that came into his head, no matter how absurd, insensitive or out of place.

"No, I don't want anything to drink, I just want to talk... about keeping a lid on those issues. They could be dangerous land mines for your White House hopes, son." They weren't sure that he knew of Roland's assassination a few months before, but he had always insisted that, in any case, each of his male sons had to become president in turn. His mind and body had deteriorated after his strokes, but he was still obsessed, as he had been for decades since his falling out with President Roosevelt doomed his own presidential hopes, with the notion of somehow keeping the presidency within the family.

"Yes, of course, Dad, but let's, uh, let those old subjects rest and talk about, er, something more current, shall we?"

"Why sure, son... ," he began, with no intention of following suit. He coughed a few times. "But..., but, those are matters of concern and we have to deal with them."

"We've dealt with them already, Dad. Believe me, that's history now." Jeff looked at him with a mixture of sternness and compassion. He was glad to see the rest of the family drifting away, not wanting to hear anything further from The Patriarch.

Nearly helpless in the supine position, it having been considered that he was not strong enough to be put in the wheelchair except for short periods, Jonathan stared back mutely. But Jeff was glad that at least he seemed to be pausing in his discussion of a subject that, to him and the whole family, was anathema.

The family secrets were a subject that Jeff Kilmory had made a point of banishing from conversation, or even the remotest allusion. He felt strongly that talking about any of them was simply embarrassing, inconvenient, and quite possibly dangerous. One never knew who might be listening.

Jeff, now the eldest male of the clan after the death of his three elder brothers, had opined that his father had not really been strong enough to be told about the assassination of a second son. The family had concurred, but realized that he might have learned about it from listening to the news or from fragments of inadvertent conversation he might have overheard.

This time death by assassination had claimed Roland, the former Attorney General, current junior senator from New York—a position known to have been carpetbagged through bribes, threats and trickery, since he was not a New Yorker—and possible nominee for president on his party's ticket. For a second time within the space of five years he had lost an eldest son and number one heir. Going back to the dwindling days of World War II, it was his third such loss within a quarter century. If, in fact, he had become aware of this latest one, he must have been utterly devastated.

Coming on a summer's day in 1968 at the height of the Viet Nam war, Roland's untimely death turned into something close to a national day of mourning. Thanks in part to the tributes paid the Kilmorys by the press, the country felt that they were akin to America's royal family, a veritable national treasure, and every sadness that happened to them was made up to reverberate as a setback for the nation as a whole. Coming so soon after the violent death of Marlin Lester Ring, and not so long after that of his brother the president, Americans were shocked and grief-stricken.

Eventually, even though they did not openly discuss it, the family concluded that The Patriarch had likely become aware of this latest, dreadful loss. Whether he was able, after his strokes, to connect the dots and realize that his own ambitions had brought about this new and overwhelming family tragedy is another story.

The fact was that this second assassination of a son of his had occurred about five years after Justin's. What probably made it more hurtful for Jonathan was that he had been the architect of the unwritten Kilmory-Mafia deal for the presidency, in which the fraudulent count in Illinois, Texas and perhaps other states had stolen the victory for Justin in exchange for a hands-off policy toward the Mob.

Jonathan was well aware of how dangerous it was to make a deal with the Mob and then not keep one's end of the bargain. It had, in fact, nearly cost him his own life when capo Francesco Castellaro had put out a contract on him in the 1950's for reneging on a real estate deal. Jonathan got wind of it and managed to convince his friend Campana—perhaps with a considerable sum to placate tempers and smooth over feelings—to intercede for him and get the contract cancelled.

He had been unable, however, to persuade his own son, Roland, to lay off the Mob when he became Tttorney General. Jonathan recalled his heated argument with Roland on the subject, not long after he had been appointed.

"You have no idea what you're getting into, son," he ventured when it was clear that Roland was going after the Mafia.

"I don't give a fuck, Dad." Roland's anger at the mobsters was, more than a matter of justice, a personal vendetta. "Those bastards have got it coming and us Kilmorys are gonna kick their ass—it's about time!"

"You don't understand. I made the deal *for* you, and it's my responsibility to see to it that we keep our end of the bargain," Jonathan pleaded. "You *have* to make good on it."

"Well, Dad, like you said, *you* made the deal—I didn't. So I'm not bound by it." Roland was fuming.

"Okay, but what's got me worried is they're not going to come after *me*. If that happened I wouldn't care—I've enjoyed a long-enough life already. How many years have I got left?"

"So you're saying they're going to come after *me* instead?"

"Exactly! You'll be the target—or who knows who else in the family." About to mention Justin, he chose to only allude to him, expecting that Roland would dismiss an outright mention of his name as being too far-fetched. "You'll probably be their top target for giving them a hard time."

"Well, fine! Let them come after me then. We'll see who wins." In full sway was Roland's old throw-caution-to-the-winds bravado.

"It's not a question of balls, Rolly." At crucial moments Jonathan invoked his son's nickname to soften up the toughness that came bubbling up.

"Well, for me it is. I've showed them I'm not afraid of them and I'll keep on doing it. When the chips are down they're nothing but a bunch of cowards anyway." Roland's eyes glowered.

"You're asking for trouble, Rolly. Mark my words."

"Let 'em bring it on."

"Well, I, I hope I don't have to tell you 'I told you so', God damn it!"

So irate that he was sputtering, Jonathan decided to say no more. He made up his mind to bring up the subject on another occasion when he could control his temper and bring more solid reasoning into the equation. By then maybe his tough-as-nails kid, taught by he himself, his own father, never to lose—and, if losing, to never give up—would be more amenable to his own way of thinking. He peered at his kid to gauge his expression.

They were both silent for a few moments.

"Wait a minute, Dad!" Roland got hold of himself, a steely calmness lighting up his eyes. "Let's look at it this way: suppose we do go after the Mob, indict them, prosecute them and all the rest? If we do away with them, destroy them, we wouldn't owe 'em anything and the slate would be wiped clean."

"I'd already thought of that, Rolly...." Jonathan enjoyed seeing his son's surprised reaction. "I didn't bring it up because I'm not sure it would work. Those guys are, you know, cold blooded. You've heard their saying when they bump somebody off: 'nothing personal—just business'? Well, if you ask me, in our case it's worse: it's both personal *and* business. Think it over."

Roland laughed lightly at his Dad's remark, recognizing its truth as he walked away, waving goodbye.

"Sleep on it!" The old man's last words momentarily relaxed his own deep-seated unease.

Chapter XXIX
GOING FOR THE GOLD

Louis Bernard Jameson knew, amid the continuing bloodshed of Viet Nam, that he would lose if he ran for re-election. Roland saw his opportunity. Once a supporter of the war, Roland had perceived its clear unpopularity and turned against it. That was not actually a great vote-getter vis-à-vis his prospective opponent, since ending the war was also one of the major planks of candidate Roger Dixon's platform.

Roland knew he was treading on dangerous ground, but felt it was his destiny and his mission to uphold the Kilmory mystique. He needed to pursue what he thought of as the shining goal: to reach the presidency and conclude the job that his brother had left unfinished. Having backed Justin's initial efforts to support South Viet Nam in resisting attacks from the North, Roland talked a great deal about ending the war there—in effect, making it an issue. But he was careful to avoid further talk of the Mafia and the need to pursue it. The Mob eyed him warily.

Unsaid as well was his conviction that the presidency would be his opportunity to use the powers of the "bully pulpit" to even the score with his brother's assassins. He was determined to identify them, search them out and make them pay. Although he had his suspicions, he still did not know, even through his own investigation, who the mastermind of the conspiracy was or what his level in government was, if any. He was also conscious that he would be running serious risks, but in a defiant, devil-may-care fashion, he chose to ignore any such dangers—in a word, to run heedlessly, recklessly. It was not a death wish, he told himself, but leaving it up to fate. He chose to think it unlikely that he would be the victim of another Mafia-led conspiracy involving who-knew-which groups, such as CIA agents or Costra-sent infiltrators.

Suspicion of having something to do with his brother's death had fallen, among others, on some disgruntled Cuban exiles who still hated his brother intensely for his betrayal at the Bay of Pigs, but Roland discounted that. The exiles were divided, disorganized and at loose ends, and would have had little motivation to commit such an act. Most of them were intent on getting rid of Costra—not Justin. As for the Mob, that was a different story. He believed that, perhaps in concert with Costra—even though the public at large ignored such an alliance—the Mafia had been involved in Justin's death in Dallas. If so, it would make sense for them to now target him as well.

Fatalistically, he concluded that if the Mob and/or its partners in crime decided to preemptively move against him before he won the nomination and then the election, there would be little he could do to stop them. He bounced this scenario around in his mind, occasionally altering his conclusions, but mostly he resigned himself to the fact that, if they so chose, they would get to him sooner or later. On the other hand, he thought, things might only get dangerous once he clinched the nomination. By then he would get Secret Service protection, so he would be safer while also taking additional steps to deal with any threats. In all, he told himself he had to go for it. In the end, everything might work out and he would revel in a glorious victory.

It was a chance that his inner voice told him he *had* to take, so he made up his mind that he just wasn't going to worry about it. The Kilmorys never cried, his dad had always said. Neither did the Kilmorys ever worry about those few things they couldn't do anything about.

As it turned out, his assessment was basically correct. If they wanted him dead, they would find a way to do it. But he hoped that the anti-Kilmory conspirators, finding that different circumstances prevailed, would be content to wait and see, letting him proceed with his quest for the presidency without launching pre-emptive action too far before its time.

But he was prepared to deal with the decision of his enemies, whatever it was. He harbored the hope that they were not going to have him rubbed out unless he posed a very real threat. If they did, he told himself, it would probably be over in a split second, and he wouldn't even have time to be aware of it, much less worry about it. He was, in a way, taunting the Mafia to take him on. In an ultimate show of fearlessness, he didn't bother to hire a security detail to protect himself during the primary campaign. His brother Justin had set the standard with his exemplary accessibility, and he was going to follow his lead no matter what.

Roland might have been a spoiled brat to some, but he idolized his presidential sibling. He truly felt that if he could implement Justin's plans, he might be able to lead the free world into one of the most prosperous and peaceful eras in history, promoting worldwide respect for freedom, democracy and human rights.

In the personal arena, Jennifer Kilmory, having lost her husband who, despite his persistent habit of infidelity, had been number one in her life, now saw herself in danger of losing her number-two man. While Justin was alive, the closeness with Roland was with his knowledge, consent and encouragement. After his death, Roland had given her the moral, emotional and intimate support she needed to keep going, and had stood by her even more closely. Who said marriage was a requirement for sex? Were Adam and Eve ever married? Anyway, it was all in the family, she said to herself with just a touch of mirth. But then she chided herself for such unorthodox thoughts.

Roland had also filled in physically for Justin at different times when he was traveling or seeing his girl-friends, and even on other occasions when Justin was busy and they could schedule a rendezvous. That was not too difficult since their get-togethers did not arouse public suspicion. Right after the assassination, Roland spent a great deal of time—both in public and intimately—with Jennifer. Then Roland's wife, Edna, put her foot down. It was too much for her when Roland was so frequently absent from the household, only to appear on television with Jennifer here and there. Sure enough, they always looked sad and serious, but Edna knew what went on behind the scenes. Women have a way of knowing.

* * * * * * *

That this rendezvous was not primarily for intimacy was quite clear to Roland as soon as he arrived at Jennifer's townhouse in Georgetown, the capital city's most fashionable, exclusive downtown neighborhood. But he had suspected that from her tone of voice when she asked him to come over.

The preliminary greeting was chilly, he was sorry to note. Sorrier, when she began to argue against his newest political campaign for the presidency.

"It's not my place to prevail on you to act one way or another," Jennifer said in her precisely clear, logical language, voiced in her upper-class tones and inflection. "But . . . ," she went on.

"But," Roland said almost simultaneously, with an indulgent smile. "You wish I wouldn't."

"Yes, Roland, I wish...." she said, close to sobbing. "It's much too dangerous—you and I—we both know it." She looked at him with something beyond love. It was affection and it showed in her eyes. Love, she knew, could be blind, unreasoning. Ah, but affection! That was something else. She didn't know when or how that had come about, but she had developed genuine fondness for him, despite his usually cold and aloof persona. Maybe it had been those light gestures he had toward her: his gentleness in caressing her hair, his caring about what concerned her, what little things she needed and *when*, his understanding, his tenderness. Perhaps it was love *and* affection. She sometimes wondered how she could have those feelings for a man who —she also knew—who could be, despite his outwardly calm and gentle demeanor, inordinately tough, hard as nails, capable of giving orders to kill.

Had he himself killed, perhaps? Sometimes she wondered, but she did not want to know. She had heard an account of how, in a fit of rage, he had reportedly thrown a black child-abuser out the window of a tall building, but that was all she knew about it—and all she wanted to.

His tenderness, she felt, came across more by approach, by touch, than by words or detached gestures. Far from being urbane and witty, like his brother Justin, he was dweebish, inept. His humor, when it came, was rarely harmless and good-natured, but attack-oriented. He could be surprisingly rude, gruff, abrupt.

She remembered how, shortly after the assassination, he had spent some time with her at the Kilmory estate in West Palm Beach. He approached Jennifer while she was sunning herself, topless, at the edge of the pool. He came over in his swimming trunks, caressed her hair and kissed her lovingly. For a period, he had gotten very close to Jennifer as a surrogate of Justin's. But after his death he had perhaps gone too far. His wife Edna had called a halt to goings-on that, although nothing new, she felt were beyond "the call of duty"; besides, it was wrong of him and neglectful of her and their dozen or so children.

Roland was especially hard on those over whom he had some measure of power. But then, he had power over nearly everyone. And of course, he and Jennifer only spent some occasional time together; *that*—as opposed to marriage, when couples spend all or most of their time in each other's company—was a formula more conducive to a harmonious, intense, magnetic relationship. There was less reason and occasion to fight, and increased sexual desire at each encounter. The two were friends and confidants, and at times co-conspirators against others they regarded as inimical to their mutual or disparate interests.

"Yes, Jennifer, I do understand," he said as he lay next to her on the bed. He looked at her tenderly. "But, you know, it's in my blood, it's the Kilmory destiny, and I can't shrink from that any more than I, or you, could shrink from our own children. I've got to do it." Roland made it clear that he would not and could not give up his race for the presidency, his hopes for a renewed Camelot for the Kilmory family's hopes of redemption and completion of a shattered but still possible dream.

"Well, you go ahead, my dear." Her tone and expression suddenly hardened. "If that's what you want." She seemed to shiver, to physically and emotionally shudder at the thought of losing him, if not to the politics, the campaign, the whole business of the presidential quest, then—before it even came to that—to the anti-Kilmory conspirators who might deny him all of that and more, the minute he began to come close to it. *They*, she was certain, would not be willing to take the chance that he might be elected. The nomination, she felt, was practically a sure thing in the trail of Justin's tragic end—but then, once in the race, if it looked at all like he might be the new Kilmory standard-bearer, those same forces responsible for his brother's wrenching destruction might come down on Roland and do him in as well.

He was desultory in caressing her half-undressed body; it was clear that, if he was in the mood, she was not.

"Please understand, won't you?" He, the tough political gladiator, sounded pleading, almost supplicating. At the moment, sex was the furthest thing from his mind. "For the sake of Justin's memory, I can't give this up. Don't ask me to."

His inner being clamored for redemption for Justin's demise. He held himself personally responsible. It had been he and none other who had insisted on prosecuting the mobsters despite his father's pleadings to the contrary. But this last quest was the only thing that managed to lift him, albeit partially, from the depths of a terrible depression brought on by his own unforgivable mistake. He had to redress the wrong.

He looked around her tastefully decorated bedroom, full of sophisticated furnishings and exquisite European taste, as if trying to find support to back up his case. In his heart, however, he realized it was useless. She had been through too much already with the loss of Justin and she could not, though he was not hers alone, bear the thought of losing him as well.

"For the sake of his memory, you should not," she said firmly. "The family can't afford another loss like Justin's, like your older brother Jonathan, Jr., killed in the war. Like your sister, killed in the plane crash. You're tempting the fates. It would be just too much, far too much."

"I understand your viewpoint, dearest." He said *dearest* as a form of address and, curiously, not as his usual term of endearment. "But my mind is made up." He became blunt and his toughness suddenly came through with stern clarity.

"I'm sorry, Robbie," she said, using a nickname generally reserved for intimate moments, "but I guess I'll have to get in touch with Ari. It's best for me—and for you—that I get out of the country and away from all of this. I just can't deal with it. I, I won't be able to take another tragedy. Ari is incredibly nice and he is... well, willing to take good care of me." She was close to tears when she said, with bursting finality: "I really can't, I can't take this anymore!"

"Go ahead, if you must. Visit him." He was serious now, slightly softening his tough-guy mode. "But for God's sake don't go making anything formal with him, okay?" He was reluctant to say "marry." Then he added: "If it has to do with... money, let me know what you need."

"No, basically it has nothing to do with that," she lied. She had always enjoyed having unlimited amounts to spend and live in a style that, though prodigal, was never quite up to her true, self-established standard. It was her hope and expectation to have enough reserves available so as to avoid ever having to worry about money again, no matter how much she spent.

It was Jennifer's feeling that the Kilmory fortune, though considerable, was already being split so many ways that the additional share he could make available to her would be too small to suit her. Besides, how could the family justify providing her with more than the fortune she had already inherited as Justin's widow?

"It's just, well, a matter of insulation and safekeeping for myself and the children. Besides, he's being extremely generous with me, leading me into temptation, so to speak." Her crystalline laughter momentarily broke the tension before she caught herself. "I mean, he's making a..., a really attractive offer, and I feel compelled to think about it..., for the sake of the children, especially. Above all, I really have to think about them, about getting them away from this violence here in America."

Jennifer wanted to prepare him for the blow, even if she herself was still unsure of taking such a big step and what it might bring... for her. For the Kilmorys, she knew, it would be nothing but bad news. But Roland could never have anything more than a now-and-then relationship with her. If he were to divorce Edna to marry her—in any case unthinkable to his staunchly Catholic mind—the scandal would be unimaginable and would never subside. Besides, despite her protestations she adored the wealth, privilege and fabulous lifestyle that Ari could provide her with—and did lavish on her at every opportunity. In contrast, Roland's life was all politics, practical matters, with little time for the graceful, sophisticated socializing she was so fond of. If anything, Roland was more politically inclined and far less sociable than Justin used to be.

"I know, I know," he said. "He's good to you. But, but he's not your type of man. The man is . . . ," he was going to say "nouveau riche," but that was applicable as well to the Kilmorys themselves, so he held back. "He's absolutely classless—no class whatsoever."

"Sure, he has his faults—who doesn't? But he is suave, gentlemanly, attentive," she replied, skirting the issue. "Besides, he's...." She used an open-arms gesture to give the idea of great wealth without actually saying so.

"Yes, I know." Roland understood what she was getting at. "I know. But please don't rush into anything, my dearest," he said, holding her hand. This time, he said *dearest* in a truly affectionate, concerned tone. "Just do me a favor and take the time to think about it, okay?" He looked deep into her dark eyes, but found them cold. It was a bad sign.

He let loose with what, to his mind, was a good parting shot: "Besides, don't forget, he has that opera singer, Cannas, as the steady always waiting in the wings!" Her reaction made him immediately regret the tactless remark.

Jennifer shrugged, but not before giving him a dagger-like, parting look. "The nerve of these Kilmorys," she thought.

Chapter XXX
THE PANTRY

Some five years prior, Mariello had turned down the plan to "take care" of Attorney General Roland Kilmory—the one Kilmory he hated and feared the most—only because, still being in power, Justin would be relentless in avenging his brother's death.

So, now that Roland was in the running for the nomination to succeed President Jameson, he relished the opportunity to toss him as well into the nether regions that, according to the Kilmory's own Catholic faith, he long-since fully deserved. There was little doubt that, after all, he was asking—no, begging for it. Another Kilmory presidency was, of course, out of the question for the Cosa Nostra, since it would spell the doom of all the Mafia families put together.

That applied as well to their allies in the CIA , FBI and Secret Service, plus other co-conspirators in the assassination of Justin. Not to mention, eventually, the mastermind of the plot—for whom Mariello cared even less than all the rest put together; but then, he despised 99% of law enforcers (1% were his own infiltrators). It would be open season on all of them—every single one.

Regardless of risk and any objective evaluation of chance-taking, the hit on presidential-candidate Roland was a no-brainer for Mariello and his fellow capos. They feared, despite Roland's poor campaign performance and so-so showing in some primaries, that at a given point nostalgia and sympathy for the Kilmorys would take over and hand him the nomination. The presidency would then be bestowed on the heir in a proverbial "lead-pipe cinch," in a landslide. Roland himself dimly recognized that he was morose, with a perennially sad, hang-dog look that hardly made him a charismatic vote-getter. Still, barring an unforeseen public upheaval or other unpredictable event, he clearly expected to win the election on his dead brother's coattails and find himself inaugurated president in January of 1969.

The unfinished era known as Camelot should, thought Roland, rise again to its rightful, luminous reign of glory, uninterrupted by that treacherous, evil embodiment from the dregs of society against which he had fought all his life: organized criminality.

Although he was quiet about them now, he would then pursue them into their lairs, their caves and holes in the ground, stamping them out, avenging their predatory destruction of the true, honest American way of life.

His father, the clan patriarch, had been wrong to consort and deal with that feral sort, but he would make up for that mistake. His deal with them might well have got Justin the presidency in November, 1960, but he harbored no doubts that the prize would eventually have been his, regardless. It would, he told himself, only have been a matter of time.

Ever the fearless, tireless, physically small but relentless competitor who had to prove his worth against all odds, Roland plowed ahead with his presidential primary campaign. Brushing aside all thoughts of peril, this train of his had been on its way since before his brother's violent death. Devil-may-care, he dismissed the need for a solid security detail, preferring to flaunt his fearlessness. He had been slated, after all, to be the vice-presidential running mate in his brother's 1964 reelection bid, replacing the hateful, brutish Jameson, who would have been sidelined—if not sent to prison—for wrongdoing per Roland's Justice Department investigation. He, Roland Kilmory, was the anointed one—and now that he was the eldest living heir to the Kilmory dynasty, so much the more. There was a score to settle and, though prudently silent for now, he planned to settle it with a vengeance.

Though it was still uppermost in his mind, Roland was careful not to mention the war on "organized crime," as he had done early in his term as Attorney General. No need to provoke the mobsters unnecessarily, tipping them off as to the sleeping serpent that would later turn around and drive its venomous fangs into them.

The question, of course, was also on the mind of his enemies: the Mob itself, the overt and covert murderers who had nearly marked him as the target before settling on his idol, elder brother "Giustino."

As far as the mobsters were concerned, there was no way Roland was going to be around to even accept the presidential nomination, much less run an electoral campaign. They were taking absolutely no chances, intent on not letting him live to get anywhere near the nomination, much less his ultimate goal of sitting in the

Oval Office and directing against them all forces governmental in a relentless and ferocious war.

Out of many opportunities to take him out of contention, the Anderson Hotel in Los Angeles was not ideal, but it was good enough. The Kilmory enemies were unwilling to wait another day—nor another minute, for that matter.

The hit was carefully planned to the last detail. As in the Justin case, they would use more than one shooter and a patsy such as Rosswell—not exactly sheepdipped but hypnotically programmed, Manchurian-candidate-like—to take the blame and deflect the heat that might be brought to bear on them. Law-enforcement officialdom itself was surreptitiously lined up to ensure the cover-up. Decades later it is still holding, even though most—if not all—of the culprits and conspirators have long-since disappeared.

Practically all significant evidence that might bring out the truth of what happened has by now vanished if not been deliberately swept away. As in his brother's case, the shots to the head were essential, while the patsy, a programmed decoy, would claim to this day no recollection of the event. In fact such a recollection would be virtually impossible: the hypnotic trance programmed him to act like a zombie and store none of it in memory. As a backstop, his relatives in the Middle East would suffer consequences if anything went awry, and their safety would mean more to him than his own freedom. Especially since being out of jail and even considering the possibility of talking could very suddenly cut off that freedom, not to mention his very life. He was so informed in no uncertain terms. The hit went off like clockwork, the loose ends gathered up and neutralized, socked away.

His brain shattered as his brother's was, Roland Kilmory was put away and the Kilmory Dynasty effectively, definitively destroyed. Younger brother Jeff would not have the guts to assume the holy mantle. If by chance he attempted it, he too would soon be sorry. There was little appetite left among the Kilmory clan for what Jonathan used to call "public service"—never "politics." One or two of the numerous Kilmory descendants would successfully run for office and win congressional seats, but their taste for it soon dwindled off and they went into other fields of endeavor.

Roland's real assassin was not the one accused and imprisoned—repetitively named Shapan Shapan—but very likely the security guard just behind Roland, since Shapan the scapegoat was a few yards ahead and facing Roland as he fell, while all indications were that the fatal bullets entered the victim's skull from behind at point-blank range. How could he have fired them?

There are as many inconsistencies in the Shapan-as-lone-assassin scenario as in Rosswell's—so many that it is unnecessary and, in the end, a waste of time and energy to pursue them all. Only a few are worth examining, since they shed considerable light on the crime itself, pointing out a number of unusual details.

A number of witnesses at the scene saw a woman in a yellow polka-dot dress, accompanied by a man. Although such attire would be unusual for someone trying to be inconspicuous, the point is that witnesses heard her say to her companion words to the effect that "we killed Kilmory." Yet this testimony by witnesses was turned away and not officially recorded, not even as hearsay. One would think such a statement would immediately attract the attention of anyone intent on investigating the crime; its truth or falsity could and should have been definitively determined via a thorough investigation. If ignoring such a piece of evidence is not turning a blind eye to a smoking gun, it is, to say the least, extremely suspicious. Despite testimony from witnesses aimed at denying or confusing the woman-in-the-polka-dot-dress story, the female so dressed would have been a prime suspect in any other criminal case. Yet no one did a timely follow-up on her, whoever she was. The attempt to discredit this vignette was implausible... and yet it prevailed insofar as the investigation was concerned.

The extra bullet-holes in the pantry of the Anderson Hotel were another mysterious factor. Not only were they not taken into account, they were made to promptly disappear by hotel maintenance people, who removed the damaged wooden panels and other materials showing evidence of bullet impacts—shades of what happened to Justin Kilmory's presidential limousine! When photographs showing the holes were brought up, investigators did not attribute them to bullets but to other, unrelated and hardly credible causes.

Over the last forty-some years, Shapan has made himself appear to be a harmless man who is still confused about what happened. He states that he had no major motive for the act other than the gimcrack impression that Roland Kilmory had voted for a bill providing fighter aircraft for Israel. Yet dozens of other senators, and not just Roland Kilmory, surely must have supported such legislation at one time or another, as the record clearly shows. What could possibly be accomplished by killing Roland Kilmory, other than providing unlikely future dissuasion for other senators to pass such bills? What was Shapan going to do: shoot every legislator who had cast a vote he disapproved of?

Shapan had a writing pad on which appeared—repeated over and over—the words "Kilmory must die," and acknowledged that the words were in his own handwriting. However, he stated that, even so, he had no recollection of having written them. Although writing that "someone must die" is incriminating, it is not evidence that the writer actually committed the act.

Finally, as noted, Shapan was yards ahead of Roland Kilmory as he advanced through the pantry and simply could not have fired the fatal bullets. Yet, over forty years later, he still languishes in prison. No one has any genuine interest in his parole nor in securing a new trial for him based on new evidence that—despite all efforts to suppress it—has been collected since Roland Kilmory died. The real assassins, as well as the authorities themselves, feel much safer keeping him in custody than letting him out into the world to raise questions and give them headaches.

There are still more bizarre and suspicious details, but there is a question as to their usefulness. It would be wasteful and tedious to engage in a full recitation, particularly since it is clear that felonious acts were carried out to facilitate the murder, together with unethical and wrongful actions on the part of law-enforcement and judicial authorities. Coincidentally, the same Dr. Naguri who autopsied Marie Moore's body in L.A. six years earlier also examined that of Roland. But it is no coincidence that in this case as well the results were doctored and misleading.

Simple use of logic, together with judicious application of the laws of chance, leads to some conclusions. Despite arguments to the contrary, the unconstrained court of public opinion makes it possible to reason, speculate and add up all sorts of evidence, regardless of its strictly legal admissibility. Such an exercise is not prosecutorial, but simply a truth-in-history quest. Whether to "convict" in this fashion is ultimately a matter of personal opinion, up to each individual, it is still worth pursuing.

Just the fact that two supposedly lone assassins with no solid motivation, special training or any kind of support network managed to shoot and kill two of the major political figures of our time—who also happened to belong to the same powerful family— brothers, no less—within a span of less than five years, strains credulity to the breaking point. The overall picture of two suspicious capital crimes committed against the first family of the land, the unanswered questions, the disputed and still-disputable facts, the sloppy and tendentious investigations, constitute—taken together—a chain of exceptionally unlikely events whose link to each other hardly seems deniable. Especially when each was attributed to a single individual who—in the first instance—was quickly silenced by murder, and—in the second—was programmed to act against his own best interests and appears suspiciously disinterested in clearing his name.

In prison and expecting that he had, in any case, not much longer to live, mobster Mariello bragged to his fellow inmates: "Yeah, we took care o' the bastards—the two of 'em."

Chapter XXXI
CURIOUS

The sailing was smooth, the weather perfect. The breeze put a pleasant chill on the warm late-June sunshine. For a change, the guests on Jeff's yacht were down to a half dozen, four of them Kilmory women gathering in the galley to enjoy some hot food and drinks, away from the political talk that their men were so fond of. Two of them, Jeff, and his nephew Jim, were alone on deck. It was one of those rare occasions when they could talk privately without witnesses, eavesdropping bystanders or unwelcome interruptions.

"Uncle Jeff, I hope you don't mind, but I'm still curious about our family history. Something just doesn't add up about what happened to my uncles—the hits they took." A bright thirty-two-year-old, Jim was intent on digging out some facts—any at all would do.

"You don't really want to know about that, son," Jeff said pointedly. "Besides, it's, uh, something that we shouldn't get into, at least now," he added defensively. "Remember that old saying, 'let sleeping dogs lie'."

"But it's only the historical truth, for my own information. You don't want me to learn about it from books, videos, all that slanted and speculative stuff that's out there in libraries, right? I don't believe most of it anyway. There's got to be, uh, something more to that whole story than just a couple of kooks who got it into their heads to kill my uncle the President, and then a presidential hopeful—both named Kilmory."

"Well, son," Jeff began, patronizingly. "You're right—there's more to it than everyone's been led to believe." No sense in denying that, Jeff thought; if he did, it would only heighten Jim's suspicion. "But that's, uh, something we prefer to keep within the family circle, as you've probably figured out already, and so I'm, uh, planning to tell you about it someday. I don't think that uh, right now, however, is the time to, er, go into that. Besides, we're likely to be interrupted any minute by, uh, Jan or Frances or who-knows-who."

"Well, if you keep postponing it I'll never know." He felt his uncle had been on the verge of telling him something about it on at least one other occasion, but held back at the last second. Jim wondered if he hadn't pressed him hard enough. "It's important for me to be informed, don't you think? If not, how will I know how to respond, how best to counter false allegations or misstatements?"

"Well, just be patient, son." Jeff's plan was to just keep putting off a disagreeable subject.

"It just seems strange that no one in the family did, er, a further investigation into these, these acts of violence." Not about to be sidetracked, Jim was determined to learn from his uncle whatever he could, always suspecting the reasons, harboring his own theories, but wanting to hear Jeff's version. The Kilmorys disliked talking about those tragic events, and Uncle Jeff's attitude followed that line precisely.

Jeff turned the wheel and the Kilmory sailboat, having been on a steady course, suddenly took a turn into the wind, near the tacking point. His plan was to cause a distraction, and would have if one of the crewmen had not dissuaded him. The timing would have made it dangerous amid the surrounding marine traffic.

"Frankly, uh, not a good idea for us and, uh, not really possible due to opposition at the very top echelons," Jeff answered, turning to leeward. He was hoping his nephew wouldn't ask any more questions.

"Why wasn't it a good idea, uncle?" he answered, not to be deterred.

"Well, uh, it might bring up things we'd rather not, uh, have in the public domain." Jeff looked less uncomfortable than he felt. He had, through years of public exposure, learned to mask his feelings well.

"As a matter of fact, many in the public have the impression that the Garrett Commission didn't do a proper job of investigating the assassination. If so, why wasn't another agency such as, well, the FBI, uh, called in to do it right?" Jim felt he also had to probe into this additional suspicious area in the complex web of mystery surrounding those tragic events whose images, thanks to technology, were still so vivid despite the decades gone by.

"Well, a number of government agencies were, uh, involved in one way or another in the investigation and, ah, worked with the Garrett Commission to help prepare its report."

"Oh? Well, it looks like they didn't do too good a job in view of all the questions and controversy surrounding it."

"Besides, as you might know, uh, your Uncle Roland conducted his own investigation," Jeff blurted out before he could stop himself.

"Really? Well, I know nothing about it," he lied. What was the result?" He had heard about Roland's investigation, but wanted to dig for more information.

"Basically, the same, uh, as the Garrett Commission's. There were, uh, only minor discrepancies, as there will be in, uh, any investigation." Jeff spoke without conviction. He was about to say more about the results of that private investigation commissioned by Roland, but decided the time was not right and the can of worms might spill out of control.

"Sounds to me like uncle Roland kept all of that pretty secret—it might be worth reading," Jim wasn't expecting Jeff to give him a copy, but it was worth a try. "Is there a way I can read it?"

"You'd make an, uh... awfully good lawyer, Jim." Jeff chose to divert the conversation by changing the subject and being patronizing. "Too bad you chose business administration." Jeff tried to throw in a weak joke and then, seeing it didn't work, quickly changed his tack. "But seriously, I don't know if it will, uh, be possible to get you a copy. I would need to look into that and get back to you." Roland had limited the report's distribution to only the closest family members.

"Well then, could you at least tell me a little *something* about it?"

"I'll tell you what. I'll check into it and do what I can to get it for you, okay? It's not, ah, all that easy... stashed away in a safe deposit box, er, somewhere." He neglected to mention that *he* also had ordered a private investigation—in the case of Roland's murder—and kept it secret, even from many family members. He had no intention of giving him a copy of either report, nor of revealing any information about his own privately-ordered investigation of Roland's murder.

There were things that were best kept secret and private, an objective only achieved by keeping those in the know to an absolute minimum.

"Okay." Jim accepted his words without too much expectation that he would come through. "But why has it never been released?" He suspected why, but was curious about hearing his uncle's reply.

"The truth is that neither your Uncle Roland nor the top people in the succeeding administration wanted to bring out anything that might conflict with the Garrett Commission's conclusions. It would open up a whole mess, give rise to needless complications."

"Why "complications"? Why not let the facts speak for themselves?"

"National security was the, uh, basic reason." The unspoken word "excuse" flashed by his brain, stopping at his tongue. "Right after taking office Jameson said, I, uh, recall, that making it all public at that time might cause such indignation as to force his hand to avenge Uncle Justin by invading Cuba. That," he added in a strangely flat, inconsequential tone, "might have brought about a war with the Soviet Union, maybe a nuclear one."

"Did you actually believe that then... or *now*?"

"I'm not, uh, sure, son," he answered evasively, turning away to signal that as far as he was concerned the discussion was over.

Then he added over his shoulder, as a parting shot, "I wouldn't want to, uh, dig into it further... and neither should you. It really wouldn't do us any good, you know. Nothing, unfortunately, can bring Justin or Roland back."

"Well, I'm sorry uncle, but I think it's important. At least for the sake of establishing the truth. There are just too many questions, too much mysterious, suspicious stuff involved in all this."

"I agree with you." His expression was serious. "But it's just, you know..., too complicated and long to go into right now." The kid is awfully persistent, he thought. "I'll either have to tell him something one day, or else figure out a way to get him off my back," he said to himself. Then he had an idea.

"Hang on!," he cried, suddenly turning the wheel so the boat went into a beam reach, making the yacht lean over forty-five degrees and quickly gain speed. Jim nearly lost his footing, grabbed a sheet and gave his uncle a surprised look..., only to see him smile mischievously.

Jeff wasn't about to discuss the subject anymore. For Jim, the mystery deepened.

Chapter XXXII
LIFE IN THE FAST LANE

David Barker looked at the stunning, elegant woman who had just come off a flight from Toronto at National Airport—as it was known then—just across the Potomac River, the dividing line between the District of Columbia and Virginia. It was Mireille Trudert, the wife of the Canadian prime minister. A decade or so older than he, but young, slim, attractive and stylish, she caught his eye and smiled at him—guessing who he was—from a dozen yards away as she made her way into the large semi-circular waiting room enclosed by expansive, curved windows. He strode up to her and introduced himself.

"Hello, Mrs. Trudert, I'm David, from Senator Kilmory's office," he said, slightly ahead of her. "The Senator asked me to drive you over to his residence."

"Thank you, that's very kind of you." She was gracious. Her eyes and expression denoted, besides a magnetic sensuality, excellent manners, breeding and intelligence. "The Senator," as his staff called him, was lucky indeed to have, if occasionally, such a companion. Known to have her choice of lovers here and there, she was spending the weekend with him at his McLean estate while his wife was away on a trip. But she was by no means the only woman who visited or consorted with The Senator on any given weekend or, for that matter, during mid-week.

Some time back, David would not have dreamed of anything like this. He had assumed that stories of The Senator's infidelity were "trash," the word used by Alice, his personal secretary, to characterize the numerous letters, news items and reports that referred to her boss's private life in an uncomplimentary manner and came into the office on a regular basis.

The Senator's preferred driver and all-around handy man—he did a little bit of everything—David had started out as a mail-room volunteer at the Senator's Capitol Hill office. But he was so adept, efficient and friendly that in a very short time he was hired as a regular staff member.

His first experience as The Senator's driver was hair-raising, but once again he did extremely well, particularly in winding and squeezing his way through traffic in Jeff's convertible. The Senator liked to show himself with the top down whenever possible, thereby getting recognized; other motorists willingly made way for him, and it kept his car from being stopped or ticketed by police, who would nod to him and practically usher him through red lights and traffic jams. David proved incredibly adept at squirming through, cutting corners and committing numberless violations with impunity, and the boss was duly impressed.

Other drivers might be angered by his aggressive attitude, but he was under orders to get The Senator to National Airport on time, and even though his boss was habitually behind schedule, he had to make it. If he missed the five o'clock flight to Boston he would have to wait until eight, and having an angry boss on hand for three hours was hardly a good prospect. Consequently, David applied all his skills to beat the traffic. Delta Airlines was sometimes able to delay a flight for The Senator—without stating the reason, they would stick to technical excuses—but only for a limited time.

Soon David was given more responsibilities and found himself rescuing The Senator from traffic accidents in the middle of the night, dealing with his wife and her drinking problem, and delicately refereeing domestic fights without hurting anyone's feelings. In this position, he began to witness things that he didn't really want to see or know and was expected to keep his mouth shut about.

It was difficult for him, since there were just too many instances of women, cocaine, corruption, poppers, and rude or improper behavior.

Singer Jane Bayez called one day to say she had to do a concert in Washington and wanted to know if The Senator "wanted to get together" with her. David picked up that they had been intimately acquainted for some time and relayed her message.

"Yeah, tell her to come over on Tuesday," he said, almost casually. "We get along well."

David made arrangements to pick up Jane at Washington's Mayflower Hotel. Accompanied by Debi, an attractive female friend of hers, David drove them out to McLean, where The Senator ushered them in and soon suggested they take a dip in the hot tub.

"You too, David, come on in," The Senator said in a jovial mood, bringing out a supply of cocaine. When he saw all three of them sitting around snorting coke as if it were coffee or tea, David lost his inhibitions and joined the party. He was not surprised when Debi began to get physical with both Jane and The Senator at the same time.

Jane and Debi then turned their attentions to David, who made no complaints. However, when he noticed out of the corner of his eye that his boss was not too happy, he gently pushed Jane over in his direction. Shortly, the two girls totally neglected him and piled up on The Senator. "Well," he thought, "I have to be thankful for small favors." At times, the two girls left both him and The Senator alone while concentrating on each other.

When he mentioned this later to The Senator, he replied self-assuredly: "Jane is not lesbian, just bisexual." Apparently he had experienced that behavior before and, with a serious authoritarian air, wanted to clear up the matter once and for all. He maintained that, ahem, bisexual women were just fine with him.

At times things were more complicated. Lauren, one of The Senator's girl-friends who flew in frequently from a Northeastern city, regularly stayed at David's house when The Senator's wife, Jan, was in town. His job then consisted of waiting like a taxi driver for The Senator to call and then ferrying the girl over to McLean. On one occasion when he was asked to board the girl-friend, things took an unexpected turn. It turned out that she started putting the make on him and, despite his protestations, she wound up taking him to bed. Naturally, David was worried that bedding his boss's girl-friend was going to get him in trouble. But if he ever found out David never heard any echoes about it, so apparently it wasn't that big a deal.

Soon enough, things went further along and he and The Senator became drinking and carousing buddies. Lauren brought along another girl one day and the four of them wound up drinking, doing lines of cocaine and eventually going to bed—although this time in separate bedrooms. At other times they would mix it up and exchange girls for a spell without so much as a by-your-leave.

David found it hard to believe he was doing all these things regularly: women, coke, poppers, pot and booze. It was the last thing he had ever expected, particularly with The Senator. When he started working for him he was very young, naïve and straight, but Jeff gradually broke him out of that. Sometimes, when David showed up in a relaxed situation, The Senator would say "Oh, oh, the Archbishop is here." Then he would joke around and say to David: "I'll bet you've never sinned once in your whole life."

Eventually, David realized that if he wanted to fit in with The Senator's life style he had to loosen up and join in the fun and games.

The Senator expected—indeed, encouraged him—to take his staff members to bed as much as he did. There was no shortage of female staff who were ready, willing and able to have occasional, casual sex with the boss and with other authority figures such as David himself had become. If you run around with them, you end up by imitating them, he said to himself—or else you find yourself alone... and, worse still, unemployed.

On another occasion David did not find the situation so enjoyable. He had established a relationship with Brenda, an attractive young woman who worked in another senatorial office. Everything was going well until one day, when the two ran into The Senator in a hallway. Right away, David was aware that his boss had his eye on her and even flirted with her in front of him. After all, that's what he heard that Jonathan, Jeff's father, used to do with his sons' dates—it was a sort of family tradition. Soon, Brenda began telling him that she was getting calls from The Senator, who was trying to go out with her. It was the Kilmory style to hit on friends' and relatives' wives and girl-friends, regardless of whatever jealous reactions might arise, so David had to acknowledge it as standard procedure, even though he wasn't happy about it.

Brenda told David that even though she kept putting his boss off, he continued to call. "Just keep saying no and eventually he'll give up," he said, not too hopefully. Once The Senator set his sights on a woman, he put on the Kilmory charm and eventually won her over. To him it was a kind of competitive game.

The Senator had the upper hand in this contest, since he controlled David's schedule and could send him out of town whenever it suited him. Soon he scheduled him for a weekend in Boston, so as to have the field to himself. He called, persuaded Brenda to join him for dinner in his mansion in McLean, shared some pot and coke with her and promptly took her to bed.

"Well, you certainly messed up my relationship," David said to him when he came back to the office on Monday. Instead of answering, The Senator concentrated on business.

David hoped that it was just a fling and his boss would leave her alone. No such luck. It continued and pretty soon Brenda was seeing The Senator more and more frequently, seemingly involved in a hot affair.

Upset and resentful at Brenda more than at The Senator's behavior, which he felt was only to be expected, David ended his affair with her. It was the first time that he had been seriously disappointed in his boss, from whom he had expected more respect for his intimate relationships.

The Senator managed to juggle a limitless number of women at the same time. He kept a little black notebook with their names and numbers, and even with his busy schedule, he kept in touch with them and made dates for weekends as well as "lunches" in his private Senate suite. Besides that, many of the women on his staff had occasional dalliances with The Senator, taking their turn as circumstances and schedules allowed. The interns, who were generally younger and more star-struck, were easy targets for The Senator's charm. At the time he seduced one of the most attractive girls she was only seventeen years old—probably his main reason. Soon afterward, knowing that she was by no means the only one, but just one more among the crowd, she stopped seeing him and went to work for another congressman. Eventually, The Senator's pursuit of women was further facilitated by his seniority, yet not at all hampered by age. He had gotten enough of it to become chairman of an important committee and qualify, in addition to his regular office, for a special suite where he could treat the women to lunch and drinks, and have sex on a convertible sofa.

Again, it was possible for him to entertain girl-friends for entire weekends in his McLean, Virginia mansion, located not far from Pine Hill, his brother Roland's sprawling estate, where the favorite sport was "baptizing" guests by tossing them fully dressed into the pool.

The Senator was generally free to entertain his girl-friends, ignoring the presence of his children, because his wife Jan, when not completely tipsy—she had gotten into a serious drinking problem as a result, it was said, of her husband's affairs—was often traveling, or simply spending time in an apartment they had in Boston. The excuse for buying it was that it gave her a chance to go and see her relatives, but the real reason was that, in view of her drinking and The Senator's incurable philandering, she was better off out of sight and therefore out of mind. They were rarely together anyway, either at home or at functions of any kind, and he even had some girl-friends over when Jan was actually home. At those times she shut herself in her room and drank until the woman's visit was over.

On one occasion when Jan had invited The Senator's mother to stay at their mansion for a few days, that did not stop him from bringing over a girl-friend and flaunting her in front of both mother and wife.

David had gradually become a valued and trusted personal assistant to The Senator and was often asked to come to his McLean mansion to take care of business. Once, The Senator's wife being out of town, he was asked to bring over a package containing a substantial amount of cocaine. He showed up to find a party going full blast. The Senator was accompanied by his brother Roland, two or three other congressmen and staffers, and more than enough beautiful women to keep them all company. When he asked The Senator's personal secretary what was going on, she raised her eyebrows and said "They're all playing together." David, who at the time was still not familiar with all the terminology, came to understand later on that, in swinger's circles, "play" is a metaphor for sex. He took care of what he was there for and promptly left the partiers to continue enjoying themselves, although by that time he had opened up and was a little disappointed that he wasn't asked to stay and join the fun and games.

* * * * * * *

Candy, one of The Senator's favorites during a certain period, began to enjoy his attentions more frequently than other girl-friends. This resulted in jealousy, competition and outright fights for his time. It did not entirely rule out sharing, however, as he frequently was able to get two of them in bed at once. When he managed to do that he not only satisfied his own sexual appetite, but by controlling himself was usually able to take care of them both in one fell swoop. "Sort of like killing two chicks with one stone," he would quip to David.

Candy was sometimes amenable to a threesome of that sort with The Senator, but lately they had been pairing off by themselves. It had gotten fairly intense when David got a call from her: she wanted to have lunch to personally discuss something confidential. "Oh, oh," he thought, "here it comes." It had become commonplace for women to want to find out from him what their chances were of getting The Senator to divorce his wife and marry them.

The story was always the same. Candy, like so many others, was extremely fond of The Senator and would do anything and everything to make him happy, take care of him in every possible way. And David's answer was always the same: forget it, it's not going to happen. He's married with children and Catholic, and if he divorced to marry another woman—even after a decent interval—his chances at being president, the top prize for all the Kilmory men, would less than nil. Even his whole political careermight be at risk. The Rantachidick incident, despite independent investigations that deemed it full of unanswered questions, was receding into the past and was hardly brought up anymore. That was not going to be a major factor. But another marital scandal on top of that could be the game-breaker.

But in this case there was a kicker: the girl suspected she was pregnant. David was not too surprised to hear it, but it was bad news for all concerned. He wasted no time in beating about the bush: if The Senator divorced to suddenly marry a pregnant girl-friend, that would be like the kiss of death for his political career and hopes for the future.

"Did you tell him or give him any hints?" David wanted to ascertain whether The Senator knew about it.

"No, I was afraid to. And besides, I might be wrong," she said, playing nervously with her food. "Suppose, for example, it's just a late period."

"Well, don't tell him," he said firmly. "It might worry him unnecessarily." He suspected that she had already confirmed she was pregnant and simply wanted to see his reaction. "As soon as you get it checked out by a doctor, let me know the result and we'll take it from there."

Within a couple of days, she called David at his home number. "I'm afraid it's true, David. I'm 'PG.' What should I do?"

"It's not my place to point out the only way to get this taken care of, Candy."

"I see," she said, her heart sinking. "But don't worry, I know what I have to do." She then expressed her appreciation to David for his support and hung up. He decided not to worry his boss by giving him news of that sort. There was no point in bringing up the matter unless complications came up. He would tell him that she had called when he was out, saying that she needed money for a trip, and would explain later. The Senator had no objection but wanted to know some details. David made up a story about a spur-of-the-moment family problem without revealing anything that might give him reason for concern. The Senator was smart enough to let the matter rest.

Within a few days Candy called David at the office and told him that she had, sure enough, taken a trip to Florida to see her parents. They never discussed her pregnancy again. He gladly issued her another check out of the office's contingency fund to cover the costs not covered by the original payment.

On another occasion, The Senator's number-one girl unexpectedly brought up a delicate matter, to the bewildered amusement of David and other guests. Sitting around The Senator's pool, the girl seemed ill at ease, squirming in her skimpy bikini. When asked what the problem was, she explained that she was feeling queasy in her most intimate area.

"What," David asked, "you mean down there?"

She replied by nodding, afraid to say *yes* out loud.

David suddenly remembered that girl-friend number two had said something similar on the phone just that morning.

"Oh, my gosh, we've got to get you checked out right away."

The symptoms sounded too much like those of a common sexual disease and, if both of them had it, the Senator probably did too. He couldn't afford to have something like that, since it was not just bad for his health but disastrous publicity if it became known.

David wasted no time in taking her to a doctor they trusted and getting her diagnosed. It turned out, as he suspected, to be what is commonly known as "the clap." He notified girl-friend number two to get herself to a doctor and get a shot of antibiotic, whether she had symptoms or not.

The amusing part was getting the doctor to come and give The Senator his own shot.

"No, I'm fine, I don't need that," he said, staring wide-eyed at the huge syringe and needle.

"Sorry, Senator, but if you don't take this you might need twice as much later." The doctor tried to sound professional but couldn't hold back a smirk.

In the face of that, The Senator had to take his pants down and take a four-inch needle into his behind. David, much amused, felt that he was getting his just desserts for his careless fun.

* * * * * * *

Being an administrative assistant to The Senator was fine for David, even if it kept him extremely busy, sometimes having to put in sixty hours or more per week. But things would get even more interesting. Unexpectedly the position of personal assistant opened up and The Senator was in a quandary to choose someone he could trust to fill it. Accordingly, he brought the matter up with David, to whom it would mean a move up. But it would imply giving up the administrative area, which he enjoyed for its involvement in Senate business, getting bills passed, working and negotiating deals, etc.

"Thanks, Senator, but to be honest, that would be a new area and I'm not sure...."

"Well, uh," he replied, before suddenly brightening. "What if you keep both jobs? You can take care of the personal stuff, but delegate some responsibility in management and just generally oversee what goes on. David, why don't you give it a shot?"

"Why, I..., I don't know, but I'm willing to try it out." He had not actually thought of it in those terms. "I'm just concerned about being able to do a really good job for you in both areas at the same time," he added. Those words were just right. He got the job. Now he would be put to the test to divide his time between two vital fields.

Being The Senator's personal assistant had its perks—more parties, women, cocaine, poppers, pot—but it also carried serious responsibilities. David had to solve major problems, be ready to rescue The Senator when he got into difficult situations, cover for him when he got into trouble, take the blame for something embarrassing he had done, etc.

And it also made him privy to numberless family secrets. One of them was erasing tapes for the Justin Kilmory Library, which was being set up in his home state. The tapes, he suspected, were full of compromising material, including Justin's conversations with many of his girl-friends, among them Marie Moore. In fact, he was hearing considerable fascinating "top-secret" information from those in charge of erasing them. There were lengthy conversations with Marie as well as with Jessica, two of his favorite lovers, with whom he maintained what were—for him—relatively long-lasting relationships.

Engaged for the "eraser job" were two trusted friends of the family. They had to be extremely trustworthy and hard-working, for there were lots of tapes to be heard and blanked out. In addition, they had to forget everything they heard and never bring it up, never comment on the contents nor the work itself, and be prepared to deny, even if asked under oath, that they ever did such a job or ever even heard of such a job being done.

One of the "erasers" once grumbled to David that he had just undergone a grueling weekend of work, and that just one conversation between the president and Marie Moore had lasted about two hours.

"Wow, you should hear the stuff they talked about," said the "eraser," raising his eyebrows.

"I assume that was when the Prez was not too busy—or else trying to make up for a time when he was, and so found it impossible to keep a date with her, right?" David grinned, slightly amused.

"Or maybe," he added, on a more serious note, "that was when she claimed that she had got, well, pregnant by him and he had to convince her to end it. She was desperate to have a child, but he could not possibly take a chance on letting something like that go on or get leaked out."

The "eraser" suddenly looked surprised.

"You knew about it?"

"Just between you and me, I once overheard something about that," David replied. "That was one of the times she supposedly had a miscarriage. Maybe she was not even sure who the father was, but her intuition told her it was Justin's." Aware that he had said too much, David then dropped the sensitive subject.

As time went on, he learned more intimate details about the life of Justin Kilmory. He found it amazing that somehow, even if affairs of state kept him extremely busy, he always seemed to find an opportunity to straighten out or sweeten up his women, keeping them on the string until he could allot them some time for personal "recreation." That a head of state with a complicated schedule could, on occasion, devote hours on end to talking to someone far beneath him intellectually was extraordinary—especially since the discussion could not broach any important issues of the day.

One exception was Marlee Penchot Meter, with whom Kilmory did develop a penchant for discussing important issues, eventually developing a fairly solid intellectual as well as sexual relationship. As the former wife of a high-level CIA operative, Marlee also became privy to secret information that may have eventually been costly to her. Not too long after Justin's assassination she was found dead on the banks of the C&O canal in Washington's Georgetown neighborhood. How thoroughly the case was investigated is a moot question to this day. Suspiciously, the murder was never solved.

To David it was more evidence of the Kilmory drive when it came to power, sex and money—in alternating order, according to circumstances.

As for the "eraser" job, he did not learn any more than necessary, nor did he want to, even though most people assumed as a matter of course that the Kilmory White House tapes would be edited "clean." The standard was to "delete anything considered sensitive, inappropriate, or that should not be heard." These tapes were, of course, precursors of the ones that later got another president in a heap of trouble because he didn't erase enough of them!

In the beginning, presidents would press a button when they wished to record something, whereas later on, after Watergate, they would press a button when they wished to *not* record something. However, since that was not always easy nor practical, it is safe to assume that there were always trusted staff members to edit the tapes before being stored away for future historians to listen to.

The use of cocaine by The Senator and by David himself had escalated to the point that he wondered if, in the event The Senator were elected president, they would be able to keep it from becoming public. He began to notice that, once the habit is ingrained, it is difficult to reduce its use, let alone give it up altogether. At one point, when the job was difficult and particularly uncomfortable, it seemed that cocaine was the only thing that kept the two of them going.

David was so trusted, particularly in the very personal area, that he traveled with The Senator on important trips. One of them was to the funeral of Pope Paul VI, where The Senator incurred the anger of President Canter's wife Alice when he turned out to be more popular than Jerry himself, as Italians cried out "Kilmory, Kilmory!" on the streets of Rome whenever they saw him. David was able to slip into the entourage of the funeral cortege itself when The Senator told an Italian security guard to let him through, claiming "he's a relative of mine." David thereby incurred the envy and anger of other staffers, who felt that they, too, deserved the VIP treatment.

The Senator and David were careful in their use of cocaine on trips such as this, usually by carrying a "bullet," a small capsule which makes it possible to bring up a dose at a time and snort it directly up the nostril, then sealing and re-pocketing the container. Thus, it is possible for a user to take a quick shot unobtrusively in a bathroom or almost anytime one can get a moment of privacy.

Many other political figures were also using the drug at the time. One of them was President Canter's chief of staff, Milton Jordener, who was involved in a scandal about cocaine use at New York's famous night club, "Studio 45." It was well known that coke and other drugs were regularly used there, generally in small, more intimate quarters, but sometimes right on the main dance floor. Apparently someone present in one of those "intimate" sessions recognized Jordener and leaked word that he participated in the drug use. A steadfast Jordener denied it until eventually the uproar died down and was glossed over.

With regard to The Senator, however, David was thankful that no one brought up the issue of drug use or, for that matter, that of women, alcohol or anything else. Oh, sure, there were rumors, but nothing solid to go on. He helped make certain that those who knew what was going on were sworn to secrecy or else paid off or taken care of in other ways.

At one time The Senator had a problem with the captain of his yacht, who knew too much about his use of drugs, liaisons with women whom he took aboard and had sex with, etc. The captain was suspiciously spending too much money on supposed repairs and supplies for the vessel and, when The Senator confided this information, David immediately recommended that he get rid of him.

"That's not possible, David," he explained. "If the man started talking about everything he knows it would be a disaster. I can't just let him go without some very substantial severance pay to keep him quiet." David later learned there were many other such cases of office and household staff who knew too much to be let go.

"All right, let me think about it," David replied without further elaboration.

A few days later, he thought he had an answer and asked The Senator if he simply had to have his own boat available all the time.

"Well, no, not really. I only use it a few times during the summer."

"In that case, I have a proposal," David said. "Let's find a buyer for the boat who'll agree to keep the captain on with at least the same salary. You get rid of the captain and save thousands to boot. You can always rent a boat any time you want to."

"Great idea! Do it," he said. "If the captain goes for it, we're home free."

In a relatively short time, David worked with The Senator to arrange a sale on those terms, with some severance pay for the captain to keep him happy and his lips sealed.

Cocaine was by no means the only drug that The Senator and David used to relax, overcome inhibitions and stimulate their sexual appetite. They frequently used poppers, Quaaludes, pot and abundant amounts of liquor. It all helped them to forget the pressures of politics, personal appearances, speeches and overall congressional pressures.

The Senator would frequently complain—sometimes in mock tones—that he wasn't having any fun and that David's attempts to control him were too close to micro-management. "Remember, I'm the boss," he would say without much conviction, since down deep he knew that David was right and looking out for his best interests.

Frequently, they would both wind up naked in the hot tub with whatever women were handy. After having experienced the joys of a hot tub, which always made it easier to help "playing" get started, The Senator just had to have one installed in his deck. He stipulated that it had to be sunk down into the deck, since that way it was easier to get into and spared his back, which still pained him from an accident with a small plane a few years back. In fact, he used his back pain as an excuse to get his doctor to certify it as a medical requirement in order to deduct it from his income taxes, although the tub was more of a sexual aid than a health requirement.

Although cocaine was a staple drug most of the time, The Senator was also fond of poppers—amyl nitrite—Quaaludes, pot and, of course, plenty of liquor. He kept these items mostly under lock and key in his desk at the office or at home in order to prevent his children from getting to them. On one occasion, however, he came upon two of his older children who were doing lines of coke and, instead of stopping the proceedings and giving them a lecture on drugs, he actually joined them and did some lines himself. He then explained to David that his idea was to get on their own level and show his kids that he was "one of the boys," thereby gaining their confidence and demonstrating that if they could not avoid using drugs, they should at least do so in moderation. Later on, one of those children developed a serious addiction that required extensive and expensive treatment. Eventually, one of his nephews was unable to give up the drug habit and died of an overdose.

Liquor was in a different category. It was freely available in his home grounds except when his wife Jan was around. Since she had a serious drinking problem and there was a concerted effort to get her to clean up her act, alcohol was quickly locked up whenever she was expected in, although her visits were becoming an ever more infrequent occurrence since she increasingly spent time away, holed up in the apartment he had bought for her use in Boston.

The marriage was deteriorating more and more, but periodic efforts were made to patch it up and make it appear acceptable, particularly at the time when Jeff decided to make a run for his party's nomination against the incumbent president, Jerry Canter. The Senator could not hope to wrest the nomination from Canter without at least the semblance of a viable marriage. The incident at Rantachidick was still a millstone around Jeff's neck, particularly when he announced that he was running. What was largely a forgotten episode—although there were still unanswered questions lurking about—began to be resurrected once he decided that he was going after the prize, intent on restoring the Kilmory mystique to what the family was inclined to call "our days of glory."

Although The Senator did make what many felt was a really serious and dedicated effort to achieve his goal of getting the nomination—Canter had a "leadership" problem and was in deep trouble as a result of American diplomats held hostage in revolutionary Iran—it was difficult to succeed against the power of the presidency. Then, too, The Senator made too many mistakes, stumbled too often in interviews and was unable to convince a significant portion of his party.

When the Iran hostage crisis came up he made an attempt to intervene, hoping that if he managed to free the American diplomats his success would easily gain him the nomination. When he was unsuccessful it actually got him in trouble. Word about it leaked out and he was criticized for acting behind the administration's back, thereby undercutting its efforts.

One mistake led to another. Even a friendly interviewer whose son he had helped by getting him an internship in Congress, confused him and caught him off guard with a relatively simple question.

"Can you tell us something about the state of your marriage?"

"Well, uh, I would say that, uh," he started, fumbling for words. "We've had our troubles like, uh, all marriages, but she's, uh, been working out her problems and, ah, I think we're making, uh, progress on a lot of things." His "uhs" and "ahs" were more in evidence than usual and denoted how uncomfortable he was with the subject.

But it got worse when another predictable question stunned the public and critics alike when he attempted an answer. It was simplicity itself: "Why do you want to be president?"

Instead of leaping in to give his vision of America's future, the aspiring candidate, incredibly, remained silent for several seconds, at a total loss for words. Was "I want to finish my dead brother's shining vision for America" clouding his mind? Eventually, he came up with a lame, unconvincing answer.

"Well, uh, I think that, er, I believe the United States should go forward and, uh, not be standing still when there is, uh, so much to be done and, ah, I think we should get, er, much more done than we are."

After that disaster The Senator tried to recover and pick up his mental energy level but he had lost what little momentum he had in the beginning of the interview, and it showed. The public began to wonder, indeed, exactly why he wanted to run for president if he was unable to handle something so basic as to articulate his philosophy in a coherent manner. In brief, the interview gave such a poor impression of his viability that, at that particular moment, he virtually lost any real chance he had to win his party's nomination. If he had intended to fumble this opportunity—not too far-fetched, really—he could not have done much better.

Some of his main supporters, including his brother-in-law, Sidney Schmidt, who was running his campaign, began to have second thoughts. This was not helped by incidents that took place in mid-campaign. When Schmidt came over one afternoon for a strategy session at his McLean, Virginia mansion, it was David who had to meet him in a desperate delaying action. The Senator had snorted some cocaine, jumped into his hot tub with a girl-friend and had a few drinks to boot. He was in no condition to discuss anything with Schmidt.

Upset and irritated beyond belief, Schmidt berated David, accusing him of not doing his job. "You're the point man in this, and you have to get him to shape up! If not, I can't do my job."

"I'm terribly sorry," David retorted, "but I'm only his employee and I can't control him. I can only do so much."

Schmidt then retreated to New York City and, out of loyalty to the Kilmorys, continued to run the campaign, but in lackluster fashion and avoiding further contact with Jeff.

There were a few minor successes and some fund-raisers here and there. But by then, even in these instances it seemed that Jeff's heart wasn't really in it. In one case The Senator met with a solid supporter who was wealthy and should have been good for perhaps $75,000, but needed to be asked in no uncertain terms.

The campaign was extremely short of funds and had found it necessary to let go a substantial number of workers and reduce its rental expenditures, overhead and other outlays. Even though David had told The Senator to ask him for a hefty donation, Jeff had simply neglected to do so. He lied and said that he had asked, but David suspected the truth when the man turned out not to have given a single cent.

It was no surprise then, that the whole campaign went downhill from there. In retrospect, The Senator might have been less interested in the success of his campaign than in ending it and going back to leading the less-restricted and -scrutinized life that he had become used to.

With the campaign over, The Senator could be more carefree and have more fun. Oh, he still had to make some personal appearances, make his peace with the incumbent president, put in a show of party unity and perhaps even do some perfunctory campaigning for him, but that was easy compared to a full-blast presidential campaign of his own. He had some fond memories of doing it for Justin and Roland, but at that time he was younger and loved the novelty and sense of adventure. Now, it had become old hat and far less attractive, not to mention cramping his style in the love-life department.

His last public appearance was at the party's convention, at which he delivered a rousing, enthusiastic speech which was much appreciated by the delegates, the critics and the press. It was easy to work up his energy for that, since it was a final exclamation point that enabled him to put the whole business behind him. His wife and kids were there to cheer him on and they, too, smiled radiantly, probably happy to see this hectic stage come to an end.

The Senator's face also showed relief... and anticipation, when he asked David to retrieve his little black book of girl-friends' phone numbers. It was time for more life in the fast lane: more fun in the hot tub with plenty of coke, booze, pot and poppers.

David wondered whether Jeff had been seriously in the race or had just gone through the motions to satisfy the hard-core Kilmorians. He was beginning to wonder just how long he could continue to put his life on hold to promote what remained of the Kilmory legend.

Life in the fast lane was beginning to be a little slower than at first it seemed.

Chapter XXXIII
CURIOUSER, CURIOUSER

After his uncle's abrupt maneuver with the boat, Jim made his way back up to his former position on deck, near the wheel, holding on securely to everything that was battened down. The Kilmorys' legendary playfulness being what it was—bordering at times on sheer recklessness—he had no doubt that his uncle had attempted to "throw" him overboard, heedless of his lack of a life jacket.

"Come on, uncle, give me a break," Jim said, in a way that referred to either his steering or not being forthcoming. "At least give me a general idea of what was going on, you know, what really happened to Justin and Roland. I can always fill in the blanks." As long as there was a glimmer of a chance to learn the truth, he had to make an effort to grab at it. "I'm aware of some background stories, such as Sal Campana's help to save my grandfather's life back in the fifties, when Castellaro put out a contract on him. But I'm not sure how it all ties in together."

Jim knew more than he let on, but it served his purpose to pretend ignorance so he could tell how much—or how little?—Uncle Jeff would be opening up. There was little doubt that he was trying to keep as much as possible under his hat. But what difference could it possibly make, since they were all Kilmorys? If it was all in the family, why was he trying to keep under wraps?

"Well, Jim, uh, that story was a little exaggerated. Something like that went on, but uh...," Jeff said, not thinking it wise to confirm the truth of that episode. "It wasn't, uh, quite that way. My dad got into a bit of trouble because he balked when they asked him to do something he didn't think was right."

"So he was not successful in arguing his way out of it?" Jim couldn't resist putting words into his uncle's or anyone else's mouth, despite the adverse reactions of some. In a dialogue, that came with the territory.

"That's it, more or less. He needed to appeal to, ah, someone who was like a third party, and not, uh, a party to the dispute."

"So he appealed to that Looney guy."

"Yeah, heh, heh, that's what they called him, 'Looney.' I see you're familiar with the nicknames." Less amused than he pretended to be, Jeff also picked up that Jim quite likely knew more than he was letting on.

"The way I see it that means my grandfather," his nephew plowed on relentlessly, "owed those powerful guys a big favor, right? A favor that was supposed to have been paid off when your generation got to the seat of power." Jim made a mistake: never answer your own question. Well, there were exceptions.

"I'm not going to deny that it, uh, might possibly have been part of it. I'm, ah, not sure myself, but that could've entered into it." Jeff stiffened, realizing he had already acknowledged too much. "I mean, those bastards might have *thought*," he backtracked, "that they had, uh, some kind of a deal like that." He congratulated himself on coming up with that escape hatch.

"Oh, come on, Uncle! Come out with it!" Jim surprised himself with his own boldness. He made up his mind that he simply wasn't going to be denied. "What else would have given the Mob a motive to put out extremely risky contracts on people of such high rank as the Kilmorys?" He couldn't afford to let this chance slip by him—or he might never get another one.

"Well, I'll make, uh, no bones about it: I'm not fond of the subject," Jeff said, trying to sidestep the issue.

"I know—I can tell," he laughed in a mocking tone. "But I think I deserve to know. Isn't *that* what happened?"

"Well... let's say it's possible." He didn't want to acknowledge too much. "They felt betrayed, er, let down, because we—Justin and Roland—didn't want to, uh, do what they expected. I think the issue was *expectations* more than specific conditions. We"—the plural meant that he considered himself to some extent involved—"didn't think the leaders chosen by the people of this country should be beholden to the underworld."

"And the underworld, of course, disagreed."

"All right, I'll level with you." Jeff felt the cat was out of the bag and drop the pretense. "We never expected that, uh, they were actually going to go so far as to do what they did." Jeff's head dropped a notch or two. "Just underestimated them. But of course there was lot more to it than that...," he added cryptically. He was going to complete the thought by saying: "It was not just the capos... we think there might have been somebody else, some high-powered guy or group behind it all." But he held back, suddenly realizing that

that would, far from putting a damper on the discussion, bring up further questions yet to be answered.

"I hate to keep harping on it, Uncle, but it's still not clear why this was never pursued," Jim interrupted, realizing that Jeff was about to pile on more of the same vagueness.

"But it *was*, uh, pursued." Tired of the questioning, Jeff was on the point of risking it and tackling the reasons for the cover-up. Yet, abruptly, he desisted, sensing that Jim had not picked up on this opening and might drop it. Also, revealing anything new might lead Jim into areas he'd rather not explore with him. "Like I said, uh, we in the family also looked into it, but, uh, it's all very complex, son."

"That's fine, Uncle, but it seems the justice system did not do its job in investigating, arresting and ultimately indicting these... criminals. Why, tell me why did they not prosecute them and punish them?" Curiosity pushed him on to get to the bottom of the story, realizing that he had barely scratched the surface.

Then there was that mysterious slaying of a fifteen-year-old girl, a few years back. Jim had heard something about that but everyone in the family chose to avoid the subject: another female slain by a Kilmory or a relative. The suspect, Mark Scarborough—Roland Kilmory's nephew by marriage—was a teen-ager at the time. It was only decades after she had been brutally murdered with a golf club that Scarborough was finally brought to trial, convicted and given a sentence of twenty years to life.

Were the Kilmory's above the law? "Thank goodness for that," Jim thought perversely. If not, more of them, especially those in public life, might have wound up with a different kind of "record."

In a moment of sheer honesty with himself, he sensed the pattern. The Kilmorys, like most, if not all, politicians, indulged with impunity in a habit of ignoring or superseding the law. Immoral and illegal acts are routinely gotten away with, thanks to power and influence and the ease with which, by judiciously applying them, the rules can be circumvented.

Physically taking people out when they get in the way was and is only slightly more difficult. The cases that he knew about involved women, but had males also been disposed of? Then he recalled that one man had been taken out of circulation in the early 1960's. It was something close to "Ngo Dhim."

He couldn't remember the exact name of the South Vietnamese leader who had been assassinated by his enemies with U.S. backing, although the instructions of his uncle, President Kilmory, had been only to depose him and let him go into exile. But he did remember that the slain leader's angry widow, Madame Ngo, had made accusatory public remarks directed at President Kilmory.

Jim had, of course, dismissed such charges out of hand when he eventually learned of them. But by now he knew a lot more.

Then he began to research his memory and read up on history. No sooner had Justin Kilmory been inaugurated than he ordered the CIA to develop a political-assassination capability called RZ/RIFLE to eliminate undesirable foreign leaders.

The number one target had been Cuba's Fingenio Costra; He had escaped death through a combination of tight personal security, cleverness and sheer luck. In that particular case, RZ/RIFLE had been a dismal failure, very costly to his Uncle Justin and to America. The Dominican strongman Trujillo was successfully taken out by using the CIA to provide conspirators with special weapons, intelligence and advisory assistance. That operation, he concluded, had eventually succeeded in re-establishing democracy, freedoms and free elections. So the U.S. had been justified in attempting to depose at least these two dictators, Trujillo and Costra.

Congolese leader Patrice Lumumba was eliminated, as far as he could recall, when the U.S. pulled out the rug from under him, making him vulnerable to his enemies. The CIA backed the plot to assassinate him for reasons shrouded in mystery but perhaps having to do with the worldwide struggle against communism.

Disposing of foreign leaders, Jim mused—especially those who posed a threat to their own people or to neighboring countries—was sometimes justified.

But had Americans also been disposed of? The question plagued him. Somehow, he had to get to the bottom of things, however shocking or distasteful they might be.

"Uncle," he addressed him one last time, in earnest, "please tell me that all of this is a fantasy.... I would prefer it that way... or else tell me the truth—the whole truth."

"Every word... I have, uh, spoken, Jim, has been, uh, the honest truth," Jeff was in what seemed to be his regular prevaricating mode, which he let on by far too many customary hesitations for such a short, declarative sentence. Then, at Jim's incredulous look, he added: "Not, er, the whole truth, mind you, since we, uh, obviously don't have enough time. Later on, I'll fill you in on more details..., don't worry." The old false cliché, "don't worry." Even as he spoke, he told himself firmly that he ought never to dream of doing any such thing.

"We're getting back to port, Jim"—he tried to sound nonchalant—"so we'll have to uh, put this on hold for the moment." *Indefinitely* was much closer to his intent. "But you've got the general idea. Pull in that sheet so we can steady the jib and bring her in properly," he said, assigning him some of the crew's duties as a distraction.

Jeff was thankful they were coming in, getting him off the hook until he could get a handle on the situation. It wasn't just that he despised discussing the subject; he actually hated to *think* about it, not to speak of dwelling on it, going back and raking over those dying but glowing embers that still left painful burns, etching trails in his brain at each and every recollection.

The less these subjects were discussed, he thought, the better. And he had said far too much already—much more than he had wanted or even expected to.

Chapter XXXIV
RANTACHIDICK

"Cheers, honey!" Jeff looked into Molly Jeanne's eyes, took only a sip and smiled mechanically as he watched her drink up.

He had invited Molly Jeanne over, together with all the "Back Room Girls" that had worked on Roland's campaign for the presidential nomination—now tragically over with another cruel assassination. Rantachidick promised them relief: a summer weekend of sailboat racing, relaxation and merry-making. The date chosen, late July of 1969, would coincide with the astronauts' first landing on the moon, a historic first for America and the world. Hopefully, the press would be too distracted to take notice of the get-together, even though there were possibilities that it might make the news. An aftermath?

"So, where are we going?" she said with innocent curiosity which, to him, sounded like something deeper. There weren't too many places to go at that hour on that small island—no bars, no restaurants or night clubs, and he didn't need to take her anywhere special if he wanted some intimacy. They had already been lovers for the better part of a year or so, and so felt comfortable with each other. Before working for Roland's campaign she had been on the staff of another senator from Florida who had been a close friend of Justin and Jeff's, so she knew her way around the ways and wiles of Capitol Hill.

"Oh, just for a drive, some fresh air. It'll do us good, and give us a chance to chat." He avoided eye contact.

"Well, okay. Maybe just for a short while," she replied, since she did want to discuss what was weighing on her mind as they walked out the front door of the cottage. He had rented it out for the weekend to host the special gathering for the girls who had worked so hard on Roland's tragically thwarted campaign.

"See you shortly," Jeff said cheerfully to the others, who were standing around, drinks in hand, trying to make amusing remarks and listening to music. He felt he had struck the perfect note, casually separating her and himself from the group.

"Let's drive down to the water's edge, along the channel," he said as he got behind the wheel. "There's a nice view by moon..., er, starlight, anyway," he chuckled, correcting himself—the astronauts' landing in the back of his mind—noticing with a smile that earth's satellite was hiding behind some clouds.

"Jeff, I'm still worried, like I said. I really don't know what to do." Her incipient pregnancy was like a dark shadow hanging over her—and him. He had been vague about his intentions. Supportive, but making no commitments. As Catholics, both were opposed to abortion—legally, politically, socially. And within the country, under ordinary circumstances, it was a practical impossibility in any case.

"We'll work something out, my dear. Let me give it some more thought."

"Well, Jeff, we haven't got much time." She hated to press him but had no choice. "Pretty soon it's going to begin to show. Then what?"

"We'll have to give it some more thought. But in any case I'll take care of you—you know that. I'm going to make sure you're taken care of... and the baby as well." He figured that he might as well recognize its existence, embryonic though it was. As he glanced at her he noticed her eyelids beginning to droop. The drug he had slipped into her drink was taking effect. It was crunch time.

"Well..., when are you, when do you think...?" She was mumbling now.

As he parked along the narrow road leading to the bridge, he observed thankfully that she was quickly falling asleep. It would soon be over with, he said to himself to allay his nerves.

"I'm going to let you get some rest here in the back," he said as he opened the rear door, picked up her light body and deposited it lengthwise, feet-first into the wide back seat.

"Hmmm, so sleepy," was the only thing she drowsily mumbled in response.

"Just rest," he said soothingly.

He then closed the back door, locked it and waited a few minutes before taking the next step. Satisfied that she was fast asleep, he started the engine. Then he fished out a wooden rod that he had improvised from a child's umbrella and secreted under the driver's seat. He wedged it between the seat and the accelerator.

He turned off the lights to make sure that, if there was anyone around, they would not easily see the car or its direction. The Pontiac's engine, in neutral, accelerated. It was a little too noisy for comfort, but no matter; there was probably no one within earshot.

He moved the wooden rod aside momentarily, drove a few feet, lined the car up and aimed it carefully down the bridge. The angle was such that the car would go over the side and drop into the water, he hoped, near the middle of the channel. As a precaution before wedging the rod again in place, he pulled back the emergency brake so the car wouldn't start rolling. Then he checked out Molly Jeanne one last time to make sure that she was soundly asleep. He paused a moment to look around in every direction before getting out of the car, engine revving. Nerves frazzled, sweating, he got out and repeated the exercise, scanning the surroundings one more time to make sure there were no unexpected witnesses.

Satisfied that everything was in order, he reached into the car and pulled the automatic-transmission lever to the "drive" position. The engine struggled to move the wheels. Finally, it was time: he pulled the lever to release the emergency brake.

The reaction was surprising. The car took off much more quickly than he had anticipated, the tires squealing slightly. He was able—just barely—to slide backward and slam the door shut as the car sped away, lightly sideswiping him.

He watched from a crouching position, thereby making himself less visible to any prying eyes. His heart dropped. The car was traveling at about forty miles per hour, much faster than he expected; worse, it was veering to the right far too soon, and would go off the side of the bridge onto dry land or shallow water, instead of in mid-channel. But now, there was nothing he could do. Within seconds, the speeding dark-blue automobile went off the side of the bridge, did an end-over-end flip, turned upside-down and flopped with a loud splash into shallow water. Momentarily panic-stricken, he made an effort to gather his thoughts and concentrate on the next step.

He looked around and to the rear, worried that the noise might have attracted unwanted attention from anyone within range. There were lights at a house perhaps two hundred yards away. But he noticed no sign that anyone there had heard anything. Seconds later, satisfied that the coast was clear, he ran over to take a look.

The car, resting just below the water's surface, was barely covered by water. So far, so good. Unless she had somehow awakened, regained her senses and scrambled out, her chances of survival were minimal. Thank goodness, he told himself, that he had thought to bring along a waterproof flashlight so he could take a good look. If the cold water had awakened her and she was trying to get out, he would have to do something about it. He shuddered to think what it would take. But he could not afford the risk of doing nothing. He would be caught in a trap of his own making.

And another thing: that incriminating rod he had wedged against the gas pedal had to disappear. If he did not fish that out, it would be a slam-dunk against him. He would have to dive in, find it and get rid of it.

He stripped to his shorts, threw his clothes down and jumped into the water, flashlight in mouth, not even feeling the cold liquid's embrace as he immersed himself. He vaguely remembered having read that, at first, extreme temperatures make little or no impression on a body geared up with adrenalin. The current nearly dragged him away before he was able to grab onto a door handle. A foot or so under water, he shone the flashlight through the rear-door window.

He could hardly believe the scene. Molly Jeanne, breathing the air trapped against the upside-down floor, was desperately feeling her way toward the rear door nearest him. When she saw the light, she spoke words he could not hear and signaled for help with her hands. Did she think he was trying to rescue her? Momentarily, just momentarily, he almost felt sorry for her. The girl had no inkling about what was going on. He shone the light straight into her eyes, blinding her momentarily. Much as he hated the idea, he had to do something.

Opening the driver's door against the current was harder than he had expected, even though the window was open. But he found that his strength—adrenalin?—was up to the task. Once inside, he responded to her muffled cries for help by reaching out to grab her by the hair as he pointed the flashlight with his loose hand through the darkness. He missed, but caught her shoulder, pulling her down below the air bubble and under the water's surface. Somehow, she slipped out of his grasp. He backed off cautiously; any bruises on her body might arouse suspicion or even become evidence that might work against him. Nearly out of air himself, he needed to go back up. What if he wound up like Molly Jeanne, trapped underwater in the upside-down car?

Struggling against the current that dragged him away, he pushed the door ajar with all his strength by bracing his feet against the seat back. He squirmed out just before the current slammed it shut and shot to the surface for a much-needed breath.

He had to hurry: suppose, by feel alone, she might be able to unlock one of the rear doors, push it open against the water pressure, and free herself?

He tried to put all these thoughts out of mind as, gasping for air, he dove back into the chilly, murky liquid. He momentarily shone the flashlight through the rear-door window and was greeted by her still-frantic efforts to signal, begging for help. She had not understood his intent, or was pleading for assistance regardless. Desperate and helpless, weakening fast and unable to save herself, her arms flailed aimlessly about. He felt a pang of pity brush momentarily past his innermost feelings, but at this point there could be no backing down. He had made a determination about what he was going to do and now he had to go through with it. If he didn't, his political career would go down the drain, and with it the still simmering hopes for another Kilmory presidency—his own.

He reached toward the passenger-side front door and, this time helped by the current, pulled it open. He reached for the steering wheel, pulled his body partly inside and pointed the flashlight toward the rear so that it lit up Molly Jeanne's eyes and face. Desperately, her lips tried to speak soundless, bubbly words. For a split second he hesitated, his resolve unsettled... Should he once again drag her head down below the bubble, underwater?

He was still undecided as he speculated that she was losing it and not going to get out by herself. Besides, he was again running out of breath, while she was actually still breathing some of the stale, oxygen-deficient air. The impulse to act then surged within him. He moved into her bubble, breathing up more of the limited air supply while grabbing her and pushing her by the neck and shoulders under the surface. It was difficult physically but, he told himself, would only take another minute or two. She slipped away and made an intuitive effort, though feeble, to regain access to the bubble.... Then she went still. He waited for what seemed another eternal minute, watching her. He could not look away from the eerie shadows—as if in a bad movie—cast by the flashlight against her body as she floated face-up, motionless. Finally, he no longer detected any movement made of her own will.

He took a last breath from the air in the bubble, and told himself it was high time he fled the scene. He swam out the still-open front-passenger door and struggled vainly with his last ounce of strength to close it shut against the force of the current. He pushed hard and paddled his feet to no avail. Then it finally dawned on him that it leaving it open would not matter and gave up.

He breached the surface and took deep breaths. Everything was now in order, he thought, except for that damned, incriminating umbrella rod. He dived once again, pointing the flashlight back and up at the driver's side floor. Miraculously it was still wedged in place. But he was on the wrong side and unable to reach it. So he climbed atop the underside of the car barely sticking up out of the water and banged his knee against the muffler. Ignoring the pain, he dropped over to the other side and, after breathing deeply, dove again. Somehow he opened the driver's-side door and, flashlight in mouth, groped around for the rod as he struggled against the current's pressure tending to close the door against him. Running out of strength and stamina, the thought crossed his mind that he might get trapped inside—just like Molly Jeanne.

A rush of relief came as suddenly, by feel alone, his hand met the rod. Grabbing it, pulling it out and breaking it in two were nearly a single motion. Pushing the front door open far enough to slip out and shoot up to the surface, he let the current close the door behind him. As he surfaced gasping for breath, he threw the pieces one by one as far as he could into the middle of the channel, where they would be carried away by tidal currents.

His heart was racing as he reached a bridge piling and held on, keeping an eye on the submerged car. What to him seemed yet another eternity probably lasted no more than two or three minutes.

Desperate to get out of there and away, he managed to hold himself in check. First, he needed to make absolutely sure that no signs of life were visible at the dim scene where the car lay upside-down. The water was cold but there was no wind; only the current to struggle with. Eventually, he had no alternative. He had to dive down one more time for a final look. What if she were waiting there, open-eyed, still begging to be saved?

Within his head, the seconds were ticking by. He could afford to wait no longer. Plunging down once more, he found himself being pushed against the car by the current. The flashlight now brought up a different scene. Molly Jeanne looked like a rag doll, very still, floating up against the rear seat. Strangely, her head was still face-up inside the bubble. Was she still breathing or just lifelessly floating? She seemed to give no sign, this time, of noticing his light. "She's already gone," he told himself hopefully. Hadn't he, after all, held her down and felt her go limp and motionless? But he couldn't be one hundred percent certain. Might she just be faint, semi-conscious?

Finally, he concluded that he was overwrought. He'd had enough. How long could anyone stay alive breathing the limited amount of oxygen contained within a small bubble? In a jumble of thoughts, one stood out: time was running out. He could not afford to stay there indefinitely, keeping watch.

On top of that he had to get his staff aboard on the damage-control effort. The back-room girls were another story: they would have to be carefully handled so as to keep them away from the press. If they could be kept at a distance and as isolated as possible, things might work out. Eventually they—and the whole episode—would fade away: an unfortunate accident in an innocent but tragic mid-summer outing to cheer up Roland's devoted staff of hard-working, faithful girls. The thought struck him that one or more of them had likely also been intimate with poor Roland—as they had with Jeff himself—without developing into anything more than an occasional fling. Who knew if they had shared his innermost thoughts and concerns? A commonplace of human nature, sex increased trust and friendship, while sometimes creating trouble by raising expectations. In that case, it could easily turn into jealousy, suspicion and enmity. Isn't the first suspect in a violent killing usually the spouse?

Now, things appeared to be under control for Jeff. He started swimming and, eventually, waded ashore. Molly Jeanne was still inside the car. Even someone fully conscious and wide awake—especially of small size and weight like her—assuming strength and alertness enough to concentrate on unlocking and opening a car door under those circumstances, would have found it extremely difficult to escape unaided.

It was time to go and deal with the aftermath, whatever it was. He brushed the cold water off, used his briefs to dry off some of his torso and put on the rest of his clothes, which stuck uncomfortably to his wet body. He pulled himself together and began trudging, shoes squeaking, back to the cottage.

With some top-notch damage-control, short of a miracle that might bring her back—thus ruining his life and career, and tarnishing the Kilmory mystique—he just might be able to echo his brother Roland's comment about the "suicide" of Marie Moore, his movie-star girl-friend: "Too bad about Molly Jeanne."

Chapter XXXV
AFTERMATH

Jeff had, ahead of time, put together a plan. He would try to get one of his top assistants, Rick Grogan, to take the blame for the accident, even though, realistically, the story might have had too many holes to be believable. Additionally, there was a risk that Rick might wind up having to do some actual jail time for leaving the scene of a fatal accident. That might be difficult for him to accept. And who knew what additional complications that might entail? Still, he was hoping that this was his best escape route. He wasn't in the car and had nothing to do with it. That's the way he had thought of it from day one. Otherwise it could get extremely messy.

Another scenario was to say that Molly Jeanne was driving the car by herself and just made a wrong turn. But no one was sure that she had a license, or if she actually knew how to drive.

Jeff got back to the cottage and signaled to Rick, who managed to slip away from the other partiers. The seven remaining girls and several male friends and staffers were still having fun and a little tipsy.

"There's been a really horrible accident," Jeff said to Rick.

"What?" Rick exclaimed, wondering what could possibly have gone wrong at that time in an area with no traffic.

"You'd better get Peter out here as well," Jeff added, holding back the details. "We need to talk."

Bringing over Peter, another staffer, Rick had a gut feeling that it might be worse than anyone expected.

"Tell us what's going on," he said once the three of them were in the privacy of Rick's car.

"The car, uh, went over the bridge and, ah, into the water, and I think Molly Jeanne's still inside." Jeff held his head low, a hand on his brow. "I don't know what to do. I need your help."

"Oh, my God! Let's get the hell over there and see if we can save her!" Rick turned around and started the car before saying another word.

Based on the estimated time elapsed since Jeff had taken off with Molly Jeanne, Rick calculated that the accident had taken place a half hour to forty-five minutes earlier. It might be too late to save a possible drowning victim, but there was always a chance.

As Jeff guided them to where the car had landed in the channel, Rick and Peter looked at the scene with dismay.

"Holy shit!" Rick was beside himself. He had not expected to see the car nearly underwater. He was even more surprised that not only was it upside down, but facing in the opposite direction from which it had apparently been traveling. It must have been going very fast, he thought, to do such a flip. Sadly, there was little hope for Molly Jeanne if she had been down there that long.

"Let's dive in and see if we can pull her out," Peter said, not about to give up.

"Right away! But first we've got to take our clothes off. We could get tangled up in something down there and get fucked up too." Rick kept his wits about him.

"Right," Jeff said mechanically. "But I, ah, tried it myself—no use. There's an, uh, awfully strong current and you, uh, get carried away."

"But you're sure she's down there?" Peter said, still incredulous. He was going to add "How come *you* got out and not her?" but thought that might sound accusatory to his boss.

"I, I'm afraid so. Well, unless she, er, got out, uh, after *I* did." Jeff did not sound as hopeful as he would have wanted to.

"Not too likely. She'd be around here somewhere." Rick was realistic. "But let's see if we can dive down and take a look. Jeff, you get up there on the bridge—don't take any more chances."

Wasting no time, he stripped and dove into the murky water. Jeff watched from above.

"It's too dark," he said, out of breath, as he surfaced.

Jeff thought of the flashlight and was glad he had taken out the batteries and thrown it away into the middle of the channel.

Rick dived down once more, now joined by Peter.

This time Rick reached in through the open front window to the passenger seat where he assumed Molly Jeanne would have been, and felt around with his hand.

"There's nothing there," he said, wondering what was going on. Things didn't seem to add up. He thought of the back seat, which he had been unable to reach.

"Well, let me give it a try," Peter cried out before plunging down near where Rick had surfaced. He also reached into the front-passenger seat.

"I can't find her!" He spoke as he gasped for breath. "Would she be in the back?"

"Uh, I don't know, guys." Jeff acted dazed, despondent.

"When did you last see her—as you got out?" Rick wondered.

"I don't, uh, remember anything about the, er, episode. I'm drawing a blank."

"Nothing? Think about it." Peter encouraged him as he held on to one of the tires with both hands. He was beginning to feel the cold water in his bones.

"All I remember is, uh, after I got ashore. But I know that when we were driving she was, ah, sitting next to me in front," he added, keeping to himself that he had put her into the back seat.

"Did you see anything at all when you dived down looking for her?" Rick looked at him intently as he swam to stay afloat.

"No, nothing. All I remember is that it was, ah, too dark and I, I was out of, out of breath; couldn't, uh, stay down that long." As if reliving the experience, Jeff spoke in strained puffs hoping to discourage more questions.

"Well, do you think maybe she got out and the current carried her away?" As he waded ashore, Peter tried to come up with a theory to explain what had happened.

"God, I hope so!" Jeff threw up his arms as he came down off the bridge. Then he sat down on the bank and, in the classic position of despondency, held his head in his hands.

"That sure would be a lucky break." Peter was hopeful. He was feeling hypothermic and also got out of the chilly water.

"But we need to find her, we need to see if there is still a chance for her!" Excited as he was, Rick made a special effort to remain calm and in control.

"Yeah, but I, I don't know, uh, what to do, guys. How, ah, do you think we can explain this?" Jeff used the plural pronoun *we*, hoping that Rick or Peter would pick up on it and volunteer to say they had been driving.

There was a momentary silence, broken only by crickets. Veiled moonlight shone through the clouds, casting shadows. Jeff made a gesture with his arms, as if reaching out to them.

"Well, just tell them the truth: you had an accident," Peter said as Molly Jeanne was momentarily displaced in his thoughts by the need to account for what had happened.

"Yeah, but do you suppose we can say someone else was driving? That might, er, keep trouble to a minimum." Jeff continued to steer the discussion away from Molly Jeanne. Equally important, he needed someone else to take the blame; Rick would be ideal if he were willing.

"Well, if that would help I would do it gladly, Jeff." Rick had studied law at Columbia University and racked his brain to recall applicable legal principles. "But we would need to get our stories straight—not get caught in any contradictions," he managed to say under the moment's emotional stress.

Peter wisely remained silent, trying not to get involved. If those contradictions that Rick had referred to came up, he realized, there might be complications making matters a lot worse.

"To avoid that and possible perjury charges," Peter pointed out, "would take a lot more time than we have available to go over all the details."

"So I'm fucked, damn it! There's ah, a possibility of, uh, serious trouble no matter what happens," he said, steering the discussion away from Molly Jeanne, "and, uh, they're going to pin it on me. Shit! My whole career is down the drain. And you guys are fucking going down with me." He thought the threat might stir them to sacrifice themselves to get him out of the jam.

Simultaneously, Rick and Peter became aware that Jeff was clutching at straws and not all that concerned over whatever happened to Molly Jeanne, but about consequences. Did he think she escaped the wreck and was out there, somewhere, alive and well? Otherwise, why would he be so uncaring about her? Would he be less worried if sure that she was still down there in the car? Then again, who knew? They were knowledgeable about how Jeff's mind worked, about how selfishness—and sometimes selflessness—could surface under stress, but had never seen him in such a situation.

Jeff decided to get away from the scene. Further discussion offered no advantage. In a sense, Peter and Rick were adrift, and neither one seemed willing to assume blame for him.

"Well then, uh, why don't you take me over to, ah, Edwardtown, Rick. My neck's really hurting. I should have a doctor check me out."

"Okay, Jeff." Rick felt that he was giving up on his plan to ask him to take the blame, but his unconcern for Molly Jeanne was still strange. At least, he thought, this would provide a welcome respite from the tension and enable them to continue the search. "We'll keep on looking for Molly Jeanne," he added.

"There's a rowboat there we can, uh, use to get across. This will, ah, give me a little time to think about this so that when I, ah, get over there, I can make a more clear-headed decision on, uh, dealing with this." Downcast, he climbed aboard, again put his head in his hands and avoided further comment as Rick got into the boat and picked up the oars. "Thanks loads for the help," were his parting words as the boat started moving away.

"That's all right, Jeff." Peter looked at him with deep concern, troubled because he wasn't worried about Molly Jeanne's disappearance. "You know, of course, that you need to report this as soon as you can. Molly Jeanne... is still missing."

"Of course," Jeff said without hesitation. "That's exactly what I intend to do. I'll, ah, take care of everything as soon as I, uh, get a hold of myself. Just don't, uh, talk to anybody at the party about this.... We, ah, don't want to worry anyone unnecessarily," he added as if it were an afterthought.

Still no mention of Molly Jeanne. Clearly, to Peter and Rick, consequences were uppermost in Jeff's mind.

* * * * * *

By the time he was dropped off at the other side and walked back to his motel at Edwardtown, near Anna's Vineyard, Jeff had made some decisions. First, he needed to take the precaution of establishing a timeline as to his whereabouts by awakening the motel manager and complaining that the noise from a party in a nearby room was keeping him awake. He asked him off-handedly what time it was, explaining that he had left his watch upstairs.

"It's two a.m.," the manager replied routinely, in a tone implying "why wouldn't you know?"

"Thanks," Jeff replied as he went back up to his room. The next morning he got up bright and early, dressed up smartly and, looking cheerful and unconcerned, started chatting with some of the other motel guests. He thought it best to look and act as if nothing had happened. The previous night's events were completely out of mind and attitude. With luck, he might still avoid taking responsibility. Possibly, in light of the situation, considering all the circumstances, he clung to the hope that Rick would not refuse him. Rick could simply swear that it was he who had been driving when the accident occurred and that, by then, Jeff had already left the party and the island. Oh, there might be some details to iron out, but Rick had always stood behind him and pulled him out of trouble, going all the way back to their childhood days. He, Jeff, would have had nothing whatever to do with the accident.

He was still chatting casually with other motel guests when he was approached by Rick and Peter. Trouble. Both were out of breath but trying hard not to look overly concerned.

"You have to report the accident right away, Jeff. The car's been discovered. Besides, it's already been nearly ten hours!" Rick was agitated, still breathless. He looked at Jeff's eyes, wordlessly questioning in disbelief.

"Why don't *you* do it?" Jeff was still desperately hopeful of avoiding blame. I expected you to, uh, come around and, er, say *you* were driving." He got a sinking gut feeling that he was wasting his time.

"I would, but like I said that could spell a lot of trouble, Jeff. I don't think it would work."

"Why not?" Jeff looked upset.

"Think about it, about last night's events. I'm afraid we won't be able to keep our stories and timelines straight. Eventually it will do us both in, and they'll wonder why I—or several of us—were lying." Rick involved Jeff by using the plural *us*. He made a gesture of helplessness, holding his hands out, palms open. "Then we'd *all* be in a heap of trouble. Besides, we're still worried that there's been no sign of Molly Jeanne." If it really had been an accident, why would Jeff try so hard to avoid admitting it?

Jeff looked at him silently as he tried to put out of mind the nagging thought of Molly Jeanne still struggling in the back of the upside-down car. He realized, reluctantly, that his plan would not work. He had to admit that one person could, but it was harder for two or more involved in a single event to keep a single story line straight. Their answers had to match perfectly. He had best face the problem alone, instead of trying to sidestep it.

In addition, time was becoming a factor. In his calls to his attorneys and other associates they had been unanimous in telling him that there should be no further delay in reporting the accident. The longer the wait, the worse it would become. It would not make sense to further postpone it, and time was slipping by.

Further, it would be too time-consuming to discuss the situation with Rick, Peter and the others and agree on a story that would follow a single, consistent timeline, taking into account the whole sequence of events, details and circumstances. That is, even if they had the presence of mind to agree on a clear, definitive version. Besides, the girls who attended the party, if questioned, would likely not give a story consistent with theirs. In sum, getting such a plan to work seamlessly would just be too complicated and far too dangerous from a legal viewpoint. Worse, it might raise suspicions that what happened was not at all an accident. For him, that was the worst lurking danger, to be avoided at all costs.

Much as he hated it, his back to the wall, Jeff gritted his teeth and placed a call to the local police. He managed to report the accident in as few words as he possibly could—the less he said the better, his attorneys had told him. The hard part would be making a coherent statement and then answering questions.

He started thinking of the words to describe what happened as they followed directions and went to the station. Rick was driving—he himself could not, after what happened, afford to be caught behind the wheel of a car. To make matters worse, he had left his license back in Washington. In minutes, they arrived at the local station.

He greeted the local police chief, Jay Aaron, who quickly recognized him and appeared deferential, perhaps overwhelmed by his celebrity.

"The car involved is your property, right?" He spoke matter-of-factly, as though the accident were not all that serious.

"Yes. I was driving it." Jeff was forthright, hoping to appear aboveboard, make a good first impression and get it over with quickly.

"Oh?" The Chief was startled. "You know, we found a dead young woman in it."

"Yes. Can I have a piece of paper so I can, uh, write a statement about it, preferably in, ah, privacy?"

"Sure," the Chief answered, surprised that Jeff Kilmory made no comment about the dead girl. There was no expression of concern, as if she had been a complete stranger and he had had nothing to do with it. It seemed odd but he chose to withhold judgment.

Quickly, Jeff became aware that he should have said something about her, but had been too worried about talking too much while pondering what he was about to write down.

Chief Aaron acceded without realizing that he should first ask him some questions, but was momentarily relieved. At least he would have a quiet moment to himself to consider the steps to take in such a potentially high-profile case.

In a few lines, Jeff described the events leading up to the accident. He said he and his passenger, Molly Jeanne, were driving back to the ferry landing to go back to Edwardtown, on the bigger island across the strait; then, being unfamiliar with the area, he had made a wrong turn and headed toward the bridge over a narrow inlet. Somehow, the car had gone off the side of the bridge and into shallow water, landing upside down. He said he was in shock and had no recollection of how he had got out of the car. He pointed out that he repeatedly dove down afterward "to check if my passenger was still inside the vehicle," but said he "did not succeed in doing so." He went on to say that he had gone back to the cottage from which they had left, got into the back of a parked car and then asked someone to drive him to the ferry landing to get to Edwardtown. He stated that once he got there he "walked around for a while," then went to his hotel room; later, after realizing what had happened, he said he "immediately" called the police to report it.

When Chief Aaron first saw him he found it difficult to believe Jeff looked like someone who had been in such an accident. He did not yet know that it had happened the previous evening, assuming only a short while had elapsed. Then he read Jeff Kilmory's written statement and realized it had occurred nearly ten hours before first reporting it. Still, that did not change his initial decision: he was going to handle it like a routine traffic accident— nothing more. Even though the law required the driver of a motor vehicle to have a license on his person or near at hand, it said nothing about a driver that walked into a police station to report an accident. The Chief could have held Jeff for twenty-four hours for not submitting his license, especially after such a delay—in a case involving a death, to boot. However, Jeff said he would attempt to locate his license and bring it in later, and expressed his intention to leave and head for his family's residence to get some rest. There, he indicated, he would still be reachable in case it was necessary. The Chief chose not to bring up anything that might stand in his way.

One of Jeff's aides, in the meantime, had arrived at the station. Realizing his predicament, he understood that an early exit was called for and arranged for an air taxi to fly him out of there from a nearby small airfield. Again, Chief Aaron seemed in no mood to obstruct or otherwise delay his departure. Instead, he helped Jeff leave the premises through a back door so as to avoid reporters and others who were beginning to arrive in search of information on the event. In a few minutes, Jeff Kilmory was driven to the airfield, got aboard the air taxi and flew away.

The reporters were starting to demand that he answer questions, but Chief Aaron held them off. Having agreed to Jeff Kilmory's request that his statement not be released or put into the record until he could consult his attorney, he felt unable to offer anything that might be considered official on the case. However, he did attempt to cover himself by calling Detective Kearney, who was in charge of investigating such cases, in order to alert him, as well as Dean Evans, the District Attorney for the southern area of the state. Evans would decide if charges were to be filed.

After a couple of hours of insistent questions by reporters, Chief Aaron had to do something. Having not yet heard back from Kilmory, he decided to give them something in hopes that it would temporarily get them off his back. So he read them the written statement Kilmory had given him.

Then he heard the news from the medical examiner. They had recovered the body of the girl after pulling the car out of the water. The preliminary examination indicated that she had not drowned, but died of asphyxiation. There was little, if any, water in her lungs. Everything indicated that she had been breathing the air trapped in the car, and once the oxygen had been exhausted, she had passed out and died. How long she had stayed alive in the overturned car was anyone's guess, but people had been known to survive for hours under such circumstances. Why such an unreasonable delay, without which she might have been saved? Aaron was beginning to regret having released Kilmory without asking him any questions, based only on a brief written statement, but it was too late.

The question of an autopsy came up. Aaron said it was not his decision to make. The medical examiner and other authorities dodged any such responsibility like a hot potato. No one seemed to want to deal with a matter so delicate and potentially consequential. The undertaker was surprised that no autopsy had been ordered, since three important reasons seemed to require it: the type of accident, the important people involved and the fact that insurance claims for double indemnity might be made.

Meanwhile, Jeff Kilmory's advisers were trying to put together a plan. While the police were deciding about investigating and other authorities were pondering the handling of consequent legal procedures without being too harsh on Kilmory, his staff was weighing how best to put it behind them.

They got their heads together, consulted Jeff's attorneys and decided that he should make a television address to the state—and to the nation at large—expressing his regrets and taking responsibility. The fundamental question of his criminal and civil liabilities would be put on the back burner.

Jeff would also take that opportunity to ask for the public's sympathy and deflect the issue of blame for the event and his having delayed reporting it until morning.

Simultaneously, all Kilmory resources would be mobilized in order to pull him through the crisis. He was, after all, the last remaining heir to the dynasty and his ascent to the presidency on the coattails of his lost brothers would be the crowning achievement for his family and followers. Vindication for the Kilmory legacy, Camelot itself, hung in the balance.

Technically, he could be charged with manslaughter. But the District Attorney would be unlikely to go that far. His attorneys would work out a plea bargain: Jeff would plead guilty to the least-serious possible charge: leaving the scene of an accident. That would avoid a messy trial with its troublesome headlines. The penalty would be something as slight as the loss of his driver's license for a year or so, plus perhaps a period of probation. If so, there would be no problem. Jeff could consider himself lucky.

His sad television address, with its reference to the "Kilmory curse," seemed to do the trick. The delay in reporting the event, Jeff would carefully explain during the broadcast, was due to shock and confusion until, the following morning, he "fully realized what had happened." The focus of the matter, however, was turned away from the accident itself by the gesture of putting it up to the people of the state to decide, as if in an unofficial referendum, "whether Senator Kilmory should resign." That was underlined as the crucial issue at stake. Prosecution and guilt or innocence were matters for the courts, but this way everything tended to hinge on whether Kilmory ought to remain in office. Although, in reality, that was a decision up to the U.S. Senate itself, it sounded as though the matter had been taken to a higher court: that of the people, who would hand down the landmark, definitive judgment.

Jeff and his whole team were pleased when the initial impression was that the public had sympathized with the Kilmorys and all the bad luck that seemed to follow them. If anyone felt that the bad luck seemed to rub off on the country itself, particularly in the foreign policy area, they did not voice such a thought. It went over well and settled the matter. No one was to push him to anything but the most harmless possible outcome, without—for appearances' sake—letting him off completely scot-free. Jeff congratulated his team for a job well done.

If the "referendum" had grabbed the headlines, behind the scenes the key to the whole thing had been the removal of the body. That had been done quickly and efficiently. Before the district attorney, the coroner and the investigating detective could agree on doing an autopsy, Jeff Kilmory's team had got Molly's parents to sign an order requesting that their daughter's body be transported to Pennsylvania forthwith. Overcome with shock and grief, they had acquiesced. The team had also taken care to bring a substantial check with them as compensation, the amount of which was never made public. Few questions or statements about it were asked by the press. Once the body was out of the state where the event took place, there was little or nothing the legal system could do or wanted to about getting it back to follow established procedure.

Molly Jeanne's parents were assured they would incur no expense whatsoever. Quite the opposite: ultimately, an undisclosed—but clearly considerable—sum was handed over to them. As expected, they cooperated completely and there were no embarrassing complications. The Kilmory machine took care of further press inquiries. There was virtually no interest from the press in interviewing her parents, the people who had attended the party, Police Chief Aaron or anyone else involved in the event. Investigative journalism was conspicuously absent.

Some years later a book with a carefully researched account of the presumed accident came out. Not widely publicized, it simply stated the facts in minute detail, without any conjectures. If the author had any personal theories, he carefully avoided sharing them. When he ran into someone who posed a delicate question about the event—that it was no accident—he appeared scared out of his wits. Was he threatened if he ever expressed any of his personal thoughts about what really happened? No need to answer *that* question.

Upon removal of the body to another state, the autopsy became a moot question. The quick burial sealed everything. Jeff Kilmory and his team breathed a deep sigh of nearly audible relief.

There did seem to be some truth to the Kilmory curse, thought Mabel, Jeff's first wife, when she finished hearing his television address to the nation shortly after the pro-forma legal proceedings convinced her that it was all a convenient arrangement to let him slip out of a difficult situation. His second wife, Anne, had precisely the same thought years later, when he married her after a long period of swinging bachelorhood since divorcing the mother of his children. Both Mabel and Anne were inclined to think that many of the Kilmorys had been caught up in mysterious events that could not *all* be attributed simply to bad luck or unfortunate coincidence.

Only Jeff and two other people who had been on his team knew that, in the Rantachidick case, the only role of luck was, for Molly Jean, a bad one. Jeff hoped that the reality would go down to the grave with him and with those who had worked with him to "clean it up."

There were others who had an unspoken, intuitive understanding of the event—he could count them on the fingers of one hand—but they had no specific personal knowledge of the facts, nor any inclination to bring up embarrassing questions or observations. Nothing of the kind would serve any useful purpose.

His first and second wives were not the only ones who wondered about the mystery of Rantachidick. The surviving "boiler-room girls" who attended the party pondered the strange, unexplained gap between the time the car splashed into the water and Jeff's call to the police the next morning, during which a life hung in the balance and was eventually lost while he himself had, as he told it, narrowly escaped with his own. Although they believed that there might be something to the "Kilmory curse," their basic opinion differed only slightly. There was sorrow over the loss of their friend and co-worker Molly Jeanne, while Jeff's scripted television address had been less than convincing to them. Harboring doubts was unavoidable, but they kept their views to themselves. They knew a lot, having been privy to a lot of pieces of the puzzle. But they were handsomely rewarded to tell no stories and give no interviews.

Furthermore, why should they get involved in something that was none of their business? Would that bring Molly Jeanne back? Why stir up such a tragic and delicate matter? Especially when they had received compensation and also warned about discussing the subject. They were, after all, loyal Kilmorians to the end .

The "boiler-room girls" were all well aware—and wary—of the Kilmorys' history of effectiveness in "taking care" of those—particularly females, it seemed—who got in their way. Molly Jeanne's case confirmed that suspicion.

Jeff Kilmory and his team were thankful for their reputation. It didn't do them any harm.

Chapter XXXVI
THE LAST CAMPAIGN

*Politics is a great career. It
enables you to fuck all the
women you want.*
— Barry Clangton

The Patriarch clearly realized that both of his sons had been targets of Mafia hits. Knowing the ins and outs of power since the days when he was close to President Roosevelt, there was no doubt in his mind that the underworld was responsible, with the likely complicity of conspirators at the highest level. About the involvement of a foreign power or pawn—such as Cuba's Costra—he was not so sure. He had no solid facts to go on, although he did harbor suspicions.

But only conspirators at the top of the U.S. government itself would have been able to back up the killers, covering up the actions leading up to the crimes and the post-assassination efforts and demarches required. In the twilight of his life, unable and unwilling to revisit the subject with anyone available, he knew in his heart the basic reason behind the conspiracies. He had no one to blame but himself and that caused him unending sorrow and inner turmoil.

Having lost some of his sharpness, a few details still escaped him. He did not grasp that the crux of the matter, with respect to the cover-up of Justin's assassination, lay in the danger of revealing top-secret national security issues and exposing the Mafia-rigged 1960 election of son Justin. These issues were also used as an excuse by the leader of the conspiracy to protect himself from being found out. As for Roland's murder, its relationship with Justin's would eventually result in bringing up those same issues, which had to be kept under wraps at whatever cost. But the pain of thinking about those events and his own feebleness of mind stopped him from delving into them further, even inwardly.

Jonathan had concluded that his burning lifelong ambition to be president—which he had transferred to his sons one after the other after he fell out with Roosevelt over his opposition to the war—had truly turned out to be the worst of his misfortunes. Shortly after Roland's death he began fearing that the next hit would be on his youngest, Jeff, should he ever run for the White House.

But Jeff himself put to rest those concerns. Fully cognizant of the mortal danger he was in, he chose to sidestep the temptation to follow in his brothers' footsteps. Needing to at least take a stab at it for appearances' sake, he made a half-hearted attempt at wresting the nomination for president away from the incumbent, Jerry Canter. He had neither expected to succeed nor hoped for it. He was all too aware that, for him, merely being *nominated* for the presidential race would mean inviting the same fate that had befallen his elder brothers.

Reasonably sure that it would be nearly impossible to stop the president from being re-nominated in 1980, Jeff felt safe. There being little chance of success, the risk was minimal. But to appease the "true believers" in the Kilmory destiny, he had to at least pretend that he was going to pursue the dream. In the unlikely event that he should succeed in denying the nomination to the incumbent, Jeff also knew that he could still find a way to lose the election and his chance at the presidency—hard as that might prove to be for him to give it up.

He was never enthusiastic about the idea, even as a dream. Should he succeed in getting the nomination he might be tempted to proceed into the national campaign. But if he deemed it unsafe, he could always come up with a way to go down to defeat; he might make "mistakes" or simply conduct a lackluster campaign. Thus, the logical fall-back position, should he win the nomination, would be to do less than his best and lose the election against the likely Republican nominee, Reginald Runyon, who would be hard to defeat in any case. So he had a number of ways to bow out gracefully. Visualizing not going through to the end, he reserved for himself in the back of his mind the option to interrupt the process at any suitable juncture.

There was little chance of anyone bringing up the Rantachidick issue, since it had happened over a decade ago and, though not entirely forgotten, was buried in the past. Neither did the press seem interested in bringing it up anymore. So by now it should not be a hindrance. No matter of regret except for its consequences, it was but a shadowy recollection that haunted his quest for more political relevance and, ultimately, his hope for the highest prize.

"It was a shame," Jeff mused in the innermost recesses of his mind, "that politicians had to be corrupt, commit crimes and misdeeds, receive bribes and payoffs under the table and engage in double-dealing to get votes and win elections."

But that was the nature of the beast. It was unfortunate that such transgressions, common to the overwhelming majority of politicians, sometimes resulted in the loss for the body politic of so many of the ablest and most talented.

His brother Justin used to jest—and was inclined to boldly tell the joke in public speeches—about what his dad had told him: "Don't buy one more vote than necessary. I'll be damned if I'm going to pay for a landslide." What was funny—both "strange" and "amusing"—was that it was the honest truth. That was how they had won most elections, including the West Virginia primary and the presidential contest. But who knew—or had the guts to call them on it? The Kilmorys were so accustomed to getting their way that they thought it only daring and fun—an inside joke as well as a public one, if in different senses—to flippantly refer to it. On the other hand, in his heyday The Patriarch didn't find it quite as funny: besides being apocryphal— although he wished he had said it—there was too much truth in it.

On another level, Jonathan took care of politicians as a matter of course. He once arranged to meet fellow-Irishman Pit O'Lean in Cleveland, promptly pulled out a sheaf of thousand-dollar bills out of his coat pocket and peeled off thirty of them. He handed them over to the congressman, who at the time was Speaker of the House, and said: "This is for Manny Di Sole." Then governor of Ohio, Di Sole had been pushed around once too often by his son Roland, and needed to be placated.

As for Justin's joke about buying votes, he felt that he could easily afford to do so. There were two excellent reasons: 1) the Kilmorys enjoyed great influence in the press, and 2) the public, consequently only vaguely aware of such goings-on, had few specifics to reach any negative conclusions about them. The family had always made sure of controlling the press by either courting or threatening them: the old carrot-and-stick method, elevated to an art form and implemented at all levels, especially that of CEO's in book-publishing. Hadn't that columnist, Walter Winger, and other, highly respectable and respected journalists, always proved their usefulness in helping the Kilmorys gain and consolidate their power?

No politician worth his salt had ever gotten very far without making friends with or maintaining control over journalists. Early on, Patriarch Jonathan had showed them how that was done.

* * * * * * *

Later, when this episode had faded from the headlines, the press once again came to the rescue of the Kilmorys. It played a part in helping them get through another difficult situation. Jeff and Walter Kilmory Smitts, a young cousin, had gone out nightclubbing in West Palm Beach one evening and, after a few drinks, picked up a couple of girls named Alicia and Janine. When they went off to a Kilmory-owned residence nearby, Janine said goodbye and went home while Alicia—closer to Walter's age—stayed and came onto him.

Jeff reluctantly conceded the prize to his nephew, but accompanied the two when they decided to go for a late-night walk on a secluded stretch of beach. Soon, the pair got some distance away from Jeff, stopped, sat down, and began to get intimate. Catching up with them, Jeff remained nearby as an observer, casually finishing the drink he still had in his hand.

Days later, Alicia accused Walter of rape. At the well-publicized trial, she testified that "while the rape was proceeding, Jeff was nearby, smiling and finishing his drink, in apparent vicarious enjoyment of what was going on."

Meanwhile, the press played up the testimony of Walter and Jeff to the effect that everything developed normally, by mutual consent, and eventually the jury returned a verdict of not guilty.

The press neglected to report that the Kilmorys engaged as a private investigator a convicted felon who pursued Janine and made threats that influenced her behavior and testimony in the trial.

The court refused to allow the testimony of three women who were assaulted sexually by Walter in separate incidents over the previous ten years. Later on, civil charges were brought against Smitts by a co-worker for sexual assault and still later, he settled out of court with yet another woman over charges of sexual harassment.

That the courts failed to convict a Kilmory in West Palm Beach is reminiscent of the case at Rantachidick. Although these were the only times that any Kilmory was brought formally into court for a crime, the case against Jeff hardly counts, the one about Molly Jean, since her death it was handled more in the nature of a minor traffic violation.

The state had given Jeff a tap on the wrist, a temporary license suspension to a man who at any rate was used to being driven around by chauffeurs. Had anyone but a Kilmory been involved, manslaughter charges would, at a minimum, would have been filed.

* * * * * * *

When considering the coming elections Jeff eventually became coldly realistic.

"No way am I going to tempt the Mafia—even slightly—into putting together a plot to see me end up like my lost brothers," he once said to himself, never repeating those words out loud within earshot of anyone. One never knew when someone was going to slip and let the cat out of the bag, quoting the remark and embarrassing the Kilmorys.

Inwardly, Jeff became convinced that even *looking* like he might win the presidential nomination—let alone actually doing so— would be suicidal. The Mob might easily see that as an engraved invitation to take him out as well.

One day, Jeff promised himself, he would finally find out for certain who, exactly, was behind his brothers' murders and make them pay for their crimes—but that would take time and careful planning. He knew that it might somehow have involved the CIA, the FBI, and perhaps even the Secret Service. He did not exclude some role—perhaps a passive one—by Vice President Jameson, but he had no proof whatsoever. He had been the main beneficiary, no doubt. But by now Jameson was no longer in this world. He had attained the heights of power, lived it up outrageously and arrived, just as he thought, at the limits of his family's longevity.

Basically, Jeff knew that the executioners, if not the masterminds, had clearly been the Mob. He was aware that Cuba's Costra had played an important part. The sworn mortal enemy of the Kilmorys had the motive, the purposefulness and the means, and if he had't done it by himself he suspected Costra of at least having participated in the assassination.

Closely involved in all this was Plan Q, a secret so closely guarded that not even Jeff had been let in on it, even though he had heard vague rumblings that intimated something was in the works. When he did learn of Plan Q he was disappointed that they had not trusted him enough to bring him in on it.

In truth he was ruled out only because information about the plan was strictly on a need-to-know basis. Everyone who lacked that requirement was kept out of Plan Q, the top-secret project to deliver a mortal blow to Costra. It called for doing away with him together with his brother Repterio while, simultaneously, a new invasion of the island would be launched by Cuban exiles from bases in Central America and the Caribbean, this time with U.S. troops standing by to move in if and when needed.

Jeff had heard that the anti-Costra Cubans, who felt betrayed at the Bay of Pigs, also had something to do with killing Justin. But, he wondered, what good would it have done them, except as an act of revenge? Costra had much more to gain from Kilmory's exit from the scene than did the anti-Costra Miami-based group.

Furthermore, the Cuban exiles who knew about Plan Q would not have wished to jeopardize it. At some point they had unwittingly compromised it by virtue of their Mafia associations, linked as they were in a three-way network by the Mafia's CIA-assigned job to assassinate Costra.

Although the exiles' primary goal was to get rid of Costra and they assumed they were working with the CIA toward the same objective, it is nevertheless true that some were more interested in the money being put in their hands by the Mafia for inside information on Plan Q. Unquestionably, the mobsters took full advantage of their double-agent role as an apparent instrument of the Kilmory plan to kill Costra while turning their guns in the opposite direction.

The facts of Justin's murder being clear enough to him, Jeff chose, like his brother Roland before him, *not* to investigate any further. It was best to disown it, to know nothing more about it. The subject might further depress him. If he did confirm all the details, how could he possibly share them with the American public without implicating his brothers in deals that had theretofore remained secret? Revealing their intimate involvement in the events that eventually caused them both to die at the hands of the Mafia would just unravel too many sensitive threads and succeed only in destroying their reputation and mystique as the best and the brightest. It would not undo any of the tragic consequences.

By now, the point men had changed at all levels. But why tempt fate and sacrifice himself at the altar of the Kilmory legend if by so doing the Mafia might succeed in wiping out the last living, politically viable member of the Kilmory clan? The mobsters were too ruthless not to deal another deadly blow to someone who could seriously threaten their powerful, lucrative organization.

When on occasion his father Jonathan had been clear-headed enough, he had urged him, as the last male standard-bearer of his generation, to keep his distance from that magnetic but costly political prize. Achieving it would put him in a position to right the wrongs done to his brothers—yet it could also mean risking the same fate. Better to be the flagship for the Kilmorys and work from the relative safety of the Senate, staying away from the dangerous precipice of the presidency. He had to keep a lower profile. Being anything more than an important lawmaker would make him a tempting target. The legislative branch, like it had so far, would be a safe place—not so being the chief executive.

Jeff made up his mind to give up any intention, under whatever circumstances, of playing the next hero just to satisfy the hopes of the family and the party for restoring the family's mystique and making the dream come true: bringing into being the longed-for, triumphant reality of another Kilmory administration. He would have liked nothing more than to achieve that goal, but the price it might exact made it an impossible dream.

The Kilmory story, despite all their hard work, was by no means perfect. But which politicians could boast of anything close to perfection? What a long history of good deeds, Jeff thought, would fall by the wayside if politicians didn't sometimes get their hands dirty?

"Unclean hands were a necessary evil in order to have an opportunity to do the things that really counted for the people, especially the poor and downtrodden," Jeff liked to proclaim to his intimates. He himself had, he was convinced, done many good works.... Yet he could not have, he felt, without playing ball with the powers that be and making secret arrangements and transactions that few could, with pride, admit to.

* * * * * * *

"Think of what happened, uh, some two decades later," Jeff reminisced as he shared a glass of scotch with Samuel Scribner, one of his favorite in-laws and a long-time family pillar. The two got along well even though, over the years, they had had occasional political and personal differences. "President Barry Clangton was able to do, ah, practically anything he wanted and get away with it. Like the, heh, heh, caper with the, uh, girl who pleasured him while he sat in the Oval Office smoking a cigar—and using it as a sex toy."

"Sure, that got him impeached only because he *lied* about it, not because he did it." Scribner smiled impishly.

"And there were other events that the public never got wind of. Did you know that on one occasion he went for a tryst with Barbie Streident, the well-known star of stage and screen, as you know— and, for some strange reason, took his wedding ring off and dropped it into a fruit bowl?"

"How could she, or anyone, not know he was married?" Scribner was amused.

"Yeah, right! And after they had enjoyed their, uh, playtime together—surely not for the first time—he promptly forgot about the ring and then had to, ah, send the Secret Service back to the place to fish it out and return it to him." Jeff talked more smoothly under the influence of scotch. "Another time he invited Barbie to spend the night in the White House when his wife Harriet had to go to her dying father's bedside. Somehow that harpie found out about it and gave him hell for a week! Then she banished Barbie from the White House whenever she wasn't there to keep an eye on both of them. A pussy-whipped president!" He laughed out loud, thinking of how the Kilmory wives put up with all those shenanigans without so much as a peep. "Then there was that mysterious Van Forester business where the poor guy was supposed to have killed himself in Ft. Marcy Park in nearby Virginia. I think he somehow did it—or got it—in his office in the White House and his body was carried out to that park overlooking the Potomac, where they put an untraceable gun in his hand."

"If you're going to kill yourself why would you bother driving out to a secluded spot when you can shoot yourself inside your office and get it over with." Scribner was not convinced of the "suicide" story.

"Absolutely," Jeff replied, thinking of another "suicide" in which his brother Roland was no doubt involved: the Marie Moore case. "Besides, it's well known that Forester and Harriet had a serious affair going on for years, since they worked together in the Ross law firm in Little Rock."

"You don't suppose that Forester was breaking down and about to spill the beans about things that could get their co-presidency in trouble?" Scribner voiced a suspicion long held by the Kilmory family, among others.

"I wouldn't be surprised," Jeff answered. "It's also a fact that Harriet not only spoke of 'our presidency' but was the architect of the whole business and wielded at least as much power as he did himself. In fact, she nearly took over the vice-president's office, relegating Gere to another building."

"The stuff Clangton got away with would fill an encyclopedia," Jeff concluded. "My brother Justin was his idol—in more ways than one—and I'm sure he beat his record in the number of women bedded just during his presidency, not even counting those he, um, 'convinced', "—he was about to say "raped" but edged around it—"prevailed upon or otherwise took advantage of while he was governor of his state. Why, his security detail's main job was to go out and procure women for him."

"Yeah," Scribner chortled despite his own strict morality code. "Meanwhile, Harriet's main job as to cover up for him, just so *they* wouldn't be run out of office. After all, as you said, she was always concerned about '*our* presidency'."

"Heh, heh," was Jeff's answer as he bobbed his head up and down in agreement.

"Well, it's good that by then times had changed somewhat. Public servants have more temptations that don't really affect their talent for governance. So to bar them for those reasons would be a disservice to the republic." Scribner had a talent for honing a phrase, especially when it applied to the Kilmorys—no less than to their emulators. "At any rate, Clangton was a past master at the game of politics and public relations—and so was his wife Harriet, who fought for him tooth and nail." In a way, he reluctantly admired Clangton's ability to slip and slide through the thorniest problems. It was as though he deliberately sought them out, Scribner thought, just so he could challenge himself and prove he could do it. Harriet, of course, had a lot to do with that with her cover-up ability.

Scribner began to think of changing the subject, aware that much of what Clangton did should best remain unexplored, keenly conscious as he was that the Kilmorys had set the examples, bad as well as good.

"As you know, there were many individuals," he said, unable to resist the temptation to conclude with an expression of moral disapproval, "who were privy to information on Clangton and mysteriously disappeared or died before revealing it or testifying about such things." He observed Jeff becoming slightly uncomfortable. "But we'd best not get into it... for our own safety," he concluded with a softening chuckle. "Water under the bridge."

"Yeah, water under the bridge." Jeff chuckled back with the old standby of repeating an interlocutor's last words to put an end to a subject.

"There was a time when the general public was much more naïve and morally sensitive," Scribner observed as a bridge to another topic, keeping to himself the personal conviction that deviations from the straight and narrow were anything but appropriate. "It viewed with great alarm and indignation any transgressions, as compared to nowadays."

"Yeah, remember," Jeff was thankful for the orchestration of the press that the Kilmorys commanded, "how we, uh, took care of Dixon?" He smiled as he slyly steered to a different tack, raising his eyebrows at Scribner to underline the statement.

"How could I forget? Our buddies at *The Washington Trumpet*—or should I call it "The Washington Roaster"?— held his feet to the fire until he was practically cooked inside and out."

"Heh, heh! The endless stream of critical articles Woodburn and Epstein charged up public opinion to the, uh, extent that he was forced to go." Jeff recollected the episode with satisfaction.

"Or face impeachment and conviction in the Senate, then maybe prison time." Scribner laughed out loud at the not-so-outlandish thought. "According to his campaign slogan, he wanted 'four more years' and he nearly got six to eight!"

"Yeah, think of that, the President of the United States doing time in Sing Sing," Jeff chimed in, "like a common mafioso. I'd venture to say that, uh," he lowered his voice in mock-conspiratorial tones, "for much less than *many others* had done!" Instead of "many others" he had almost said "my brothers" in a burst of boastful honesty, but at the last split second chose to sidestep it, but with special stress and wide-open eyes. "All he had to do was erase more of those tapes—but he just didn't have the guts."

"He should surely have destroyed them," Scribner replied, picking up on Jeff's comment as he recalled that Justin's own White House tapes were cleaned up of anything that would reflect badly on him or his administration. "Barry Clangton, on the other hand, was so sly and lucky! He committed his transgressions practically in the open, made statements tantamount to confession and then lied, contradicting himself. It was a good thing that Harriet was behind him to orchestrate his defense and 'stand by her man' like Tammy Wynette. But hey, Dixon deserved everything he got," Scribner concluded.

"Ha, ha," Jeff guffawed, deflecting further speculation about his brothers. "I am not a crook!," he crowed, imitating Dixon and banging his fist on the table. "How could anyone say anything so stupid?"

"Don't forget Jerry Cantor's 'I won't lie to you'! Hah! As if everyone didn't do it, one way or another—including him!" Who really knows what constitutes "the truth, the whole truth and nothing but," as the legal oath goes. Scribner thought Canter liked to play the role of modern-day saint. "And let's not forget his never-ending flirtations with Costra." To him, the naïve ex-president had committed the mortal sin of turning over the U.S.-built Panama Canal to a relatively unstable and not overly democratic Panamanian government. The country's dictators have before and since been Costra's partners in crime, to top it off!"

"I could've done so much more, Sam, if I had, uh, actually got to be president or even gained, sooner rather than later, an, uh, higher-ranking position in the Congress." Jeff waxed nostalgic.

"Well, Jeff, sometimes it's necessary to bend with the prevailing winds to get anywhere and do some good where it counts. It's difficult to change the reality of how politics works. You've done very well and that deserves a lot of recognition," he concluded, giving him a figurative pat on the back.

"Yes. 'Politics is the art of the possible'," some unscrupulous politician famously said. Jeff's smile was bitter. "It might have been someone called, within our family circle, 'the Usurper'." He needed not clarify, of course, that he referred to Jameson.

Chapter XXXVII
EXIT JENNIFER

Jittery as usual when she watched political events—reminders of Dallas—Jennifer was in her comfortable Georgetown townhouse, tuned to the live television coverage of Roland's victory in the California primary. It was unsettling. About to turn the set off, she heard shots ring out. She knew, without a glance at the screen, that yet another tragic event in the Kilmory saga had unfolded. The shots, the shouts—and her intuition—told the story, making further description unnecessary.

"Senator Kilmory's been shot! He's been shot!" The newscaster shouted. Against her instincts to know more, Jennifer flicked it off, not wanting to see nor hear anything further. She was absolutely certain of his murder, as she herself had predicted to him.

She thanked her lucky starts that son Justin, Jr. and daughter Candice were out of the country, staying in France with a close friend of the family. Still, Jennifer shuddered to think of having to tell them the news. Mercifully, they would probably hear of it before she could call them. But first, she had to get in touch with the Kilmorys at the family compound in the Northeast quadrant. She would, as soon as she could stop crying and shaking, and get control of herself. Emotionally, she felt shredded, weakened, barely able to think. Despite their break-up, she had always had fond feelings for Roland. It was only natural, considering that he had been her lover and brother in law.

Now, she was determined to do one thing. It was time to call Aristide—her "ace in the hole," as she thought of him. She had suspected—no, expected—this turn of events all along, so it really came as no surprise. Even though she always hoped against hope itself that it wouldn't come to this. Now, for her, there was no question about it. She had to get out of this malaise, get her children away from "this muddle of mayhem and murder," as she was inclined to refer to American society. In time, perhaps, it would change. But, for now, "flight—not fight" was the order of the day.

* * * * * * *

"I can't tell you how delighted I am to hear it, my dear." Aristide spoke smoothly, trying not to sound overenthusiastic when, in fact, he was thrilled beyond words. "We'll do it quietly, on my island, of course."

"Of course, Ari," she answered quietly. "As long as it's secluded enough from those nosy, irrepressible journalists," she added emphatically. "You know how I feel about them." In recent times she had been hounded by journalists and photographers to an extent less and less tolerable.

"I will arrange that; don't worry yourself, my dear. We'll make it a very intimate affair, happy but as quiet and private as possible," he reassured her in his Greek-accented English. "Why, no one can land on my island without my permission. It's the ultimate refuge." He felt ecstatic. He would finally marry the woman considered the most desirable on earth—at least for him and, he felt, for most of the Western world as well. Sophisticated, refined, elegant, beautiful, shapely, stylish, still young and desirable, and most of all extraordinarily prestigious. The closest thing to American royalty. "I'll have my lawyers draw up the paperwork to make sure you'll be secure no matter what the future may hold for either of us." His inflection made it plain what he left unsaid: "together... or, if it comes to that, separately." He knew that's what she wanted to hear or at least feel that he implied—particularly in the financial picture— even though under the circumstances he could have breezily dispensed with anything like that altogether. But, at his age, he was well aware that nothing lasts forever.

"Let me know when you want me to send over my private jet so you can come over comfortably."

"I will, Ari dear, as soon as I can make my arrangements. Give me a few days." Jennifer tried to sound slightly more upbeat than she felt. She gave herself a mild shock by thinking that she never would have expected a wedding decision to be so sad an occasion.

For Aristide, it was sheer joy. He screamed with delight as soon as he put down the telephone, startling his butler and servants. It couldn't have worked out better he thought perversely, his malevolent side momentarily taking over—if he himself had actually planned the hits against the two Kilmory brothers. But he brushed aside such absurd thoughts. Others had unwittingly done the dirty work for him, and his hands were clean: he had had absolutely nothing to do with it. Hoping (he had previously met and entertained Jennifer—platonically?) was not something he could be blamed for; he absolved himself, his conscience clear. Besides, it hadn't cost him anything, financially, materially, morally or intellectually. The essential point was that his life would soon be complete.

And Marcia Cannas would be waiting on the sidelines for him, as usual. He could always—well, nearly—count on her to be at his beck and call. She would be unhappy over his decision, but soon get over it. At their next get-together, he would shower her with his usual lavish gifts to help her forget. Ah, life was sweet!

Jennifer, on the other hand, in a strange way, felt relief. The Kilmory political era, for all intents and purposes, was over in America. Over, also, was her own role in it. Gratefully, she could be physically and emotionally distant and aloof from it. It would be up to others to drive on with Camelot the political arena, and to chronicle the history of the Kilmorys' rise and fall.

Chapter XXXVIII
EXIT JAMESON

Jameson sat morosely, sipping a drink of his favorite whisky, Cutty Sark, in the living-room-headquarters of his vast Texas-hill-country ranch, known by his ever-present initials, "LBJ." He had bought, built and furnished it with the proceeds of his corruption and that of his partners in crime, thanks to the impunity provided by the powers of high office.

He was content to have achieved his childhood dream of getting to be America's chief executive, but it still hurt that he never got to run for re-election after his first full term. He missed the power.

"It was a miscalculation," he explained to Jasper, one of his closest friends. "Being a war-time president, I never thought I wouldn't get my second full term like I was s'pposed to."

"I guess you underestimated the enemy in that war, Louie." Jasper was condescending. "And by that I don't mean necessarily the... North Vietnamese." He smiled impishly.

"You're absolutely right about that, my friend," Jameson said without returning his smile. "The enemy was in China—and here at home. But in the overall scheme of things," Jameson waxed philosophical, "I thought I would get away with it, just like I did with everything else." He nearly said "...including the Kilmory business," but held back. Since Jasper knew about it, he could have bragged about it to him and others, heedless of consequences now that his life expectancy was down to perhaps a few weeks or months. How could they possibly hurt him now? His place in history was well taken care of by journalists and biographers beholden to him or subject to his control.

"But it was mainly those god-damn' Chinese, Jasper. They were the bastards who wanted to do me in, to throw America out of Asia, kick our ass and keep us on the defensive."

"No question. The North Vietnamese couldn't've done it by themselves."

"My military advisors let me down, Jasper. That's what it boils down to." Jameson liked to use the armed services as his scapegoats and had avoided associating with his top officers as soon as he left the presidency.

"Now, you were jus' followin' Kilmory's long-term plans when you went in there." It was a statement and simultaneously a question.

"'Course. When 'e lost Cuba he hadda make it up somewhere else and picked Viet Nam. I was jus' followin' in 'is footsteps." Jameson artfully lied to make up his own versions of history. He had perfected the art, having assiduously practiced it all his life with single-minded, self-promotional zeal. "But the fucker couldn't do anything right so I had to get 'im outa the way." He, finally, could not resist bragging. "If I'da had *my* way he wouldn'a lasted *that* long."

"And look at the legislation you passed as soon as he was out!" Jasper spoke matter-of-factly, acknowledging a well-known fact. Why Kilmory couldn't ever 'ave got a single one o' those laws passed if he'd spent the rest of his life workin' on 'em." He looked around the room at the framed pictures of Jameson signing bills and proclamations, surrounded by a multitude of congressmen and civil rights leaders.

"Yeah, an' those stupid bastards never knew what hit 'em. They always thought it was the Mafia, the Cubans, the CIA and the FBI. I don't think they ever suspected *me*."

"You'd think Roland woulda done somethin' about it if he had suspected anything. He thought of 'imself as a real macho guy."

"You betcha, Jaz. Thass what he thought 'e was, the snotty little ass-hole. But if 'ed ever 've tried something, I'da got him first with my 10-gauge shotgun." Jameson's laughter filled the room. "Did I tell you 'bout the time he came out here and I got 'im to go huntin' with me? I gave 'im the 10-gauge and said 'try it out', and when 'e pulled the damn trigger the contraption knocked 'im flat on 'is ass and smacked a cut right inta 'is forehead. I said to him, real patronizin', 'Son, you gotta learn to handle guns like a man.' Boy, was 'e stinkin' mad!"

"Bet he, heh, heh, never wanted to do that again!" Jasper laughed through nearly every word.

"I hated that little runt son of a bitch, an' so did the Mob. I sure didn't have to persuade *them* to get rid of 'im. They were mad as hell at the Kilmorys an' 'rarin' to go. Why, they were ready to go for 'im first, 'stead o' Justin."

"You talked 'em out of it?"

"Why, hell yeah," Jameson lied. "My plan was to take over the top job, not just knock off that li'l ol' runt. That wouldna done no good."

"He wanted to inherit the presidency and build the Kilmory dynasty for the rest o' the century, ain't that right?

"Why, 'course. Their plan was to force me out an' make the li'l shit-ass vice president in the '63 election. I guess after that they woulda put up the next li'l brother in the presidency, jes' like a dynasty."

"So I had to stop those cock suckers. They wanted to take over America lock, stock an' barrel for the next hunnert years."

"You stopped 'em in their tracks, Louie. Still, later on, he was wantin' to take over. The runt was dreamin'. You think 'e coulda been elected?"

"Hell, no. But we couldn't take that chance. I told the Mob to go ahead and git 'im. Told 'em I'd hold the line for 'em so they didn't have to worry 'bout any investigations or nothin'."

"Blamed it all on that Middle Eastern guy, huh?"

"Yeah, 'nother patsy like Rosswell. Stopped ever'thing 'cold in its tracks' like I said." Jameson was on the same wave length with Jasper. "Hooper covered for us just like 'e did in the Kilmory case. Same thing with the L.A. police. A lone nut did it. Case closed."

"What made 'im think he could actually run without the Mob doin' nothin' 'bout it?"

"Them arrogant Irish bastards kep' on thinkin' nobody could touch 'em. Bunch o' fuckin' dummies."

"You jus' ran rings around 'em, din'cha, Louie."

"Yup, startin' in 1959. I tol' Justin he'd better put me on the ticket if he wanted to win the election, or else."

"Or else?"

"Or else I might jus' tell some stuff I knew that I got from Hooper over the back fence. All kindsa crap—women, drugs, venereal diseases like the clap, you name it." Jameson looked smug as he warmed to the subject. He had to tell somebody about it and Jasper was a good, safe listener.

"So you scared 'im shitless."

"He caved in so fast, for a minute I thought 'e was ready to switch places an' ask *me* to run for president with him in the, heh, heh, second spot."

"Then you had 'im."

"You betcha. Had it all planned. A heartbeat away from being president. All I had to do was wait for sump'n to go off." Jameson laughed heartily as he turned his right hand into a mock gun and pointed it playfully at Jasper's head.

"It was the surest way to get to the top," Jasper said, ducking slightly to play along with the sign-language joke.

"Abso... lutely! Otherwise I might've had to wait eight to twelve years. That was just too long an' I wouldn'a made it, considerin' my family longevity."

"Their family never suspected anything?"

"They might've but they never did nothin' 'bout it. Don' think they knew what him 'em." He smiled mischievously, almost fiendishly.

"You did a good job of organizin', takin' care of all the details." Jasper knew enough about his host to visualize a vast, detailed but unwritten plan that only Jameson capable of dreaming up, following through and implementing to the letter.

"You have no idea how much work was involved in it. I had 'least three levels o' what they call 'plausible deniability' to cover my ass. My girl-friend Mandy knew 'bout some of it, more even than mah wife." He savored the bit of bragging more than the Cutty Sark.

"Oh?"

"Yeah, the night of the big party, November 21, 1963, at Masterson's in Austin, when me an' all the guys who were in on it with me got together in that room—Hooper, General Le Maine, Hunter the financier, Dixon the future president, McClayson. Some were a bit on edge, but I was anticipatin' the big day—you might remember that," he bragged, forgetting that Jasper was not there. "I tol' Mandy. I grabbed her soon's I got out 'n said: 'Startin' tomorra those goddamn Kilmorys'll never embarrass me again—an' thass no threat, thass a promise'," Jameson said in his best Southern accent, which he could partly turn off if he put his mind to it. "You shoulda seen 'er face!"

"I can imagine, Jasper chuckled."

"You have no idea. She was the only person not workin' on the plan who knew in advance." Jameson smiled as he thought back at her good looks at the time.

"How'd you explain your Haley Plaza picture?"

"Oh, haw, haw. You mean the one where I *ain't*?"

"Yup, that one." Jasper smiled knowingly, having done his homework.

"Well, you know, I jus' told 'em I was hunchin' forward tryna hear agent Youngblood's radio communications. They was comin' up with ever'thing goin' on durin' the parade. Even mah wife Laura Bertha din't know what I was doin'. She was busy wavin' at the crowd."

"Good excuse, Louie. But you knew..."

"Then, just as the bullets started flyin', Youngblood jumped into the back seat where I was an' jus' sat on me until it was all over. I gave 'im a medal for it, remember?" Jameson had crafted a credible story that Secret Service agent Youngblood had saved his life and repeated it so often that eventually he believed every word of it. It had, in fact, diverted attention from the fact that Jameson had ducked out of sight thirty to forty seconds before the firing started. A picture taken by the presidential photographer in a car ahead of him made that clear. Few, if any, had taken notice.

"I was glad after that was over, 'cuz you never know what can happen when shots are fired. But then, heh, heh, I started actin' like I was scared to death an' while I was givin' orders an' tellin' ever'body what to do, I kep' sayin': 'We gotta be careful, I think they're tryin' to kill us all!' I do believe, heh, heh, they ate that up. It wuz a pretty good cover, if I say so mahself. Made me look like 'nother innocent, potential victim!"

"Well, that's what anybody would expect from a man in your position, Louie."

"I won't go into the complicated plan to get Kilmory's body into the back-up plane—while everyone thought it was traveling on Air Force One with me and Jennifer, the president's widow. By the way, I felt a little sorry for her. She was the only Kilmory that was always civil to me."

"Yeah, she hadda go through a lot." Jasper commiserated.

"Anyway, the back-up, Air Force Two, passed our plane en route just like we planned and landed ahead of us at Andrews Air Force Base," Jameson went on. "Kilmory's body had to undergo some cosmetics so it would fit in with the 'lone-nut' scenario, since the bullets were all supposed to come from the rear."

"Otherwise, fergit it, right?" Jasper encouraged him to go on.

"Exactly. Later, after we landed, Kilmory's body was switched into the empty casket unloaded from Air Force One."

"An' what happened to the Cuba angle?" Jasper was curious.

"That was Plan B, the international commie conspiracy that was s'pposed to have triggered our invasion of Cuba, planned by the Kilmory brothers. But we had to make it look like Rosswell was an agent of that conspiracy and that got too difficult when they di'n't bump 'im off right away. I wanted to git that son-of-a-bitch Costra, but that woulda got too tricky."

"So then you had to stick with the 'lone-nut' theory."

"Yup. Plan A. Once Rosswell was taken care of 48 hours later, the way was clear for us to take that route. Director Hooper told the FBI to back us up all the way, as he was s'pposed to." Jameson recalled the events. "We had CIA people high up the ladder who also did their part. To throw 'em off the scent even more, long after the whole thing was over, I intimated that I believed in the connection between Costra's DGI and Oswald."

He was about to say those CIA agents had been responsible for recruiting the Mob, but he curbed himself, not in the mood to go on into that angle. Maybe some other time he would tell Jasper that James J. Ambleton, Chief of Counter-Intelligence, had brought into the picture experienced killers and Cuban exiles disgruntled with Kilmory's betrayal at the Bay of Pigs against Costra.

"That's a fascinating story, Louie." Jasper was eager to hear more about it.

"Okay, I'll tell you briefly," Jameson said. Jasper's interest gave him a boost. Besides, telling his war stories energized him and helped put things into perspective. And what did he have to lose? "What happened was that Ambleton had signed on to our plan when he heard through his contacts with journalists that Kilmory was using some of them—including a Frenchman named Pierre David and reporter Linda Harrow—as go-betweens to arrange a "peaceful coexistence" deal with Costra. For Ambleton that was the straw that broke the camel's back."

"He wasn't gonna take any chances that Kilmory would let Costra off, huh?"

"Hell no! Besides, Linda Harrow was smitten with Costra intellectually and sexually—seduction was part of, heh, heh, Costra's power and pubic, I mean public relations strategy." Jameson smiled slyly, thinking of his own power-trip sexual adventures on all levels of "public service"—giving new meaning to the term. "Linda saw 'erself as a player on the stage of history and took pride in acting as a mediator toward makin' a deal between Costra and Kilmory. That might have been what she really fell in love with and what she took to heart."

"I'll bet that eventually got her into trouble," Jasper said wryly, recalling that, not too long afterward, Harrow had disappeared from the scene.

"Well, Jasper, to tell you the truth, I believe it did." Jameson chose not to go into the details of how he had ensured that, upon the death of Kilmory, her efforts would come to "a dead end," as he called it. "She was plannin' a book containin' a lotta confidential information and, naturally, we tried to dissuade her. But then she solved the problem 'erself by, er, committin' suicide."

"Too bad." Jasper said in a mock-sentimental tone, picking up on Jameson's intimation. "But hey, she ran some risks, didn't she?"

"Ri-i-i-ght." Jameson chimed into his innuendo by lengthening the vowel. An' she was a nice lookin' girl, too. But you know, this guy Ambleton, who was a top CIA counter-intelligence fella, turned out to be our point man. He was the one who directed Rosswell's handlin', sheepdippin'," Jameson smiled proudly on demonstrating his knowledge of intelligence terminology, "an' preparin' him to do his job." He was about to add "as scapegoat," but thought it obvious enough.

"Quite a guy, huh?"

"Sure. An' you know, Ambleton couldn't stand that bastard Costra no more 'n that son-of-a-bitch Kilmory. Why, he was sure that Kilmory was only bidin' his time to tear down the CIA, jus' as he'd promised, and replace it with an agency of his own creation, responsible only to him, like an expanded DIA."

"You were lucky, Louie."

"Yeah, then I was. But I did have to duck," Jameson laughed as he went back to the Dallas story, "'cuz I knew a deadly crossfire was gonna start any second, an' a stray bullet coulda messed me up too," he added, flashing back to that iconic, personal moment. "I jus' don' know what the country woulda done, rudderless, if I'da been incapacitated.

"I'll bet. You jus' had to protect *yerself.* An' at the same time you sure musta had a lot on your mind, concentratin' on gettin' everythin' jus' right, not lettin' any 'o them loose details screw up the works." Jasper looked in awe and admiration at his host, who had never discussed with him such a wealth of information about subjects so secret. He felt, more than amazed, privileged that his friend, neighbor and fellow-Texan would confide all this in him. When he momentarily felt a little uneasy, he reminded himself that it was more like a death-bed confession and there was little likelihood of any consequences for him. Could this be their last conversation? He hoped not. His curiosity was far from satiated.

"Those guys were firing from every direction you could possibly imagine," he commented wryly, building up his role as dashing and near-heroic. "Poor Jesse Donnelly got some o' those slugs, 'cuz I couldn't convince Kilmory to switch Yarborough with 'im. I woulda preferred 'at two-timin' congressman Yarborough to take 'em slugs 'n' have Jesse safe with me, but—crap—Kilmory insisted that he ride with him."

"You were hopin' to kill two birds with one stone, eh?" Jasper smiled knowingly.

"Hell yeah, *that* woulda worked out a lot better," Jameson laughed at Jasper's not-so-subtle play on words.

"Jesse took it like a man, though."

"'E sure did. I could always count on 'im, no matter what."

On another occasion, Jameson thought, he would go into other things he would like to get off his chest. Right now he was feeling the effects of his illness and needed some rest.

"Well, it's nice of you to drop by, ol' fella. Always enjoy talkin' to ya." He signaled to one of his staff to come escort Jasper out.

Jasper glanced up at the framed sign on Jameson's living room wall: "If you're talkin' you ain't learnin' anything". In that case—he amused himself—Jameson was hardly ever learning, since he did all the talking.

* * * * * * *

There were other stories Jameson wanted to relieve himself of. After all, it wasn't that often that he could enjoy an appreciative audience like Jasper, one that he would hardly have to worry about repeating anything that ought to be kept under wraps. As far as he could tell, the man's lips were always sealed once he got off his premises. As well they should have been, since he was perfectly aware of Jameson's fearsome reputation. His best and most loyal friends swore by it and knew how dangerous it was to cross him.

Jameson did avoid discussing details of his service in the Navy during World War II. He had managed to use his influence to get assigned some soft jobs, mostly within the continental U.S., which enabled him to do some travelling to "inspect" Air Force bases in western states. And he finagled his way into getting a brief, cushy overseas assignment in the Pacific. It lasted only a few weeks, but long enough to work in a twenty-minute ride in a bomber. Although eluding combat in the brief, routine reconnaissance mission, he did take full advantage of it to claim a heroic flying accomplishment and convince General MacArthur to award him the Silver Star. Although none of his fellow servicemen were able to corroborate any of it— they emphatically denied it and were upset that he got it—he claimed to be one-hundred-percent worthy of that distinction.

"In fact," he claimed, "they wanted to give me a bigger medal, but I turned it down." He lied with a big, proud smile.

The deal with MacArthur was that, in exchange for the medal—which Jameson used thereafter in his campaigns as evidence of his «distinguished» service—he would lobby Roosevelt to allocate more funds and materiél to the Pacific theater.

During his adult life Jameson had gradually perfected a natural but extraordinary ability to plan and orchestrate very complex schemes designed to promote himself to ever-higher power and influence. He spent years cultivating the most powerful figures in the House and the Senate. His reverence and obsequiousness to congressional leaders like Sal Rayman was legendary. Eyewitnesses said that he would greet Rayman in the halls of Congress and kiss the top of his bald head. His kow-towing to Rayman was crafty and careful. Jameson would go to Rayman's house to pick him up on Sunday mornings and invite him for breakfast at his house, where his wife, whom he renamed "Laura Bertha"—her real name was soon forgotten—would tend to him hand and foot. They would read the papers, exchange gossip and commiserate when anything did not go exactly according to plan. Eventually, Jameson won over Rayman, who solidly backed his every move until he became Speaker of the House. He then paid a little less attention to him.

Jameson pursued all sorts of questionable personal and public activities, enriching himself through unbridled corruption; he got away with it all through the powers of office, influence-peddling, bribes and threats. His number one mistress, by whom he had a child, as well as former associates have spoken of some seven murders ordered by him, all covered up during his lifetime by those involved and by his friends in the press. His hit-men, surnamed Yeats and Waller, were quick to dispose of enemies and dangerous individuals on his orders. Waller was so slipshod and left so many clues that he was caught and prosecuted for one of the cases. He had walked in on a popular golfer who had previously been going with Jameson's older sister and shot him point-blank. Waller's car was identified as having been in the vicinity, he had a bloody shirt in his possession and was found to have a cartridge of the same caliber used in the killing. It seemed to be an open-and-shut case. Though convicted of first-degree murder, Jameson's string-pulling managed to get him off with a five-year suspended sentence. Even for Texas, it was an astounding case that, said one newspaper, "was unusual from start to finish" and had left the people of Austin "quizzical and in a state of shock." It was afraid to label the trial as an out-and-out fraud.

The TFX scandal, involving a highly lucrative contract in which Boeing and a Texas-based company competed tooth and nail, was one of the most glaring cases in which Jameson had a controlling hand. Despite Boeing's considerable advantage in cost and experience, Jameson managed to get the contract awarded to the Texan company, in which he had an interest and that got him a generous "commission." Texas newspapers exonerated him, stating that, regardless of corruption charges and suspicious manipulation, Jameson "had done right by his constituents." He probably also did right by the Texas newspapers.

He was highly praised for his comprehensive civil rights plan. Knowing the nature of the man, historical perspective brings up the underlying suspicion that his purpose was not so much ensuring civil rights for victims of discrimination as getting the black vote. There is no doubt that he did a lot for racial equality but progress in this area was nil during his vice presidency, when he had been entrusted with guiding the bills through Congress but did everything in his power to stall Kilmory's civil rights initiatives.

Did he want the credit for himself and fully expect to get it, in time, when he took over the Oval Office? That he longed to get the recognition and had the black vote in mind was something he himself put into words on numerous occasions. He was fond of saying that his efforts in this area had "nailed down the black vote for my party for the next two hundred years."

On the other hand, he had no compunctions about using the "n" word on occasion when berating non-whites who had crossed his path or given him an excuse, however flimsy, to loosen his volatile temper. There was never even a hint about such incidents, although some of his victims eventually dared to talk. A black driver was once the target of his sharp tongue when he ventured a harmless remark intended to compliment him about his actions for racial equality, but happened to rub him the wrong way. Jameson minced no words and sternly put him in what he thought should be his place.

At the time, none of that made the news. But it has later become public knowledge that many congressmen were also subject to pressure and abuse—not to mention threats and outright bribes— to get his bills passed. The threat of black violence in U.S. cities was unsparingly used by Jameson as a weapon to force politicians of both parties to agree to his demands or else, as he was inclined to warn them in threatening tones, "we're gonna have a long hot summer." Haunted by the death of the president, Congress was cowed into submission as Jameson knew how to push the right buttons. The "Jameson treatment," as it was called, seemed to work wonders. He would corral his prey into a corner, put his own face an inch away from his, and give him a lecture full of warnings, bribes and threats until his quarry gave up.

During his vice presidency, Jameson bought the mansion owned by a famous society dowager, Perle Mesta, regardless of the fact that it carried a racial clause preventing its sale or lease to "anyone of Negro or Semitic blood or extraction." Jameson had an answer ready: "I wanted to buy it in order to cast aside such an unjustified discrimination." Nobody brought it up, but he still said so in private.

Even good friends were not exempt from the infamous Jameson temper. When drinking—his capacity was limitless—he was inclined to display a mean and aggressive attitude. Texas Governor Donnelly for example, once got a taste of his unpredictable irascibility when he arrived slightly late to one of LBJ's innumerable receptions at his ranch. For no apparent reason other than his lateness, Jameson turned on him in front of all his guests, called Donnelly "a lousy son of a bitch" and continued pouring invective on him, nonstop. Finally, Donnelly and his wife walked back out, tail between their legs.

Although it wasn't mentioned in polite company, one of Jameson's favorite "tricks" was to invite his male guests to partake of the institution of "skinny dippin'" in the White House's indoor pool. He would lead them all into a separate room and invite them to strip while he did the same, all the while bragging about "Jumbo," as he called his penis.

While he didn't have a hot tub on Air Force One, he did like to have his own brand of fun with his personal secretaries and other women who were handy and attractive. Even when his wife Laura Bertha was on the aircraft—or especially when she was—he would take such women into a separate room and have his way with them. If the woman put up any resistance, he would smoothly say in his most engaging style: "You're not going to say 'no' to your president, are you?" If the matter was brought to his wife's attention in any way she would just brush it off and say something like "it's only natural because everybody loves him so much."

Among other mildly shocking things he did that were never public knowledge while he was in office was a habit of giving dictation to secretaries or instructions to staff members while sitting on the toilet defecating. The idea was to give the victim a dose of intensely perfumed, demeaning treatment while pretending that nothing out of the ordinary was happening, acting as though that were the most normal thing in the world. Once while driving through his ranch, he stopped his car, got out and urinated on the leg of a Secret Service agent, who told him: "Mr. President, you are urinating on me."

"I know. I'm doing it on purpose because I can," Jameson replied smoothly. The agent accepted the humiliation because his job depended on it and he had a wife and family to support.

LBJ also liked to drive at wildly unsafe speeds while drinking—no doubt because he "could." Needless to say, nobody ever dared to give him a ticket.

Jameson was caught in a compromising situation by no less an authority than a Captain J. Spock, head of the local law enforcement division of the Texas Game and Fish Commission, who happened to be hunting on an adjoining preserve along with two of his wardens one evening. While Spock and his party were picking up their birds, they heard shooting still going on nearby. On further inspection, they ran into the Jameson group, led by a judge named Murchison, a local banker and another man. Jameson retreated to his car, where he sat still, hatted head down, while his friend and companion dealt with the situation.

The sheriff was not impressed with their status and asked: "Who's that big-eared, sorry-looking s.o.b. sittin' in your car?"

"Why, that's Mr. Jameson, the Majority Leader in the U.S. Senate in Washington," he answered.

The captain, a man who believed in doing his duty regardless, was unimpressed. Hunting was forbidden after sundown and the pair were clearly in violation of the law; besides, the two hunters had refused to let the officers check their game bags. Accordingly, charges were brought in the nearest town, Jameson City (which Jameson used to say was named for his family). Mysteriously, the charges were soon dropped. Seven years later—Jameson had an elephant's memory for any hint of a slight against him—when Jameson's friend Jesse Donnelly was elected Texas governor, it was payback time. Jameson reminded Donnelly that they had a score to settle, and the captain, his deputies and another state employee involved were summarily fired on the excuse of a departmental reorganization.

Not long thereafter, Donnelly appointed this same Judge Murchison who had gone hunting with Jameson—by the way, labeled by a neighboring colleague as "the greatest game outlaw" in the area—to be a member of the Texas Game Commission.

On one occasion Jameson told his pilots to fly his private airplane overnight to his ranch—he needed it the next day. Since the weather was very bad and the lighting on the ranch's runways was not the best, the pilots demurred and tried to postpone the flight. But Jameson called and berated the men until they finally agreed to his demands. On the way, the pilots crashed into a hill and died. The accident was attributed to pilot error and quickly covered up. Why, the aircraft didn't even belong to Jameson, they said, but was being "borrowed" on the spur of the moment.

Jameson once viciously scolded a female staff member who suggested that she call the pilots of a waiting aircraft to let them know that Jameson was on his way so they would have more time to get ready. Among instances of cruelty and boorishness to his staff, he yelled insults at a secretary for a typing mistake. And he once verbally abused an interpreter who had just arrived for duty at the White House and, to prepare himself, asked Jameson a pertinent question while waiting for the arrival of the German-speaking guest of honor.

Jameson's corruption, ill temper and inclination to punish those who stood in his way by firing, destroying them economically or otherwise, made many people wary of crossing him. He was inclined to demonstrate, on the slightest excuse, his unlimited power and unchecked ability to apply it brutally and indiscriminately.

In December 1963, barely a month into his sudden accession to the presidency, LBJ was driving along a highway in Texas with a well-known *New York Times* reporter when all of a sudden, while driving by a ranch, he was hit by the notion to buy it. Duly impressed by his ability to appraise an enormous piece of property by whizzing by it over the legal speed limit without even pausing to put down his beer, the reporter wrote approvingly of the president's amazing talent. Why, "the question of money didn't even seem to enter the picture," the reporter pointed out, as if the President's perceptiveness were virtuosity personified.

Wasting no time, Jameson called his manager and told him to get the details taken care of. In a couple of hours, before Jameson took off for Washington, his man walked in with the paperwork and the deal was done. Not that he needed another ranch, since his main one had over 400 acres and included a 6,000-foot aircraft runway (built at government expense).

One should not, after all, be too surprised at the affluence of a man who had become a multimillionaire within a few short years on a congressman's salary. Jameson attributed it all to his wife's "management ability and good sense" to run business operations, which he claimed to "have nothing to do with."

There is no doubt whatsoever that, based on his office, many improvements to the LBJ Ranch were legally made at taxpayer's expense. But some were clearly questionable. One of these was a forty-foot hunting tower complete with elevator, comfortable quarters, bathrooms, dining rooms, lavish food and bar services and other amenities. From the top-floor vantage point, Jameson and his guests—in safety, comfort and without the slightest danger—could wait for nightfall, when hunting is *illegal* in Texas. Contrary to law, the host would shine a spotlight on the unsuspecting bucks or other game that happened to come by, either attracted by lush, well-fertilized fields, or else "herded" in their direction by his ranch hands. Then, at their leisure, the "hunters" would fire away at will. Little more than target shooting, it was only a sporting proposition from the viewpoint of the hunters.

When things got really tough, were actual human beings considered fair game as well? The methods were more subtle. When the Willy Paul Testes scandal broke in 1961—its enormous scale made it the greatest in the history of Texas and possibly the country—no one believed that Testes could have stolen millions from the taxpayers without accomplices in very high places. At one point Testes planned to confess and make a clean breast of things; however, he had a sudden change of heart, decided to plead the Fifth Amendment and do his time quietly. He later remarked that, in reality, he was scared to death; if he had gone ahead and talked, he said, he would have been "dead within twenty-four hours."

Strange things seemed to happen to loose tongues. One such belonged to Harry Mitchell, a minor Department of Agriculture official assigned to investigate the mysterious jungle of cotton allotments and other suspect operations conducted by Testes.

One day, on a remote area of his Texas farm, Mitchell was found dead. A few days later, a justice of the peace pronounced him a suicide *without* ordering an autopsy, despite protestations by his wife that he was "not the type to kill himself" and had no reason to. Later, evidence came out that Mitchell had been murdered with five bullets fired at intermediate range from the front. The jury "could not agree" to convict the suspect, Jameson's hit-man. The case was eventually closed and no one ventured to connect this crime to those who had been behind it.

One of the most notorious rip-offs was the case of a government contract to build a facility on a Pacific island that should have cost about $5 million, but was eventually awarded to a Jameson-backed company for an outrageous $18.5 million (in 1970's dollrs) —nearly four times as much.

In his more sedate moments Jameson liked to talk about his friendship with Felix Gresham, who owned the Washington Trumpet and helped promote his pal LBJ whenever he could. A kind man, Gresham reportedly suffered from bouts of depression. The problem, according to inside sources, was that he and his wife did not get along well at all. So, unlike "suicides" who had made political enemies, Gresham's enemy was domestic. After a bitter argument, according to some sources she shot him and then explained tearfully that he had killed himself in a fit of depression. The newspaper, now hers, duly reported the story according to her version.

Without missing a beat, LBJ forgot about Felix and switched his allegiance to the heiress and new owner, thus ensuring continued good publicity. With a backer like that, the case was promptly shelved.

Later, upon the assassination of Justin Kilmory—one of the great favorites of The Trumpet and its successive owners and editors— Jameson continued to enjoy the friendship and support of Mrs. Gresham and other high Trumpet executives and journalists. Any news or speculation about a conspiracy conflicting with the single-assassin theory—or who was behind it all—was automatically squelched by the Trumpet or, at best, put into the back pages.

No one suspected that Jameson, the master dissembler, had anything to do with it, although he had the most to gain from it—as well as, had the crime not been committed, the most to lose. No one observed that he had the opportunity and power to arrange it and cover it up. If so, they chose not to print it.

Toward the end of his own life Jameson became depressed, probably over the exponential reduction in the scale of his power. He just loved to throw his weight around and bully others to his heart's content, like he did with hundreds of thousands of innocent Americans and even greater numbers of Vietnamese. But, out of office, that was no longer in the cards and it was too humbling for his ego to have lost its prerogatives to such an unimaginable extent.

That, he did not recall much of—nor did he want to. Forgetful, he would stop in the middle of a story, completely lost as to what he wanted to say. It was too bad, he thought, that he couldn't have a teleprompter while talking privately, like he did when delivering his speeches. That would enable him to talk endlessly about himself without worrying about what his next line would be.

Now that death was near, it was good to bask in his memories of having outwitted the whole country and gotten to the presidency through the back door with no soul being the wiser.

But that would have to wait for another day. He retired for the night and never woke up. To his dying moment, he had gotten away with it.

* * * * * * *

As we have seen, in U.S. public life, corruption, theft, rape and other felonious crimes are seldom, if ever, prosecuted or punished if the criminals have sufficient power and status... or if they own another country.

And Getting Away with Murder is par for the course.

* * * * * * *

Now, let the Court of Public Opinion hand down its verdict.

You, dear reader, are part of the jury.

13212502R00183

Made in the USA
San Bernardino, CA
14 July 2014